I0777473

The Singularity series:

Redshift
The Observer Effect
Uncertainty Principle
Quantum Entanglement
Event Horizon
Point Singularity

Prequel
Ani, or, the care and feeding of your great tree-
dwelling venomous tentacled land-devil

QUANTUM ENTANGLEMENT

R.M. OLSON

ISBN-13: 978-1-990142-21-5

Cover by MiblArt

*To Grandma Olson.
Even though there's probably too much "space stuff" in this one for you to
have read it, I know you'd have proudly shown it off to all your friends.
<3*

"There are, however, instances where two or more particles are linked or interact in such a way that the quantum state of any one of them cannot be measured independently of the others—in simple terms, no matter the physical distance of such particles, their states remain linked."

-From a quantum physic textbook, Sao Martim University, Vila Nova do Sol, Colorida

1

Aran

"Aran!"

Aran didn't even turn at Dessi's voice, just hitched Istvay's knapsack higher on his shoulder and continued his quick stride across the clearing towards where he and Istvay had left the stolen attack pod.

"Aran! Wait! You said—"

He paused at a small copse of trees to gently loosen one of Ani's winding tentacles from across his mouth. "I'm sorry, sweetheart, I love you, but I still need to breathe," he whispered.

She gave a pathetic little whimper of protest, suckering the rest of her tentacles down across his back and neck. When her attempts to comfort him hadn't worked, she'd settled for huddling into a miserable ball on his shoulder and trying, apparently, to completely envelop him in her tentacles for reassurance.

Dessi had started after him, he could hear her footsteps.

Dessi might be small for a raider, but she was still a good head taller than he was, her ice-pale skin, blood-red eyes, and sharp fangs giving her face a nightmarish appearance. Her black hair was cut short, rather than allowed to grow long like the other raiders, which, he'd been told, meant she hadn't actually made a kill yet. She was a scientist, and a pacifist.

But she *could* kill him easily, if she wanted to. The part of his brain that was still thinking rationally was trying to tell him that was important. Even a pacifist like Dessi could probably be induced to violence now that Aran was blatantly and unequivocally breaking the promise he'd made to her in exchange for all the humans' lives.

But that was before Istvay had been kidnapped. Before Aran's entire world had stopped spinning on its axis. Before everything in the damn universe had lost its meaning, except for one thing: he was going to find Istvay, and he was going to bring them back.

Above the tree line, in the distance, there were the quick, bright flashes of light as the yibo military ships took off, heading Mystery-knew-where with the rest of the humans. Hopefully to safety.

"Aran!" Dessi's voice came from right beside him.

"I know," he said through his teeth, without turning. "I promised I'd come back with you to your research station. But—damn it, I have to get Istvay back. I have to, I—" his voice choked.

He couldn't think about it, not right now. He couldn't afford the paralyzing, overwhelming horror that had almost drowned him minutes before, when he'd gone to find his friend, and instead, found a slit in the back wall of the tent where they'd been waiting. Signs of a struggle, raider footsteps leading away. Blood on the ground.

"Aran," said Dessi in a placating voice. "You're never going to—"

Some instinct pinged a warning in Aran's brain, and he turned and shoved Dessi, hard. She broke off her sentence with a startled yelp, and he tumbled to the ground almost on top of her, Ani hissing angrily on his shoulder, as a cluster of shots hummed through the space where both their heads had just been.

"What the hell—" he started.

Dessi growled something that was probably a raider curse. "Sharda. The one who took your Istvay. She must have set a trap for the captain."

Ani hissed again, and Aran rolled out of the way of another shot, and then he and Dessi scrambled to their feet and ducked behind the sparse cover of the thin copse of trees.

Raiders were boiling out of the forest behind the attack pod, their black and grey armoured suits marking them as Sharda's crew, the captain who'd been hunting Aran and Istvay for days now.

The one who, if Dessi and Captain Krevai were correct, had kidnapped Istvay.

Aran swore through his teeth. He didn't damn well have time for this.

Krevai glanced up from where he was standing, deep in conversation with a couple of his raider crew, beside the tent where Istvay had been kidnapped. He was taller than Dessi by a good head, and significantly broader, his skin the same ice-pale and his eyes blood-red, but his black hair hung down past his knees. A group of Sharda's raiders had spread out, and were approaching him with the air of hyenas stalking a wounded plains-lion.

And then Krevai sprang, grabbing the closest of Sharda's raiders, and with a motion that was almost too quick to follow, snapped the unfortunate creature's neck with a vicious twist. Before the limp body had finished falling, he grabbed the next raider, snatched their weapon from their hand, and fired at the others, yanking his captive around in front of him as a living—although not for very long— shield. The captive's body jerked with weapons fire as Krevai fired, dropping four more raiders.

The rest of Sharda's raiders had started towards Krevai at a run, but Krevai's crew was bursting out through the trees on the other side of the clearing, sprinting for their captain.

Aran closed his eyes as another raider's shriek was cut off abruptly when Krevai jammed his knife through their stomach.

No help for it—the ship he needed to go after Istvay was on the other side of the pitched raider battle. And he couldn't afford to wait one more second.

He jumped to his feet and started off at a sprint across the clearing.

Dessi gave an exasperated shout, scrambling to her feet and pelting after him. "God's sake, Aran—"

He ignored her.

Find Istvay. Bring them back. Everything else would take care of itself.

The heads of at least a dozen of Sharda's crew turned towards him, and he cursed and dived to the ground as a shot hummed over his head, then rolled to his feet and took off running again. Shots whistled around and over him as he dodged through the battling raiders, his heart pounding in his throat.

Damn it to hell. Damn it to actual hell, he couldn't afford to get hurt, not here, not now. Not like this.

He was half-way across the clearing now. Ani was hissing like a teakettle, and he could feel her tense, then she launched herself from his shoulder. He could follow her trajectory by the location of the high-pitched scream that accompanied her landing.

"Aran!" Krevai shouted, looking up from where he was grappling with two other raiders. He turned briefly to shoot a third, who'd come up behind him. "What are you doing? Wait, we can talk this over when—"

"Aran! Stop!" Dessi gasped, and something in her voice made him look up.

Three raiders stood in a close semicircle in front of him, their pistols pointed directly at his head.

He risked a quick glance behind him.

Another raider had grabbed Dessi, and they were holding a wicked-looking knife to her throat. Dessi's face had gone even more pale than usual. Of course—she was a pacifist, and she hated violence even more than he did.

"Well, look what we found," said one of the raiders, their grin showing their fangs to full advantage. "Krevai's other pet human, and his little tame scientist." The speaker was tall, almost as tall as Krevai himself, and towered over even Dessi. Aran, standing at full height, would probably have been staring at the creature's sternum. They gestured, and the raider holding Dessi shoved her forward, not taking the knife from her throat.

"Take them back, or eat them?" he asked, his own grin wide and threatening.

"Sharda doesn't need any more captives—she made her point," said the first. "We'll eat these ones."

Aran gritted his teeth. Ani could kill them, easily, but he wasn't completely sure she could do it before the raider standing behind Dessi slit Dessi's throat.

Predators. They were predators, and yes, they thought like humans, more or less, and he'd never been all that good at humans, but these particular predators had a keen sense of smell, and probably decent eyesight if he remembered properly. Certainly they had spectacular hearing.

The raiders' eyes were fixed warily on Ani, who was growling on Aran's shoulder. "Watch out for the thing," one of the raiders began, gesturing. "The humans had it when we tracked them down a few days ago. It's dangerous."

Aran edged his hand into his supply pouch, his fingers sorting quickly through the jumble of supplies.

Ani growled.

"Duck," he mouthed at Dessi. Then he jerked his hand out from his supplies pouch and tossed a light flare and a sound flare, igniting them both as he threw them.

The raiders staggered back at the combined assault on their senses, and Aran palmed the canister of the concentrated musk-dog urine he and Istvay used when they had to cover their trail, and threw it with all his might.

It hit the tallest raider across the forehead, shattering on impact, its contents spraying across Aran's attackers. They stumbled into each other, coughing and choking, their eyes streaming, and the raider behind Dessi dropped to his knees, clutching at his throat.

Aran held his breath and grabbed Dessi's hand, hauling her clear. "Get out of here," he hissed, gagging a bit at the smell, and pushed her in what was probably a safe direction.

Then he turned again and ran for the pod.

He hadn't made it more than another twenty metres before another raider stepped in front of him, grinning, her fangs glinting in the reflected sunlight.

"Hello, human," she said.

Aran yanked out his pistol and shot her in the chest. Her armour absorbed the hit, but it made her step backwards momentarily. He snatched out another flare and set it off directly in her surprised face, shoving past her as she blinked, momentarily blinded.

Almost there. He was almost to the pod.

And then someone grabbed his shoulder, spinning him around. "Aran, listen!"

It was Dessi.

He managed, barely, to stop himself from shooting her in the face with his pulse pistol.

The clearing was a cacophony of noise, pounding in his ears. Krevai was still shouting something from across the clearing, two more raiders had started towards Aran, and three from Krevai's crew were running to intercept them. The weapons fire hummed and buzzed across the clearing, the shouts and curses of raiders fighting, Ani's piercing whistle, and the high-pitched screams of her victims, and Istvay was gone, damn it to hell, Istvay was gone—

"Shut up!" he shouted, grabbing Dessi's wrist and yanking her hand off his shoulder. "Just shut the hell up!"

She stared at him, eyes wide.

"Shut up, and leave me the hell alone. What the hell is wrong with you? Leave me alone, or I'll set Ani on you!"

Dessi's mouth gaped open.

Across the clearing, Krevai was staring as well, and so were the three members of Krevai's crew who'd started towards Aran.

"I'm taking that damn attack pod, and I'm going after Istvay, and if you want to stop me, you'll damn well have to kill me, if you can manage it." His voice was shaking. He turned to where Ani was finishing off another raider. "Ani!" he said, his tone harsher than usual. "Come! We're leaving."

Ani bit her victim one last time, then slithered down, looking sheepish.

Aran scooped her up off the ground and started off again at a run for the attack pod.

The chaos resumed behind him, but the raiders seemed to have realized that coming after him when Ani was on his shoulder would not be a wise idea.

And then he was there. He pulled himself inside the attack pod hatch, slamming it shut behind him.

The sudden stillness was a relief that was almost overwhelming, and he leaned back against the wall of the small alien craft, sucking in a deep breath. His heart pounded, and his head ached, and the panic that he'd managed to shove down when he'd realize that Istvay might still be alive and he still had a chance to save them was clawing at the edge of his consciousness again, trying desperately to work its way loose and take over his entire brain.

He drew in another deep breath, and then another, then forced himself to straighten and make his way through the small corridors until he stepped inside the cockpit.

Then he stopped, staring blankly at the lines of controls laid out in front of him.

If he could just remember how to start the damn thing up, that would be something, at least. He just had to remember—

For the briefest moment, his mind pulled up a picture of Istvay in the pilot seat, grinning up at him with that mischievous expression on their face.

He gasped, grabbing at the wall to steady himself.

Istvay was gone.

He almost fell into the pilot's seat and dropped his head into his hands, trying to force himself to breathe.

Istvay was gone, Istvay was gone, Istvay was gone. His brain couldn't seem to move past that thought. Istvay was gone, and Aran was the only one who could help them, but … hell, he was so far out of his depth right now that he was drowning without even knowing which way was up. He'd never even flown a damn ship out of atmosphere before, Istvay had always done the piloting because they knew how much Aran hated it. And now Aran would be taking an unfamiliar ship out into space, on his own, with no Istvay there to help him through the panic attacks that would inevitably follow, and Istvay was gone … Istvay was gone—

He could hear, distantly, Ani's soft, distressed noises, feel her touch on his arm, but he couldn't make himself focus on anything except the desperate, leaden fact that Istvay was gone, and Aran would have to fix this on his own.

He didn't even remember how to start the damn pod.

There were heavy footsteps in the corridor. Some part of him wondered if it was one of the raiders come to kill him, but he couldn't really bring himself to care.

"Aran?" Dessi's voice was quiet. "Can I come in?"

She must have taken his non-answer as acquiescence, because her footsteps came closer, and then there was the creak and groan of the copilot's seat as she sat.

"Aran," she said, her voice still quiet. "I'm—sorry. But can you at least hear me out?"

He didn't answer.

"I wasn't trying to stop you," she said. "I know how much your Istvay means to you. Remember how I let you go to shut down the portal, because I told you that I can't work with lab animals who are pining away? You must think that I'm exceptionally stupid if you think I didn't realize that losing your Istvay would kill you. But—" she paused. "I hope you'll excuse my bluntness, but you don't stand a chance. You don't know where Sharda went, and her people will come after you until they shoot you down. And I doubt you have much experience flying raider ships."

Aran almost laughed at that. If only she knew.

"I thought you said you weren't trying to stop me," he said instead, in a dull voice.

"I wasn't." There was so much surprise in her tone that Aran lifted his head. "I was just coming to tell you, you should wait until Krevai's finished out there. He's going to want to come. And since you're my only remaining research subject, I'm coming as well. I'm sure I'll get all sorts of interesting data, and while it would be unethical to purposefully put a human into distress, I'm hardly going to not take advantage of the opportunity to study this when it's handed to me."

He stared at her, not completely sure he'd understood her correctly.

"You—you and Krevai—" he began.

Dessi sighed. "Of course we're coming. You know Krevai, do you really think he could let an insult like that pass? When he made you and Istvay part of his crew, that comes with obligations. He can't be seen as abandoning one of his crew. And besides, now that the portal's down, there's almost certain to be a leadership war. Krevai was out hunting during the last two leadership wars, but he's not going to sit this one out, not against Sharda. Especially not when she's attacked him and captured one of his crew. And she knows it, too—why do you think she left an ambush in the clearing after she'd taken your Istvay?"

Aran was still staring, his mouth hanging open. "I—" he began, then stopped, because he had no idea what to say.

"You'll stand a much better chance with us," said Dessi reasonably. "Krevai knows people—he'll be able to figure out where Sharda's gone, and the other raider crews will talk to him, rather than try to eat him, like they would you." She paused a moment. "At least, most of them will talk to him instead of trying to eat him, I assume."

From behind him, there was the thud of heavy boots in the

corridor, and then Krevai poked his head into the cockpit. Blood stained his uniform and dripped from his hands, but most of it seemed to belong to someone other than himself.

He grinned when he saw them. "Ah, there you are," he said in a stage-whisper. "Did you finish explaining things to Aran?" He turned to Aran apologetically. "I'm sorry, I know you don't like loud noises, but I think I killed most of the people making noise out there, so you're alright to come out. You can pilot the pod by yourself if you want, but I suspect you'll be more comfortable in our ship. Didn't your Istvay say you humans didn't like space travel? And besides, I owe you a favour for keeping my little scientist safe—I saw the whole thing from across the clearing. I'm impressed!"

Aran was still staring.

"Come on Aran," said Dessi, nudging him gently. "The sooner we get on the ship, the sooner we can go after your Istvay."

Aran took a deep breath. "Yeah," he said, his voice coming out a little strange. "I ... guess you're right." He glanced around, then closed his eyes and drew in a long breath.

Maybe, just maybe, he stood a chance after all.

He managed a weak smile at Dessi. "Let's go."

2

Alba

By the time the yibo military ship hissed, shuddered, and stilled, and the shouts and calls of the crew members made it clear that they'd landed, the exhaustion of the mad, absurd previous few weeks had sunk deep into Alba's bones.

Every muscle in her body felt weary. But it was more than that. The strain of the previous—days? Weeks? She had no idea—had become a weight sitting on her entire consciousness, crushing her body and soul into a sort of numbness.

Perhaps it was for the best. If for one moment she had the time or energy to think about everything that had happened, everything they'd been through, the unalterable, unthinkable consequences of her decisions—she wasn't sure she'd survive it. This numb, exhausted shock was likely her brain's survival mechanism. At least now, she could think, coolly and with detachment, about their future.

Whatever future they might have in this strange, alien system.

She glanced around at the others.

They looked as exhausted and shellshocked as she felt.

Joska, Rafel, and Beni had met them halfway through their journey, and the yibo had allowed Joska's battered ship to dock on the onboard hangar bay.

Savina wasn't with them. Joska hadn't offered an explanation, but there had been a grim cast to her expression, and Beni had looked sick—silent and pale and almost on the verge of passing out. Nicolau had come running at the ship's arrival, and his expression had gone sharp with dismay when he hadn't seen Savina, but Joska took him by the arm and drew him off into a corner, speaking quietly. When they returned, Nicolau had been as quiet and pale as Beni, but hadn't said another word.

At some point, Alba would have to ask them—simple curiosity aside, it was dangerous to have an assassin with unknown intentions on the loose. But that wasn't a situation she felt she could face at the moment.

There was a tap on the door of the small deck that had been given over for the humans, and then Jair, the human who'd been travelling with the yibo military, ducked inside. He glanced around, then nodded. "Good, you're all here. Come with me. General Riit has called in ahead, and they've set up some temporary housing."

He waited as they gathered their meagre belongings, such as they were. At this point, it was hardly enough to be worth gathering. When they were finished, he gestured for them to follow, and led them out of the ship.

Alba could feel the eyes of the yibo soldiers on them as they walked past, and she tried not to pay attention to the stares and whispers that followed them.

It wasn't the fact that they were human that was so uncommon— she knew that well enough by now. It was the fact that they were humans who'd escaped from Kachik and his yibo nativist supporters.

Humans who'd taken down the portal mechanism the nativists had seized, meant to open a portal into the Joias System and allow them to wreak destruction on the unsuspecting human inhabitants waiting on the other side.

She and the remainder of the diplomatic crew had destroyed it, likely beyond repair. It was a victory, by every measurable account —millions, billions of lives saved.

But there was a bitter aftertaste to the victory.

She glanced surreptitiously back at the ragged group of humans walking behind her—her clerk, Feliu—her oldest friend, although she wouldn't have thought to call him that before this mission—his pink cheeks and round face now chalky and almost cadaverous with exhaustion and illness, his hair gone completely grey, not even streaks of its original dark brown remaining; Yosip, with his friendly smile and a weary slump to his shoulders, his shaved hair growing back a ragged grey-white against the brown of his head; Joska, her tawny face more ashen than usual, lips pinched tight with worry, and her crew, Rafel, scowling with it, the pallor even more evident on his pale skin; Beni and Nicolau huddled together, faces drawn with grief, their complexions a matching olive-brown, his hair and the roots of Beni's, where it had grown out, a matching incongruent auburn. Alba's young interpreter, Ines, with her slight frame and dark skin and the soft halo of black hair surrounding her face, had her arm around Nicolau, looking as if she was supporting him, although he was so much taller and broader than she was.

They and every other human survivor from the diplomatic ship were trapped here, for likely for the remainder of their lives. And how long their lives would be depended entirely on the goodwill of their yibo hosts.

As their small, ragged party stepped down from the gangplank and onto the streets of the yibo city, Alba glanced around at this new place.

The architecture—the soaring, graceful lines, the tall buildings—was broadly consistent with the other yibo settlements she'd visited thus far. But this place had an entirely different feel to it then the yibo city they'd fled days earlier. The buildings here, though still tall and graceful, were weathered with age, the streets full of not only yibo transport vehicles, but pedestrians. The air was warm and dry, not the sticky heat of the jungle, and there was a bustle and drive here that seemed to permeate the very air itself. Even the soaring buildings and the tall, delicate architecture seemed designed less for aesthetics than for practicality, although there was a certain beauty to the austerity of it.

"Come on," said Jair gently, turning back to take her by the elbow. "Let's get the lot of you somewhere you can rest. You look exhausted."

Alba managed a wan smile.

She felt somewhere beyond exhausted, on the verge of collapse—as if the only thing holding her up was the fact that her legs had not yet figured out how to let her fall.

Jair led them to a small, utilitarian transport, and they climbed in wordlessly, finding their places on the stained, uncomfortable seats covered by faded, torn upholstery.

There were to be no special diplomatic privileges afforded them here. Here, they were no more or less than refugees.

Alba stared sightlessly out the grimy transport windows as they passed through the streets, the buildings blurring before her eyes. She didn't know if it was from tears or sheer weariness, and she hardly had the energy to care.

At last, the transport came to a halt in the cramped courtyard, with a large, stark building squatting in the centre, taking up most of the space. The walls were of glass and stone, and it reminded Alba of nothing more than a port-district warehouse back in do Sol—useful, but with nothing at all of beauty to it.

"Quarters have been set up for you in there," said Jair, gesturing to the building as they disembarked. "We're currently supporting a few other human refugees who fled from areas that Kachik and his nativists have become the de facto ruler of—you won't find humans in their territory if we can avoid it. But as you're from a different system, the yibo have set you up with your own rooms and dining area, at least."

He led them through the door and into a large, echoing room set with bare tables and benches, where curious humans, ragged and tired-looking, watched them pass. A few children played, chasing each other around the tables, but they stilled when they caught sight of the newcomers.

At the back of the room, Jair opened a locked door and beckoned them down a bleak hallway. "You'll find your rooms at the end there. General Riit instructed they be stocked with your basic necessities, as we assumed you wouldn't have many supplies to bring with you."

Alba nodded, then, with an effort of will, turned to look him full in the face for the first time since they'd arrived.

There was pity in his eyes as he watched them. She wasn't accustomed to pity. But she swallowed down the bitter dregs of what remained of her pride.

He'd done more for them than he'd needed to. And looking at him, she guessed he, too, had experienced the odd, weightless disorientation of losing one's home, one's identity, one's place in the world.

She'd learned, only days before, of the destruction decades previous of the Labirinto System, Jair's original home, wiped out by a combination of yibo pride and raider aggression. And she still hadn't had even a moment to process the full horror of it.

"Thank you, Jair," she said softly. "We are in your debt."

She hadn't meant for her voice to crack on the words.

He smiled, a small weary smile. "We humans need to look out for each other." He hesitated. "Alba. I—understand that you're the leader of this party."

Alba glanced around at the others.

For the first time in her life, she wasn't entirely sure of her answer.

It hardly mattered, though—Jair seemed to take her non-answer as confirmation. "The Advisory Body contacted General Riit as we were on our way in. They asked if one of you would be willing to appear before them tomorrow and give testimony as to what happened." He must have noticed her look of confusion. "Yibo government officials. Something like your equivalent of a Council meeting."

Alba could scarcely stifle a groan. She felt as if she could sleep for a month, and would still wake up exhausted.

"Surely the soldiers saw enough that they could explain," she began.

Jair cut her off, shaking his head. "Soldiers could tell the story. But this is about more than that. You probably don't know about the politics here. But ... the status of humans in this system has been a topic of debate recently. For obvious reasons, there are none of us in government, and so we rely on the goodwill of the yibo politicians willing to speak up for us. But you—you're from a different system. You're a new voice, and a new factor in the equation."

He hesitated again, and she could see the hint of desperation in his face. "Things are not going well. The advisors and the Synod don't want to risk war with the nativists over the fate of humans. Your voice and your perspective could help. And we need all the help we can get right now." he paused, glancing around quickly. Now that Alba was listening more closely, she could hear the crack of exhaustion in his tone. "We're starting to hear rumours of a leadership war among the raiders. That could lead the Synod to consider joining forces with the nativists, if it means some solidarity against whatever hell the raiders are going to set loose. And if that happens …" He trailed off.

Alba drew in a deep breath. "So. You'd like me to speak with these … advisors." She had to fight back bleak amusement at the resigned horror in her own tone.

What she would have said back in do Sol, had someone suggested she'd find herself hesitant to stand in front of a group of alien politicians and argue for the lives of the humans she had made herself responsible for.

But if her time in this system had taught her anything, it was the hard, uncompromising limits of her own capabilities.

She sighed. "It's not that I'm unwilling." That was a lie, but no one but her needed to know it. "However, I'm … not sure that I am the most capable person for this. I suspect Yosip would be the best choice, although I'm certain Feliu would also do very well."

"Alba," said Yosip quietly from her elbow, where he'd come to stand, almost unnoticed.

She'd noticed him, though, she realized, because of the way she'd felt herself relax at his presence.

"Yosip. Jair has told me that they are in need of humans who can —"

Yosip shook his head. "I heard." He paused, hesitation clear in his face. "Alba. I know you're tired. You've done more than should have been expected of any of us. And I'll do it if you ask me. But … this is not my strength."

"Not your strength?" Her voice was unintentionally sharp. "I've seen you make friends with aliens with whom you share no common language, within an hour of meeting them. How is this not your strength?"

He gave her a small smile. "I appreciate your confidence. But I'm not a politician. And this calls for more than simply remembering the names of someone's children, or swapping recipes. This is your expertise, more than any of ours."

She stared at him for moment. Then she almost laughed. "This mission I was sent to lead has been a disaster from the first moment. What happened back in the city with Kachik, then closing down the portal—"

Yosip smiled again, a hint of his customary twinkle in the expression. "I do remember," he said softly. "I remember how you held out despite all the best efforts and threats of Kachik and his people until you knew what their objective was, despite pressure that would have overwhelmed a less practiced diplomat. I saw you outmanoeuvre the mayor in the yibo village, and befriend the villagers such that they were willing to give us the information we needed. I saw you work with two field scientists who, for all their strengths, are not accustomed to working with anyone but themselves." He laid a hand on her arm. "Believe me when I say, if any one of us can make an eloquent plea for the humans in the system, it would be you."

Alba looked at him for a long time.

She'd always been certain of herself. She'd seldom, if ever, taken a step without having planned out to the last detail every possible move and countermove.

And in this situation, she didn't know enough to make even the first step of a plan. Worse than that, the nagging uncertainty— uncertainty as to the rightness of her own actions, uncertainty at her ability to do what needed to be done—gnawed at the edge of her confidence like a rodent on a scrap of dry biscuit.

"The Council trusted you enough to send you as head diplomat," said Yosip. "And I, at least, still trust you."

Alba closed her eyes.

When she opened them, she turned back to Jair. "I shall talk with the rest of my company," she said, trying to keep her voice steady. "If they are in agreement that I am the best person to go—" She paused. "You may inform the advisors that I shall be happy to appear before them tomorrow."

3

Savina

Savina glanced quickly over the streets that surrounded the small, dingy transport hub on the edges of the yibo city she'd left so precipitously the day previous.

Kachik's city. Chrr. The place where she'd been captured, twice —once by yibo criminals, and once by Kachik himself.

She'd thought she'd left the place behind forever. And she would have left it behind forever, if it hadn't been for bloody Reka. The woman she was following.

The woman she was going to kill.

Tension knotted in her stomach and burned in her muscles.

She'd almost been killed here. She was still limping from her injuries. And now, like a complete idiot, she was back.

The memories still haunted behind her eyelids when she closed her eyes for a moment: the cell where she and Reka had been thrown together, captured by Kachik's guards. The sharp, searing pain in her leg where the yibo had shot her, the taste of blood in her mouth, the desperate, frantic realization that she was going to die. Joska and Beni and Rafel hijacking the ship where Savina was to be killed. She and Reka in the gun tower shooting down yibo ships, desperately, hopelessly, and preparing to die when their firepower finally wasn't enough. The portal closing.

And then, when against all odds Joska had landed them safely, Reka calmly telling the captain to stand aside and let her take Savina in.

Despite the fact she and Reka had just saved each other's lives ... Savina had more than half expected it. Reka had never made any secret of the fact that she didn't trust Savina, and she didn't intend to let Savina leave here alive.

What she hadn't expected, though, was for Joska to step in front of her and tell Reka, in her matter-of-fact way, that if Reka wanted Savina, she'd have to do it over Joska's dead body.

For Rafel to agree with her.

For her sibling, Beni, to grab Savina's arm and whisper that if Reka tried to hurt her, they and everyone else who'd come with Savina through the portal were willing to die themselves to keep her safe.

And that couldn't happen. Savina had realized at that moment, firmly and irrevocably, that it couldn't happen.

Reka would never stop trying to kill her. And she'd seen how easily the others could become collateral damage. The only way to prevent it from happening was for her to kill Reka herself.

So when Reka had left, headed back to Chrr to save the trapped humans Kachik still had locked up there, with a comment over her shoulder that she'd give Savina a day's start, Savina had waited on the ship, pretending her injuries were worse than they were. And when Joska had gone into a small yibo village to resupply before heading back to meet up with Alba and the others ... Savina had slipped out, turned off her wavelink so the others couldn't track her down and get killed for it, and caught a ride with an unsuspecting yibo man back to the city where she'd almost been killed so many times.

But this time, she wasn't intending to be killed. This time, she was here to kill.

She drew in a steadying breath, her hand resting reassuringly on the hilt of her knife. Then she slipped into one of the smaller alleys.

Now she was back in Chrr, tracking down Reka should hardly be a problem. Reka might be intelligent, and incredibly dangerous, but she honestly seemed to believe she had some glorious mission to bring forth justice, or something ridiculous like that. Killing her would be like putting down a sick animal—believing in those kinds of ideals made someone too damn stupid to live. If Savina didn't kill Reka, someone else almost certainly would.

She made her way down the twisting alleyways, reorienting herself to the yibo city. That was one advantage, at least, of having spent time in the alien criminal underground—you either got to know the back alleys, or you died.

It didn't take her more than an hour or two of walking before she caught sight of the government compound in the distance. If Reka was right, somewhere in the compound was where the rest of the humans who'd come through the portal on the Joias System's diplomatic ship were being kept. Where Kachik was, apparently, holding them until he decided how and when to murder them.

Savina wasn't completely sure how recent events would play into his calculations, but she knew well enough that he bore no love for humans. If they weren't dead already, they would be soon. And she knew just as well that Reka, idiot that she was, would never be able to leave that alone. She'd show up here, heedless of her own safety, like she always did if she thought it was for a good cause.

It was only a little after midday, and Savina slowed her pace to a casual walk. She circled the outside of the loose cluster of government buildings and their surrounding courtyards and walkways until she came to a likely looking walled structure, inside the compound, but under its own protective force field.

Judging from the number of yibo guards surrounding it, she'd found where Kachik was holding the humans.

She smiled to herself, running her fingers along the hilt of one of her throwing knives.

For once, she was excited to see Reka again.

She walked carefully around the building, keeping to the shadows, and found a place to wait that would provide her a view of the compound while keeping her mostly out of sight. Probably no one in this particular city harboured friendly feelings towards humans, after she and Reka had sabotaged the yibos' negotiations with Cavaco's people, followed by shooting down a not-insignificant number of yibo ships over the city and generally causing mass chaos.

The drone of insects hung in the heavy air, the wet, sweltering heat draped over the city like a suffocating blanket.

More and more guards arrived as the day wore on, and Savina frowned to herself as she watched. Had she been too late? Maybe Kachik intended to execute the humans this afternoon and, most likely, Reka with them, and her work would be done for her.

She tried to ignore the sharp twinge of discomfort at the thought, and pressed her back up against the alley wall, the surface sweaty in the heavy jungle heat. It wasn't like she cared about anyone inside those walls. And as long as Reka was killed, it hardly mattered who did it.

Still, she found every time a guard approached the entrance to the compound, she was holding her breath.

As the sun at last began to set, another troop of guards arrived at a jog, sweaty and breathless. They didn't go inside the compound, though, just spoke quickly with the captains of the guard troops already there. The captains moved back to their units. And then three of the four guard troops formed up and marched off.

Savina stared, her breath coming short and quick in something that might be relief. Then she shook herself.

Whatever the hell the guards had been building up to in the human compound—if Savina had her guess, it would have been a mass killing—it appeared there had been a change of plans.

This was as good a chance as any.

She got to her feet and walked purposefully towards the compound entrance.

The guards at the gate frowned as she approached, but they were clearly distracted by whatever orders they'd just received.

Savina batted her eyes at them. "I'm so sorry, one of the other guards sent me out to run an errand, and I got lost. I'm just getting back now."

The guard looked at her for a moment blankly, then nudged his neighbour, and they conversed in low tones. Then one of them stepped aside. Savina gave them a grateful nod and slipped past into the compound.

The humans' makeshift prison consisted of a large, open courtyard, and behind it, a small, self-contained cluster of buildings that must comprise living and sleeping quarters. The courtyard was crowded with people enjoying the approaching cool of the evening, now that the heat of the day had passed. A few people looked up curiously at Savina's entrance, but no one seemed to find anything particularly alarming in it.

It only took her a few moments to locate a small corner at one end of the courtyard, mostly obscured by the jutting edge of one of the buildings, that would offer a clear view of the doorway to what looked like the main building, and was within easy throwing distance. If someone should, for instance, have a knife designed for throwing.

She made her way over casually and, once there, crouched so she was hidden in the shadows, leaned back against the wall. Then she blinked to bring her wavelink online and dialled in the retinal screen to a higher magnification, scanning the crowd.

There was a small group in one corner, and the way they were clustered together, the unconscious glances over shoulders, told Savina that whatever they were discussing, they didn't want the yibo guards to overhear.

And there, in the centre of the cluster, stood a familiar figure, dressed in a familiar stained and travel-worn grey suit, her movements marked by a familiar, dangerous grace.

Savina pulled her knife carefully from its sheath, playing it over her fingers.

She'd have to wait for a clear shot. But it was twilight now—people would be heading back inside soon.

All it would take was a flick of her wrist, and she'd be free.

Reka seemed to be talking to the group, her voice pitched low enough that Savina couldn't make out her words. Whatever it was she was saying made her listeners uncomfortable—their postures were stiff, their shoulders tight, and they glanced nervously at the yibo guards more than once. A frightened-looking young woman, dressed in the stained outfit of cargo crew, stepped closer to her, whispering something, and Reka said something Savina couldn't hear, the corners of her mouth turning up in a small, almost imperceptible smile. The young woman's posture relaxed, her eyes lingering on Reka as Reka turned back to the rest of the group.

Savina gritted her teeth.

Stupid. This whole thing was stupid. Reka had no right to be—like this. Cool, and collected, and heroic, and unconsciously, stupidly attractive.

At last, the group of people surrounding Reka began to disperse, moving in small knots towards the building. Reka stayed back, speaking with one or two of the stragglers, then moved to follow.

Her face was grim, but there was a familiar purposefulness to her steps as she walked. Her throat was bare, her skin, a little darker than Savina's own, glowing in the reflected light of the setting sun.

A perfect target.

Savina checked her knife again, running her finger unconsciously along the smooth hilt. Her breath was tight in her chest, her heart jumping in a quick, unsteady rhythm.

This would be easy. As easy as falling asleep.

At the entrance to the building, Reka paused, half-turning as if to respond to some question. And for just a moment, she was fully exposed to Savina's position.

Despite her grimness of earlier, her posture was relaxed when she turned. Her mouth curved up in a smile, and there was that trace of softness in her eyes Savina had only seen in those brief, rare moments when Reka let down her guard.

Whatever the person had said, it must have been funny, because Reka gave a low, soft chuckle, the sound painfully familiar.

Savina stood still, hand frozen on the hilt of her knife.

Reka turned back, her gaze passing over Savina's hiding place without the faintest note of alarm.

Then she stepped into the building, and was gone.

Savina leaned back against the wall of the building, knife still clutched in her fingers. She was lightheaded, and it was only that that reminded her she still needed to breathe.

Reka hadn't seen her, hadn't even suspected. This should have been the easiest kill she'd ever made.

She sank slowly to the ground, her back still pressed against the building, and forced her fingers to uncurl from her knife.

She felt sick to her stomach.

She'd been right, back in prison—something had broken inside her. The thing that had kept her alive all these years, kept Beni alive, allowed her to protect her baby brother, was broken.

She was broken, and she didn't know how to fix it.

She stared sightlessly into the emptying courtyard as the sun disappeared, the last brilliant flare of colour fading into darkness. She stayed there as the moon rose, and then, finally, she pushed herself slowly to her feet.

She glanced around, then crept carefully to the door of the building. A warm light spilled out of the opaque glass-like material of the structure, and shadowy shapes moved on the other side, the muted hum of conversation floating out on the breeze.

Savina closed her eyes against a sudden, sharp ache in her chest.

These weren't her people. They hadn't grown up in a compound, like she had, born into a heretical sect whose beliefs had marked them for persecution and death for hundreds of years. These people, if they'd known who and what she was, would hate her and everything she stood for.

At least, that's what she'd always been told. That's what she'd been taught, since she was old enough to understand language. That's how she'd always justified her kills—kill them before they had a chance to kill you.

But maybe they didn't, in fact, hate her for that. Maybe her entire life had been a lie, and they'd never hated her the way she'd been told they did, because of who she'd been born. They only hated her because of who she was now. Who she'd become, because she'd been so convinced of their hatred.

And Reka—that damnable, noble, stupid Reka—was inside as well, talking and laughing with them. She didn't need to hide who she was or what she stood for, not in front of these people. And she was alive because Savina had had a chance to kill her, and … she hadn't done it.

She couldn't.

Even though she'd known that by not killing Reka, she was dooming herself and everyone she cared about.

Slowly, she pulled a writing instrument and a paper out of her pocket and scrawled a quick note. She stared at it for a few moments, and then she knelt, slipping it under the door. Her hands shook, just a little.

Reka would understand it, even if no one else did.

She straightened and made her way to the outer gate, waiting in the shadows until the guards' replacements came, and slipped out without anyone noticing.

It didn't take her long to leave her second message. The streets were dark, but she knew where she was going. She couldn't help but hope that Reka would find her message first, that she'd understand and come. But she couldn't afford to take chances.

The stuffy, residual heat of the day was slowly clearing as Savina made her way down the streets, replaced by the soft cool of the night. The streets were dark and probably dangerous, but the yibo criminals here should still remember her. And if they didn't, she'd do what she did best—play innocent, then slit their throats.

She walked slowly, breathing in the strange, sweet perfume of some night-time flower, strong enough that she could catch the scent of it over the garbage and mold and mildew of the streets. She checked to make sure her wavelink was still off.

For a moment, she debated turning it back on again, just for a minute, calling Beni or Joska … but she didn't.

Things were better left as they were.

4

Aran

"Aran!" One of the raider crew came striding down the corridor towards him, and Aran cracked an eye open, sucking in a breath for the first time in what felt like hours.

Dessi had suggested that Aran go back to his cabin during the flight. But he didn't think he could handle stepping through the door to see Istvay's spare jacket casually discarded on the floor, the faint indent of their head in the pillow, the blankets tossed back in a messy pile where they'd pushed them off when they'd woken, and still maintain his grip on the thin thread of control he was clinging to with both hands. So instead, he'd elected to sit in one of the ship's interior hallways, back pressed against the cold metal of the wall, eyes closed and teeth clenched.

But now that the floor had stopped moving, he found himself much more capable of pushing back the panic.

"Aran, the captain's calling for you! You best get yourself into the cockpit before he decides you're too edible to resist." The raider was grinning, but Aran got the sense she'd have been grinning whether her words were a threat or an attempt at a joke.

He pushed himself to his feet, grabbing onto the wall for support for just a moment, his legs still shaky from the terror.

"Human! What's the matter, didn't you hear—" The raider staggered as a blow hit her upside the head.

"He doesn't like being shouted at," snapped Dessi, massaging her knuckles. "And after everything I've gone through to get these specimens, I'll be damned if I let you damage this one."

Aran almost expected the raider to turn on Dessi and start a brawl to the death in the middle of the hallway—Dessi was significantly shorter than the other raider, her build not nearly as muscular—but her position as either crew mascot or special friend of the captain's seemed to be enough to quell any argument.

Aran looked between Dessi and the crewmember, who'd turned away, scowling to herself. "I ... thought you didn't believe in violence."

Dessi raised her eyebrows. "I don't."

"You just hit that woman in the head."

Dessi's face cleared, and she laughed. "Oh, that? That's not violence, that's just clear communication. Are you ready? We're back on-planet, at our main trading city. If we're going to hear word of where Sharda's gone, this is where we'll find it. She won't have stopped here, I don't think—she'll have gone on to wherever she plans to wait for the challenge, because after the portal was shut down, she won't be popular. But rumours spread."

She looked Aran over critically. "I'll get you body armour—you'll probably need it. Everyone here will see you as food, so it would be wise for you to wear something that will at least turn their teeth until the rest of us have time to explain the situation."

Usually, a comment like that would have significantly increased Aran's anxiety. At this point, however, he was so far beyond the limits of his comfort zone that the thought of being chewed on a few times before he managed to explain what he was looking for seemed hardly worth noting.

"Go on, I'll catch you up," said Dessi. "There're some old armoured shirts of mine that might work. They'll be big, but it'll certainly be better than trying to fit you into something of Krevai's."

She turned and started off cheerfully, leaving Aran to make his way to the cockpit.

Krevai turned at his entrance. "Aran! Good, you survived your space trip. I always assumed humans had to be sturdy enough to take space travel, but I wasn't completely sure after what your Istvay told me the other day, about you getting stressed out by space travel and crowds and loud noises and so forth. But you're not too stressed? You're still able to function?"

Aran sighed and nodded. At this point, he wasn't sure that "too stressed" was a concept that held any meaning.

Dessi ducked into the cabin a moment later, and Krevai grinned at her. "Dessi! You're coming, of course—it's been too long since you've been in the city. Who knew it would only take Sharda kidnapping one of your research subjects to get you back here!"

Dessi shot him her signature scowl. "Just because I prefer my own company does not mean that I'm frightened of the trading city," she said haughtily. "I was just going to get some armour for our human, so the first time someone takes a bite out of him, I don't lose all the effort I've put into this research."

The captain narrowed his eyebrows. "Speaking of effort, one of these days you're going to have to explain why you thought letting the humans go and shut down the portal was a good idea."

Dessi snorted. "I don't like violence, you know that perfectly well," she retorted. "What did you expect me to do when his Ani tried to eat me?"

"And it's just a coincidence, I suppose, that the first time his Ani has ever threatened you was the time that forced you to let the humans shut down a portal, when it just so happened that you were opposed to us going through this portal in the first place?" Krevai's voice had lowered into something close to a growl.

Ani, sensing the tension in the room, chimed in with a growl of her own, and Aran put a cautioning hand on her tentacles.

Dessi sighed deeply. "Assuming, despite all my objections, that you're correct, if the portal had stayed open, Sharda would be the undisputed leader of the raiders. I assume that that's not exactly your ideal outcome."

Krevai stared at her for a long moment, his eyebrows still lowered.

Dessi, who didn't look cowed in the least, glared back.

At last, Krevai chuckled, shaking his head. "Dessi, what are we going to do with you? You're right, of course. But I let you get away with far too much, my friend."

"Because I'm a status symbol," Dessi snapped back. "You're the only raider captain with an in-house scientist."

Krevai burst into genuine laughter. "Ah, Dessi," he wheezed, wiping it his eyes. "This is why I keep you around. You're always good for a laugh. Almost as much as our little human and his Ani. You always were, ever since I picked you up as a scrawny little runt off Rak's crew."

Dessi smiled reluctantly. "And you were such a very important captain then? Bilge-sweep, I think you were. You kept me around because I was the only one willing to be seen with you."

There was a fondness in both their expressions that told Aran that this was an exchange that had played out more than once.

Dessi tossed the armoured tunic at Aran, and he unstrapped his knapsack and nudged Ani off his shoulder as he pulled the heavy cloth over his head. It was significantly too big for him, and he had to roll up the sleeves in a way that reminded him, suddenly and sharply, of the many foster homes he'd spent time in where none of the clothing actually fit him, and was always passed down from someone else.

"Bring your Ani," said Krevai, standing. "She'll come in handy if someone tries to eat you."

Aran sighed, trying not to imagine Ani's reaction to an entire city full of raiders who would apparently see him as nothing more than a snack on legs.

On the other hand, with as clingy as she'd been, leaving her behind would have been impossible anyways.

"You stay with him, Dessi. I'll leave a couple of the crew with you as well, in case we get separated—shame for you to have to break your pacifist streak." He shot her a sharp grin, and she gave an exasperated sigh.

"Don't worry, Aran," said Krevai cheerfully. "I'm sure someone will know where Sharda went. And if they don't want to talk to us —" his grin widened. "Well, it's been a while since I let the crew hunt."

Ani had wound herself around Aran's face again, making muted sounds of concern, and Aran prised a tentacle away from his mouth. "Easy, girl," he whispered. "If you behave, I'll give you a treat when we get back." He reached into the pocket of his battered jacket and pulled out a bit of energy bar, and she took it with one tentacle, clicking her beak in satisfaction.

He grinned to himself. She didn't actually like energy bars, she just liked the fact that she was getting the same food he and Istvay ate—

He had to cut off the thought quickly.

He could think about it later, when he was alone in his room. When they found out where Sharda had gone, and were on their way after her.

When he could fall apart, and no one was depending on him to hold it together.

Krevai's crew was made up of what Aran guessed to be around two hundred people, but the landing party Krevai had picked out was comprised of seventeen—five that Krevai had assigned to him and Dessi, and who were eyeing Ani dubiously, and the rest gathered up behind Krevai.

"Listen, you lot," Krevai bellowed. "We're here to find out where Sharda's run off to. She just declared a leadership war with her little stunt, and I intend to win it. Don't kill anyone unless you have to. It would be a shame if we ran out of raider crews to be leader of." He grinned, and in his grin, Aran read a very loose definition of the concept, 'unless you have to.'

The other raiders shouted their agreement, apparently unconcerned by the thought of a leadership war with themselves at the centre of it.

"If anyone of you gets killed, make sure someone calls it in," said Krevai with a casual wave of his hand. "Don't want to be waiting around for someone who's not going to show up. And besides—" he grinned wider, his teeth showing sharp through the expression. "It'll give us our next target to go after once we kill Sharda. And you lot," Krevai turned to the five raiders with Aran and Dessi. "You're to keep our scientist and our human safe, or don't bother coming back —I see you back here without them, and the rest of us will be eating your hearts for dinner." He paused, then grinned. "I don't think you have to worry about protecting the Ani. She seems capable of holding her own."

The raiders, grinning and laughing, shoved and jostled their way down the gangplank, Krevai striding ahead of them like a proud mother duck with her ducklings.

Dessi watched them go, shaking her head. She turned back to Aran. "Shall we?"

Aran nodded, swallowing hard, and stepped down the gangplank after her, their assigned bodyguards following close at his heels.

As he stepped off the gangplank and out into the crowded bustle of the port city streets, the noisy chaos of the place crashed against him like a physical blow. The sun, high in the sky, glinted off the bright white walls of the buildings and the puddles of water or refuse that gleamed in the streets, and the place was crowded with raiders, jostling, shouting, calling loudly to each other, sometimes in whatever the raider language was called, other times in the human Common Dialect.

Aran raised an eyebrow, his curiosity engaged despite the chaos. "Do all raiders speak Common Dialect?" he shouted at Dessi.

She glanced back at him. He could tell from the set of her posture that she wasn't any more comfortable in the chaos than he was. "We use it as a bit of a trader tongue," she called back over the noise. "Most of the yibo understand it, and the humans do as well, at least, the domesticated ones the yibos' keep. And you put a raider crew on their own on a long enough hunting mission, and their children come home speaking something the rest of us won't even understand. Common Dialect is the one we all go back to—makes things easier."

Aran nodded.

The discomfort of too many people in too small a space was crawling up his spine and itching under his skin, prickling a twinge of nausea into his stomach, but he swallowed hard and pushed it back. He'd dealt with worse than this before. And he'd deal with a million times worse than this again, if it meant getting Istvay back.

The raider city looked like a cross between the inner city of do Sol, where Istvay, and by extension Aran, had grown up, and one of the larger and more lawless Rim Mountain villages. The buildings were low and squat and constructed of a rough material that somehow seemed to retain its whiteness despite the dirt, grime, mud, and what looked like blood spattered against it. There were no peaceful tree-lined avenues as in the yibo city—this place had clearly been built for utility rather than looks—but there was plenty of greenery—vegetation springing up unbidden in cracks in the street or between buildings, scraggly evergreens growing wherever they could get a foothold, and the raider town simply forming itself around them.

"Stay with me," Dessi called. "We'll follow Krevai for as long as we can, until he gets into a fight. That will at least take us into the middle of the city, I suspect."

Aran nodded, not bothering to attempt a reply. The shouts and laughter of the raiders, the ring of boots on the rough surfaces of the street, the glare of the sun against the bright white of the buildings, had already started a dull headache pounding behind his eyes.

He breathed in deeply through his nose, his hand resting on one of Ani's tentacles. She'd wrapped herself around his shoulders, plastering her bulbous body to his back, and was growling softly to herself, her protuberant eyes peering around for any sign of a threat.

"This is one of our biggest trading cities," Dessi shouted as they walked, her voice barely enough to carry over the clamour around them. "With all the ships gathered to wait for the portal to open since Sharda sent out the call, it's busier than it usually is this time of year." She grinned a little. "And I suspect most of them aren't very happy with Sharda at the moment—she promised them a system full of humans to hunt, and now the portal's shut down and she's gone."

Someone shouted, and Aran spun just in time to see a raider grab another by the hair, swing them around, and slam them face-first into a building.

The victim gave a grunt of pain and staggered back, yanking out a weapon, and there was a bright spurt of blood as a knife slid through the belly of the raider's would-be attacker.

Dessi looked away, her expression faintly sick, and Aran swallowed hard.

No one else seemed to think the interaction worthy of note, though, the rest of the city simply stepping around and over the body without so much as pausing conversations.

Dessi must have caught Aran's expression. "There are reasons raider crews tend not to congregate in one place. Our society is built on immense loyalty within crews, which tends to lead to … interpersonal conflicts when crews mix. And besides, if there are raiders who become each other's mates, and they're on different crews, it becomes an unofficial peace treaty between the two crews for as long as it lasts. No captain wants to be burdened with a peace treaty unwillingly, so they try to make sure their crews have as little peaceful interaction with another captain's crew as possible." She paused, then muttered sourly, "And Krevai always asks me why I don't want to come with him on his supply runs."

He could still make out Krevai ahead of them, the raider captain's brilliant red cloak bright against the drab raider uniforms, his broad shoulders cutting a swath through the crowded streets. It seemed he hadn't oversold his reputation—no one appeared eager to get in his way.

As they got closer to the centre of the city, the noise and bustle around them rose in volume and pitch. Twice, the bodyguards Krevai had set him and Dessi stepped in front of them, shoving a path for the two of them through a brawl or a murder—Aran wasn't entirely sure he could tell the difference at this point. His head was pounding, and he could feel his chest tightening and his breath coming quicker, despite his best efforts.

Damn it to hell, getting kidnapped by raiders he could handle. Things trying to eat him he could deal with. But why the hell did he have to be shoved into the middle of a noisy, crowded city, people jostling and bumping up against him, the sun shining off the white buildings brilliant enough to give him a headache, the smell and heat of too many bodies in too small a space pressing on his senses like a thick blanket, and endless, exhausting noise that wouldn't stop no matter how much he tried to shut it out?

"Ah, I see you brought a snack. Mind if I try some?" A raider, not from Krevai's crew, stepped forward, grinning at Dessi.

"He's mine, don't touch him," Dessi snapped, and the raider's grin widened.

"You're not much of a fighter, are you?" The newcomer gestured casually at Dessi's short hair. "Forgive me if I don't wait for permission."

She stepped towards Aran, grabbing for his shoulder as the bodyguards from Krevai's crew leapt forward.

She got a handful, instead, of Ani's tentacle.

She had just enough time to look surprised before Ani spat. The raider woman staggered back, her screams of agony fading to muffled gurgles as she fell, writhing, to the cobblestones.

Aran winced.

There was a moment of silence, as what felt like the entire street turned to look at him and Dessi.

Then Krevai's bodyguards, who'd been standing, hands frozen on their weapons, whooped. "You don't mess with Krevai's scientist and her pet, not if you know what's good for you," one of them crowed.

Aran sighed internally, trying to force himself to draw in a full breath. Ani gave a questioning little chirrup, touching his face delicately. He managed a small smile and patted her head. "Good girl, sweetheart," he whispered. "You did a good job."

She vibrated with a contented purr, and reattached herself to him.

"Ani, sweetheart …" he muttered, prying a tentacle off his mouth again.

It was just crowds, nothing he hadn't dealt with before. Granted, he usually dealt with it by finding a quiet place where he could have a silent panic attack, but still—

They caught up with Krevai again a couple of streets down. He was in the middle of a packed crowd of raiders, bellowing greetings and good-natured threats to all and sundry. His eyes lit up when he caught sight of Dessi and Aran. "That there, that's my human," he shouted, pointing at Aran. "And the raider is my scientist. If anyone tries to eat them, I'll rip your heart out and eat it myself, it's been a while since I've had fresh meat." He laughed heartily at his own joke, but from the expressions on the faces around him, it wasn't entirely a joke.

"Sharda kidnapped one of my humans as a leadership challenge," he continued, his voice loud enough to carry over the chaos. "I say, if she wants a leadership challenge, I'll give it to her. But she's run off, and I need to know where to find her. Anyone who wants to come talk to me, declare yourself before the contest starts, I'm sure you'll get more than your share of favours out of it. You all know how I treat people who are loyal. And how I treat those who aren't."

The gathered raiders were shouting and talking, a garbled mix of Common Dialect and raider dialects that Aran had no hope of understanding. He'd half-way turned to ask Dessi what was happening when he saw from the corner of his eye a raider behind Krevai yank out a pistol.

"Krevai!" he shouted, although across the crowded square, there was no chance the captain would hear him. Krevai seemed to have sensed something, though, because he spun, just as the other raider brought his pistol level.

"Sharda's explained what happened," the raider hissed, and fired directly into Krevai's chest.

Aran sucked in a quick, horrified breath.

Then Krevai, moving with the deadly grace of a striking snake, flattened his attacker with one blow of his fist.

There was a moment of silence.

Then Krevai's laughter echoed through the square. "You thought I wouldn't come with an armoured vest?" he chortled. Then his grin turned dangerous, and he spun around, yanking out a long, vicious-looking knife as another raider leapt at him.

Krevai's crew were shoving their way through the crowd to his sides, whooping with delight as more raiders piled into the battle, and the street devolved into screams and shouts, growling and snarling, the hiss of weapons and the metallic ring of knifes clashing or the bloody squelch as they found flesh.

5

Alba

The city around her probably should have caught more of Alba's attention, now it was daylight and she was awake enough to see it. Instead, at the end of the transport ride, she couldn't have told anyone who asked even the faded colour of the transport seats. She hadn't noticed the exterior of the building as they entered, except for a vague impression that it was large and grand.

Despite her exhaustion, she'd hardly slept at all the previous night, and now her brain buzzed with a sharp, over-bright clarity condensed from too little sleep and too much strain.

Jair stopped at the security checkpoint. "The interpreter will take you from here," he said quietly.

Alba gave the man a curt nod—he deserved more, but she didn't have the mental capacity at the moment—and turned to the yibo waiting for her in the hallway on the other side of the checkpoint. He looked bored, as if this was a common but unpleasant duty, and she was reminded uncomfortably of how little status she currently had.

The halls of the yibo government building were long and narrow, and her guide walked quickly enough that Alba was constantly in danger of being left behind. At one point, she actually lost him, reaching a fork in the corridor and pausing, unsure of which direction he'd gone. She stood there for a humiliating, helpless few moments before she heard his brisk footsteps returning, and, with a long-suffering sigh, he gestured her to please keep up.

At last, she was brought to a small, claustrophobic room with a door on each side.

"They'll call you when it's your turn to speak," said her guide. "I'll translate as you give your speech. Please speak slowly and clearly, and pause after every sentence to give me time to finish before you go on."

Alba tipped her head in acknowledgement, the yibo gesture coming now almost as naturally as a human nod would have before. And then she waited, leaning up against the side of the wall, as the room seemed not to have been provided with even one of the uncomfortable stools.

At last, there was a tap on the outside of the door. The interpreter stepped forward, pushing the door open, and gestured Alba to follow.

The room Alba stepped into wasn't the rotunda of the Council Hall back on Colorida, but there was an air of grandeur to the place that Alba recognized in her bones—a place for important people, who knew that the impact of the decisions they made here would reverberate throughout the system.

The interpreter said something in the yibo language that Alba's wavelink translated as a meaningless string of words—likely a ceremonial greeting of some sort. As he spoke, Alba tried to calm her nerves by observing her surroundings.

The hall was decorated in what Alba had come to consider yibo aesthetic—the walls mostly windows, with the greenery of potted plants climbing artfully around the trusses, their spreading leaves opening overhead to form the illusion, almost, of standing under the canopy of a forest. The yibo government officials were arranged on tiers of branching seats that rose up towards the ceiling, out of view in the shadows. The irregularity of the arrangement, combined with the greenery and the yibos' lemur-like appearance, gave Alba, for just a moment, the impression of being watched from the trees of a jungle by a conspiracy of curious animals.

She pushed the image out of her head, scolding herself internally. Differences in culture were not an excuse to dehumanize one's galactic neighbours, after all. Still, something primal in the back of her brain buzzed at the perception of a threat.

"Go ahead, human," said the interpreter, turning back to her. "Explain how you came to be in our system, and what happened with closing the portal. Slowly and clearly, please."

Alba nodded, straightening. She had no idea how the seating or the seniority was arranged, but some political sense told her that the yibo woman seated on one of the higher tiers, with dark brown eye patches and the wrinkles of age, was the person to whom she should address herself.

"Advisors," she began. "As I'm sure you are aware, I and a number of my compatriots were sent on a diplomatic mission through a portal which appeared unexpectedly in our system, to open up relations with whatever sapient species were on the other side. Shortly after our ship passed through, however, the portal itself closed, and our ship was destroyed by the resultant release of energy."

Even now, weeks removed and with so much that had happened between, the memory of the ship's death—panicked people pushing and shoving and trampling each other for any means of escape, looking through the window of the escape pod at the icy shards, remnants of the ship and the frozen, lifeless bodies of the crew mingled, spreading in a deceptively peaceful halo through the vacuum of space—still had the power to catch her breath in her chest.

She cleared her throat. "Those of us who survived the break-up landed on the nearest inhabited planet, which was under the control of Kachik and his people. We were taken to Chrr, and unaware as we were of the politics here, we understood Kachik to be the head of government. He did all in his power to maintain that deception during our time with him."

There was a quiet murmuring around the room as the interpreter translated her last few sentences, and Alba noticed the older yibo's face darken.

"During the course of our negotiations," Alba continued, "Kachik appeared interested in arranging an alliance. Although I believed at the time that I was negotiating with a legitimate authority, the things he asked for—an unequivocal promise of military alliance, in particular—made me uneasy of his motivations. There were, however, other members of our diplomatic party who, although unauthorized by our own legitimate government authority to negotiate, had no such qualms, and were more than willing to promise mutual military aid in exchange for a perceived political advantage back in our home system. When I learned, through carelessness on Kachik's part, of the true nature of Kachik's plans for the so-called alliance, I realized they would result in the entire destruction of my home system. My compatriots and I were able to ascertain the location of the mechanism that controlled the portal Kachik had opened, and we determined that our best chance at preventing a genocide was to destroy the portal mechanism."

"And what, may I ask, led you to believe you had the authority to do this?" asked another yibo politician in a bored voice. They didn't bother speaking in Common Dialect, and as she had not yet explained her translation program, Alba waited for the interpreter to translate.

It also gave her an additional moment to bite back the sharp retort that wanted to slip from her tongue.

"As I explained," she said when the interpreter had finished, "at the time we were unaware there was another government entity. We believed we had exhausted our avenues of appeal, and it was act, or allow our system to be destroyed. We—I must admit, we did not expect to live past that point, and I believe it is only through your intervention that we did so. For that, I express our deepest gratitude."

There was a small rustle among the assembled yibo, heads tipped to one side in acknowledgement.

"And the raiders?" asked another of the yibo. "What of them? We heard reports that there were raiders battling around the site of the portal mechanism."

Again, Alba paused. "They were … pursuing members of our party," she said at last. "And although I cannot say I am an expert in raider society, it appeared two opposing factions arrived in pursuit, whereupon they engaged in battle, allowing us to take down the portal."

She wasn't entirely sure how to explain that her diplomatic party's resident scientist and his assistant had tracked the raiders down, on purpose, in order to collaborate with them on scientific research, had then, at her urging, stolen a raider attack pod and escaped, been recaptured, and had then been set free again by a raider scientist who was apparently worried about how the destruction of the Joias System and its negative impacts on her test subjects' psyche would impact her studies, in a way that was in any sense believable.

Had she not spent the amount of time she had with Aran and Istvay, she wasn't sure she would have believed it herself.

The yibo politician leaned closer. "And two of your party went with them?"

Alba sighed. "The scientist who accompanied us and his assistant agreed to go with them, yes. In exchange for our freedom."

"And you, as leader of this mission, let them?"

"As the alternative was allowing our entire party to be killed and eaten, the portal to remain open, and my home system to be wiped out of existence, I hardly felt myself in a position to forbid them," Alba snapped, too exhausted for a moment to put on a facade of politeness.

The yibo politician gave her a disapproving look.

"We keep a close eye on the raiders, for reasons I'm certain you'll understand," said another politician. "And now, it appears, there are rumours of a raider leadership war, along with rumours of a crew with a human on it. Is that one of yours?"

"I cannot be certain, but it is certainly possible," she said cautiously.

"And what of the other survivors?" asked the yibo woman who Alba had judged to be in charge of the proceedings. "You left them with Kachik?"

Alba drew in a steadying breath. "When we took our leave of Kachik," she said at last, feeling out her words, "we escaped from a prison that was meant to hold us until the execution he had arranged for us the next morning. Under the circumstances, fleeing for our lives appeared to be the only viable option left to us at the time. We could no more than hope that Kachik would keep the remainder of our party alive during the course of the negotiations."

She tried to keep the trace of sarcasm from her tone. She'd love to see anyone of these yibo who were sitting in judgement think lucidly about both the future of their system and the lives of their fellows, weigh them against each other, and come up with a more productive solution, all with the threat of execution by yibo, or murder and dismemberment by raiders, hanging over their heads. "That itself was the reason I asked to speak with you today—I had hoped you would intercede with Kachik and allow the survivors of my party to be brought here. Aside from my own personal interest in this matter, I can tell you that Kachik intends to oppose you, with violence if necessary, and he intends to use the humans, as unwilling as they may be, to assist him in doing so."

The yibo woman nodded slowly. "I suppose I can see how you might have come to the conclusions you did. Still, although I can hardly judge you for your actions, you must see how this puts our government in something of a bind. Our relations with Kachik's Nativists have been strained for some time. In taking you in, we've offered asylum to humans who have caused an unspeakable amount of damage to the Nativists' infrastructure, no matter how ill-gotten that infrastructure might have been. And now you're asking us to intercede again." The woman's gaze was sharp and calculating. "Having spent time in Chrr, human, what is your opinion on the danger facing your fellow humans?"

Alba clenched her hands in the sleeves of her tunic to stop them trembling. "Not to put too fine a point on it, I hold out very little hope for their survival if your government doesn't step in. Kachik's plans were to use our system to gain an advantage in a war. I didn't know at the time against whom the war would be fought, but the logical conclusion seems to be, against yourselves. He treated us very well until he realized that I would not give him what he was looking for. The moment he came to that conclusion, he instructed his guards to lock me up in preparation for my execution the next day. I suspect now that he realizes he can't get what he's looking for from the Joias System, he will see very little profit in keeping his human prisoners alive."

"Which is more or less what we had expected," said a younger politician. "I think we all know his philosophy on humans as a species."

"Perhaps," said another politician, glancing up. "But I would argue that makes our situation that much more delicate. This raider war is going to bring more trouble than we already have, and for whatever reason, at least some of these humans seem to be involved in it. These humans, as this one has already admitted, are—you'll excuse my crassness, but with the portal closed, they are an asset that has lost its value. Kachik, she says, won't see humans as valuable enough to keep alive—perhaps the question should be, are they valuable enough to us to start a war over, especially now, with this unrest among the raiders? Kachik didn't send an army through the portal after them, they made the choice to come through on their own, and their ship broke up when the raiders took down the portal. Neither of those occurrences were properly our fault. So it seems odd that they should expect us to pay a political price to save them from their own errors." They shook their head. "We have more important things to worry about than a band of humans who may or may not be in any real danger."

Alba bit down hard on her tongue. The politicians were speaking yibo, and even if they hadn't been, interrupting a government proceeding would be unlikely to win her any political favours.

"Still, I would argue we bear some responsibility for humankind—they are sapient lifeforms after all, and we count a not insignificant number of them among the inhabitants of our system," another politician chimed in.

Alba watched, memorizing the faces of those who appeared friendly.

"If I may," she said at last, turning to the interpreter. "What are they saying?"

The interpreter waved a hand. "They're talking about internal political matters," he said.

"If it would be appropriate, I would like to give more detail as to the humans who are in Kachik's clutches at present," she said, trying very hard to keep her tone polite despite her rising irritation.

The interpreter hesitated, then, with a long-suffering sigh, said something into the next pause.

The yibo woman who appeared to be in charge glanced at Alba curiously, then tipped her head to one side. "Go ahead, human, what did you wish to add?"

"I simply wished to inform you that many of the survivors from our ship have expertise in technical matters—engineers, mechanics, etc. Our technologies differ substantially from yours, and their insights would provide a valuable resource. Kachik is preparing for an armed struggle. And while we may not have raiders in our system, I'm certain that our knowledge base could provide options to protect your cities and yourselves that may not otherwise be possible. Even placing to one side the ethics of leaving innocent refugees to be slaughtered, it seems unwise to allow such a resource to be destroyed, or put to use by your enemy."

"That is true," said the young politician thoughtfully. "The Nativists can hardly claim that the humans belong to them merely because their ship crashed on the planet the Nativists are occupying. I see no harm in at the least requesting that the humans be brought to neutral ground and negotiated over."

"It would be a good opening bargaining point," said another politician. "But the humans' knowledge, while interesting, can't be that much different from what we know from the other humans who live here. It certainly isn't going to give us enough assistance against the raiders to offset the effects of focusing on this when we should be focused on the survival of our settlements. I suggest that we use the humans as a concession we can offer the Nativists in exchange for closer relations. After all, with all due respect to the human inhabitants of our system, any value that their society could provide ours has already been given and taken. This is an emergency situation that we're facing. I hardly think we can argue that the value of human lives would outweigh the inevitable suffering of our own people should we be unable to protect ourselves against the raiders, or bridge our disagreements with Kachik's Nativists."

"And how many more humans are going to show up at our gates, demanding that we sacrifice ourselves and our comforts in order to provide them refuge? We are already providing, on the public purse, accommodations and food for—how many human refugees do we have here at the moment? I've lost count. And they keep coming in. What these new humans are asking is something a step beyond even that. This isn't providing for citizens of our own system, this is strangers actively interfering in the delicate balance of our own internal affairs."

"We don't know the Nativists will mistreat them. The only reason we have to believe this is the humans' own suspicions. This is all conjecture. If it's true that humans are valuable, I hardly see Kachik wasting that resource. Chances are, they'll be treated as well there as they would be here."

Alba listened, too numb to feel horrified.

The worst of it was, the voices were reasonable, their words calm and thoughtful, not a fanatical heat-filled rant. Words she could almost, in a different context, imagine herself saying, arguments that she could perhaps see herself making in another situation.

She might, in their shoes, have believe the arguments herself.

She might have, had she not seen the icy hatred in Kachik's face when he ordered her execution.

"Please," she began, turning to the interpreter, but he cut her off impatiently.

"I believe they've heard everything they need from you. You may come back on their invitation, and I'm sure they will issue such if they require further information."

"Please, I need to—"

He cut her off again, pulling the door open and gesturing her through. "You are dismissed," he snapped. "I suggest you leave before I call the guards."

For half a moment, Alba was tempted to simply shout out her argument to the crowd, interrupt the decorum of the setting. But she'd heard enough and seen enough from the other side of the benches herself to know that that would be no use—she would only brand herself as a fanatic, and it would just make it easier for them to disregard her words completely.

So she stepped out through the doors, the bitter taste of hopelessness in her mouth.

6

Savina

The yibo tavern keeper had recognized Savina on sight—not that surprising, considering that the last time she'd been there, she'd shot a raider in the face.

That had been—a while ago. Savina was a little hazy on the details at this point. She was also a little hazy on the number of drinks she'd consumed.

She probably could have figured it out by counting the empty glasses on the bar in front of her, but she didn't really feel the need.

She felt light, and happy, and a little floaty—probably something to do with whatever was in the blunt the trembling tavern keeper had handed her when she'd yanked out a knife and held it under his chin.

It was still smouldering, and she brought it to her lips and took a long pull of the fragrant smoke, holding it in her lungs for a few moments before she blew it out.

The whole world had gone soft, and a little fuzzy around the edges, and she smiled to herself, leaning back in her seat. Her body was loose and light, her blood slow and soft in her veins, like maple syrup.

The tavern keeper was huddled against one corner of the wall, and she beckoned to him, pointing at her empty glass. He darted over, refilling it quickly, then pushed it across the bar, his hands trembling.

Savina laughed, a low, delighted laugh.

"It's not," she tried, but her tongue was thick, her words slow and sticky, blending together on their way out of her mouth. She tried again. "'T's not—it's not like you're going to have to put up with this for long. Reka's on her way, she'll be here any minute now." She picked up the drink, although she had to try a couple times before she got her hands firmly around it. When she did, she raised it in a drunken salute to the tavern keeper. "And when she does, you can watch her shoot me right in the head." She giggled, and brought the drink to her lips.

When she tried to put it back down on the counter, the surface wasn't where she'd expected it to be, and the drink tipped over, spilling everywhere. She watched the puddle spread across the surface of the bar, glistening in the low light.

It was so pretty. Everything was so pretty—the way the light glittered off the liquid, the way it spread and dripped down the edge of the counter and pooled on the floor.

Everything here was so beautiful, the lights, the colours, that nice, nice yibo tavern keeper, cowering in the corner.

Why was he afraid again?

She laughed.

Of course. He was afraid of her. Because she'd cut his belly wide open the moment he did something she didn't like.

The door to the tavern burst open, and Savina turned.

Then she choked on her breath.

Reka Soler stood silhouetted in the doorway, the backlighting from the streetlights outside making her glow around the edges.

She was … stunning.

"Reka Soler," Savina slurred. "I've been—" she hiccupped. "I've been waiting for you."

Reka spun, staring at her, and Savina leaned back in her seat, half closing her eyes.

She'd never truly appreciated, until now, how beautiful Reka was —that sharp, icy gaze, her sensuous mouth, the curves of her body that Savina's eyes could get lost in, the muscles in her arms and shoulders, shapely and defined and perfect.

"Savina?" Reka's voice was sharp and incredulous.

Savina grinned. "I thought you'd be happy to see me. I've been— I've—" Dammit, why weren't her lips working? If she focused hard enough, maybe— "I've been waiting for you," she enunciated, then smiled proudly.

Reka was still staring. "Savina! What the hell is going on?"

Her lips were so perfect. So perfect, and so pretty, and … how would they feel against Savina's lips? On her skin? It was an intriguing thought, and it captured Savina's full attention.

"Savina?"

She blinked back up at Reka, then smiled and gestured around her expansively. "I've been—been—waiting for you."

She'd said that already, hadn't she? Why was Reka still asking the same question?

"I—I tried to kill you. And then—and then I couldn't. So I thought—" she hiccupped again, and laughed, because it was funny. "So I thought, since you were going to kill me anyway, I may as well enjoy myself before you did."

Reka was still staring at her.

"I'm glad it's you who's going to kill me," Savina said, leaning forward confidentially. She had to catch herself against the bar, because the room was swaying around her. Like it was dancing. "You're— you're—" she was having a hard time remembering the word she was trying to say, so she waved her hand vaguely.

Reka was smart. She'd understand.

Savina leaned back in her seat again, because it was dangerous, trying to move around when the whole world was swaying.

Maybe this was what heaven felt like. Everything slow and soft, every muscle in her body relaxed, everything so perfect, this feeling of floating just a little above the floor.

She let her eyes drag over Reka's body again. She wanted to run her hands along Reka's curves, feel the muscles under her skin, lick away those small beads of sweat that had formed on Reka's upper lip.

Reka's cheeks were flushed, her posture taut. But she shook herself out of whatever reverie she'd been in, and strode over to Savina, grabbing her by the arm. "Savina," she snapped. "I don't know what the hell you did, but word got around. There's a whole band of yibo outside, probably your former coworkers. They all want to kill you, and the only thing holding them back is that none of them wants to be the first one to walk through the door. But that won't last forever. At some point, one of them will get up the courage to check, and if they see you in this damn state—"

Savina giggled. "I don't want them to kill me. Just you. Only you. I've been waiting for you."

Reka leaned down.

Her face was so close to Savina's, those beautiful, sensuous lips so close, and Savina could feel the heat gathering low in the pit of her stomach that she'd always fought back, before.

She couldn't remember why, though, and she was about to die, so it hardly mattered.

She leaned forward, catching Reka's lips with her own.

Reka's mouth was warm and sweet, her lips so soft, better than anything Savina had ever imagined. Little sparks exploded through her whole body, and she groaned in pleasure. It was so good, better than anything, better than the blunt she'd been smoking, better than the alcohol. She leaned in, deepening the kiss, and Reka's lips parted slightly at the pressure of her tongue, her hands catching Savina's shoulders. Savina moaned again, and there was nothing in the entire world but Reka, the taste of her, the warmth, the way her touched sparkled and hummed in Savina's blood …

Reka jerked away, her face flushed, her eyes wide and startled.

Savina laughed, low and lazy. "Come on, Reka, I'm all yours. Whatever you want. Kiss me or kill me. Or both. You could do both, if you wanted."

"I'm not here to kill you," hissed Reka through her teeth. "And I'm damn well not here to kiss you. I'm trying to save your damn life."

Savina blinked at her, then pouted. "I went to … to all this work."

"Can you walk?" Reka snapped.

Savina wanted to kiss her again, but she wasn't sure she could move anymore, because she wasn't really sure her head was attached to the rest of her. Or that her limbs were. It was all very confusing.

But Reka was so pretty. If Reka wanted her to walk—

She slid off the stool. Her legs gave out completely, and she landed in a heap on the floor, laughing.

Reka bent over her, which was exactly what she'd been wanting, probably. Her arms came around Savina, lifting her, and Savina sighed in satisfaction.

"You're so strong," she slurred. "You're so—so—" she hiccupped again, and was caught with another fit of giggles.

Reka sighed in exasperation, hoisting Savina up so her face was buried in Reka's shoulder, her feet dangling off the ground. Savina laughed in sheer enjoyment. She was pretty sure Reka was supposed to be killing her, but this was even better than being killed.

Dimly, she heard the tavern keeper shout, heard Reka curse. She lifted her head enough to slur out a curse as well, since that seemed to be the appropriate response, and then dissolved into helpless laughter.

Yibo were shoving through the door, shouting, pulling out weapons, and she watched them through half-lidded eyes.

None of it made sense, and Reka's arms were so strong, and Savina couldn't remember ever feeling this good. She trailed her hand down the muscles in Reka's back as Reka spun, cursing steadily, and shot two yibo at point-blank range. She ducked as a shot impacted against the wall behind them, then grabbed one of the yibo in her free hand, shoving them up against the wall so their skull hit the glass with an audible *crack*, then spinning them around, sending them flying into the crowd still pushing through the door.

"Dammit, Savina, of all the damn times to pick to get wasted—" Reka muttered, the words making a soft rumble where Savina's ear was pressed against the side of her throat.

Savina hummed in contentment and turned her face, pressing her lips to the warm skin that tasted of salt and sweat and soap.

Reka's body tensed, her arm tightening reflexively around Savina.

"Reka. You're so—you're so—" Savina let the sentence trail off, because her lips didn't want to make words anymore, and it seemed a bit unnecessary, anyways.

Weapons were firing, yibo voices shouting. Reka had jerked back into action and was shooting and shooting, one-armed, shoving her way out of the tavern, but it all seemed hazy and distant and dreamy.

She just—she needed another drink, that's what she needed, because the world was spinning too much and it was too loud and she was—she was tired, she was so tired, which didn't even make sense, she'd been waiting for Reka to kill her and—

And Reka was so warm, the soft hiss of her breath, the rapid gallop of her heartbeat singing through Savina's whole body.

She nestled her head into Reka's shoulder, and closed her eyes, and sank into unconsciousness.

7

Aran

"There's no way Sharda should have been able to come here!" Dessi half-shouted, her voice barely audible over the sudden chaos. "The crews should have torn her to pieces, after she let the portal go down!"

Aran didn't answer, so far past the limits of sensory overload that he wasn't sure his brain was even capable of parsing what had just happened.

Dessi gave him a worried look. "Come on, let's get you somewhere quieter," she shouted over the noise. She reached out to grab his arm, then stopped abruptly. "May I?"

If one more person touched him, Aran thought he might actually lose his mind.

He shook his head numbly, bracing himself for her to ignore him, but to his shock, Dessi just nodded and gestured with her head. "Follow me, then. You can have your Ani kill anyone who tries to touch you on the way."

Aran sucked in a breath through his nose and followed Dessi out to the back of the crowd, across the street that was much quieter now than it had been a few moments ago, the inhabitants having piled into the main square either to join into the fight or to watch it, then down a mouldy-smelling, crumbling set of stairs and through a decrepit doorway into a small, dark room that smelled sharply of alcohol.

He took a deep breath and closed his eyes, the sudden quiet an almost physical relief. When he opened them again, he blinked, trying to adjust his eyes to the dim inside of the bar.

"I thought this place might be empty if there was a fight outside," Dessi said. There was an unusual tension in the set of her shoulders.

"Is Krevai going to be alright? Should we go back to the ship, let the rest of the crew know?" He'd probably feel guilty, at some point, that his spike of panic had less to do with Krevai's wellbeing than it did for the fact that, without Krevai, he was unlikely to ever see Istvay again. Right now, though, he hardly cared.

Dessi's expression was worried. "He'll be fine, he'll call them if he needs them. It's just, this isn't usually how leadership battles go. And Sharda shouldn't have been able to find supporters so fast." She shook her head, as if brushing the matter from her mind. "Come on, we'll go sit in the back. It'll be quieter there, and from the look of you, you need it." She paused, peering at him curiously. "So humans are more sensitive to noise or being touched than we raiders are, then?"

Aran swallowed, still trying to push back the jittering panic of the noise and crowds from earlier. "It's … I mean, yes, but it's not really all humans. Istvay thinks I'm probably autistic, which would mean I'm more sensitive to that sort of thing than Istvay is, for instance, but—"

Dessi, who was listening with rapt attention, held up a hand. "Wait, let's sit down first. I want to take notes."

He followed her to a small table in the back corner. From the corner of his eye, he caught the bright streak of light when the door opened, and recognized the newcomers as Krevai's bodyguards. Once they noticed him and Dessi sitting peacefully in the back, though, they seemed perfectly content to pull up stools in the front of the bar and call out their orders.

"This is absolutely fascinating," said Dessi, pulling out a chair. She glanced up at Aran, gesturing impatiently to the chair across from her. "Go on, have a seat, no one's going to try to eat you here. They all know Krevai, they wouldn't dare. Now. You say that there are some humans who have less acute senses than normal? And your Istvay is one of them?" She pulled out her data pad. "Is it genetic? Do you have a name for it?"

"Um," Aran said. "I mean, people who aren't autistic are … I guess you'd call them allistic, and yes, it has a genetic component as far as we know, but it's not really … I mean, they aren't …"

Dessi was writing furiously on her data pad. "You say they aren't as sensitive to noise and touch and crowds, so I assume the genetic variance must affect their senses and their sensory reactions to some extent. Anything else I should know about them? I want to be sure to be sensitive to your Istvay's condition when we find them again." She shook her head, standing. "Wait here a minute, this might be a long conversation. You humans can drink alcohol, right? I'll get something for both of us, then, but I'll tell them to make sure yours isn't very strong. I'd hate to damage you on accident."

Aran refrained, with an effort, from sighing. If there had ever been a moment in his life where he could have used a strong drink … Still, at this point he was hardly going to argue.

As Dessi leaned against the bar to make her order, he glanced around. The neighbouring tables were occupied mostly by raiders who, by the looks of it, were either too old, or too inebriated, to bother with the fight outside.

"You here as a meal?" slurred one of them, leaning over towards Aran. "That one with you, she's that scientist Krevai picked up, isn't she? You think she'd share?"

Ani was growling, low and threatening, but she hadn't tried to leap off his shoulder to get at the man yet, which probably meant she, at least, didn't see the raider as much of a threat.

"No, I'm—I'm not here as food."

"He's part of Krevai's crew, and if you know what's good for your health, you'll remember that." Dessi had returned to the table with two large mugs. She dropped one in front of Aran and scowled at the raider.

The man leaned back, raising his hands in surrender. "No need to get upset. You know as well as I do you don't see many humans on crews these days."

"Well, this one is," Dessi snapped.

The raider shrugged, raising his mug to his lips. "Hear Sharda has one too, she was flaunting it around the other day. Status symbol, they're turning into."

Aran's heart almost stopped beating completely. "Sharda has a human on her crew? Not one she's planning to kill?"

The raider shrugged again and took a long pull from his mug. "From the sound of it, this one defected from Krevai's crew, asked to sign on with hers. Something like that, I don't know all the details. She was in here not too long ago, wanted everyone to know that Krevai's people are jumping ship like a bunch of space-lice when her crew shows up."

"Do—do you know the human's name? Or where Sharda's taken them?" Aran's voice was hoarse.

The man laughed. "We don't usually worry much about humans' names—around here, we mostly call them dinner." He chuckled at his own joke. "She said she'd sent coordinates to the captains who swore to follow her, and she'd kill whoever leaked them. Had a juicy prize for those who'd swear to her, too, she said. But I'm not getting in the middle of that, I'm too old."

Aran closed his eyes. He was lightheaded, and his lungs felt like they couldn't pull in enough oxygen

It was Istvay. It had to be Istvay.

The raider was still speaking. "Me, I'm used to the old-fashioned way, free-for-all and the victor wading through rivers of blood to claim their reputation. But Sharda's never been one for following tradition for tradition's sake, and she knows damn well the only one who'll challenge her is Krevai. And she'll have to have a quick crew or a foolproof plan to kill him. Crafty old bastard, Krevai."

"Did—did the human say anything while Sharda was showing them around? Anything at all?" Aran was trying, desperately, to keep his words casual.

The raider furrowed his brows. "No, the human didn't say much, only repeated what Sharda told it to. But in human words."

"What did they say exactly?"

Istvay wouldn't have done this without a reason. He knew Istvay, and short of actually killing them, Sharda wouldn't have been able to convince them to be paraded around like a trophy unless they had some reason to agree.

"People were angry about the portal, but Sharda told everyone she had a strategy. She said there'd be a leadership battle, and best start choosing sides now. And so did the human, when she nudged it. But it said …" he paused a moment, eyes pointed to one side as if trying to remember. "It said something about, we may as well pick sides, or Sharda is going to come after us like … what did it say? Something about a grey … something or other after a herd of mouse?" He laughed. "I'm sure that would've sounded impressive if you were a human."

Aran closed his eyes, sucking in a quick breath. "A southern greyback after a herd of doe-mice. Was that it?"

The raider peered at him more closely. "Yes, that may have been it. What did it mean?"

Aran closed his eyes for a moment.

"Aran? Are you alright? Is there too much noise? I can get them to—" Dessi's voice sounded distant, and distinctly worried.

Aran shook his head dazedly. "No, no, I'm fine."

Istvay had been trying to tell him something, they had to have been. There was no way they'd chosen that analogy on accident.

The door to the bar slammed open, the sudden light from outside all but blinding Aran. Krevai was silhouetted in the doorway, and in the brilliant backlighting, Aran couldn't make out either his expression, or the details of what he was holding.

The shape of the thing, though, was uncomfortably familiar, as was the sharp, warm scent of blood.

"Dessi?" Krevai hissed in an exaggerated whisper. "We've killed all the ones who were making too much noise, you can bring our human out again. And I brought you some nice fresh heart, in case you were getting tired of a vegetarian diet." He glanced at the object in his hand. "Do you think the human would like to—"

"No," said Dessi firmly. "Humans have very strict cultural rules about eating other humans, and considering that we're genetically related, I assume that would carry over." She paused. "Although there are some human cultures that allow it, I've heard, depending on the circumstance." She turned to Aran. "How would you feel about eating a raider heart, hypothetically? I know you prefer cooked meat, so—"

"Um. No, no that's fine, you enjoy it," Aran murmured. He was hardly listening to the conversation, his head spinning, his pulse pounding quick and loud in his ears.

Istvay was alive. And they'd left him a message, if he could figure out what the hell they were trying to tell him. He shoved his stool back from the table and stood. "Um. Dessi, can—can we go back to the ship? Or—or at least, somewhere we can talk in private?"

Dessi gave him a puzzled glance, and then glanced up at Krevai. When he nodded, Dessi stood as well, and Aran followed her out of the tavern, the captain falling in behind them.

They reached a narrow, filthy alley that smelled of refuse and the sharp, familiar sent of stale urine. Aran noted it in the back of his mind—the fact that the smell was so similar to human urine likely said something about raider physiology that he would be interested in learning, once his most pressing concern had been taken care of— but that was something he'd focus on later.

"What did you want to talk about?" Krevai wasn't frowning, exactly, but he didn't look entirely pleased to have been called away from what was apparently a very enjoyable pitched battle.

"Listen," said Aran. "I … think I know where Sharda's gone."

Both raiders turned to stare at him.

"We met someone in the tavern who said that Istvay had signed on with Sharda as part of her crew," said Aran, turning to Krevai.

Krevai's face darkened. "If that human—" he began.

Aran shook his head impatiently. "I've known Istvay my whole life. They wouldn't do something like that without a very good reason, you have no idea how damn stubborn they are. And I'm pretty sure they agreed to sign on with her because they thought they could figure out how to tell me where they were, and how to get to them." He turned back to Dessi. "Can you pull me up a star map?"

Dessi rummaged through her pockets and pulled out a small sphere. She tapped it against her knee, and a galaxy map sprang up around it.

"Where are we?" asked Aran, his eyes scanning the map for familiar features.

Dessi pointed out a small dot on the map. Aran nodded, orienting himself quickly.

Then he sucked in a sharp breath. "Here," he said, tapping a small cluster of three planets on the outskirts the map. "She's headed out here."

Krevai glanced at the map, then back at Aran. "How do you know?"

"Back on Colorida, Istvay and I almost got eaten by a group of greybacks who were going after a herd of doe mice. We almost didn't notice because they drew us into a bowl between three hills and ambushed us. We got out, thankfully, but I'm certain that's what Istvay was trying to tell me. They said Sharda would come after us like greybacks after a herd of doe mice. And this is the only planetary system that has a setup anything like the place we were ambushed."

"That almost sounds like they were warning you that it's a trap," said Dessi, but Aran shook his head impatiently.

"I'm sure it's fine."

Krevai was still frowning, but his expression was more thoughtful now than angry. "It's—not what I'd have expected her to do. But it's not a bad plan," he said slowly. "Hide out near Katran to gather her strength, then set an ambush for us."

Dessi nodded as well, glancing between Aran, the captain, and the star map. "It's possible," she said. "But unless we head out there, we have no way of knowing for sure whether—"

She broke off as one of the crew came sprinting around the corner. The raider woman pulled up sharply in front of Krevai, grinning, her fangs and lips dripping with blood. "Captain," she panted. "I found someone from Olec's old crew. His sister is still mates with someone on Desvar's crew, and *her* mate's best friend is mates with someone on Sharda's crew, and I persuaded him to tell me where Sharda's gone. He said that they're headed out towards Katran."

"Katran? You're certain?" asked Krevai.

The raider nodded.

Krevai and Dessi shared a look.

Then Krevai grinned and reached out to slap Aran on the shoulder, pulling himself back at the last second. "Well! I suppose I won't be able to just eat your Istvay if we find them again." He ignored the dirty look Dessi shot him and turned back to the raider. "Tell the crew to finish gathering supplies and get back to the ship. Best to go after her and try to catch her before she's found too many allies. Or before she figures out what your Istvay is up to and slits their throat, and we don't get any more leads. And you can tell the others—I've put our human in charge of setting our course. The navigators will talk to him directly. That will free me up to plan out the battle strategy."

"Yes, Captain," said the raider, nodding her head respectfully. "I'll tell the others." She disappeared out of the alley.

Aran stared at Krevai. "I—" he began. "You want me to—"

Krevai chuckled. "Like you said—your friend is going to be passing you messages, and Dessi and I certainly aren't going to understand them. We've never been hunting greybacks in your Joias

System. Although maybe we'll change that one day, if the yibo ever open another portal. Anyways, I'll need to be planning our battle strategy. Sharda's much too intelligent for us to just come blazing in without being on the lookout for a trap. So—" he gave Aran a toothy grin. "This is your mission now, human. Don't let me down."

He turned and strode off down the street, back towards the ship.

Aran stared after him, mouth hanging open.

At last, he turned to Dessi. She looked inordinately pleased.

"I—I can't—Dessi, I'm not—there's no way—" he stammered.

Dessi laughed comfortably and turned, beckoning him to follow. "Your Istvay is leaving you messages, right? So I agree with the captain—you're the best one for the job. And you seem highly motivated to get your Istvay back before Sharda figures out what they're doing and kills them. So I'm not worried about you leading us wrong."

She strode off after the captain, and Aran stared after her for a moment before he could remember how to make his legs move.

He sucked in a breath through his nose, trying not to panic.

This was fine. This would be fine. Yes, he was now apparently responsible for an entire crew of raiders, and for finding Sharda before the leadership war began. And yes, he was once again the sole person who had any chance of keeping his best friend safe, the person he'd been in love with his entire life, whose absence cut through him like a damn knife, and yes, if he wasn't fast enough, or he missed something, Istvay would be killed in the most brutal fashion he could imagine, but—

He closed his eyes for a minute, trying to keep from hyperventilating.

It would be fine. He could do this.

If he ever wanted to see Istvay alive again, he had to.

8

Savina

Savina groaned. Her head throbbed, her mouth tasted foul, and she could smell the sour sent of vomit.

What the actual hell had happened to her?

Cautiously, she blinked her eyes open.

She immediately squeezed them closed again, swearing. She'd just had time to make out the fact that she was in a small room, probably dimly lit, but the flickering light pulsed against the backs of her eyeballs like a jackhammer.

She groaned again, trying to fish some sort of memory out of the muddy goop of her brain.

She'd left Joska and the others behind, she remembered that. She'd found a ship to take her to the yibo city, following Reka.

Had Reka done this to her? She had some hazy recollection of seeing the woman.

No, that hadn't been it. She'd been the one to find Reka. And then—

She sucked in a quick breath as the memories filtered back.

The way she'd stood there, frozen, staring at her enemy, the woman who wanted to kill her, and she'd been unable to throw her knife. Unable to move at all.

The sick realization that she was broken. That she couldn't escape Reka, and she couldn't kill her, and so there was only one option left if she wanted to protect the people she cared about.

The note she'd left for Reka. The trip through the city to the tavern.

More memories settled into the thick mud of her thoughts, and she winced, blinking her eyes open again.

"Savina." The voice was dry and amused, and uncomfortably familiar.

Savina swore.

"I was wondering how long you'd be passed out. I'm almost impressed."

Savina scowled, turning her head gingerly to find the source of the voice.

Reka sat cross-legged on a small mattress, leaned back against the wall, watching Savina in unmistakable amusement. There was a cut across her left cheekbone, but rather than marring the elegant perfection of her features, it only made her look more dangerous— and more irresistibly attractive. Although honestly, Savina wasn't sure she was in any state of mind to make judgements about anything right now.

"What the hell did you do?" she mumbled. Her tongue felt thick and heavy, and her head pounded, her stomach churning uneasily.

Reka raised an eyebrow. "Well, to start with, I saved a very drunk, very stoned idiot from at least a dozen yibo who were trying to kill her. I feel like that's worth noting."

Savina closed her eyes and slumped back against the wall. Dammit, she was too hungover for this. "You were supposed to kill me," she muttered. "Didn't you get my note? Or did you just want to make sure I was sober and in pain and could see it coming, is that what this is about? I know you hate me, but even for you …"

Reka let out a long-suffering sigh. "Dragging someone in a drunken, and apparently very horny, stupor out through a crowd of criminals trying to kill her, just so she can be hungover rather than wasted when you finally shoot her yourself, seems like an impressive amount of effort."

Savina tried to scowl without opening her eyes, but even that hurt. Everything hurt, and dammit, she hadn't thought it would matter, because she hadn't thought she'd be alive to regret it.

Her head ached too much to try to make sense of whatever this was.

"Listen, Reka," she said flatly. "I don't know what you're after. I don't know what the hell you want. But whatever it is, would you please get it over with? I'm not in the mood to play games."

Reka gave a low, soft chuckle, and Savina heard her get to her feet.

She should probably stiffen, get ready for whatever torture Reka had planned for her, but she didn't have the energy.

"Savina." The voice came from very close.

Savina ignored it.

"Savina."

Something was shoved into her hand, and she blinked her eyes open in mild surprise.

It was a cup, filled with a clear liquid.

She glared at it suspiciously.

From beside her, she heard Reka let out another long-suffering sigh. "Savina. It's water. Drink it. Because I'm tempted to just dump it over your head to see if that will sober you up."

She raised the cup to her lips reluctantly, sniffed it, then swallowed.

She hadn't realized she was thirsty. But the cool liquid on her tongue reminded her, and she sucked the water down gratefully.

Reka crouched beside her, watching, her usual indifferent expression still marred with a hint of amusement.

When Savina had finished, Reka took the cup from her shaky hands. She placed it on a low table, then turned back to Savina. "Now," she said. "If you're sober enough to listen—"

Savina leaned back against the wall again and closed her eyes, scowling in Reka's general direction. "Believe me, I'm sober. You're much more fun when I'm drunk."

There was a moment's pause. "Speaking of that," said Reka, "you really should ask before you kiss someone."

Savina's eyes shot open. "I didn't—" she began furiously.

And then she remembered, and groaned, sinking back against the wall again.

Damn it to hell.

She'd honestly thought she'd be dead by now. She shouldn't have had to worry about this, because you couldn't be embarrassed about something when you were dead.

"What the hell, Reka?" she snapped. "What the actual Mystery-damned hell are you doing this for? Why are we here? I just wasted a hell of a lot of alcohol, and a hell of a lot of—whatever was in that blunt, to give you the chance to kill me, and you didn't bloody well take it. I'm hoping that at some point, you'll come around to telling me why the hell not?"

Reka was quiet for a few minutes. At last, she said, her voice quiet, "I need your help."

There was a moment of silence as Savina let the words filter through her sluggish brain.

She tried to figure out if there was any possibility that they meant something other than what they appeared to mean, but there didn't seem to be an alternate interpretation.

She blinked her eyes open again and glared at Reka. "What. The actual. Hell," she said flatly. She didn't have the energy to be as angry as she probably should be, her head still throbbing, her muscles shaky, the taste of vomit coating the back of her throat even after the cup of water. "Why in the actual hell do you think I would help you? Especially after that trick you pulled the last damn time we spoke."

Reka sat back on her heels, watching Savina. "If you were anyone else," she said at last, "I'd tell you it was because there are almost two hundred people being held captive by Kachik who are going to be killed at any moment." There was a weary, defeated note to her voice that Savina hadn't heard there before.

Savina pushed herself up painfully. "But you know damn well that that kind of argument's not going to work on me," she said through her teeth. "Because you know damn well that as far as I'm concerned, every single human on that diplomatic ship could be chopped into pieces and cooked into a raider's morning porridge, and I wouldn't shed a single tear over it."

Reka sighed again. "Yes. I'd gathered that." Her tone was dry.

"So then why the hell did you think this was a good idea?" Savina hissed. "I'm not going to do it, Reka. I'm not going to help you. I will walk myself straight into the Void before I help you again. So if you have any sense of fairness at all, you'll damn well get me some more alcohol so I can get drunk again before you shoot me. Because your options are, shoot me, or let me walk free. And I promise you, if I walk out of here, the first thing I'm going to do is find a knife and stab you in the back."

Reka raised an eyebrow. "I found the place where you must have been hiding in the courtyard. You could have killed me if you wanted to. While we're explaining things, would you mind telling me why you didn't? Why you decided instead to leave me a note telling me where you'd be, and then get drunk off your skull and wait for me to kill you?"

Savina mumbled a few curses, dropping back against the wall.

Reka was silent, waiting.

"Yes," Savina snapped at last. "Yes, I would mind."

Damn Reka Soler to hell.

Reka was quiet for a while. At last she said, "At any rate, I'd already gathered that wasn't an argument that would work on you. So I propose something else."

She paused for long enough that Savina cracked her eyes open again.

There was a look on Reka's face Savina couldn't quite read, and her head hurt too much to try.

"I … accepted a warrant on you, Savina," said Reka slowly. "I've never lost a warrant. Never. But …" she paused. "If you help me, I … won't come after you. I'll let you go, you and all of your friends. I've spent enough time around you to know that's failing my duty as a government agent, because you're not going to stop doing what you're doing. I don't even know if you care. I don't even know if you think murder is wrong. I don't know why you kill people without any reason and without any remorse, and I don't know why you didn't kill me when you had the chance. But …" She shrugged, a small, hopeless gesture. "I can't do this on my own. And Cavaco's soldiers are mixed in with the civilians, and Mystery aid me, you're the only person here I know well enough to trust."

She laughed, sharp and bitter. "At least with you, Savina, I know you have no morals other than your own self-interest and saving your friends, and you'll burn the world if it'll help you do that. So you can't surprise me."

Savina stared at Reka.

For the first time, she realized how exhausted the woman looked, the circles under her eyes dark and pronounced, her posture drooped with weariness. Had she even taken the time to sleep since she'd walked off Joska's ship a day or so back?

Knowing Reka, she probably hadn't.

"Of course," Savina said at last, her voice flat. "Just like the last time we worked together, right? When we saved each other's lives. And then as soon as we were safe, you turned on me. I know how far I can trust you, too."

Reka was still watching her, and Savina expected her to smile at the memory. But instead, she dropped her eyes.

"I … have been thinking about that," she said at last. "I did it because I thought it was my duty. But I …" She looked up again, a strange reluctance in her movements. "I'm sorry, Savina. It wasn't well done."

Savina stared at her blankly. Then she pushed herself upright, anger burning hot and clean in her chest, strong enough to cut through the throbbing in her head and the strange muddiness in her brain. "Listen to me, Reka Soler," she hissed. "We are enemies. I don't need your apology. I don't need you to take care of me. I don't need you to worry about me, and I sure as hell didn't need you to walk into that tavern and drag me out. You were supposed to kill me. I *wanted* you to kill me." Her voice was shaking.

Reka didn't move, didn't pull back. From this close, Savina could see the small cut in one corner of her mouth, the bead of dried blood crusted on her bottom lip. And just for a moment, Savina's mind flickered back, involuntarily, to the taste of Reka's lips on her own, the warmth of them, the way they'd parted for Savina's tongue, the thrill that had jolted down the pit of Savina's stomach, hot and urgent.

She wrenched her gaze away, just in time to see Reka's eyes flick up from Savina's lips, her tongue brushing her own lips in a small, unconscious gesture.

For a moment, the two women stared at each other. Then Reka leaned back, breaking off the gaze abruptly.

"I thought Kachik would try to kill everyone last night. But something happened. He changed his mind. I didn't have a chance to do much before, but there's a chance now." There was a rough edge to her normally cool voice. "I don't like this either. Believe me. If I could handle it myself, I would. But as I'm sure you've noticed, we both have limited options."

"You have limited options," snapped Savina. "My options are what they've always been, because I'm not agreeing to this."

Reka leaned closer, and Savina's heart gave a strange little jump. "When Kachik had us locked up, you were ready to burn the system to the ground to save your baby brother. I know why you're here, Savina. I know why I found you drunk and defenceless in that tavern. You don't want him to be hurt. You were going to let me kill you so I'd have no more reason to go after him or any of the others." Her voice was low and compelling, her gaze cutting through Savina like a scalpel, leaving her stripped naked, shivering and vulnerable.

"Listen," Savina began, her voice coming out hoarse and strange.

"I'm giving you another option," whispered Reka. "You can keep your baby brother safe without dying for it. And in an alien system like this one ... there are all sorts of ways an idealistic young man like Nicolau could get himself in trouble, without a big sister to protect him."

Slowly, Savina leaned back against the wall. It was easier to think when she wasn't in quite such close proximity to Reka. "Even if I agreed, there's no way this will work. We can't get that many people out from under the noses of Kachik's guards. One or two, maybe, but not all of them."

Reka's expression smoothed once more to one of cool amusement. "I can't on my own, certainly. But if there were an innocent, helpless little Rim Mountain girl who managed to fool the guards ..." She shrugged. "The city knows you're here by now, certainly. You weren't being very subtle last night. They'll be on the lookout for you, and probably me as well. But I think with both our skillsets, we'll manage."

Savina glared at her for a few moments, until the effort of glaring made the pain in her head too much. Then she collapsed back against the wall, half-closing her eyes. "This is a damn suicide mission. I told you, I don't do suicide missions."

"Really?" said Reka dryly. "Because from what I saw, your alternate plan was to get completely plastered and wait for someone to shoot you."

Savina swore quietly.

Damn Reka Soler to hell.

"You'd burn the system to protect Nicolau, you said it yourself. Surely this can't be worse," said Reka. There was a bitterness in her tone, and Savina wasn't sure if it was for her, or for something else.

Savina drew in a long breath. "Fine," she said at last, flatly. She didn't bother to open her eyes. "Fine, Reka. Like you say—you haven't exactly left me with a lot of options."

9

Alba

Jair was waiting with the others when Alba arrived outside the refugee quarters. All of them had expressions of such identical concern on their faces that Alba had to bite back a small, incongruous laugh.

"It's no use," she said quietly as she came in, closing the door behind her. "They seem to have made up their mind. I attempted to convince them that the humans would be valuable enough to be worth negotiating for, but with the unrest among the raiders, they seem entirely committed to keeping the peace with Kachik. Even if that means bargaining off the rest of the diplomatic crew in exchange for peace. And I hardly see what I can do to convince them—if I were in their place, I don't know that I would say differently."

Jair shook his head grimly. "Once they start using human lives in their negotiations, all of us will be the losers for it. There are more and more refugees coming in from areas controlled by the Nativists. If the government signals that those lives are negotiable, who knows where it will end? Certainly Kachik doesn't relish the thought of humans leaving his occupied territories—it's a blow to his pride, if nothing else. And I hate to imagine what he has planned for those who stay."

Alba shook her head in frustration. "The issue is, they have no reason to listen to me. I'm no one here. If I had even a modicum of political sway—even some reason to be able to speak up in their debates—"

"Telling them who you are won't provide that?" asked Joska. "You are one of the three most powerful people in our system."

Alba gave a weary shake of her head. "From what I saw, they have no interest in our system. My position in Joias is irrelevant. Here, I have neither power nor influence."

Jair nodded. "I was young when the yibo came through to Labirinto. But from the stories I hear, there was no more respect for our head of government there than there was for any of the rest of us."

The tone of his voice made Alba very certain that she did not want to know further details, at least not at present.

Not until she'd dealt with this crisis, and had the luxury to mourn her own dead.

"There were some politicians who seemed more interested in the plight of the humans than their colleagues were," she said instead. "From what you know, do we have a chance with them? Is there a way we could get a private meeting?"

Jair frowned. "It's possible," he said at last. "But our issue has always been, humans have no positions in the government. Even if by some miracle we were able to get the ear of one of them, the only ones willing to listen tend to be the younger and more reckless advisors. As far as political clout, in our terminology it would be the equivalent of being a junior clerk to a first-year counsellor."

They were silent for a few moments.

Then Feliu looked up at Alba, a small gleam in his eye. "A junior clerk to a first-year counsellor," he said slowly. "Madam. It seems to me that we have in our midst someone who was once a junior clerk to a low-level counsellor. Someone who rose from being a junior clerk to a low-level counsellor, and is now one of the three Joint Heads of Government."

Alba frowned, staring at him. She opened her mouth to protest—it had been a different time, she'd been young, it had taken her years to build up the political acumen—and then, slowly, she closed it again.

Because as absurd and outlandish as Feliu's suggestion was—he wasn't incorrect.

Alba had never considered herself an adventurer, or a saboteur. Escaping from yibo captivity, twice, fleeing for her life, helping Aran blow up the portal mechanism, would rank among the most uncomfortable and entirely unpleasant experiences she had ever had the misfortune of dealing with.

This, on the other hand …

"Jair," she said, turning to the man. "There was a younger yibo politician, sitting in the fifth row from the top, three seats in on the left-hand side, with pale fur and pale eyepatches."

"That would be Tika, I believe," Jair said.

Alba nodded briskly. "He has more liberal views on humans, correct?"

Jair nodded again, slowly. "That's my understanding. There are a significant number of humans in his territory, and if they're given more political weight, it would directly benefit him."

"Do you think you could use your influence to get me a meeting with him?"

Jair frowned. "He is one of the most junior advisors in the ranks at the moment," he said. "Getting a meeting would be easy enough, but his influence will be small."

"I've worked with less in the past." She wasn't completely certain it was true, but she hoped she sounded more confident than she felt.

Jair sighed ruefully. "I'll see what I can do. As you say, it's not like we have many other options. And whatever Kachik has planned for your fellow survivors, we won't have long to prevent it."

Alba nodded. Her stomach was a tight knot of worry that Feliu's confidence did nothing to assuage.

"Then I shall wait here to hear from you," she said.

Alba slept poorly that night, her dreams restless and troubled.

She dreamed of the look on Ines's face, when the girl had talked about being taken from her family and brought into do Sol for schooling, through the program Alba had spearheaded.

It had been six years before Ines had been able to see her parents again. No wonder she was quiet and timid.

And Istvay. Alba's bill to provide for the homeless population of do Sol. She hadn't for one moment dreamed that anyone could possibly object to such a thing—after all, Aran and Istvay were touted as the best-known successes of the program: a homeless child and a foster child who had, against all odds, succeeded brilliantly, because her bill had taken them from the streets and allowed them to go through university on the public purse.

And then Istvay had stood in front of her, cold and furious, and told her about their friend who'd died in prison, because she hadn't met the criteria for any other program to get off the streets.

Weeks ago, back in do Sol, Alba might not have given it a second thought, confident in her own analysis of the situation. But that had been before she had witnessed, first-hand and personally, the stunning disaster this diplomatic mission had been. Before she'd looked into the faces of people she'd have to condemn never to return home, and made that decision for them, without giving them so much as a voice. Before she'd finally been forced to see the human cost of the choices she'd made so glibly in the past.

She'd had to do it. She'd had to shut down the portal. Not doing so would have meant the destruction of the entire Joias System, and everything she'd seen since had confirmed to her that her decision, in this case, had been the correct one.

And yet—

She opened her eyes, staring up sightlessly at the ceiling of the small, dark room. She could hear the soft breathing of the others on the cots around her, and she wasn't sure if the sound was comforting, or terrifying—more people she was responsible for. More people who her decisions had affected and would continue to affect.

More people who'd trusted her, and who she'd failed.

She grimaced, and sat up painfully on the small cot. She wouldn't be falling back asleep again, not with her mind racing as it was. Besides, if she was going into a political meeting for which she was entirely unqualified, the result of which could possibly have a direct impact on the lives of more people than she liked to think about, the least she could do was what she'd done when she was a young clerk —make up for lack of confidence and qualifications by sheer, panic-fuelled preparation.

She didn't know how long she'd been pouring over the notes on her retinal screen when a soft creak startled her into glancing up.

Yosip was sitting up on his cot, yawning. The room had shifted from pitchy black to a soft grey, and dim light accentuated the lines on Yosip's face, making him look older than he was, and weary beyond words. Still, he smiled when he saw her looking, and she smiled back unconsciously.

"Preparing for your meeting?" he whispered.

Alba nodded. "I've been going over the few notes I have," she whispered back.

"I'll send you the notes I've taken as well," he said. "I'm not a politician, but I am a diplomatic aide. Noticing nuances is my job, so there may be something helpful."

Alba closed her eyes, surprised at the rush of relief his words brought. "That would be appreciated," she said at last.

Yosip nodded, the movement barely visible in the semi-darkness, and a moment later something winked in the corner of Alba's vision —an incoming transmission from Yosip's wavelink.

She accepted it and pulled it open, scanning quickly through the notes.

Despite herself, she was impressed. Yosip had picked up on subtleties in the yibo speech and dialogue that she'd missed entirely. She glanced up at him, raising an eyebrow.

He smiled at her self-deprecatingly. "Like I said—this is something I was trained for."

"You've worked as a diplomatic aide for a long time, then," she said. "Your entire life?"

The question was hardly pertinent to their situation. But she'd gone over her notes enough times now that she could recite them in her sleep, and she knew herself well enough to know that going over them again would add more to her stress levels than to her knowledge base.

Yosip's smile was distant. "No," he said quietly. "I only began work as a diplomatic aide maybe … fifteen years ago? Before then, I clerked in the government for a few years."

Alba watched him, curious. "And before that?"

He chuckled. "Oh, nothing particularly interesting. My father was a farmer, and I spent the first decade or so after I was married teaching at the primary school in the village. My son spent his childhood catching spotted lizards and climbing trees and playing in the dirt on a Rim Mountain farm."

Alba found herself smiling at the picture. It hardly surprised her— the way Yosip related to people, his calm, quiet, friendly manner, spoke more of someone raised in the countryside than someone who'd grown up in the bustling rush of do Sol.

"And you?"

She glanced over at him, startled. It had been a long time since anyone had asked her about her own life. She was either too important, or too intimidating for that. And besides, her life had been a matter of public record for quite some time now.

Yosip smiled, the wrinkles creasing the corners of his eyes. "I don't mean your history in politics. Every schoolchild on Colorida knows that. But what made you go into it in the first place? If you don't mind my asking."

Alba was silent for a moment.

Her older brother's face danced in her memory as she recalled it as a child, laughing, his eyes glinting mischief. And transposed over that memory, the memory of his body in a casket, the blank, sickly silence of his face then.

How she'd shouted at her father, screamed at him that they could have done something to save him. How she'd determined that she'd never sit there and do nothing while terrible things happened, things she might be able to change. To fix.

"I ... suppose I thought I could change the world," she said at last. The words sounded ridiculous as she spoke them, and she gave a small, dry laugh. "It turns out changing the world is easy enough. The difficult part is ensuring your changes do more good than harm. At that, perhaps, I did not succeed as much as I had hoped."

Yosip's gaze was searching and curious. "Perhaps you didn't," he said quietly. "But if you'll excuse my saying so, Alba—no one does."

She frowned at him. "Perhaps no one's record is unqualified. But I sincerely doubt that a rural primary school teacher's miscalculation does the amount of damage a Chief Justice's does."

He chuckled. "I won't say you're wrong. You've caused harm, Alba, and your power means the harm you caused touched a significant number of lives, just as much as any good you caused did. But—" he shrugged. "I suppose what I'm trying to say is, you've said good intentions don't save us. It's true. And neither do regrets. I would go back, if I could, but I can't any more than you can. All of us have caused harm, and none of us can change what we've done, much as we might want to. But any one of us can use what we've learned to choose our path going forward. That's all I meant to say."

Alba stared blankly ahead.

It was both more uncomfortable, and more comforting, than she'd imagined, to hear her own flaws laid out in Yosip soft, compassionate tones. If he'd tried to sugarcoat the harm she'd caused, she'd have known, instinctively, she couldn't trust what came next.

But he hadn't. His words had been every bit as condemning as her own thoughts. But it wasn't her he'd condemned, in the end.

She wondered, idly, why it mattered so much. When the opinion of a diplomatic aide—or, for that matter the opinion of a ship's captain, or a diplomatic linguist, or the harried research assistant to an eccentric young scientist—had begun to mean anything at all to her.

When she turned, finally, Yosip was still studying her, the look on his face that unconscious friendliness that seemed his trademark. He smiled, and there was a sincerity in his eyes that was almost disconcerting. "Alba. As a friend, I'll tell you this—from what I know of you, I don't see you as a person who will hold onto the mistakes of the past so tightly they're unable to change the future."

She stared at him, and his smile widened, just a little, kind and amused. Then he sighed, pushing himself to his feet. "And now, I suppose I'd best figure out where Joska put our luggage, or at the very least, if the yibo have given us clothes to change into. I don't know about you, but after the last few days I'll be more than happy to wear something that isn't stiff enough from the dirt to stand up on its own."

Alba smiled to herself as she watched him leave.

The others were stirring as well by now, and she could hear soft conversation from the corner where Nicolau and Ines were sleeping, their cots pushed closer together, perhaps, then they'd been when the group of them had arrived.

Still, it certainly wasn't Alba's business.

And glancing over at them—Nicolau's auburn hair tousled and standing up on one side, his face animated, his hands gesturing to emphasize his words, and Ines, her normally petrified expression replaced by one of quiet happiness—Alba found herself smiling at the scene.

Every half-formed fear from her restless dreams was likely true— she was, in fact, as out of her depth here as she had been the first morning she'd walked into the Council Chambers as a young clerk.

But what Yosip had said was true as well. Perhaps what had brought her here were layers of politics and bureaucracy and, to be quite frank, personal ego, more than idealism. But there were people here who she'd come to care about, with a depth of sentiment that was almost uncomfortable. This was no longer about the entire Joias System, the disembodied mass she'd always pictured herself representing in the Counsel. It was about—people. Nicolau, Ines, Feliu, Yosip. Joska and Rafel, Beni, who looked so much more frightening than they were. Aran and Istvay, the way each of them looked at the other when they thought the other wasn't watching, the softness in Aran's eyes, the tenderness in Istvay's. These people —their familiar smiles and frowns and worries and joys—mattered to her, in a way that nothing had when she was back in Vila Nova do Sol.

She sighed and got to her feet, stretching the aches from her muscles.

She was—or at least, she had been—a politician. She'd always seen it as her job to speak for the many, not the one. But here, with the loss of the comforts, the security, her confidence in her own self and the confidence of others, she'd lost, as well, the need to keep everyone and everything at a safe arm's-length to maintain her impartiality.

And that simple fact added a touch of sweetness to the bitter.

By the time Jair arrived to fetch her, Alba had managed a cleansing shower in the utilitarian facilities provided to the refugees, and had changed into one of the plain tunics the yibo had supplied. Feliu, predictably, had been irritated on her behalf, grumbling that if the yibo knew they were dealing with a foreign head of government, they might provide Alba, at least, with the facilities she deserved, but Alba had shaken her head at him fondly.

And the knowledge that his concern wasn't for his image— because they'd left that behind long, long ago—but for her comfort, was unexpectedly touching.

"Alba." Jair smiled, but she could see the worry behind the expression. "We should get going. Tika has agreed to a meeting, but he wasn't enthusiastic. Best not to keep him waiting."

Alba nodded, hardly trusting herself to speak.

It was absurd, really, that she should be just as nervous going into a meeting with a low-ranking politician now as she had been at seventeen. Although in fairness, no one could argue that these were circumstances she could have anticipated.

"Well then," she said briskly, pressing her hands tightly against her thighs in an effort to still their trembling, "I suppose we should be on our way."

10

Aran

"Here we are." There was satisfaction in Dessi's voice.

Aran glanced up, startled for a moment out of his spiralling panic, and realized they'd reached what must be the ship's map room, with a long central table that had metal divots set into the surface every ten centimetres or so.

Dessi rummaged in the table drawers and pulled out a handful of spherical items Aran recognized as starmaps, and popped one into one of the divots near the centre of the table. A spherical holo-projection appeared around it in a glowing display that took up most of the table.

"This is where we are," she said, indicating a small red dot in the centre of the map. Aran could hardly hear her through the rushing in his ears. "And here's the planetary system you mentioned earlier. Now what I need you to—"

"Dessi, please," he managed. His voice was harsher than he meant it to be. "I just … I need a minute. Okay?"

There was a moment's pause, and Aran didn't look at her because that probably wasn't how people who had just been put in charge of a damn attack mission were supposed to act. But hell, he didn't have the energy to try to figure out how he *was* supposed to ask because he was barely clinging on to his sanity as it was …

"Of course," said Dessi. "Do you need … food? Anything?"

He needed Istvay, and a stiff drink, and to be off this ship and out of this nightmare of a system and back in his comfortable, familiar base camp in the Rim Mountains.

He needed Istvay …

"No, just … I need to be alone. Just for a minute."

She nodded and stepped outside, closing the door firmly behind her, and Aran sank to the ground, burying his face in his arms.

He drew in a deep breath, then another.

The weight of Ani, still plastered to his shoulder and making little humming sounds of concern, helped to ground him.

He wasn't alone. He had Ani, still. And as much as Istvay's presence had been woven into the very fabric of his life for as long as he could remember … he'd had to survive without them before. There had been that time when his then foster family had moved to the outskirts of do Sol, and he'd only managed to slip away to visit Istvay and Istvay's mom once or twice in the course of a year.

He knew how to do this. He'd done it before. He just had to remember.

"Ani?" he whispered.

She slithered around, shoving herself under his arm and poking her head up so her bulbous eyes were blinking innocently directly into his.

He let out a soft breath of laughter and stroked her head. "Ani, listen," he said. "We can do this, alright?"

She gave an inquisitive chirp, and he found his smile came a little easier this time.

He sighed, and leaned his head back against the wall. "I was going to go on this trip on my own, remember? Except Istvay was too damn stubborn, and insisted on coming with. And then you and I were going to get onto that pod and go through the portal ourselves, when we thought that was our only option." He paused, and reached up to pull a creeping tentacle off his face. "Sorry, sweetheart, I know you love me, but I do have to breathe."

She grumbled, and settled for winding her tentacle tightly around his arm instead.

"So. This isn't all that different, is it?"

It was different. Because this time, he didn't have the comforting knowledge that whatever happened to him, Istvay was home and safe. And it wasn't just him and Ani he had to worry about—he was on a ship crewed by raiders, whose default volume seemed to be just below the level required to actually split Aran's eardrums, and whose constant chaos seemed designed to drive him to actual madness. And he was working against the clock, every second he delayed driving up the chance Istvay would be found out by Sharda.

"But I've done this before," he whispered. "Almost a whole damn year, and you weren't even there, and my foster family was …" he broke off, but Ani must have heard something in his voice, because she perked up a little, growling and peering around the room.

He laughed softly. "It's alright, sweetheart, they probably just …" he trailed off. "Anyways, the point is, I have you now. And we can do this. We'll be fine."

He wasn't actually sure he'd be fine. But Ani was cuddled against his chest, draped over him like a weighted blanket, and he'd done this before. He'd survived without Istvay before.

He just had to remember how.

At last, he pushed himself to his feet and detached Ani gently from his chest. She resisted, suckering on to his jacket with all her tentacles and growling a little in discontent, but he managed to pry her off at last and set her back onto her usual perch on his shoulders. Then he opened the door and went looking for Dessi.

She wasn't hard to find—she'd retreated down the corridor to wait, and was pouring through something on her data pad.

She looked up when she saw him, and smiled. "Are you ready? Good. Here, if you don't mind, I'm going to do a quick scan for your pulse and vital signs ..." she held up her data pad without waiting for an answer, then glanced at it and tapped in some numbers. "This is excellent. I did a scan before I left, and I'm getting some really fantastic measurements as to how humans in distress react biologically. Now." She started down the corridor at a brisk pace. "Let me show you the map room, and we can get started on getting your Istvay back. I suspect I won't get a really good baseline reading of a human not in distress until they're back with you."

Aran shook his head ruefully and followed.

When they were back in the map room, and in front of the glowing holomaps once again, Aran frowned at them. "You said this is where we are now?" He touched the glowing red dot. "Which means that this would be the planet we were on when we took down the portal."

Dessi nodded, and Aran turned back to the map.

It was much more detailed than the tiny, glitchy, half-complete thing he and Istvay had been working off when they'd come here in the first place. But now that he was oriented, he was beginning to see how it fit together.

He bit his lip, frowning. "And at top speed—Dessi, show me how long it would take to get between these two points with a raider ship." Now that his mind had fixed on a problem to be solved rather than the overwhelming terror of what solving that problem entailed, he was finding it easier to push back the panic.

Dessi reached in and hit a button on the spherical projector, and a tiny blue dot appeared between the planets Aran had indicated. "I'm not completely sure how humans measure time while you travel in space," she said. "We use days as an informal measurement, either when we're planet-side, or if we're not, then based off the day-night cycle of our main planet. But for technical measurements when we need precision, we use radiation pulses of the system's central sun. Which, if I am correct about your human time measurements, would be about—" she squinted one eye. "Something like twenty-seven hours, thirteen minutes, and forty-two seconds per pulse. At our ship's top speed, we can travel about this far in one pulse cycle." She flicked a finger, and the blue dot moved forward, leaving a glowing trail behind it.

Aran nodded, chewing on his lip. Istvay usually worked the math, but he could do the calculations if he had to. "What about at normal cruising speed?"

"At normal cruising speed, we'd go about this far in a pulse-cycle," said Dessi, marking another blue line with her fingers.

Aran nodded absently, his brain already busy with finding patterns in the chart. "These mark the terraformed planets, I guess?" he murmured, touching one of the illuminated spheres.

It took a moment for her confirmation to penetrate his concentration, and when he glanced up, she was watching him with amusement.

"I'll leave you to it, then," she said. "I'll be in my lab if you need me."

When the door to the room slammed open again, Aran almost jumped. "Krevai?" he said, when he'd reoriented himself to his surroundings. "I thought you were going to get supplies."

Krevai laughed and strode over, raising his hand to slap him on the shoulder, then dropping it hurriedly. "Sorry, I always forget your human customs. But we've got the supplies. It's been almost a third of a cycle since I talked to you. So. What have you come up with?"

Aran took a deep breath and turned back to the map glowing across the table, and the notes he'd jotted down on the data pad Dessi had left. He tried not to let his fingers fumble. "Sharda couldn't have stayed here long, because there's no way we're more than a cycle behind her, and it looks like a lot of her time here was spent talking to the other raider crews. I doubt she had time to fully resupply, and it looks like it's about a five and a half cycle trip to where she's planning to make her stand, or whatever it is she's planning. And Istvay is obviously in her good graces right now, and they know I'm looking for them. We could try to get there first, if that's your plan. But if you plan to try to catch her before she makes it ..." He rotated the map with his fingers.

"Back on Colorida, whenever Istvay and I got split up in the field, we'd meet up at the body of water nearest to our last position. They'll know that's where I'll look for them. So I'm guessing we're looking for a planet with a lot of water, terraformed probably, something that's got enough flora and fauna that Sharda can resupply her ships quickly. From what I can see from the map, this is our most likely place. I assume you can resupply a ship here?" He glanced up at Krevai.

Krevai glanced down at the map, then up at Aran, his eyebrows raised. "It's possible. I'd have expected her to go over here—" He thrust a finger at another glowing planet a few pulses' travel away.

Aran shook his head absently, his attention back on the map. "No, they haven't gone in that direction. Pishti would have said something."

Krevai's eyebrows raised higher. "I don't know your Istvay like you do," he said slowly. "But they never told us any of this, correct? It's all conjecture. No, I don't see why this planet wouldn't be just as likely."

Aran glanced up. "Istvay would never do that. They don't like to run things to the wire if they can help it, at least not with supplies. If Sharda didn't fully resupply here, Istvay is going to be pushing her to resupply as soon as possible. If she's listening to them, which it sounds like she is, she won't wait that long. Besides, Istvay's always been interested in efficient systems. Going that way would add a solid two cycles to the trip to the Katran planetary system, and the ship would have to retrace its steps here. That would open the ship up to attack, and they'd have to resupply again sooner. It would drive Istvay crazy, and then Istvay would drive Sharda crazy."

There were a few moments of silence. He glanced up again to see Krevai watching him, although he couldn't read the raider's expression.

"And your Istvay," said Krevai at last. "They've decided to work with Sharda. Betray my crew. We'll bring them back, of course, for honour's sake, if nothing else—I won't let Sharda get away with kidnapping one of my crew and besides, if there's going to be a leadership war, I prefer it to end with me in charge. But—" he paused. "How much can we trust them?"

Aran blew out a short breath. "I once found Istvay literally halfway down the throat of a mottled land-shark, because I'd asked them to hold onto something and not let it go no matter what. I don't know what Istvay thinks about Sharda—although I'd guess it's not complimentary. But I can promise you, they wouldn't ever, ever do something they thought would hurt me. They may be working with Sharda, if that's the only way they could think of to stay alive. But if they leave a message for me? I'd trust it with my life."

Dessi had come in while he was speaking, and now both raiders were watching him. Krevai turned to Dessi with a questioning look.

"I have read multiple accounts of humans risking their own life or safety for people in their social groupings," she said with a shrug. "Especially close groupings like the ones these two seemed to have. It's not outside the realm of possibility. Our social structure revolves around crews, but humans' social structures seem much more loosely defined. It's possible his Istvay saw renouncing your crew as less of a betrayal than being killed and leaving their Aran on his own, so this could be more of a cultural difference than a purposeful breach of trust. Both of them seemed willing to get eaten to save the other when they first met you."

Krevai turned thoughtfully back to Aran. At last, he nodded. "Alright, human," he said. "We'll follow your lead. But if your Istvay is doing what you say they are, you'd best hope we get to them before Sharda catches on. Because I know her. Your Istvay won't last longer than the time it would take her to pull out her butcher knife."

Aran closed his eyes, trying to push back the stomach-churning panic. "I know."

Krevai grinned. "Good! Well then, it looks like you've given us a plan of attack. You're right, I'd rather catch her before she reaches the Katran system. It looks like she's trying to lure in allies, and even if we don't catch her before she reaches it, if she's worried about staying a step ahead of us, she won't have time to set up much of an ambush or find too many more allies." He turned. "I'll tell Landru to set the coordinates, and maybe we'll get lucky and catch up to her before she reaches Katran."   He strode out of the chart room, leaving Aran staring blankly at the chart in front of him.

It was sometime later when the door burst open again. Aran jerked his head up from his data pad he'd been pouring over in a desperate attempt to distract himself to see Krevai standing in the entrance. "Ah. My little human scientist!" he said jovially. "And how is your—your little science going?"

"Dessi and I are actually making progress in a comparative analysis of the human and raider genomes, which theoretically, should—"

"Good, good! Sounds like you've been very productive!" said Krevai, with a hearty laugh. "Now, I put the ship down a little ways away from the normal landing area, just in case Sharda's still here, and we're going out to have a look around. Are you coming?"

Istvay could have been here, on the same planet he was. They could still be here, although admittedly that wasn't likely.

He managed a nod, and started after Krevai.

He made his way quickly back to his own quarters to grab his supplies, and paused at the door to brace himself. Then he pushed it open and, for the first time since he'd left it with Istvay in their mad escape, he stepped inside.

He paused for a moment, his foot half-way to the ground.

Istvay's old jacket lay on the floor, the blankets that had served as a bed bunched together and shoved to one side, just the way he and Istvay had left them the night the two of them had snuck off the raider ship to take down the portal. A couple spare shirts and trousers were folded neatly in one corner, and a jumble of equipment from both their knapsacks that the two of them had emptied to lighten their load for the flight through the forest surrounding Dessi's research station lay in a pile beside the blankets.

Aran swallowed hard and made himself walk over to the pile of blankets.

He dropped to his knees beside the supplies, and, forcing himself not to think too hard about what he was doing, he rummaged through them for any equipment he might need.

"There will be new creatures out here, Ani," he whispered as he worked. "Things we've never seen before, probably."

Ani chirruped and detached herself gracefully from his jacket, wandering around the room looking, probably, for any leftover treats.

Aran found the battered sensors he'd been looking for and shoved them into his supplies pouch. Dessi had warned him the planet's surface was mostly frozen, so he pulled on the warm tunic she'd lent him, then shrugged Istvay's spare jacket over top of his own. Then he stood, glancing around the cabin one more time, and fought back another wave of something that felt like homesickness.

Could you be homesick for a person? From available data, Aran was hypothesizing that you could.

He sighed, held out his arm for Ani to scramble up, and started back out towards the main deck of the ship.

When he reached the loading ramp, Krevai and the rest of the landing party stood talking in what Krevai probably considered quiet tones, which were loud enough they rang off every available surface. He glanced up as Aran came in. "Good, good, our human is here! You can stay with my party, or you can head off on your own, whatever you like. Call if you see signs that Sharda's still here, but you have your Ani, so you shouldn't be in too much danger. As long as you move quickly, that is." He laughed. "I've sent a party to the main landing site, which is probably where Sharda will have come. If anyone find signs of Sharda or of your Istvay, they'll let us know.

Dessi gave you a communicator, yes?"

Aran nodded silently.

"I should probably warn you," Krevai continued casually. "There are xaxiks on this planet. They sense ship vibrations when we land, but it takes them a while to make their way over, so we usually have a few hours. But depending on how long it's been since Sharda's been here, it's possible they'll get here quicker than usual. If they do show up—well, best hope you can run faster than they can, is all I'm going to say." He grinned and hit a control on the wall panel, and the hatch on the raider ship slid open, an icy blast of air thick with the hint of snow swirling into the ship.

Aran tightened the jacket around his shoulders, pulling on his mitts and shoving the toque down over his ears. Ani grumbled in protest, flattening herself against his shoulders.

"Come on, sweetheart," Aran whispered, cracking a small grin. "You've been out in colder weather than this. You've just gotten used to the jungles here, haven't you? Look, you can crawl into my coat if you want."

Despite their rowdiness in the ship, Krevai's crew executed his orders with impressive alacrity. They split into two smaller teams, one following Krevai, the other following another raider who Aran was pretty sure was Krevai's third in command, and within moments, both had started off into the icy landscape.

Aran sighed and started forward after them.

He pictured the map of the planet in his mind, and headed off at a slight angle to the path Krevai had taken.

Krevai was heading towards where Sharda had most likely landed. And judging from the topography, if Istvay wanted to get somewhere away from Sharda to leave a message, and do it quickly, they would almost certainly have gone in this direction.

He'd been walking for almost an hour, face bundled against the cutting wind, when his foot sunk through the crust of the snow more easily than it should have.

He glanced down, startled out of his thoughts.

The ever-present wind had swept the surface of the snow clean, forming a stiff crust that he had to break through with every laborious step, but where he'd just stepped, the crust had quite obviously been broken earlier.

He crouched down, touching the surface of the snow gently with one hand, and squinted at the snow around him, scanning the area quickly.

His heart was beating quick and strange in his chest.

There were more depressions, a steady line of them headed away from him.

It didn't mean anything, necessarily. This was a planet where the raiders stopped semi-frequently to stock up on supplies, and considering the supplies they were talking about were probably not fruits and vegetables in a climate like this, that probably meant prey animals.

Still, it wasn't impossible these were human prints.

Which meant, it wasn't impossible that Istvay had been here, not too long ago.

He looked up quickly, surveying the frozen landscape.

In the distance, through the blowing snow, he could see the outline of—something. Hills, maybe, or mountains.

He glanced down at the tracks again, and pushed himself to his feet. "Krevai," he whispered through his communicator. "I've found something. I'm going to go check it out. Ani's with me, so don't worry about us. I'll meet you back at the ship."

Krevai grunted an affirmative through the communicator.

Following the trail wasn't easy, with the wind blowing snow in his face and piling it up in drifts, erasing the tracks on the surface of the snow-crust almost before they had a chance to form. But it certainly wasn't the most difficult tracking he'd done—he couldn't even count how many winters he and Istvay had spent in the highest parts of the Rim Mountains, tracking some obscure species or another.

Sweat beaded on the back of his neck, even in the frigid air, and froze in his hair.

Besides, he recognized this trail. He almost didn't have to look down to follow it—the way it hesitated at a steep slope, then edged up at an angle, like whoever was making the tracks didn't want to scramble all the way up, but was too impatient to go around. He wasn't tracking a creature he'd never met, trying to guess its habits or predilections. He was following Istvay, he was almost sure of it. Someone he knew almost better than he knew himself. And Istvay knew he'd be following, and was trying to give him all the help they could.

He was starting to lose feeling in his fingers and toes when he stopped at last and looked up to realize he was at the base of the hill he'd seen in the distance. He blinked up at it for a minute, squinting through the blowing snow.

Then he grinned.

At the top of the hill, a saddle dipped down, exposing the tips of a few desolate, windblown rocks.

And he could hear, in words some variation of which he could recite verbatim because of their familiarity, Istvay's voice in his head —*for hell's sake, Aran, I don't care how much easier it is to see the nesting site from there, we're setting up camp in a damn windbreak. I'm not sleeping in a wind tunnel again, I'm too damn old for that.*

"You and your windbreaks," he whispered, and had to swallow

back a knot in his throat.

He scrambled up the slope, no longer bothering to try to follow tracks, and came out at the top a few minutes later, breathing heavily.

Once he ducked down into the hollow between the two hills—it did, in fact, cut the wind an impressive amount—it only took him a few moments to find what he was looking for. Behind the largest rock was a small hollow in the snow.

He brushed away the freshly blown snow, holding his breath.

Inside, tucked up against the rock, was a small, rolled piece of the waterproof parchment he and Istvay used sometimes for leaving messages in the field.

With trembling fingers, he unrolled it.

It was nothing but a sequence of numbers, in Istvay's spidery handwriting.

Aran stared down at the writing for a few minutes. His chest ached, and tears burned behind his eyes.

Istvay had been here. They'd been here, not very long ago. And they'd been alive.

At last, he shook himself from his daze and pulled out his data pad, jotting down the numbers. He wasn't completely certain what the numbers meant—he'd need to go back to the map room to check—but he was pretty sure when he had a map in front of him, the numbers would add up to coordinates, in the shorthand he and Istvay had developed over the years.

No one else would understand it, which meant that even if Sharda's crew had found the message, it wouldn't be particularly incriminating.

He managed a watery grin, then shoved the parchment into the inside pocket of his jacket. It was hard to make himself let go of it, even then—something about holding it in his hands made the possibility of seeing Istvay again real, for the first time since he'd come to find them and found, instead, the site of their kidnapping.

Ani peeked one bulbous eye out from the front of Aran's jacket, then reached out the tip of a tentacle and touched him gently on the cheek.

"It's alright, sweetheart," he murmured, patting the lump under his jacket. "We'll find them, okay? We'll get them back."

He straightened, glancing around. His trail had been completely obliterated by the blowing snow, but he'd been keeping track of his direction as he went, so he wasn't worried about getting back to the ship.

"Dessi?" he said cautiously, tapping the communicator device she'd handed him. "Can you hear me?"

"Aran? You should start back. Krevai and the others are on their way—Sharda was here, but she'd been gone half a flare by the time we got here. Which means the xaxiks may still be close to the surface of the ice, so we need to get going. He'll be back here within a quarter of a flare."

Aran ran the quick calculations in his head—just over three hours, then. That should give him plenty of time.

"I'm on my way back. But listen, Istvay did leave a message, and I'm pretty sure it's coordinates. As soon as I'm back to the ship we can figure it out."

"That's fantastic!" Dessi's voice was almost as excited as his. "And when we're done, I'm going to have some questions for you, too—I'm very interested in your Istvay's ability to know where you'll look, and yours to know where they'll leave you a message. I'm thinking of starting a new study on inter-human relationships, and its influence on your culture ..." she trailed off, and Aran grinned to himself, picturing her grabbing her data pad.

When no more communication was forthcoming—apparently she'd been distracted enough that she'd forgotten about him—he tapped the communicator off, took his compass bearings—the planet did have a magnetic field, although it was weaker than the one back on Colorida—and started back the way he'd come.

He watched the snow-covered terrain, almost too bright to look at even in the anemic light from the distant sun, for signs of life as he walked. There weren't many, but he could see, here and there, tiny tracks—possibly small rodents, or insects of some sort. "Ani," he whispered, nudging the sullen lump that had migrated half-way up his chest. "There's got to be some sort of body of water under the ice here."

Ani stirred sleepily and gave a distinctly unenthusiastic chirrup in response.

He hardly cared. He had to think of something to keep himself from going absolutely crazy thinking of Istvay, and research was always a reliable option.

"If these temperatures are typical of the planet, which, according to Dessi, they are, you couldn't expect much plant life on the surface. But there are animals that live on the surface, which means they'd need some source of food. And the most likely source would be a body of water under the ice. Just because it's cold on the surface doesn't mean there aren't warmer vents under water, like in the Gardile Trench back home. There could easily be enough aquatic life to sustain whatever lives up here."

Ani grumbled to herself and snuggled deeper into his jacket.

He closed his eyes and touched the spot on his jacket where Istvay's parchment was tucked into the inner pocket.

He could do this. Just keep walking. One foot after the other, and worry about everything else when it came to it.

He couldn't have been more than twenty minutes from the raider ship, and he was beginning to recognize landmarks, when there was a startled curse through his communicator. The sound pulled him out of his thoughts, and it took him a second to remember how to turn the thing on. By the time he'd hit the line, the sounds coming through his earpiece were already loud enough almost to drown out Dessi's words.

"Dessi? What's wrong?"

"We have a problem." Dessi's voice was tight with strain. "The xaxiks are—"

The communication broke off.

11

Savina

Savina, still nursing a headache, scowled at the woman standing just ahead of her at the door to the tiny, rundown apartment she'd apparently used as a safehouse.

This whole thing would be … easier, somehow, if Reka would just act like the damn monster that she was. Like someone who hated Savina, wanted to hurt her, who was threatening everyone Savina loved and cared about. Someone who'd sold Savina out as easily as if they'd been two strangers.

So why the hell did Reka smile at Savina with that rueful, fond smile of hers, like there was something between them other than mutual hate and mistrust? Why had she bothered to hand Savina painkillers to take the edge off the nauseating ache pounding behind her eyes?

It was too much to think about right now. Even without the blinding hangover.

"So, what's your plan?" Savina whispered, making no effort to hide the irritation in her tone. "If you're willing to work with a criminal like me, I assume you must have a plan."

Reka turned over her shoulder, her gaze as startlingly intense as it always was. "Savina," she began, then paused, as if unsure what to say next.

"What?" Savina shot her a mocking look. "Harder to talk about how much I deserve to be killed now that you're doing it to my face, instead of trying to turn my friends against me?" The words came out more bitter than she'd intended.

Reka shook her head slowly. "You're dangerous, Savina. You're not just an assassin, it's not just that. I've gone after plenty of killers. But Captain Joska—she's a moral person. She's the type to care about every life lost, even yibo trying to kill her. And yet still, knowing who you are, she would have let me kill her before she let me bring you in. I've filled warrants on people who were much more skilled with weapons than you are. But you don't need that. You make people trust you. You make people care about you, even when they shouldn't. That's what makes you so dangerous."

She paused. "And I made the mistake of thinking you didn't have the capacity to care about them back."

Savina felt like a bug under Reka's gaze, pinned to a board, everything inside of her laid out on display to the curious onlooker.

She scowled. "I fooled Joska and Rafel, and Beni only follows me because they have no other choice. But you? You know damn well who I am. And yet here you are, saving my life. Working with me. Rescuing me from the consequences of my own decisions, just like Joska did. Are you sure you're not just as easily fooled as she was?"

Reka was silent a moment. At last, she gave Savina a tight smile. "Perhaps I am," she said in a low voice. Then she stepped quickly out of the doorway, leaving Savina staring after her.

Belatedly, Savina started after her. "Reka," she hissed. "What the hell—"

Reka held up a hand for silence, and Savina gritted her teeth.

The streets were heavy with yibo police and soldiers, many more than there had been the evening before.

Maybe Reka was right, and Savina's adventure in the yibo tavern had spread to more people than just Reka and some of Yuur's thugs.

She scowled. In fairness, she shouldn't have had to worry about that.

They were almost seen more than once as they crept down alleyways towards the centre of the city, and more than once Reka pulled them both into a hidden opening between two buildings, or a small space behind a waste disposal unit. At first, Savina was almost surprised at how well Reka knew the city—but of course she did. The weeks Savina had spent as a prisoner of a yibo crime boss, Reka had spent trying to hunt her down.

Savina might have been a prisoner, but she'd had friends, allies— Beni, Joska, Rafel, Nicolau. Even Yuur's people, who'd been acting as her guards, had a vested interest in keeping her alive. Reka had had none of that, completely on her own on the streets of a hostile city. And even then, it made Savina's blood run cold when she thought about just how close the woman had come to succeeding.

She cast a sideways glance at her companion as they walked, and shivered.

"Kachik hasn't made his move against the humans yet," Reka whispered as they neared the government compound. "He obviously knows you're here, but I checked while you were passed out—he doesn't seem to be trying to kill the prisoners. I don't know why, or what changed, but we're flying without nav equipment until we get more information."

"So what's your plan?" Savina whispered back.

Reka raised an eyebrow. "Surely you've done reconnaissance

before."

"Beni does the reconnaissance. I kill people. So unless your plan involves killing people—"

Reka gave her an amused smile. "Don't sell yourself short, Savina. You're very good at getting information if you want it." She paused. "We're going to use your handy little interpreter, since you're the only one here who has one, to listen in on Kachik's conversations. That's the plan."

Savina glared at Reka in outrage. "Oh, so you don't actually need my skills after all, then? All you're concerned with is the translator in my wavelink?"

Reka's grin widened. "I have nothing but respect for your skills at killing people. Your skills at listening to Ines's translator in your wavelink, though, happen to be the ones I value most right now."

Savina bit back a retort—Reka would probably only think it was funny—and swore under her breath. It really wasn't fair to have an archenemy who happened to have a drier sense of humour even then bloody Joska.

When they finally reached the courtyard outside the government buildings, Reka stopped, and Savina barely avoided bumping into her. Reka half-turned as if on instinct, catching Savina's arm to steady them both.

For a long moment, neither of them moved. Reka's lips were half-parted, and her eyes ran down Savina's body, lingering a moment on her curves, then flicked back up again almost guiltily, her hand tightening just a little.

Savina's breath was caught somewhere in her chest. She was standing far too close to Reka, close enough that she could feel the warmth from Reka's body against her skin, the heat of Reka's hand on her arm.

Reka dropped her hand quickly and turned away. "I can get us inside," she whispered, her voice not quite as calm as usual. "Best to go in tonight, I think, and find a place to hide until morning."

It was already close to sunset, the orange glow of the fading sun glinting off the glass and steel of the buildings.

Savina shook her head a little to clear it, and leaned back against the wall of a building, and resolutely did not look at Reka.

They waited until it was fully dark, and then they waited for a while after that. Savina tried not to think about the cold fear that bubbled up inside her at the thought of walking back into the yibo government building—the memories, all too clear, of guards shouting, blood streaming down her leg, pain so sharp and intense that she could hardly breathe through it.

At last, when it looked like most of the occupants of the buildings had left, Reka stood. "Let's go," she whispered. "You ready?"

"Yes," said Savina, clipping off her words.

She turned away quickly when Reka turned to look at her. It had been a long time since she'd felt this afraid, and there was no way in hell she was going to let Reka see that.

"Savina?" Reka asked quietly.

"Shut up," Savina snapped, and to her shock—Reka did.

For a place full of light and windows, the shadows the buildings cast across the open courtyard were thick and plentiful. It was easy enough to stay within their shelter as she and Reka made their way across the open courtyard in the quiet of the night. The soft hum of the transports and whatever it was that powered the city purred softly, almost concealed beneath the buzz and chirping of the night insects. Even after dark, the thick, sticky heat of the jungle clung to Savina's body, sweat gathering under her clothes and beading in her hairline.

It was only the heat that was making her sweat, of course—it wasn't because she was afraid.

She closed her eyes and forced her mind away from the last time she'd been in these buildings. Forced herself not to think about the fact she was walking back inside, of her own accord, beside a woman who'd sold her out without a qualm days previous.

And then, at last, they were at the walls of the building. Reka glanced back to check that Savina had followed, then pulled out a small metal device from her pocket. She put her hand up to the clear surface of the building walls, then hesitated.

"It's possible there's more security than there was last time we were here," she whispered. "If an alarm goes off, we'll have to be fast. Find somewhere out-of-the-way, and stay hidden."

Savina opened her mouth to hiss something about if she'd wanted to be an athlete, she would have chosen a different profession, but Reka's hand had already slid across the smooth glass.

An opening appeared.

And at the same time, an alarm wailed across the courtyard.

Savina cursed under her breath, and then Reka had grabbed her by the upper arm and pulled her through the gap before it closed.

"Let's go!" she hissed, and Savina glared up at her in disbelief.

She was grinning. Reka Soler was actually grinning.

She didn't have time to focus on the sheer unbelievability of it, because Reka had already started off at a run down the corridors.

Savina stumbled after her, cursing through her gasps.

She hated running. She'd always damn well hated running.

Reka seemed to know exactly where she was going, dodging down hallways and through corridors, and Savina did everything in her power to keep up.

"Mind the tripwire," Reka hissed over her shoulder as she stepped lightly over the dim laser, almost invisible in the darkness.

Savina jumped it, a little more clumsily than Reka had, but damn it to hell, Reka had height on her, and apparently some sort of masochistic enjoyment of this type of thing.

Already in the background she could hear the boots of yibo soldiers, the shouts and curses. Her wavelink translated their words.

"What is it?"

"After-hours intruders, it looks like."

"Any idea who?"

"No sign of anyone yet, but we'll comb the building just to be safe. After what happened, we can't take risks."

"This way," Reka whispered, slipping down a corridor.

"Have we checked down here?" The voice came from the far end of the corridor they'd just ducked down.

Savina cursed and grabbed Reka's shoulder. As Reka spun, surprised, Savina snatched the device neatly from the woman's hand, slid it across the doorway of one of the empty conference rooms, slid her foot through as if to enter, then pulled it back. She jogged to the next doorway, dragging Reka behind her, and did the same, then the next, and the next. When at last they reached the end of the corridor, she pulled them both behind a small plinth with vines cascading down its sides and dropped to the ground, gasping for air. Reka crouched down beside her in the darkness. In the silence Savina could feel her own heartbeat in her ears, hear Reka's quick breathing from beside her.

The soldiers reached the first room where Savina had triggered the alarm—or at least, she hoped she had—and they opened a doorway and stepped inside.

Savina held her breath.

At last, they reappeared, shaking their heads. "I think it must be a malfunction," said one of the soldiers. "Every alarm on this hallway was triggered, and there's not a sign of anyone inside."

The other officer gave an audible sigh. "Always with the security malfunctions," she grumbled. "We'll have to check every room to be sure, either way. But I suspect you're right."

Savina and Reka crouched behind the plant for what felt like hours. Savina's leg cramped halfway through, but she couldn't move without making a sound, so she gritted her teeth and bore it.

At last, the sound of the soldiers faded in the distance. Reka turned her, eyebrows raised. "Not a bad idea," she whispered.

Savina batted her eyelashes. "Unlike some of us, I only look stupid."

This time, Reka actually did chuckle. "I learned that the first time I met you."

Savina turned to stare at her, but she was already on her feet, her lean, muscular body poised and ready, and dammit, Savina was *not* paying attention to Reka's body …

"We're going to trigger all the alarms again," whispered Savina. "But this time we'll go into the room you want us to hide in. I doubt they'll look very thoroughly this time."

Reka gave her a look that could almost have been admiring, but she only nodded.

As Savina had predicted, when the soldiers came back a second time, they hardly bothered to glance into the rooms. "I'm half-tempted to shut off the security until tomorrow, and they can fix it," the captain grumbled, her voice muffled from outside the door to the room where Savina and Reka had taken refuge. "Keep an eye on it, anyway—we'll get someone into look at it tomorrow."

Their footsteps faded away, and at last Savina and Reka stepped out from their hiding place in the farthest corner from the entrance.

Reka surveyed the room carefully, then gestured over to a narrow alcove in one corner. "That should have enough space for both of us," she whispered.

"And also no way out if they see us," Savina grumbled.

Reka glanced at her. "Were you planning on getting caught?"

Savina glared, and Reka chuckled.

And for some reason, standing in the dark, so close together that Savina could have reached out and run her hand down Reka's cheek, the chuckle sounded … warm. Intimate. Like something between friends. And the thought made something catch in Savina's throat.

She studied the woman from the corner of her eyes as they made themselves comfortable in the tiny, cramped space. But Reka didn't speak, and Savina wasn't sure what to say.

She must have dozed off at some point, because the sound of boots and voices startled her awake. She blinked her eyes open to see Reka already crouched at the entrance to their hiding place, her entire body alert, her expression focused.

The sunlight dripping through the walls caught on the black shine of her hair and trickled across her dark skin, lending it a rich glow. As if she'd sensed Savina's eyes on her, Reka half turned and shot her a small grin, beckoning her over with a jerk of her chin. Savina grimaced, and crawled over to where Reka crouched.

She had to lean close enough that their shoulders were touching if she wanted to be able to see. Which was fine. Proximity born of necessity, just like every other time she'd touched Reka.

Again, her mind pulled up the hazy memory of her lips pressed to Reka's, the way Reka's lips had parted, the softness of her mouth against Savina's …

Well, almost every time she'd touched Reka.

She peered down in time to see the yibo members of government chatting and laughing amongst themselves as they took their seats. When Kachik arrived at last, the chattering the room fell silent.

"I won't lie to you," he began, once he'd made his way to the front of the room. Savina noticed, with no small sense of satisfaction, that he seemed to have aged ten years in the last few days—his eyes bloodshot, his posture stooped. "Our position here is precarious. We were counting on technology and soldiers from the humans in our battle against the Synod And now, my spies tell me, the Synod is conspiring against us with the humans themselves. I'm certain you've heard the rumours—that some of the humans involved in the disaster are back in the city. I do not know if this is true, and I have all our peacekeepers out on the streets, so if they're out there, we should find them quickly. Nonetheless, it is a disturbing rumour. With that said, however, it's not all bad news. Negotiations on the alliance are progressing well, and I think we can still turn the situation to our advantage. So our human guests may prove useful after all."

Savina frowned, unease crawling up her spine. She couldn't think of any context in which someone like Kachik calling humans 'useful' would be anything other than horrifying.

"And how secure is our ally's position?" an older yibo woman asked, her voice hard. "The results of a miscalculation would be nothing less than catastrophic."

Kachik smiled, but the expression was cold. "Don't underestimate how badly she needs us. She's been pushing to get her prize early, but until her position is secure, the humans will stay with us—a promise, no more. I'm putting every pressure I can bring to bear on her to ensure she deals with the uprising as quickly as possible. Her people told me they'd be ready in five days at most." He turned to the woman who had spoken earlier. "And to assuage your concerns, we're keeping the humans who are most likely to prove useful. Mattin and that scientist and a few of Mattin's soldiers, I think, comprise most of them. If anyone will have information on human weapons technology we can use, it'll be them. They've already proven they're willing to work against their compatriots' interests, as long as they are given sufficient motivation. And I think we're all satisfied that once the rest of the humans are turned over—there will be no inadvertent passing on of information."

There were scattered hums of amusement throughout the assembled politicians.

"That, at least, I agree with," said the yibo woman. "But the others—sufficient motivation?"

Kachik nodded, still smiling that death's head smile. "Friendly persuasion, at the moment. But every one of them is aware of what happens when friendly persuasion ceases to work. And I grant them the minor favours they ask for that are easy to grant—this one saved with the others, that one killed. Things like that."

"Five days, then," said the older yibo woman.

Kachik nodded. "Yes. And once things are finalized, we'll be in a much stronger position to negotiate with the Synod. Within five days, we should have the political capital to ask for almost anything. And I think that inadvertently, the humans may have given us that option."

Savina glanced at Reka. There was a look on her face that told Savina that even if she hadn't understood the words, she'd understood the tone behind them. Savina gestured back to the recesses of their hiding place, and Reka followed her.

"How bad is it?" Reka asked, when they were far enough back that they were unlikely to be overheard.

"In five days' time, they're trading the humans in exchange for an alliance," said Savina in a flat voice. "And it doesn't sound like anyone thinks the humans will survive it."

Reka nodded grimly. "Alright, then," she whispered. "You and I have five days to figure out how to save them."

12

Alba

Alba studied Jair as they walked together out into the city streets, already busy this early in the morning.

She didn't know much at all about him. He looked as if he might be in his mid- to late forties, although with the deep lines in his face and the grey in his hair, he could be older. He'd have been past his childhood when the yibo and the raiders had destroyed his system and massacred almost all its inhabitants—a teenager at least, if not an adult.

He hadn't spoken of it, other than to tell them to be grateful they'd stopped it from happening to Joias.

She fought back a shudder.

That could have been her. Her system. Her people, slaughtered in cold blood. Even now, she wasn't certain she'd prevented it— perhaps all they'd managed was a delay of the inevitable.

She forced her mind resolutely away from the thought. There would be time to deal with that when they'd solved the current crisis.

"You're comfortable with the details I gave you yesterday?" Jair asked. She looked up, startled, and nodded.

Jair let out a quick, nervous breath, turning back to his route.

The yibos' political situation was unfamiliar—but then, she was very accustomed to reading through the dense political treatises disguised as briefings that Feliu habitually prepared for her. And ultimately, although there were differences in the structure of the government and the training of the politicians, there was an echo of sameness to the underlying political system.

In Joias, the governing body that debated and passed the laws was the Council; here the governing body was called the Synod, made up of fourteen Hierophants, who passed laws based off proposals passed up by the Advisory Body, and in accordance with something called the Tenets of Clarity. The Advisory Body was made up of individual advisors, and it functioned more or less like the Counsel back on Joias, although without the final ability to pass laws. There were differences in how the politicians were appointed, as well—the Hierophants, for instance, were generally started in the discipleship as children, and had to spend several years of religious study, plus years of something called "ascetic wandering," before they were eligible for a political position, and the advisors were nominated as children by their districts and sent to specialized schools for a chance at an advisorship—but the grinding gears of politics beneath it all seemed familiar enough.

Alba glanced around her as they walked. They were in the middle of the yibo city now, and she found that, despite her own worry and strain, the odd beauty of the alien architecture caught her eye, the sun painting the edges of the venerable buildings in the soft glow of early morning. The streets were old, crafted of a textured cement-type material that bore the marks of years of foot traffic. The patina of centuries had overlayed the place with a feeling of dignity and permanence, rather than one of decay, just like on the ancient stone buildings in the Old Quarter in Vila Nova do Sol. But the craftsmanship itself was delicate and intricate, worn from centuries of use, and poignant in a jarring way that Alba had not expected from an alien civilization, in an alien system.

And oddly enough, the sight made her wonder, for the first time since the diplomatic ship had broken up, spewing its dead in frozen dust across this harsh, unfamiliar system, if perhaps there was a way for their two civilizations to coexist peacefully. Two species who, for whatever reason, valued craftsmanship and beauty enough that, even in a desperate struggle to survive, they'd take the time to make something necessary into a work of art.

She sighed and shook her head. Of course, all this was theoretical. Any chance for peace depended in large measure on the yibos' willingness to see humans as sapient creatures in the same oddly disorienting way that Alba was learning to see the yibo.

Well, that, and her ability to convince those in power that treating the humans as such would be in their best political interest, morality aside. If the yibo truly were anything like humans, that was probably the most important factor of all.

Jair glanced backwards at her and slowed his pace, and she bit back an unexpected spark of resentment at the pity mixed with condescension in his expression. But the past few weeks had taught her that her dignity was no match for the ache in her muscles or the exhaustion that seemed to have lodged in her bones themselves, so she forced herself to give him a short, grateful nod for his consideration, and said nothing.

The shape of the yibo government building, when they reached it, was entirely different from the shape of the ancient Council Building back on do Sol, but there was a gravitas about the place that felt entirely familiar.

Jair spoke with someone at the door to the building, then turned back to Alba. "Tika has agreed to meet with you. He'll be with you shortly." He paused. "My function is the human liaison to General Riit, and the advisor can't be seen to take an aide based on my recommendation. It wouldn't look good, in his position. Best if I leave you here."

The words shouldn't have shot a quick bolt of panic through Alba's body, but they did. She'd be once again alone, trying desperately to find the correct words or gestures or arguments that would convince an alien species, with their alien ways and their alien culture, not to kill her and everyone who looked to her for protection.

But she was no child. No Ines, with this her first foray outside the realm of her own comfort.

And Ines, who was little more than a child, had shown a courage that would put most people Alba had known to shame. Alba could hardly countenance doing less herself.

So she simply nodded, forcing her face into a pleasant smile. It took her a moment to realize that she had copied the close-lipped smile of the yibo without thinking, in the same way Jair had.

He turned away, leaving her standing alone outside the doors.

When at last the doors were pulled open and an expressionless yibo attendant beckoned Alba inside, she held her head high and stepped through the doors, forcing the fear from her expression.

She walked down the wide central corridors, their walls mostly translucent, as in most yibo buildings she'd entered. Now that she was paying attention to her surroundings, she realized it was darker inside than she'd expected—the walls were covered, yibo-style, in a riot of greenery, but even the greenery felt different in this building than it had in Kachik's—rather than the bright yellow-green of vines trailing down the sides of plinths, this was the darker, older green of trees, roots and suckers reaching into cracks in the old stone or petrified wood supporting the walls, branches pressed up against and almost obscuring the huge windows—if you could call them "windows" when they took up most of the wall—in a way that spoke of age and centuries.

"The advisor is waiting to see you inside," the yibo guide said, stepping back at last and gesturing Alba to a door.

Alba set her teeth to keep from a frankly ridiculous shudder, and stepped inside.

A young-looking yibo man, dressed in heavy ceremonial robes, glanced up from his desk with faint irritation in his expression. "Yes?" His words were passible Common Dialect, although spoken with a heavy accent. The annoyance in his tone, however, was also very clear.

"Advisor Tika," said Alba, tipping her head in the yibo form of respect. "Thank you for agreeing to meet with me."

"How could I do otherwise?" There was an expression on his face that said this was politeness, not sincerity. "Please do tell me how I can help you …" he consulted his communication device, "Alba."

There had been a time when this man not knowing her name would have been highly irritating. Now, she realized with wry humour, she was absurdly grateful to be acknowledged at all.

"I had hoped, in fact, that I could be of some help to you," she said.

He frowned. "I'm sure I'm very appreciative of the offer, but I'm not sure you'd be able to help with anything I need at present."

Alba cleared her throat. "If I understand your politics correctly, you're the advisor over a district in which there are a large number of humans, correct?"

He was watching her warily, but there was a spark of interest in his eyes that hadn't been there before. "I am, as a matter fact," he said at last. "However, as you are not from this system, I don't know that you could give me any appreciable insights into their needs or culture."

"As a human, however, I am familiar with human social structures in way that I assume that many of your colleagues are not. My system communicated regularly with the Labirinto System for centuries, and I am very aware of their culture and politics prior to their meeting you."

Tika gave her a slightly condescending smile. "I'm sure your offer is well meant, and you comported yourself well in the hearing yesterday. Unfortunately, our political documents are not written in your language. So while I appreciate your offer, I'm not certain how helpful your skills would be."

"There is a linguist in our crew. She's managed to make a translator that allows us to understand your language. She is working on an additional component that would translate our speech into yours, and I assume she'll have it ready shortly. But in the meantime, you needn't worry that I won't understand, at least."

They'd discussed this the night before, for hours—the advantages of keeping a secret of their knowledge of the yibo language, versus the advantage of having Alba in politics.

In the end, it had hardly been a contest. If Alba didn't succeed, chances were they would live out their lives as little more than prisoners—whatever the yibo government said now, humans who had destroyed a portal mechanism would likely be too dangerous to let wander free. Understanding the yibo language would certainly not be enough to save them in that case.

She gave Tika a small smile. "And in my home system, I was a high-ranking politician. I have experience working in human politics, and experience in crafting policies that would be acceptable to a broad swath of my fellow politicians. I realize that our systems of governance are different, but there are similarities. And if you had someone to consult with, someone who could assist you in crafting policies that would give the humans you represent some say in the governance of your system—surely that would be as much an advantage to you as it would to me."

He watched her for a few moments, and she could see the calculation on his face. At last, he nodded slowly. "Very clever. I get your assistance in crafting advisories that will be palatable to all concerned, and you get a voice for humans in the Synod."

Alba nodded, trying not to let the relief flood through her prematurely. He hadn't said yes, not yet.

"In addition," she said, "while our systems of government are different, I imagine even here, it is never a detriment to have an extra set of eyes and hands to perform research or draft speeches."

It felt disturbingly like begging. But at the very least, this system had given her an expansive amount of experience in swallowing down her pride.

Tika watched her, considering. At last, he gave a small, close-lipped yibo smile, and nodded. "It is an intriguing offer," he said. "A former human politician. As I said, you impressed me yesterday. I'll take you up on it, on a temporary basis. The raiders, you may have heard, are currently in the midst of a leadership war, and between that and the situation with the Nativists, basic governance matters are getting more and more difficult to push forward.

"I am to make a proposal tomorrow in front of the Advisory Body. I'll give you all the information, access to the current draft of my speech, and some articles that may be helpful. If you're as experienced a politician as you claim, I'm certain your input will be most helpful. And if I find your assistance on this proposal to be useful—" he twitched his tail in a yibo shrug. "Then I'd be more than happy to have your help. As you said, it does appear that our political goals are aligned, at least at present. I shall let the security guards know that you are to be allowed into the building and shown to my office when you arrive."

Alba returned his bland smile and tipped her head in acknowledgement. And she tried not to let her expression show anything of either the exhilaration, or the terror, that his words had caused.

13

Aran

Aran hit the line open again. "Dessi? Dessi, are you alright?"

There was no response.

He swore and started off at a quick jog towards the raider ship. He was already tired from his slog through the snow, and his muscles burned in protest, but even from here he could see the brilliant flashes of the raiders' energy weapons. He pushed himself harder, stumbling as his numb feet broke through the crust of the snow.

And then he reached a rise overlooking the ship, and stopped abruptly.

What looked like an outright battle was going on in the shallow basin around the ship. The raider crew were swarming out of the ship, firing their energy bolts into—

Aran frowned, yanking out his battered pair of binoculars and squinting through them.

Whatever the attacking creatures were, they weren't anything he'd seen before—long, slender bodies, with grasping claw-like pincers on the end of flailing tails that looked something like those of scorpions. Their bodies were snakelike, but thicker than what he'd expect on a snake, their colour an almost translucent whitish-pink.

The raiders were firing indiscriminately, and Aran winced unconsciously as one of the creatures was hit, and rolled backwards in the snow. The shot seemed to have bounced off its hard exoskeleton, though, because it rolled back upright, shook itself, a long series of undulations rolling down its body, then launched forward again into the battle.

Aran's communicator crackled, and he jumped.

"Aran! The xaxiks have latched themselves onto the communicator box, so I may lose contact in a bit here. Don't come back to the ship yet, we're going to try to hold them off."

"These are the things Krevai was talking about?" he asked quickly. "What do you know about them?" He was trying very hard to keep the fascination out of his voice—this was probably not the time.

As he watched, one of the crew abandoned their weapon and launched themself at one of the creatures. Aran stared in horrified fascination through his binoculars as the two danced around each other. The snakelike animal struck, and the raider leapt back, then jumped forward again, raking claws down the creature's back. Black blood oozed like tar from the wound, gleaming in the fading light.

Opposite the small battle, another raider wasn't faring as well—their weapon seemed to have jammed, and they were backing up against the side of the ship, frantically trying to reset it. One of the creatures had followed, head low and weaving back and forth. It struck, the movement almost too fast for Aran's eyes to follow, and when it pulled back, it was dragging the raider's limp body.

There was a moment's pause. "We don't know too much about them," said Dessi, a note of caution in her voice. She sounded a bit like Istvay usually did in these situations. "They live under the ice, and we assume they feel the ship's vibrations when it lands, which draws them to the surface. That's why no one stays long here." She paused a moment, muttering a curse. "Krevai is almost back. Stay away until he gets here, and I'll call you. You should be able to slip in while he's distracting them."

The communicator clicked off, and Aran stared down at the scene playing out below him, biting his lip.

Already, there were limp bodies on the snow, raider and xaxik both, and brilliant scarlet or shiny black stained the snow.

"Ani," he whispered. "When Krevai gets here, they'll slaughter those things. Unless the xaxiks slaughter him first, which they might. So. what do we know about xaxiks?" He dialed up the magnification on his binoculars and focused in on the fight.

At a closer look, it was easy to tell the creatures had very little eyesight, although he'd guessed that already from what Dessi had told him. They seemed to be homing in on the location of their prey by the vibration of their movements. In fact—

He squinted into the binoculars. One of the creatures near the back of the battle had stopped, pressing its long body to the ground as if trying to sense something.

Holding his breath, Aran stamped a foot lightly against the ice.

The beast's attention swivelled in his direction, and he grinned broadly.

He was at least two kilometres away. They must have incredibly sensitive tactile receptors.

"Look at that, Ani," he whispered.

Ani gave an uneasy growl.

The creature, who was near the back of the group, turned in a slow, sibilant motion, and started towards him, its movements cautious and somewhat hesitant. Aran's grin widened, a giddy excitement bubbling in his stomach. "Look at that, Ani," he whispered, taking care to keep his voice as quiet as possible. "I haven't moved since that one stamp, but it can tell exactly where I am. That's incredible!"

The thing was moving slowly, but steadily.

"I wonder," Aran murmured. He reached inside his supplies pouch, careful not to make any sudden movements, and pulled out an energy bar. He tossed it away from him across the icy snow, where it bounced, landed, and skidded a couple metres before coming to a halt.

The creature froze, body flattening down against the ice. Aran practically held his breath.

And then the creature's head swung back towards him, and it resumed its forward progress, movements a little more certain now.

Aran was grinning so wide his face hurt, and the cold air stung his teeth. "Ani!" he whispered. "It must be sensing the vibrations of my heartbeat and breathing, something like that. Look, we didn't fool it at all!"

The creature was coming faster now, its movements smooth and sinuous, and Aran watched in utter fascination.

At this rate, it would reach them in minutes.

He sighed and pulled his eyes from the creature's hypnotic approach, glancing around quickly. No point in trying to run—that thing was much faster than he was, and the moment he started running, he was pretty sure it would get a hell of a lot faster.

"Don't worry, sweetheart, I'm sure it's just hungry," he whispered reassuringly to Ani. "It's not anything personal."

Ani's eye pouches were bulging out, and her uneasy growl had turned into a low hiss. She seemed to have decided that, regardless of whether it was personal on the creature's side, it was utterly and terminally personal on hers.

"It's beautiful, isn't it?" Aran whispered, raising his binoculars to his eyes for one last look.

The animal's movements were graceful and sinuous, its hide—or perhaps more of an exoskeleton, he really needed to see it up close— seemed perfectly suited for the ice, smooth, but with ridges like those he'd seen on waxless skis, allowing it to move forward easily, but catching and gripping to keep it from sliding backwards.

"Alright, Ani," he whispered, rummaging in his supplies pouch. "I'm going to set my wave-scanner to …" he pulled it out, glancing down at it as he turned the dial. "We want it a little faster than a normal heart rate, I assume this little beauty is used to coming after prey with elevated heart rates. I'm going to set it to about a hundred and twenty beats per minute, that should be in a believable range." His own heart rate was probably at least that, considering how absolutely fascinated he was right now. "There," he whispered to the still-growling Ani. "Let's see if our friend can tell the difference."

The creature had picked up speed. It was probably less than five minutes away, at this point.

Aran hit the controller on the sensor, and it began to buzz gently.

The creature perked up and started moving faster, powerful muscles bunching and releasing to push it forward.

"Easy there," said Aran. "Easy there, beautiful—let's see what you think of this." Gently, he tossed the sensor away from him, and the moment it hit and bounced, he took a few quick steps in the opposite direction, stopping when the device stopped.

The creature paused, its head whipping back and forth between Aran and the device.

Aran grinned to himself. As close as the beast was now, he could study it much more easily. The claws on its tail were hooked slightly, longer and slimmer than he'd expect if its usual prey was land-bound.

"I was right, sweetheart!" he whispered under his breath. "It looks like their mandibles are designed to catch aquatic creatures. Look, that's almost certainly designed for spearing, not a pincer grasp. It's not proof, but it looks like it could wait by the edge of the water and spear its prey. With hypersensitive tactile receptors like that, it could feel a fish coming and pinpoint its location easily." His grin was so wide his face hurt. "Oh, you beautiful, beautiful creature, you."

The animal's semi-transparent exoskeleton—it was clearly an exoskeleton, now that he saw it closer—was stiff, but flexible, a series of narrow, overlapping plates. It had no external eyes that he could see, but then, it hardly seemed to need them. It did, however, have heavier plates near the tip of its snout, which could very well cover some light-receptive organ, since he could imagine sensing the amount of light could help the creatures measure their depth and orient themselves.

He wished, desperately, that he had the time to take a quick scan.

The creature was still hesitating, swinging its head back and forth between Aran and the sensor, when Dessi's voice crackled through the communicator, loud enough to make Aran jump.

"Aran, listen! Krevai and the others are close. You'll have to try to make it in with his team. You won't stand a chance otherwise. Then we'll have to hope we can get them away from the ship long enough to let us take off." Her voice was sharp with strain.

Aran bit back a curse, his mind jerked abruptly back to the urgency of the matter at hand. These stunning creatures—and, incidentally, much of the raider crew, if he was any judge—were about to be slaughtered.

He couldn't just stand here and let it happen.

The creature's head swivelled towards him, its attention once again fixed on the place he was standing. Then it sprang forward with a sinuous, deadly grace, covering the short distance between them with unimaginable speed.

Aran leapt back as its tail spike impaled the ice where he'd been standing, trying to hold Ani under his coat as she struggled to shove her head out. The sensor was still ticking, so the only thing that had changed was the sound through the communicator.

"So you can sense sound waves, somehow," he gasped, scrambling back again as the creature recalibrated its aim and plunged its tail spike into the ice millimetres away from his foot. Its tail swung around, practically sweeping him off his feet, and he dived out of the way and rolled in the snow, then curled into a ball as the spike hammered down again, barely missing his head. He fumbled in his pouch and yanked at the controller for the sensor, cranking the vibrations higher, then scrambled to his feet and dived, sliding and skidding, into a wide, shallow depression in the snow.

Ani had got the tip of a tentacle out of the neck of his jacket, and was attempting to haul herself out by main force.

He fumbled in his pouch as he slid down the icy snow crust, yanking out the self-inflating sleeping mat. He pulled the tab, and as the mat inflated, he rolled on top of it, pulling Ani against his chest protectively.

He held perfectly still, hardly breathing.

If he was incredibly lucky, the padding from the mattress, muffling the vibrations of his breath and heartbeat against the snow, combined with the louder vibrations from the sensor, would be enough to distract the creature.

For a few moments he lay completely still, waiting for the dark bulk of the xaxik to appear in the opening above him, silhouetted against the sky—but nothing came.

Cautiously, he lifted his head.

And then, abruptly, he heard the vicious crunch of something sharp spiking through ice, and at the same time the sensor control in his hand flashed and died.

He grinned to himself, a little shakily.

"Well, Ani," he said, keeping his voice barely audible. "I guess it worked. And did you see how accurate it must be? That sensor was only a few centimetres wide, and our little friend spiked it first try." He drew in a long, regretful breath.

What he wouldn't give to have a few days to study these gorgeous animals …

He shook his head. This wasn't the time, there was always the chance that he'd make it back here again. That he and Istvay would make it back here …

He gritted his teeth.

The problem he really should be focusing on right now was first, how he was going to get back to the ship, and second, how he was going to keep these things and the raiders from killing each other for long enough that they could get the ship back into the sky.

He turned his head carefully in the direction of the massive creature a few metres away from him across the snow.

Which might be a little complicated, all things considered.

But …

"Ani," he said slowly "I might have an idea."

He yanked the battered remnants of his supplies out of his supplies pouch and laid them out carefully on the mat, wincing at the shape they were in. He and Istvay had been on other expeditions that had gone pretty far sideways, but usually by this point they'd have had a chance to at least stop by their basecamp and restock.

He chewed on his lip, looking dubiously at the assortment of mismatched parts.

"Well," he murmured Ani, "at least we're used to making do."

He wasn't any sort of a mechanic, but he had enough experience performing frantic slapdash fixes on equipment in varying degrees of hostile terrain that it didn't take him too long to rig a makeshift amplifier.

"Alright, sweetheart," he whispered, loosening the neck of his jacket as she squeezed her way out. "I think this'll work. I'm going to need your help in just a minute here. But I think we better warn Dessi first." He tapped the communicator. "Dessi?"

"Where are you? I was worried you were dead!"

"I'm fine, I just—look, I'm going to try something. I'm not sure if it'll work, but if it does, the xaxiks might leave you alone for a minute. If they do, get everyone back in the ship, maybe we can get away without killing any more of them."

"What exactly are you planning?" There was something like dread in Dessi's voice.

"Don't worry, I'm pretty sure it'll work." He tried to disguise the excitement in his voice. "And if it doesn't, I guess—" he trailed off. "I think it'll work, though," he added hastily. He tapped the communicator line off before Dessi had a chance to respond, and took a deep breath. "Alright, Ani," he whispered, turning over the handful of amplifier nodes in his hands, "guard."

Her body perked up, bulbous eyes peering around suspiciously, and she let out a low growl. Aran held the amplifier up to catch the sound, then hit the controller to play it in a loop, and tossed the nodes out across the snow in a wide arc.

If Istvay were here, they'd have been able to do some quick calculations to ensure the sound waves would reverberate through the ice the way he wanted them to. But he wasn't as fast with maths, and he didn't really have time to worry about it. He was just going to have to give it his best guess, and hope it was close enough.

Ani's growl rumbled through the amplifier nodes, making the snow shake.

For a moment, nothing happened.

Then there was the rough rasp of something sliding rapidly over the snow.

"I think it's working!" Aran whispered jubilantly.

The creature's head appeared at the lip of the depression.

Ani's growl increased, and the amplifier picked up the sound, high enough that even Aran could feel the reverberations through the snow.

The creature's body whipped towards where the nearest amplifier node was planted, then to another, as if confused by the overwhelming sensations.

Aran scrambled up the side of the depression and took off across the snow in a flat run.

The creature spun, tracking his movements, and he dived to one side as a sharp tail spike skewered the snow exactly in his path. He rolled franticly over, waiting for the next strike … but it didn't come.

The creature had already turned back to the rough semicircle of amplifier nodes.

Aran scrambled to his feet and kept running.

He could already see the creatures around the raider ship turning in the direction of the amplifier nodes as he approached the ship—or rather, he hoped they were turning in the direction of the amplifier instead of just watching him and Ani, although honestly, either was possible. The creatures nearest the ship were still focused on their prey, but the ones in the back were beginning to peel off, gliding across the ice towards him.

In a few moments, the ones in the centre of the pack began to turn as well, until even the creatures nearest the ship seemed distracted, turning uncertainly back and forth from the raiders they were attacking to the place where Ani's amplified growl reverberated through the snow behind them.

"Dessi, get everybody in the ship!" Aran shouted through his communicator. "Tell the crew to stop fighting them, and I think they'll leave!"

"What in God's name are you talking about—" Dessi began.

"Just trust me," Aran panted.

There was silence from the other end of the line. He closed his eyes for half a moment, praying to any deity available that the raiders would damn well listen.

Then there was a sound ahead of him on the snow.

He opened his eyes, glanced up, and swore.

Most of the creatures were heading for the amplifier nodes, but the creature nearest him had turned towards him and Ani, exoskeleton scraping across the snow.

"Dammit, dammit, dammit," Aran muttered. He'd left the inflatable mat back in the depression in the snow—although in fairness, he'd been a little busy at the time—so holding completely still wouldn't do him any good. They'd already proven they could sense his damn heartbeat.

It had picked up its pace, sliding towards him with deadly focus.

It was moving deceptively quickly. Aran glanced around, looking frantically for survivable options, and by the time he turned back, the thing was almost on top of him.

"Damn it to hell," he gasped as it raised its tail to strike.

And then Ani launched herself at the beast in a hissing, deadly ball of pent-up rage.

"Ani, no!" Aran began. But the creature was already swaying uncertainly, Ani latched like an oversized tick on the back of its neck.

It dropped to the ground with a *thud*, and Ani growled, looking very pleased with herself.

Aran looked ruefully at the fallen beast, shaking his head, as Ani clambered back to her perch on his shoulder, preening.

Then he looked over into the faces of three raiders, who'd been running towards him, weapons drawn.

They stared between him, Ani, and the creature.

"It's—it's, um, it's fine, Ani took care of it," said Aran weakly.

The raiders were still staring.

Aran cleared his throat, settled Ani a little more firmly onto her perch, and picked his way quickly down the ice towards them. He'd have liked to stay long enough to take some samples, since the creature was already dead and it was a shame to waste it—but at this rate, if they didn't get off the planet quickly, it was looking like there would be a lot more dead animals to take samples off than he was really comfortable with.

"Did—did she—" began one of the raiders, gesturing between Ani and the massive, limp carcass.

Aran sighed, putting a hand protectively on one of Ani's tentacles. "She—she really only does that when she's trying to protect me. She's actually very gentle."

The raiders didn't speak, just fell in with him, although, he noticed, they kept a cautious distance from Ani as they walked.

When they crested the small hill, Aran saw Krevai and his small, handpicked crew striding towards them in the snow.

"Aran!" Krevai shouted. "Here Dessi told me we were walking into the middle of a battle! I'm disappointed! What happened, did your Ani eat them all?" He laughed heartily.

"No, just the one," said Aran quickly. "But, um, I think maybe we should—"

"The Ani just took it down," one of the raiders beside Aran shouted, her voice thick with admiration. "She was magnificent! She jumped on it, and two seconds later it was dead! And our Aran! You should have seen him, standing there like he was out for a morning stroll. Didn't even draw a weapon on it. You picked good ones, Captain!"

Krevai beamed.

Aran groaned.

Then he noticed something his brain had been trying to tell him for a few moments now.

The growling through the amplifier had stopped.

He cursed.

It had only been a matter of time—the creatures had proven they were exceptionally accurate with their tail spikes. "I think we should get inside the ship—" he started.

The first of the xaxiks appeared over the crest of the hill, moving at speed.

Krevai followed Aran's gaze. "Our Aran is right," he bellowed. "No point in feeding those things any more of us than what they've already taken."

The group of them reached the loading ramp mere metres in front of the first xaxik, and someone hit the controls, slamming the hatch shut.

"Landru, take us up before they latch onto the ship," Krevai shouted, striding down the corridors towards the cockpit. He paused a moment, glancing back at Aran. There was a look on his face, half of amusement, half of mild admiration. "Go on back to your cabin, I know you don't like space flights. But after we're up and you're feeling better, I would really like to hear about what just happened out there."

14

Savina

"How in the hell are we supposed to break almost two hundred people out of here, let alone find a safe place to take them, in under a week?" Savina hissed once she and Reka were safely outside the building. It was dark, and the light from the two moons glowed dimly under a thick cover of clouds.

"I don't know." Reka's face was grim.

Savina managed to stop herself from pointing out the obvious solution—walk away and leave these idiots to handle their own problems. Reka wasn't any more likely to listen to that line of reasoning then Joska would have been.

"Listen," she said instead. "From what Joska said, there are—other planets in the system where the yibo might be more sympathetic to humans."

Reka nodded slowly. "I remember Joska mentioning that. So, what are you suggesting? Steal a ship and get them off planet?"

Savina nodded reluctantly. "I think if you're set on going through with this stupid rescue mission—which, by the way, is a terrible idea —getting them on a ship and getting off planet sounds like the best option we have. And since, thanks to you, I don't have any other option than to go through with this, I'd rather have a survivable plan."

Reka bit her lip, and Savina absolutely did *not* find her eyes drawn to it like iron shavings to a magnet. "That still leaves us with the problem of getting everyone out. And it means we need to find a ship." She gestured with her head back down the alleyway, and led the way to a small alcove of sorts between two of the buildings.

She ducked inside, and Savina followed warily, looking around in mild surprise. The place was set up as something of an emergency shelter—a space blanket folded neatly and tucked against the wall of one building, some packages of something Savina guessed must be food, a couple small bottles of water.

She glanced at Reka again, curious, but Reka just gestured her to take a seat on the blanket.

It wasn't a large space, and they ended up sitting closer together than Savina meant to. She tried to ignore the warmth of Reka's body where it brushed against hers as Reka pulled a sheet of paper and a writing stick out from of the pockets of her suit and spread it out on the blanket between them.

"This is the layout of the government compound," Reka said in a low voice, sketching out a quick outline. "And here is where they keep their ships. The loading pad is back here behind the buildings, and there's usually one or two ships standing ready at any one time."

Savina nodded, leaning in over the map.

"Over here is the compound where the humans are being kept. They've posted guards at all the entrances. There's a force field over the top, so no way in or out except through the doors."

"They didn't seem too hard to get past when I went in," whispered Savina. "With one of us on the inside and one on the outside, I think we could take them out fairly easily. Just like when Kachik locked us up—I provide the distraction, you take out as many as you can, and when they notice something's wrong, I finish them off."

Reka frowned, her entire attention on the diagram. "We'd have to be fast. If they have time to get out an alarm—"

"There's no way they get an alarm out fast enough to trap us in there," said Savina. "The moment we hear an alarm, we finish off everyone who's seen us and slip out, and whoever shows up has no idea what happened. The yibo weapons vaporize people, and I have a knife that makes the death look like a heart attack."

Reka glanced up, eyebrows raised. "Wait. That business magnate back in do Sol two years ago? The one where they were certain it was a murder, but it looked like …"

Savina nodded curtly. "Yes. That was me."

Reka looked mildly impressed. "Alright, now that I've agreed not to fill your warrant—how many people, exactly, have you assassinated that we thought were accidental deaths?"

Savina rolled her eyes. "Enough that we probably don't have time to chat about it. I'm good at my job, alright? Now, if you don't have any more questions about my personal life, maybe you could get your mind on the damn job, isn't that what you're always telling me?"

Reka looked like she was biting back a grin, but she nodded and turned back to the diagram. "I'm less worried about them catching us than I am about them locking down the security. From what you told me, this new alliance Kachik wants is dependent on his allies getting the humans at the end of it. He's not going to want to risk losing them. If he sees guards dying, it won't matter whether it looks like a heart attack, he'll lock everything down. Getting back in would be next to impossible."

Savina sighed. "What about this, then—we kill the guards as planned, and with any luck things go smoothly, and they don't get off an alarm. But as a precaution, we arm the humans first. Maybe those of Cavaco's soldiers who are going to be sold off with the others. They make a distraction, the guards focus on that, you and I get the rest out."

Reka glanced up at her. "What happens to the people providing a distraction?"

Savina smiled, showing all her teeth. "We tell them we'll come back for them, as soon as we get the others out." She shrugged. "Their boss was willing to sell out the entire Joias System, so I hardly think they can complain about us not being completely honest."

Reka stared at her for a moment, as if unsure whether or not she was joking. And then she huffed out a small laugh. "I won't say it's a good first option. But I suppose as last options go—"

Savina blinked. "You—agree?"

Reka chuckled again, and again, the sound sparked something warm in Savina's chest. "I'd rather save them all. That is and will continue to be our objective. But if it comes to a choice between the soldiers and the civilians—" she shrugged. "The soldiers made a choice when they agreed to participate in a mutiny and force the ship through the portal. Like you said, I hardly see how they can complain when they're held to it."

Savina was still blinking at the woman. She'd gotten used to working with Joska over the past few weeks. Joska, who, for all her good qualities, had no sense of the necessity of the occasional murder.

It was ... refreshing, to be working with another person for whom murder was a necessary part of the job, rather than completely anathema.

She smiled. And to her surprise, Reka smiled back.

"So," Reka whispered, turning back to the map. "Our first task is getting the weapons. Then we'll have to find ourselves a ship. We may have to clear a path to get there, but with you and me both armed, we should be able to get where we need to. In the worst-case scenario, we let our soldier friends put their skills to some use."

"You're willing to trust the soldiers?" Savina whispered.

Reka turned to her, an amused gleam in her eye. "Oh, absolutely not. But I think we can ensure that they don't do anything we don't want them to. I'm intimidating, and you're … easy to underestimate. I think watching their ringleaders' throats slit will do wonders for the others' morale."

Again, Savina found herself smiling unconsciously. She turned quickly back to the map, trying to school her expression before Reka noticed.

"We'll try to speak with the prisoners tonight," Reka continued. "They'll need to be ready to get out on a moment's notice. And then we'll do some reconnaissance for weapons and ships. We have five days. No point in showing our hand before we're ready."

Savina nodded, and Reka pulled a small incendiary out of her pocket and held it to the map. They watched as it turned to ash, then Reka crushed the pieces under her foot. "I'll scout things out," she whispered. "You may as well get a nap in. We'll head in around sunset."

Savina probably should have argued. But she hadn't slept nearly long enough in the cramped corner of the government conference room, and if Reka wanted to act the hero, Savina certainly wasn't going to fight her over it.

* * *

When Reka nudged her awake, it was evening, and the sun had already set. "Time to go," she whispered.

She still looked residually exhausted.

Which was her own problem, not Savina's, and Savina refused to let the knot of guilt in her stomach take root.

They moved quickly, the sound of their footfalls on the street hardly audible. When they reached the compound that housed the humans, though, Reka slowed abruptly, holding up a hand.

The compound was brightly lit, and much busier than it should have been—guards striding back and forth, people shouting orders.

Savina glanced at Reka.

"Something's happened," Reka whispered. "It shouldn't be this busy."

They crept closer, keeping to the shadows, and Reka paused again where they had a clear view of the courtyard. "What are they saying?" she whispered, turning to Savina.

Savina gave a tight shake of her head. "I need to be closer."

The two of them crept closer still up the small alley they'd been sheltering in. By now, they were close enough that they could make out the faces of the guards in the flickering light, hear the shouts and calls clearly.

"—don't know why we're doing this in the middle of the night," one soldier grumbled.

"Kachik's orders," another responded. "He said he's not taking chances on any of them either getting away or getting stolen, not with the news coming in from everywhere else. Get them in the cells, keep them safe until the raiders pick them up." He shook his head. "Besides, you remember what he did to the two guards from a couple days back? I'm not about to make myself a target."

"I suppose you're right," said the first, and the voices faded.

It took Savina a moment before the import of the words hit her.

Then she had to grab for the alley wall to steady herself.

The raiders. That was what Kachik had been talking about. That's who his mysterious ally was. He was going to trade the rest of the diplomatic ship's survivors to the raiders.

She wasn't sure she'd ever stop having nightmares of those glistening fangs, the hunger in those red eyes as the raider captain looked at her.

Reka glanced over, concern in her expression. "Savina?"

For a moment, Savina hesitated.

Even the thought of the raiders had started a cold, unreasoning fear in her chest. And if Kachik had made promises already, she and Reka would be stealing the raiders' prey out from under them. And she knew, bone-deep, that the raiders wouldn't hesitate to hunt them down for it.

If she said nothing … if the humans were taken inside the government compound, the chance of her and Reka getting them out alive was slim to none. Even Reka would have to see that. She could tell Reka they'd only been talking about increasing security, or they were doing an emergency drill tonight, so the two of them should come back the next day. Reka wouldn't know until it was too late.

But—

She bit back a groan.

What the hell had happened to her? A few weeks ago, she wouldn't even have had to think about it. A few weeks ago, the thought of the disappointment in Joska's face, the sick despair in Reka's, wouldn't have moved her at all.

She scowled. Anyway, it wasn't that. It was just that Reka would probably insist they try anyway, and then they'd both be killed for sure, and Reka had made damn sure she didn't have an option other than going through with it.

"They're moving the humans into the cells inside the building," she whispered reluctantly. "Tonight. And ..." she paused. "And it sounds like they'll be traded to the raiders."

Reka swore viciously under her breath. And for just a moment, Savina thought that maybe, just maybe—

Then she noticed the look on Reka's face. Her expression was determined, her eyes narrowed, that small, grim smile pulling at the corners of her mouth, the smile Savina had seen all too often when Reka was about to do something she thought might kill her.

"Alright," she whispered. "I guess we go in now."

15

Alba

"How was it, Alba?" Yosip's voice was warm, his brows crinkled with a concern that Alba knew perfectly well was as much for her wellbeing as it was for their position.

She didn't even fight the now-familiar, aching relief at the sound of his friendly voice, the way she could let herself sag with weariness, and not worry about who would see the weakness as a point to attack.

"He was willing to give me a chance, which is as much as we can ask for, I suppose." She tried to disguise the hopelessness in her tone.

"Alba," he said again, quietly.

She sighed. "I am welcome to be his assistant, as long as I'm able to create a proposal for him to present to the Advisory Body tomorrow, and as long as that proposal is successful. Which would be much simpler if I had any idea at all of what type of proposal would be acceptable to a yibo government official." She gave a bitter, exhausted little laugh. "Unfortunately, I find that is not exactly within my knowledge base."

Yosip nodded, his eyes dark with sympathy. "I'm not sure that it's within any of our knowledge bases," he said. "But I'm sure you know as well as I do how skilful Feliu is in matters of politics, and it's possible that Ines learned something about the yibo culture and priorities as she studied the language. And I'm sure Jair will be more than happy to help, and he's spent most of his life here—married, raised children."

Alba had to bite back a quick smile. She'd had no idea of Jair's familial status, but of course Yosip did. Yosip probably knew his favourite food, and had already asked him for the recipe.

She took a deep breath. Asking for, let alone accepting, help still felt more like admitting defeat than she really wanted to think about.

"I'll get the others," said Yosip. "In the meantime, you can rest for a minute, have time to look through whatever he sent back with you."

Alba nodded, and took a seat on a low, hard stool pulled up beside one of the rickety tables.

It wasn't long before there was a small group of them huddled on the uncomfortable stools around the table—Yosip, Feliu, Ines and Nicolau, who seemed to have become all but surgically attached to the young translator, a silent, haunted-looking Beni, Rafel, and Joska, the dark circles under her eyes showing clearer than words that she was as worried about the missing assassin as Beni and Nicolau were.

"What are we working with, Madam?" Feliu's words were sharp and precise, and Alba found that, despite everything, the sound made her smile.

"This is the proposal Tika gave me," she said, gesturing to a holographic document projecting onto the uneven tabletop. "I certainly can't speak to the advisor's political acumen, but unless the yibo culture is very much different than I suspect, I am not sure this is a winning proposition."

Feliu scanned it quickly, then gave a snort of disapproval. "The idea itself is—not terrible," he said at last. "At least, I assume so, after the time we spent in that agricultural village. Finding a more efficient way to get agricultural products to market seems like one that should be broadly supportable. But he hardly points out a single benefit of the proposal at all, and it's worded in a way that will almost certainly create opposition. Is that a yibo trait, or is this advisor just not particularly skilled at his work?"

"Ines?" asked Yosip, turning to the perpetually terrified-looking girl.

"I—" she began, her eyes locked on Yosip, and studiously avoiding Alba's glance. "I don't know, really. But when I was listening in to find patterns for my language program, I was able to sit in on a couple of political debates. I may be remembering wrong, but it seemed to me that they were just as interested as our politicians are in whether a proposal would benefit them. I can't say for sure, but I would guess it was an oversight on the advisor's part."

Yosip smiled. "Thank you, Ines. I appreciate the insight." He turned to Feliu. "What do you think? Can we find enough information on the potential benefits of the program that we could comfortably write them into the speech?"

Feliu was peering at the holographic documents in front of him, his face creased in a frown. "It's certainly possible," he began slowly. "I can do my best, at any rate. I doubt I could possibly make things worse."

Alba nodded. "If there is a way to resolve this, Feliu, I have every confidence in your ability to do so."

He looked up at her with a small smile—an easy gesture that

would have seemed a shocking breach of decorum to both of them only a few weeks earlier—and turned back to the documents.

Alba watched the holographic image, frowning as her wavelink translated the documents. The words that danced in front of her face had an almost disturbingly familiar ring to them. The sort of thing she might have written, months previous, when she was still Alba Espina, Chief Justice of the Joias system, instead of a nameless political refugee.

"Yosip?" she said quietly, leaning towards him. "How likely is it, do you think, that—that Hrrr would appreciate this particular piece of legislation?"

He looked up at her, and she saw his expression change as he realized what she was asking, a slow smile spreading over his face. "Well," he said slowly, "I suppose we could ask her."

Alba stared at him.

Yosip's smile widened, his eyes twinkling. "She gave me her communicator line so she could send me pictures of little Prii trying on the hat I left behind. And I told her I was going to be trying out the porridge recipe, and she told me to give her a call if I ran into problems."

Alba sat there blankly for a moment. And then she began to laugh, a genuine, hearty, unconscious laugh, like she hadn't in far too long.

By the time she recovered herself, everyone around the table was staring at her.

With an effort, she schooled her face back into a serious expression. "I'm sorry," she said. "I think it would be wise to consult someone with more experience than ourselves in yibo agriculture to find out if this proposal would be helpful in the way that is intended to be."

She didn't miss the sudden tightening in Ines's jaw, the way her posture went tense.

"Do you—disagree?" she asked, frowning at the girl.

Ines drew in a quick breath. "No. I don't," she said quietly. "I just —I wish you'd thought of that eleven years ago."

There was a sudden, fraught silence around the table. Alba didn't miss the way the young crewmen, Nicolau, tightened his arm protectively around Ines, or his challenging expression as he looked at Alba.

Alba closed her eyes and drew in a deep breath.

"So do I, Ines," she said at last, quietly.

Ines stood quickly, turning away, and Nicolau jumped to his feet and went after her.

There was silence around the table. Joska was watching Alba, but Alba found she couldn't meet the woman's steady gaze.

"Madam," Feliu began.

Alba shook her head.

"Shall we see if Hrrr answers her communicator?" asked Yosip softly. "It should be just after midday there, but maybe she'll be willing to step away from the knitting circle for a few minutes to talk to old friends."

Yosip was right—Hrrr answered after only a few moments, and her familiar, friendly voice made Alba smile unconsciously.

"Yosip!" Alba could hear the smile in the yibo woman's voice. "How are things in the city? We heard about what happened. The mayor was furious. But you're all alive, I take it? You're well? And Alba, how is she?"

Alba blinked, startled, and Yosip smiled. "She's doing well. She's right here, actually—she wanted to ask you something."

"Good! Good, put her on! My little Prii said the funniest thing yesterday, and I thought Alba would appreciate it."

Alba swallowed hard and cleared her throat as Yosip held out the communicator. "Hrrr. How are you?"

Hrrr insisted on hearing about all everything that happened since they left the village, and recounting with delight exactly how angry the mayor had been about the whole situation, and then Alba asked about Hrrr's granddaughter, and how things had been back at the village after they'd left.

It … wasn't the type of conversation she was used to. But the sound of Hrrr's voice, her thick yibo accent, brought Alba back to the small knitting circle in the tiny agricultural village, where conversations like that had been the only thing keeping her from spiralling into abject despair. And she found that, despite everything, she did, in fact, want to hear about the funny thing Prii had said.

"But I assume that you are not calling just to hear about my granddaughter," said Hrrr. Alba could picture the perceptive glint in the woman's eyes at the words, and she smiled to herself.

"You are correct," she said. "I asked Yosip to call you because, as it turns out, there is an advisor here in the city who asked me to assist him in a proposal. And as the proposal had to do with the transport of agricultural goods, I—thought perhaps it would be productive to speak with someone who the proposal would impact, before trying to offer my opinion."

There were a few moments of silence. At last, Hrrr said, "We're not generally given that much consideration when those in the city put agricultural policies into place. But I appreciate the thought." She paused. "Read me what they're proposing."

Once Alba had finished, there were a few moments' silence from the other end of the communicator. "The idea behind it isn't bad," said Hrrr at last. "But there's no way it'll work. We'd have to be able to predict crop cycles in advance, and we can't do that—the weather isn't that consistent, and we can never tell for certain if there's going to be arliks eating the crops, or how much rain we'll have. Too many variables. No, if they're going to try to schedule the transport ships in advance, the number and location would have to be flexible."

Alba nodded slowly. "I—can see what you're saying," she said.

"Listen," said Hrrr. "I'm happy to help, but I'm no politician. If you give me a quarter cycle or so, I can talk to Prrran and Eeta—they're more involved with getting our products ready to ship out. They may have a better grasp on all this."

"I would ... appreciate that," said Alba, through the lump in her throat. "And the rest of the proposal? What do you think of that?"

There was another pause, as if Hrrr was considering. "I'm not sure. The proposal on documentation will be unworkable, though. During harvesting season, everyone is so busy we can hardly breathe. Add on something like two hours per day of administrative paperwork, and people are going to start burning things." She chuckled. "Or, more likely, they just won't comply."

Alba nodded, jotting down notes.

"I'll let you know if I think of anything else," said Hrrr.

Alba nodded. "Thank you."

Hrrr made a soft hum of amusement. "Not at all. It's what friends do for each other."

The line clicked off, leaving Alba staring at the blank screen.

When she looked up, Yosip and Feliu were both watching her, both with smiles on their faces.

She cleared her throat. "Alright," she said. "Hrrr has very kindly pointed out some problems with the proposal. Therefore, I believe the least we can do is try to think of some feasible solutions while

Hrrr is making inquiries on her end."

It was, by Alba's calculations, well past the middle of the night by the time Hrrr's line appeared on Yosip's communicator. He tapped it on.

"I have a few possible solutions, but even more logistical problems for you," said Hrrr without preamble.

"Good," said Alba. "Let me know what they are, and when you're finished, I'll tell you some possible fixes Yosip and Feliu and Joska and I came up with in the meantime."

By the time the small, weary group of them finally got to bed, the sun was already beginning to brighten the edges of the horizon outside the windows. Alba was so tired she could feel the ache of it through her entire body. But the proposal that was now sitting on her communicator screen, wordsmithed to Feliu's exacting standards, was something Hrrr had given her grudging approval to. And looking at it, Alba could see that it was, in fact, significantly more practical than the original proposal had been.

"I can't guarantee they'll like it," Feliu had muttered darkly, as they'd finally gone to their beds. "I don't know enough about yibo politics to say. But I can tell you this—the proposal itself is as sound as we can make it, considering we had one night to put it together."

Alba hardly had time even to smile at the memory before she was asleep.

"Alba. These are some … very interesting changes you've made to the proposal." Tika watched Alba with an expression she couldn't read.

She wasn't sure if he was happy with the result, or irritated that Alba had seen fit to change what he'd given her. But this was, after all, exactly what he'd asked her to do.

She gave him a bland smile. "I'm glad you think so. I spoke with a friend of mine who works in agriculture, and she was able to offer insight into some of the matters that I was not fully certain I understood properly. She assures me that this will lead to a much easier implementation."

Again, he watched her, for long enough that, had she not been so practised in working within the Joias system government, she might have blinked.

At last, though, he smiled, giving a soft hum of amusement. "Very innovative of you," he said. He glanced back down at the proposal. "I won't say I disagree with the results—even with the changes, you've done a fair job of making it sound palatable. But I suppose we can reserve judgement on whether your skills were helpful until after we present this at the meetings today."

Alba nodded, not letting her face show anything other than the expression of polite interest she'd learned as a young clerk. Her heart, though, was pounding, her stomach tight with a combination of strain and dread.

The meeting was that afternoon. She spent the morning performing a handful of menial clerk duties for the advisor. Normally, she would have resented it. Now, she found herself grateful for the distraction.

Then it was afternoon, and time to present the proposal.

"Advisor Tika?"

The yibo man stood and pulled up the proposal to broadcast on the holoscreen in the centre of the government building. "I'd like to present a proposed advisement on regulating transport of agricultural products."

The advisors listened attentively. When he'd finished, one of the other advisors stood. "And why should we not simply standardize the transports to each village, based on the previous year's production?" she asked.

Tika gestured to Alba. "My assistant will explain."

A translator stepped forward, and Alba stood.

Here, at least, she was in her native element.

By the end of the question period, more than a few heads were tipped to the side in tacit agreement with her words.

She wasn't sure, yet, that it would be enough. She wasn't sure, yet, if she'd convinced them. And if she hadn't—if the proposal they'd crafted together with Hrrr was ultimately shot down—

She glanced at Tika, sitting beside her. He was frowning, watching the faces around them, his body tense.

She doubted very much that, if this proposal failed, he'd be willing to entertain a second attempt. In all likelihood, she'd be blacklisted permanently.

It seemed like an eternity before the vote was called.

Alba held her breath.

And then the Master of Readings stood. "It appears your proposal has the requisite support to move forward to a second reading," she said, tipping her head in Tika's direction.

Alba leaned back in her seat with a small sigh of relief.

Tika was smiling as well, his face a picture of satisfaction. But looking around the room, Alba could see on the faces of some of the other counsellors a different emotion.

She wasn't certain she was reading it correctly. She really hadn't been here long enough to pick up the political pulse of the place. But if she had to make a guess, she would have said there was more than one counsellor here who was not thrilled with a human having a say in yibo government affairs. And if she had been back in the Joias

System, the looks they were giving her would have been enough that she would have asked for a security escort on her walk home that night.

16

Aran

There was a pounding at the door to Aran's cabin, and he looked up, startled, as Krevai cracked the door open. The raider captain peered inside, grinning broadly. "Aran! There you are! Come into the map room, we're talking about our plans."

Aran bit back a groan. The last thing he wanted to do right now was to stand in front of a sea of charts, Krevai peering over his shoulder, half the raider crew crowded in around him.

This was for Istvay. He could do this for Istvay.

He took a deep breath, swallowed hard, and nodded.

When he got to the map room, he stiffened instinctively. Ani growled on his shoulder, her posture suddenly more alert. He sighed, and tried to make himself relax. "It's okay, sweetheart," he whispered. "It's just—it's just a lot of people, is all."

Ani tightened her suckers on his shoulder, her posture making it clear that she'd be happy to ensure there were a lot fewer people if he were to give the command, and he managed a small grin as he stepped into the crowded map room.

"Hey! Let the human through," Krevai shouted jovially, and

raiders stepped back to clear him a path, laughing and shoving. As Aran got close to the table, one of them reached over as if to slap his shoulder, but Krevai leaned over to catch the woman's wrist. "Don't touch him unless you ask first," he snapped. "That stresses them, and it's dangerous for humans to get too stressed."

"And considering this particular human likes fighting with xaxiks, that would be a shame!" called one of the other raiders.

The entire crowd burst into laughter, and Aran took another deep breath, fighting back his instinctive panic at the press and the noise.

"And what exactly did happen with the xaxiks back there?" Krevai bellowed cheerfully as Aran reached the table. "Landru said they were right in the middle of a fight when all the worms turned tail and took after you!" He laughed heartily. "I never would've thought that a human had it in them to do something like that!"

"It's—it really wasn't anything," Aran mumbled. "I just—I mean, it seemed a shame for them to be killed, they seem like very intelligent creatures—"

Krevai stared at him. Then he burst out laughing, head thrown back, hand on the table for balance. At last, gasping and breathless, he turned to Aran, shaking his head. "Aran! I truly have never met anyone who makes me laugh like you do! The longer I know you, the more I think that maybe Dessi's right, you humans are related to us raiders somewhere!"

Aran squeezed his eyes closed for a moment, the heavy, choking discomfort of too many people and too much noise crawling up his throat in suffocating waves.

He could do this. He could push through this, he had to.

"Listen," he said through his teeth. "I found a message from Istvay. And I think—I think this is what they were trying to tell me." He touched the starmap, and as it sprang up around them, half a dozen raiders crowded in, trying to peer over his shoulder, chattering loudly to each other in a mix of Common Dialect and whatever raider language they spoke.

He clenched his teeth until they ached, fighting to stay calm.

"Aran! Do you need help with the map? I'll show you if you want —" Krevai had leaned in close as well, shouting to be heard over the noise.

Aran straightened abruptly, his heart pounding, and spun on the startled raider crew. "Get the hell back," he snapped. He hardly recognized his own voice. "Get the hell back, and leave me the hell alone. If you can't bloody well respect my space, I'm going to damn well take a pod and go after Istvay on my own, the rest of you be damned!"

The cabin fell abruptly silent.

Aran was breathing heavily, almost dizzy with the desperate rush of emotions.

Damn it to hell, that was stupid, he hadn't meant to shout. He never meant to. But he was used to having Istvay here, who always seem to know when and how to speak up without causing too much trouble. Who knew how to say things, how to ask for things.

And Aran ... well—

He could still feel the choking desperation of trying to explain to his foster parents why he'd run away from them in the hot, crowded bustle of the do Sol streets, why he'd hide in the bathroom of the children's group one set of foster parents used to send him to, eyes closed, fists clenched, trying to remember how to breathe. And how every damn time they'd shut him down—sometimes with blows, sometimes with derisive remarks, sometimes just with laughter.

How they'd never, ever understood.

He'd thought he could just push through. And now he was here, with this whole damn crew of raiders who could actually kill him and eat him, and who also held the only damn chance he'd ever have of getting Istvay back, and he'd done it again, lost his head, panicked and shouted, and now …

Krevai's eyebrows were raised, and he was staring at Aran. Aran thought that maybe the sick knot in his stomach would rise and choke him.

Then Krevai turned on the rest of the crew. "Out!" he said, in an exaggerated whisper. "Go on, all of you! You heard the human, he needs his space. I'll brief you afterwards."

Aran blinked in surprise.

The rest of the raider crew shuffled awkwardly out of the cabin, muttering apologies over their shoulders.

In the sudden silence, he forced himself to look up at Krevai.

"I'm sorry, Aran, I wasn't paying attention," the captain said, gesturing around the cabin. "I'll remember next time. Are you alright, or do you need some time? I'd hate for you to get stressed and die …"

Aran was still staring, dumbfounded. Finally, he cleared his throat. "Um," he said weakly. "Thank you. I'm … I think I'm alright now."

"Good, good," said Krevai cheerfully. "Just shout at me if I forget again. Now. The maps."

Aran realized his mouth was hanging half-open. He clamped it shut. His heart was still pounding, adrenaline still flooding his veins, but he managed to take a deep breath and steady his shaking muscles. "Um," he said, leaning over the map. "I've … I've been studying the map on my palmscreen, trying to compare it to what Istvay told me. I think they're trying to tell me that Sharda is heading … here." He touched his finger to one of the smaller moons around a large planet a few cycles' travel distant.

Krevai examined the map, frowning. Then he glanced at Aran. "It's not a bad strategy," he said slowly. "That's where we go to hunt … you humans call them giant sand crabs, I think. If she set up her base there, no one would pay much attention, because there's always a hunting camp set up, and she could bring people into her camp without attracting attention—no one pays much mind if someone is flying in that direction." He turned, and shot Aran a grin. "At this rate, you'll lead us to Sharda in no time! I knew you were an extraordinary human." He chuckled. "Even before you saved a good portion of my crew on the planet back there. I am going to ask you about that one of these days. Now, you get some sleep, and I'll wake you when we get there."

"I—um, it really wasn't—" Aran began, but Krevai had already turned and started off.

"Aran!"

There was a pounding on Aran's cabin door, and he jerked upright, staring around him in confusion as his brain tried to piece together where he was and what he was doing.

"Aran?"

The voice was a raider voice—Captain Krevai, his brain helpfully supplied—and he cleared his throat, blinking the sleep from his eyes. "Yes, I'm here, just give me a minute." He pushed himself to his feet, pulled on his trousers, and stumbled across the floor to the cabin door.

By the time he had it open, he'd mostly managed to bring himself back into full alertness.

The ship must have landed—he couldn't feel the soft hum under his feet that he had to consciously ignore when they were in space, in order to keep from losing his damn mind. Outside, he could hear the typical bustle of raiders in the hallway, calling out orders or jibes.

"We're here." There was a note of undisguised anticipation in the raider captain's expression. "Our sensors picked up a ship signal. The atmosphere on this place messes with our sensors, so I can't promise she's still here, but if she's not, it's been less than a quarter cycle since she left. We landed the ship a little ways away at one of the further safe landing spots, so we won't show up on her sensors easily if she is still here. Meet me at the loading deck with your Ani in two centi-cycles."

By the time Aran reached the loading ramp, Ani perched comfortably on his shoulder, his heart was beating so rapidly that he felt almost dizzy with it. Krevai arrived a few moments later, a dozen or so raiders in tow. He turned to them, eyebrows lowered. "You're to stay back unless I call you," he said sternly. "We're going to let the human go in first, see if he can find any messages from his Istvay. And I'll stick close to him, in case Sharda thought she'd be clever and set a trap for our human."

The other raiders grinned, and the looks they sent in Aran's direction felt almost friendly.

Krevai handed Aran a breathing mask, and then pulled on his own. "Does your Ani need a mask?" the captain asked, voice muffled through the apparatus.

Aran shook his head, his breath coming so quickly he couldn't have spoken if he'd wanted to.

Istvay was here. Istvay could be waiting here, and in just a few minutes …

"Good, good," whispered Krevai. He hit the control, and the hatch hissed open.

The thin, compact mask over Aran's mouth and nose was

surprisingly comfortable as he stepped out into the arid landscape, the hood of his protective shield pulled up over his face. Dessi had lent him her suit, which fit over his ragged clothing like a flexible skin, covering his hands and pulled over his boots, and the material was light enough that it didn't press or itch too badly. He'd have to ask her later what it was made from—it was nothing like the hot, stiff, uncomfortable protective gear he and Istvay had used back on Colorida.

Although in fairness, he wasn't sure if anything he and Istvay owned wasn't a few years old, and much the worse for wear after having gone through a few of their expeditions.

The landscape around the ship was barren rock, and even with the protection and the temperature control of the suit, Aran could tell it was far too hot for human comfort. The glare of the sun mingled with the radiant heat from the rocks under their feet, causing sweat to bead under his hairline and between his shoulder blades.

Ani had spread out lazily across his shoulders and seemed to be thoroughly enjoying the change of temperature.

Krevai walked swiftly enough that Aran had to half-jog to keep pace. The raider captain's eyes narrowed, and every so often he lifted his head, as if scenting the breeze. And again, Aran was reminded with a jolt that, as friendly as Krevai was to him, these raiders were, first and foremost, predators.

"Be careful," Krevai whispered as they walked. "This place is dangerous."

Aran was just opening his mouth to ask what Krevai meant when Ani went rigid.

"Get back," Krevai snapped, and then he felt the slight tremor through the rock.

The two of them scrambled for higher ground, the rock surface they'd been standing on crumbling under their feet. Krevai's larger stature meant he reached safety first, and Aran threw himself forward in a last-ditch effort as the ground under his feet collapsed to reveal a massive pit beneath. He caught the edge of the rock ledge with the tips of his fingers, gritting his teeth and clinging on for dear life.

Krevai reached down, then hesitated. "May I touch you?"

Aran had to bite back a snort of half-hysterical laughter. But he managed a nod, and Krevai grabbed his arm, hauling him bodily to the safety of the firm rock.

"That seems inefficient," Krevai said, still frowning, as Aran leaned over, hands on his knees, gasping for breath and trying very hard not to think about what had almost happened. "I mean, in a situation where a human wouldn't have time to answer, there would be problems—"

Aran raised his head weakly. "If I'm about to die, you can safely assume permission."

Krevai grinned. "Ah. Good to know." He turned and started forward again. "As I was saying, the ground is unstable, so watch your step."

Aran followed, testing his footing a little more cautiously now. Although in fairness, that wouldn't have actually helped last time— the ground had felt solid enough, until it had fallen away beneath him.

They had to scramble for safety twice more as they traversed the flat, arid plains. Both times, it took several minutes before Aran's heart stopped pounding wildly and he was able to push the shakiness from his muscles.

Once they reached the place where the flat ground around them turned into the jagged beginnings of the odd, spiky mountains that marked their destination, Aran was no longer sure if the shakiness in his muscles and the pounding of his heart was due to his recent narrow escapes, or to the mixture of excitement and dread weighing in his stomach like a stone. He was so focused on the path ahead of him, trying to force his brain to keep from panicking, that he almost didn't notice the hint of movement out of the corner of his eye.

He swore and leapt forward, shoving Krevai with all his might.

The raider was a solid half-metre taller than Aran, and significantly bulkier, but Aran was no lightweight. The raider captain stumbled forward as Aran plowed into him, and half-turned, his mouth drawn back into a snarl—and then his expression turned to one of alarm as the rocky peak he'd been standing under crumbled, boulders the size of the attack pods crashing down where Krevai had been standing.

Krevai looked between the boulders and Aran, his eyebrows raised. At last, he shook his head. "Perhaps I was smarter than I realized when I took you onto my crew."

By the time they reached the area where Krevai's scanners had picked up the energy signature of a ship, Krevai and Aran were both walking silently, eyes and ears straining for any sound. It was difficult on this planet, where at any given moment you could hear the rough, thundering rumble of rocks collapsing or solid ground caving in. But then, Aran was used to listening for subtle sounds amidst the noise. And the thought that Istvay might be here, somewhere, had every single nerve in his body on a knife-edge.

They came around the edge of one of the rock outcroppings, and paused.

In front of them was a large, flat area, just large enough to accommodate a raider ship.

But it was empty.

"That's where she must've landed," Krevai whispered, pointing out the scorch-marks on the ground.

Aran nodded, swallowing hard.

Istvay had been here. Istvay had been here maybe hours before.

They were close.

His entire body was shaky.

Krevai was watching him.

Aran took a deep breath, straightening. "I'll head down there," he whispered. "If Istvay left me a message, this is the place to start looking."

Krevai nodded. "I'll stay back here and keep you in my weapon sights, in case Sharda thought she'd set a trap." His teeth were bared in a grin of anticipation. "It's been a long time since I've gone up against an opponent like Sharda. I can't tell you how much I've missed it."

Aran closed his eyes for a moment, wiping his sweaty palms on the inside of his protective suit, and then stepped out.

He was braced to dived to the ground if there was a shot, but nothing but silence greeted him as he clambered cautiously down the rocks and into the open clearing. He reached the place where the ship had once stood, every nerve in his body on edge, every sense alert, the hair on the back of his neck standing up a little at the openness around him, the countless hiding places the rocks concealed.

There was a dark stain on the dusty red-rock surface just outside of the area of the scorch marks, and he frowned and walked over.

He knelt, something cold and uneasy twisting in his stomach, and ran his fingers along the dusty ground.

"What is it?" Krevai whispered through his communicator. "Did you find something?"

"I—I found something," said Aran slowly. "But I don't think it's a message. It's—blood. Lots of blood."

There was no reason to be uneasy, not really. After all, he'd seen for himself how easy it was for someone to get injured here—very likely, one of the raiders had been in an accident, and the blood was where the rest of the crew had laid their injured companion for a moment before bringing them on board.

But somehow, the thought didn't chase the tension from Aran's muscles.

He glanced at the dull red powder on his protective gloves. "Krevai," he whispered into the communicator. "Would you be able to tell by scent who the blood is from?"

"I suppose if there's enough of it," came Krevai's voice after moment. "What, you think it was Sharda?"

Aran shook his head slowly. "No. Not Sharda."

Krevai heaved a sigh through the communicator. "Well, the rest of the crew are within hailing distance now, so if this is an ambush they'll be able to take on Sharda's people. If we can't fight our own way out, that is." He sounded far too happy about the prospect for his concern to be entirely genuine.

Aran was still crouched beside the dark stain on the ground when Krevai arrived. Ani, who'd been peering over Aran's shoulder, slithered to the ground, her attention caught by something in the rocks, but Aran was too distracted to pay her much mind. Besides, Ani was eminently capable of taking care of herself—even on this planet, it was doubtful there was anything that could pose her any real danger.

Krevai glanced down at the blood. "Likely just one of the crew injured," he commented, stooping. "If they were wounded badly enough, she'd have slit their throat and let them bleed out, give them a quick death." He didn't sound particularly disturbed by the possibility. He swept a finger across the blood and brought it to his face, holding it against his breath filter.

Then he frowned, and Aran could see the way his posture changed, just a little.

"That's—it's not raider blood, is it?" Aran said softly, dread coating the back of his throat.

Krevai looked up at him. "No," he said slowly. "It's not raider blood."

Aran's whole body felt cold, despite the heat of the planet around them. "Can you tell, for sure, who it's from?" he asked quietly. He saw the expression on Krevai's face, and added, distantly, "Don't lie to me. Please."

Krevai put his hands on his thighs and pushed himself to his feet, shaking his head. "I'm not lying, Aran. I can't tell which individual the blood belongs to. Maybe if it was fresh I could, but the planet is hot enough that the heat destroys the smell to some extent. I can only tell you that it's a human."

Aran nodded. He felt numb, and icy, icy cold.

"It doesn't mean it's your Istvay," continued Krevai. Aran could hear the words distantly, as if they were coming through a haze. "There's always the possibility that Sharda's crew went hunting, picked up other humans to eat. And even if it was your Istvay, they could have just been injured, and taken back aboard to be cared for."

Aran nodded again. He was clenching his fists so tightly that his fingernails cut into his palms.

Krevai was right. Blood didn't mean death, necessarily.

But there was so much blood. Looking at it, he knew, instinctively, that if any one human had lost this much blood, they were already dead.

And then there was a scream, and he and Krevai both whirled. Aran's eyes scanned the rocks around them where the noise had come from, and he'd already started towards it before he had time to think.

Someone staggered out from behind one of the rocks, an angrily growling Ani wrapped around one of their legs, their build marking them, even under their protective gear, as human.

For a heart-stopping moment, Aran almost thought that maybe, just maybe —

And then he realized that this person was the wrong build, their skin too pale, hair a light blond rather than a smooth black, and his heart dropped.

"Get it off me! Get it off me!" the man was screaming, and automatically, Aran held out his hand to Ani.

"Hey, sweetheart, come here," he coaxed. Ani clung to the man's leg, hissing. "Don't move," Aran said curtly, turning to the stranger. "If she spikes you, there's nothing I can do. You'll be dead in seconds."

The man froze. Something about the terror on his face told Aran that this was someone who knew very well what land-devils were.

With her victim finally subdued, Ani, grumbling, detached herself from the leg of his protective suit and skittered across the rocks towards Aran. Aran held out his arm to let her climb up, then crossed over to the newcomer, who was still standing frozen, face pinched in terror.

"Thank the Holy Mystery," the man gasped. His accent was familiar, something Aran wouldn't have been surprised to hear on the streets of do Sol. "Thank the Holy Mystery. She—she killed—"

his voice choked off, and he dropped to his knees, burying his face in his hands.

"Who? Ani?" asked Aran, glancing around reflexively. It wasn't that Ani *couldn't* have killed an entire group of humans when he wasn't paying attention, but she generally wouldn't, unless they were posing an active threat to his or Istvay's life.

"Who the hell is Ani? I'm talking about Sharda! The raider captain."

"What—" Aran began. "Why are you—did she try to capture you?"

The man shook his head, his voice wavering. "No. We—that yibo governor, Kachik, wanted us to go, and Captain Mattin gave the orders. We were—we were supposed to meet with her, negotiate. There's a yibo watchpoint on the planet you followed Sharda to, and Kachik heard about what happened, whatever weapon you used to get rid of the xaxiks. He wanted us to warn Sharda. There was a human with her, so we thought we'd be safe enough, and then—" he swallowed hard, his eyes haunted.

"And then what?" Aran's voice was clinical and cold, his brain in that odd, numb state that emotion didn't seem able to penetrate. "Who was killed?"

"Sharda figured out that one of the humans was planning to sell her out. And—and she was angry, and she was going to kill us all, I ... I didn't have a choice. I didn't want to do it, but she was going to kill us—"

"What did you do?" Somehow, his voice was still steady.

"I ... I saw him trying to send a message. And—and Sharda would have killed us all, it wasn't my fault, I ... I only told her who it was so she wouldn't kill all of us. But then she—she marooned us here, and there was a cave-in—I think I'm the last one alive. I was sure that—"

"What happened to the human you sold out?" Aran interrupted.

The man buried his face in his hands again, his voice coming out a choked sob. "She killed him. Just took her knife and—" he made a motion with his thumb, like gutting a fish. "And she took the body, and I—I'm sure they're going to—"

"You're sure they were dead." Aran's voice was still flat.

The man nodded, looking sick. "Unless you know a way someone could survive with a broken neck, and their entrails in a heap on the ground. She … she made her crew gather them all up, all the pieces. I think she didn't want them going to waste …" he turned, and from the retching sounds, he was vomiting inside his protective suit.

Aran just stood there, staring at the man.

The man was still kneeling, his whole body shaking, his face sick with horror.

Krevai was watching Aran. His forehead was creased in a frown, but he made no move to interfere.

Aran knelt beside the man. He still felt that odd, icy cold that nothing seemed to be able to penetrate. "That person you sold out was my best friend."

The man glanced up at him. "You can't blame me." His tone was frantic. "She would've killed me. She was going to kill me and eat me, if I hadn't distracted her—"

"Their life is worth a hundred of yours," Aran said, still quiet. There was a hot, compact ball of rage in the back of his brain, burning its way through his self-control.

This man, who was willing to work under yibo orders, whose mutiny on the diplomatic ship had killed most of the crew and stranded the survivors behind the portal—this man had sold Istvay out to save his miserable life.

Aran's hands were shaking, and he realized it only distantly.

"What are you going to—" the man began in a terrified squeak.

Aran reached out, grabbing the man's protective hood. The man's hand twitched, as if to clutch at Aran's wrist, but Aran shook his head. "One move, and I'll set the land-devil on you."

The man froze.

All it would take was one twist of his wrist. The man's hood would fall open, and he'd choke to death in the poisonous air, coughing his lungs out until he drowned in his own fluids.

Not quite what he'd done to Istvay, but a fitting enough end.

For a long moment, no one moved.

Aran's heart was pounding, nausea churning in his stomach.

At last, he dropped his hand to his side and stood quickly, turning away.

In the end, he couldn't do even that. Because in the end, no matter how much this man suffered—Istvay would still be gone.

"Aran?" It was Krevai. Aran realized, distantly, that the captain sounded worried. "Are you going to kill him? You don't need to worry about me, I'm happy to give him to you—it's the least I can do."

Aran shook his head, glancing up at the captain with a small, wan smile. "No," he said. "He may know something about where Sharda's gone. Probably worth questioning him, at least."

The captain nodded slowly, still watching Aran. "I've called Landru," he said. "She's bringing the ship down here so we don't have to worry about the walk back."

Aran nodded. "Thank you." It was funny, really, how his voice seemed to work just fine now. "I'll wait for her, then."

17

"We're working on a tight schedule," said Reka, stepping back into the shelter of the alley. "We won't have time to find weapons to arm the humans. But the yibo guards will have weapons, so as long as we're careful as we're killing them, that should at least give us something to work with."

Savina closed her eyes and tried not to swear out loud.

"I suggest we wait an hour," Reka continued. "I've been studying the guards' patterns. They should be changing the guards soon, and that's probably our best bet to get inside."

Savina didn't deign to answer.

"Do you have anything to add?" Reka was studying her, frowning.

"No," said Savina in a mock-friendly voice. "It seems to me that you've covered all of the possibilities." She turned away deliberately.

Her hands were shaking, and she couldn't tell whether it was from anger, or fear.

She shouldn't be afraid of raiders. She shouldn't be afraid of dying, not after all the ridiculous things she'd lived through so far.

But she was. She was horribly, viscerally afraid.

Reka hesitated, and from the corner of her eye, Savina could see the tension in her posture.

Damn Reka to hell. Reka didn't care about dying, did she? As long as she was doing her duty. And now she'd dragged Savina into this somehow, and there wasn't a way out. There wasn't any damn way out that wouldn't put her siblings and Joska and Rafel in danger, and she couldn't do that, not again. And so here she was, condemned to walk into something that would kill her, and there was no damn way out. Why the hell hadn't Reka just shot her in the yibo tavern and been done with it?

"Listen," said Reka at last, in a low voice. "I—know helping me do this wasn't your first choice."

Savina whirled on her. "Not my first choice?" she snapped. "What choice are you talking about, Reka? This isn't any choice of mine. I'm here because it's the only way I can keep you from killing someone I care about. And I'm going to die for it, because you're too stubborn to listen to me and just leave these people. So don't for one second stand here and talk to me about 'first choices.'"

There was a long silence. At last, Reka said quietly, "Savina." She paused, and Savina was almost shocked at the hopeless expression on her face.

Reka took a deep breath, glancing between the compound and Savina. "When I ... when I made that bargain with you, I thought we had a chance. But you're right. This is likely a suicide mission. And you're right that I—can't ask you to do that. So ... all I ask is that you don't betray me to the yibo on your way out." She gave a small smile. "Give my regards to Joska. Tell her she was right. I didn't appreciate your help back in prison nearly as much as I should have."

Savina stared. She felt like her brain had completely shut down.

Reka turned away, her usual calm dropping over her face like a mask.

"What the hell—" Savina began at last, when she was finally able to form words again.

Reka glanced over her shoulder. "You'd best go quickly," she said. "Don't worry, you did what you agreed to, up until things went sideways. I'll keep my end of the bargain. I won't be coming after you again, after this. Alba will have to set out another warrant." She paused, a wry smile on her face. "Even if I wanted to, I think the chances of me being in the position to do so will be slim."

Savina just blinked at her.

This was exactly what she'd wanted. This was everything she'd wanted. She could go back with Nicolau and Beni and Joska and Rafel, without worrying about the fact that her very presence would put them in danger. She didn't even have to worry about whether she could kill Reka, or if the woman would keep her word. This was a damn suicide mission, and Reka almost certainly wouldn't survive it, not on her own.

Everything Savina had damn well wanted …

Reka was surveying the compound, facing away from Savina, that cool, indifferent expression apparent in the elegant lines of her jaw and cheekbones, tension in her shoulders. That same air of quiet desperation she'd had back in the yibo prison cell.

"You're a damn idiot," Savina hissed.

Reka faced straight ahead, the way her jaw tightened the only indication she'd heard Savina.

Savina stepped closer. "Stop bloody well ignoring me, Reka Soler," she snapped. "You honestly think you'll be able to do anything against that many guards? You admitted this is a suicide mission—why the hell are you still planning on going through with it? How will dying in here with them do anything at all? I thought you got over your death-wish when we were trapped in Kachik's cell."

At last, Reka turned. Her expression was weary. "Listen, Savina. You have people you care for. You'd burn the world down to save them, and they'd burn the world down to save you. I don't have that. If I die here, no one will even know. No one will miss me. All I have—the only thing I have—is what I believe in. What I believe to be the right thing." She turned away. "If I walk away and leave these people to die … I have nothing."

Savina's heart was pounding. "Alright, tell me this before I go," she hissed. "You say you have to do the right thing. So why did you save me, back there in the tavern? Why didn't you just shoot me? You could have."

Reka was quiet for a long moment, still facing away from Savina. At last, she said, "I could ask you the same thing."

"But we're not talking about me right now, Reka. We're talking about you. And I asked you a damn question."

Reka was quiet for a moment longer. Then she sighed. "I suppose I have come to realize that people are … more complicated than I like to believe." She paused. "And that sometimes, you need help, whether or not you want it. Whether or not you deserve it." Her voice was almost bitter.

"I didn't need your help!" Savina snapped. "I never asked for—"

"I wasn't talking about you," said Reka, in a low voice.

Savina closed her eyes.

She could still see Reka's rare, unconscious smile from those few endless days in Kachik's cell, feel the gentleness in Reka's hands as she'd treated Savina's injuries on the ship. Things she'd been able to convince herself to ignore, because Reka clearly didn't mean any of it. Because Reka would kill her, if given the chance.

And now, she didn't even have that.

Damn it, this was stupid. It was sentimental, and stupid, and utterly ridiculous.

And she was going to do it anyways. She wasn't going to be able to help herself.

She sucked in a long breath through her nose. "Well, too bad, Reka. I guess your sanctimonious morals are just going to have to suffer. Because apparently you can't damn well take care of yourself without someone watching over you, so I guess I'm stuck here."

Reka stilled, then turned, slowly. There was honest confusion on her face. "What—"

Savina scowled. "I don't give a damn about anyone from the diplomatic ship. As far as I'm concerned, the raiders can have them, and may it be a joy. But I … I can't sit here and watch you ruin this job, like you would have back when Kachik had us in prison. Your best plan was to throw yourself at one of the yibo politicians and die before you had a chance to do anything at all. You're pathetic."

Reka was staring at her. "What are you saying?" she asked at last.

Savina just glared.

"Are you … are you saying you're going to help?"

"I'm saying I'm a damn idiot," Savina muttered bitterly.

Reka opened her mouth, and then closed it again.

Savina swore quietly to herself. Her heart was pounding, her hands shaky in a confusing way that she was trying very hard to avoid thinking about.

Because if she sat down and tried to think about it—about why she'd agreed to stay with Reka and risk her life to help a group of people who meant nothing to her—it would lead to thinking about things that she really, really did not want to think about right now. Or maybe ever.

On the bright side, since they were all bloody well going to die, she might not have to worry about it after all.

"Thank you," said Reka quietly.

"Shut up," said Savina through her teeth. "If we're going to do this, we may as well get going."

Reka had been right—it wasn't long before the stir and bustle of the guards changing shift slowed into a few moments of relative quiet.

"We won't have long," said Reka, her eyes trained on the guards. "Same plan as before?"

"Unless you've come up with a better one in the meantime," Savina snapped.

Again, there was a brief flicker of a smile on Reka's face. "I haven't."

"Then there's your answer," said Savina sarcastically.

Her heart hadn't stopped pounding, and she felt like she might be sick.

She didn't bloody do suicide missions. What the hell was she doing here?

Reka nodded and started forward on silent feet, and, swallowing down the bile in her throat, Savina followed.

When they reached the compound, Reka paused, glancing at her. Savina braced herself, then stepped forward out of the shadows and into the glow of the artificial lights, her eyes wide, her expression faintly bewildered.

The first guard started violently as he caught sight of her. "What —" he began in yibo, raising his weapon. A moment later, Savina was surrounded by six guards.

"What are you doing, human?" the guard growled, this time in heavily accented Common Dialect.

Savina blinked, letting tears well up in the corners of her eyes. "I —I got lost, and I got locked out, and I … I didn't know how to get back in."

"Who let you out?" the guard snapped.

Savina sniffled and brushed the back of her hand across her eyes, trying frantically to remember any yibo name she'd heard recently. "Ittit," she whispered at last.

It was a politician's name. But seemed to do the trick—the guards looked at each other in mild confusion.

From the corner of her eye, Savina caught a glimpse of movement, a dark shadow detaching itself from the shadows behind the guards.

She bit back a small smile.

Whatever you could say about Reka—and there was plenty she'd like to say about Reka right now, none of it complementary—the woman was good at her job.

There was the soft hiss of pulse pistol, and a guard dropped, blood welling from his mouth.

Before the other guards had time to so much as react, two more had fallen, the soft thud of their bodies against the concrete the only sound marking their collapse.

It took a split second for the survivors to realize what had happened.

One of them open their mouth in a shout of alarm. Savina yanked out the knife she'd been toying with and jammed it upward into the man's chest through a crack in his body armour. He went limp, body sliding off the bloody blade, and as the other guards turned in horror, she slid the bloody knife across the throat of the second guard in a quick motion, and then shoved it between the rib cage of a third, angled up and to the side so as to neatly penetrate the heart.

All of them were dead before they had time to make a sound.

Savina smiled herself as she bent to wipe the blade on the edge of one of the fallen guards' uniforms. It was nice to be doing something she was good at, finally.

When she stood, she was face to face with Reka. The woman had a pistol in her hand and a small, wolfish grin on her face, and there was something about the fierce heat in her gaze as she watched Savina that made Savina suddenly very aware of her own body.

She cleared her throat and looked away as Reka stooped, grabbing the weapons from the limp bodies of the fallen guards, and jerked her chin towards the inside of the compound. Savina pulled the key card from one of the guards' uniform jacket, wiping the blood from it carefully. She tapped it to the gates, and then the two of them slipped inside.

The courtyard was mostly empty—it seemed the humans had been herded inside the building to wait.

"You go in," Savina whispered. "They're more likely to listen to you. I'll stay out here in case anyone comes to see what happened."

Reka nodded and slipped inside the building, and Savina settled herself against the courtyard wall into the shadows to wait.

She didn't wait long. It was only a few minutes later that the first guard stepped into view, glancing around curiously. "Kata?" she called.

Savina straightened, but at the soft sound of her feet on the courtyard, the guard spun around.

Savina smiled innocently at her. And in the brief moment where the guard was clearly trying to figure out what was happening, Savina shot her in the face.

She glanced down at the small pile of ash that was all that was left, and sighed. Yibo weapons made much less of a mess, but she'd now vaporized any weapons the guard may have been carrying. She'd use the pulse pistol next time, and deal with the mess.

"But there'll be more where you came from, won't there?" she muttered, brushing the stain from the concrete.

The next guard appeared a couple of minutes later. This time, Savina was ready for him—she waited until he was inside the courtyard, then stepped silently up behind him and slit his throat. He managed to get out a strangled wheeze before he died, but hopefully it wasn't loud enough to attract attention. At this rate, she had no idea.

She dragged the body back into the shadows, relieved it of its weapons, and took up her position again. "Hurry up, dammit!" she muttered into her wavelink.

Her muscles were tense with worry. It wouldn't take long before there were too many guards for her to deal with alone.

She spun at a soft sound, in time to see the door to the compound building swing open and Reka silhouetted in the entrance. She couldn't repress her sigh of relief, and Reka shot her a small grin.

"What the hell—" came another voice, far too loud in the silence. The man who'd stepped out behind Reka stared at Savina, wide-eyed.

She glanced down at herself, the blood spattered across her clothing and the bloody knife in her hand, and gave him her most innocent smile.

He looked less than reassured.

"Reka, who is this?" he began, turning quickly back to Reka.

"I'm Reka's associate," said Savina.

The man glanced between them, skepticism in his face. "Your

associate? I thought you said you were working alone."

Reka sighed. "She's my … girlfriend."

Savina blinked, then grinned to herself. "Alright, sweetheart," she whispered, widening her eyes even more than usual. "What's the plan now?"

Reka shook her head, but there was a hint of reluctant amusement in her expression. "I suppose, darling, we get these people out to safety."

Savina's heart skipped in an odd, giddy little way at the words. She ignored it resolutely. "Go on, you first," she whispered. "I'll take up the rear."

Within a few minutes the courtyard was full of ragged, terrified survivors. They were whispering quietly among themselves, faces drawn with fear and strain.

"Follow me," Reka whispered, just loud enough to be heard. "Remember what I told you. And be quiet—if we're found, you'll be taken back here to be killed, one way or another." She gestured them after her, then slipped out the gate past the dead guards.

Quietly, the rest of the group followed, organized into small groups that were probably Reka's doing.

Savina was practically dancing with impatience as they filed out the gate.

They had maybe a minute or two before the guards would be there en mass, but at the same time, there was no way to hurry this many people along without causing panic, which would be even more certain to bring the guards after them.

She stepped back into the shadows of the courtyard, waiting with clenched teeth for the inevitable sounding of the alarm.

It came later than she'd expected—they'd almost all made it

through the gate when three yibo guard stepped around the corner.

They took in the scene, their eyes wide—their companions' bodies slumped haphazardly on the ground, the dark bloodstains pooled in the courtyard, the open gate, their captives slipping through it into the street.

And then Savina slipped out of her hiding place and, with a quick flick of her wrists, sent three knives flying with deadly accuracy.

The guards fell one after the other, blood spraying across the courtyard in a brilliant arc and pooling around their fallen bodies. None of them had had time to make more than a gargled moan.

When Savina turned, a human woman was watching her, eyes wide. Savina shot her an innocent smile. "Reka's taught me a lot of things since we became girlfriends," she said in a breathy whisper.

The woman swallowed hard, avoiding Savina's gaze, and scuttled after the group.

Then there was a shout from behind the walls.

Savina cursed, looking around quickly, and grabbed two of the stragglers in ragged military uniforms.

"What the hell—" one of them began, but Savina stooped and grabbed the weapons off two of the fallen guards, shoving one into the woman's hand, and tossed another to the man beside her.

"You can help, or I'll kill you like I killed them," she snapped.

To their credit, they didn't argue, just caught the weapons and turned to face the yibo guards. Whatever could be said for their morals, at least they didn't seem to be physical cowards.

A cluster of yibo guards pounded around the corner, skidding to a stop when they saw the tableau.

Savina turned, a picture of wide-eyed innocence, and gestured at the soldier. "That man! He was trying to hurt me! He stole a gun, and—"

The guards hesitated.

Savina gestured impatiently with her hand behind her back, and at last, the human soldiers seemed to catch on, yanking up their weapons and firing on the yibo. As the yibo guards turned to face the threat, Savina snatched up another weapon and shot three of them from behind.

But the delay had been more than enough. An alarm blared across the courtyard, a loud wail that could have probably been heard anywhere in the damn city. Savina grabbed the closest soldier by the arm and shoved him out the gateway after Reka, gesturing with her chin for the other soldier to follow.

The woman hesitated a moment, turning to aim at one of the remaining yibo guards.

A shot hit her, and she dissolved.

Savina swore and took off after the remaining soldier, who'd already started through the gate. "Wait! Help me, you idiot, or we're both dead," she hissed. He hesitated, then turned reluctantly to help her shove the gate into place. Savina fired her pulse pistol into the lock, turning it into a melted, jammed lump of metal, then the two of them took off running.

"I have a troop coming up the street those two are headed down," Savina heard someone shout in yibo from behind her. She grabbed the soldier's arm, yanking him around and shoving him down another alley. They'd have to go around, then, and meet up with Reka on the other side.

"What the hell—" she heard from behind her. "She understood us! Kachik's right, they must have been sent by the Synod."

She didn't hear anymore, because they'd turned the corner of the alley and were running for their lives.

18

Alba

Alba slumped in her seat, trying to ignore Feliu and Rafel's bickering in the background, and pushed her hands against her eyes in a gesture that reminded her, suddenly and starkly, of her first political clerkship.

That one had taken place when she was much younger, and even then, the sheer, bloody exhaustion of it had all but destroyed her.

Still, she'd survived it once. Now she'd simply have to survive it again. At the very least, this time she had friends to help her, and enough wits about her to understand which tasks were utterly necessary, and which would be no more than a waste of her time.

"Tika wants to bring this advisement in for a first reading, correct?" asked Yosip, looking up at her from the holoimage pulled up over the table in front of them.

She nodded wearily. "They have two readings before it's sent up to the Hierophants. But at the very least, this puts it on the schedule. If it's shot down, Tika won't be able to bring it up again for another year, if then. From the looks of the rest of the Advisory Body, I expect that this may not be a popular proposal among certain factions."

Yosip nodded. "I was talking with some of the junior clerks the other day," he said. "Kachik's position on humans is a minority one only because of the radical means he proposes to enforce it. There are more than a few of the advisors who would be happy if the human problem simply … resolved itself on its own. They wouldn't go so far as to propose genocide, like the more radical Nativists have done, but as far as they're concerned, we are no more than an inconvenience. And the sooner we become someone else's inconvenience, the better for everyone."

Alba started to open her mouth to ask him when and how he'd found time to strike up conversations with the yibo clerks, and then closed it again.

Instead, she sighed, frowning down at the holographic documents. "Perhaps it would be worth our while to speak with our friend Jair."

If Jair was surprised at having been woken so early, he didn't show it. His face was tight with its usual worry when he arrived, despite the reassurances they'd given him over the communicator.

"So you are truly just discussing a political advisement," he said, when Alba had explained what they were working on. He shook his head and chuckled dryly. "I was convinced this was a code to tell me we were in more trouble than any of us knew how to handle." He sank back in his seat, frowning. "This is Tika's proposal to give some political power to the humans, correct?"

Alba nodded. "He wants to give the humans a voice, but only insofar as it would ultimately benefit him. But we need something that will allow us to get the survivors from our system to safety, and this may be our only chance—the longer we wait, the less likely there will be anyone alive to rescue. However—" she hesitated, and cleared her throat. "I have, in the past, made decisions that I thought were wise ones, without consulting the stakeholders of those decisions. It was … perhaps not the best way of pursuing politics."

Jair raised his eyebrows. Then he chuckled. "Maybe not," he said. "But it does seem to be the universal method. Back in Labirinto—" he stopped abruptly, pinching his lips together. "At any rate," he continued after moment, his voice quieter. "I appreciate you asking."

He bent over the proposal and scanned through it quickly, then gave a sharp shake of his head. "This is what they offer every time, more of the same. I'm not sure if they don't understand it won't work, or if they truly don't care." He sighed wearily. "And it certainly won't do much to get your friends to safety."

"We might be able to work with it, still," said Yosip quietly. "There's no guarantee, but from what Alba tells me, with the political climate as it is, the advisors were willing to accept more feedback from her than any of us anticipated.

Jair shook his head. "I'm not sure you understand how deeply suspicious the yibo are of humans. They see us as self-centred villains, whose entire identity is built on destroying the yibo culture and replacing it with our own—contaminating yibo society for our own nefarious purposes." He gave a small, wry chuckle. "We're hardly a fully sapient species to them. You won't be able to change anything long-term."

"But it's that way because you don't have power," said Alba. "You don't have influence. You don't have any way to shape the narrative. If you could get enough political leverage that they'd have to start taking you seriously, perhaps then …"

Jair glanced up at her. "I'll lay out the bare minimum that might eventually lead to us having some form of autonomy. But—" he shook his head again. "I'm warning you, it won't be a popular suggestion. You may lose any political capital you've managed to gain just by suggesting it."

Alba gave him a wry smile. "And what, pray, did you think the point was of this political capital that we may or may not lose?"

Jair chuckled dryly. "I suppose you're right." He paused a moment, then leaned forward, sketching out a quick outline on the holoimage in front of him. "Under Tika's proposal, humans are counted towards the number of citizens who comprise a district. And each district can send ten of its children to be educated as advisors, one of whom, after the tests are administered, will be passed into the Advisory Body. In theory, it sounds good—humans now have a voice. In practice, there are no districts where humans are the majority. Practically speaking, no human child will ever be nominated. And do you know what the Hierophants do during their ascetic years? They spend two years in each stratum of the yibo social order—the agricultural villages, the labourers, the shipping crews, so on. They do that so that they will have experience to draw from when they pass their laws. Humans aren't included in that. So after this proposal comes into play, Tika gets more voices in the Advisory Body that have the same interests as he does, because they come from what's now his district. And we get nothing. However—"

He sketched a small diagram overtop of the first. "In the Labirinto system, we had, as you know, several political factions that came up over the centuries after we'd made our home in the system. About two hundred years back, there was a civil war, and the loss of life was tremendous. However, we did learn from that how to allow minority voices enough representation in government that their rights would be protected without allowing them an undue influence over the majority. If humans were given an autonomous district of our own, self-governing within its borders but beholden to and protected by the yibo state in exchange for taxes and trading rights, if we were given an independent voice in the Advisory Body, and if human society was officially added into the social structures that the Hierophants learn …" He sketched out another quick diagram, and Alba watched, frowning.

He was right—the Joias system had never had anything similar, but then, no matter how tense things had gotten between the Belt and the Rim Mountain settlements, and no matter the admittedly ugly spectre of the Holy Wars, the Joias System still hadn't had to deal with the decades of deep mistrust that the Labirinto civil war had engendered.

She thought back, with a guilty start, to the look on Ines's face when she spoke of the Rim Mountains.

Perhaps the Joias System political divide was, indeed, deeper than she had imagined, from her sheltered political office in do Sol.

"So essentially," she said at last, looking at Jair's sketch, "the crux of it is giving the humans a direct voice instead of a yibo representative."

Jair nodded. "That, and autonomy to deal with our own internal affairs—places the yibo law can't overrule. But as I said—no matter how much you were able to impress Tika, you'll never get either him or the Advisory Body to agree to this."

Alba nodded, frowning. He was right—from everything she'd seen, presenting this proposal as a serious one in front of the Advisory Body would be no less than political suicide.

But—

"What if the objective wasn't to get you everything you're asking for at the moment, but to put yourself in a position where an expansion of your rights would be much more likely? That would still be ultimately more helpful than passing the proposal as it stands, correct?" she asked.

Jair frowned, but nodded slowly.

Feliu caught Alba's eye and gave a small grin that told her he'd figured out what she was getting at. "Madam. I've been going through the Tenets of Clarity during my spare time. Perhaps in the past, it would have been a difficult argument to make. But with political matters as they are now, I think we could make an argument that granting the humans an autonomous self-governing space would be both the practical and the ideologically correct solution."

Jair shook his head, frowning. "It's been suggested before, more than once. They won't accept it. Even if they did, it would never happen in time to save your friends."

"Except before when it was suggested, there wasn't a threat of civil war, with humans at the centre of it, was there?" said Alba. "Any proposal that would allow the government to shift the blame for accepting the refugees who are streaming in from territories that the Nativists hold may bear more merit in the eyes of the advisors than it did before. Especially with the unrest among the raiders. If they agree to fast-track the readings and possibly use the emergency provisions, it's possible they could declare a temporary autonomous zone in less than a month. That would allow the human autonomous region to accept any refugees it wished, correct?"

Jair nodded slowly, a gleam of something like hope in his eyes now. "You're right. And I've heard rumours about some supposed new weapon the raiders seem to have discovered, judging from our surveillance cameras on the ice planet—they managed to frighten off an entire pit of xaxiks a day or so back. No one wants an argument with the Nativists until we figure out what's happening with the raiders, and what they've discovered. Perhaps you're right that this is the time to try the argument again. Then it would only be a matter of negotiating with Kachik to keep the prisoners alive until we can officially request them. But first, you'd have to convince Tika to bring forward an advisement that would leave him with less influence than his original proposal. How do you intend to convince him to go along with this?"

Feliu looked up. "It takes … how many years are children educated before they're eligible for advisorships? Twelve? Fourteen?"

"Fourteen," said Jair.

"What if we were to suggest that, upon humans gaining their autonomous region, they can submit children for the advisorship training as is the usual yibo procedure, rather than have a human appointed for an advisorship immediately? And in the meantime, the yibo districts that housed the refugees each get a portion of the advisorship voice, in proportion to the number of humans they'd been housing in their districts? That would give Tika the largest voice, correct?"

"I may be able to convince him to agree to something like that," said Alba slowly. "It would mean less autonomy for the humans for the first few years, but it would give us a chance to at least get it heard. Jair, what are your thoughts?"

Jair gave a small, wry shrug. "It's not perfect. But it is certainly better than what Tika is proposing. It may be the best we can do." He looked up. "And as you say—if there's a time to suggest it, it's now."

Tika glanced up from the document Alba had presented and studied her thoughtfully. "I'm sure I don't have to tell you, Alba, that I'm a little surprised at your recommendations."

Alba forced her face into a studied serenity. "Of course," she said. "However, I think if you consider my proposal, you'll recognize the long-term benefits for your district. You're the advisor with the majority of humans in your district, which means you'll have the largest portion of the extra voice in the Advisory Body for fourteen years. And you'll get that advantage without having to use your district's resources on more humans. And it will likely be more palatable to the other counsellors as well, if we can frame it in a meaningful way."

He was still watching her. At last, he nodded. "There's an argument to be made, I suppose." She had to fight to keep from stepping back at the sharpness in his gaze. "As you know, this is a proposal that is very important to me politically. Based on your performance on our last collaboration, I'm willing to give you the benefit of the doubt." He leaned forward. "But if this goes badly, my goodwill will run out completely. I know what you're doing, Alba. And I'm not blind to the mutual benefits we provided each other. But please don't try to make me believe that this is pure altruism on your part."

"Of course not," Alba murmured. "You and I both know the best proposals come when all parties will benefit thereby." Her heart was beating quickly, and she managed a wry amusement at her own reaction.

The moment she'd entered the political arena, most of the decisions she'd made had been life-and-death to some extent or another. It was just that before now, she wouldn't have felt their affects with the same gut-clenching urgency as she would certainly feel these ones.

The time for the meeting of the Advisory Body seemed to take simultaneously years, and no time at all, to arrive. Alba's impatience was bordering on actual pacing by the time the meeting was called to order. And, once the meeting was called to order, it seemed at least another eternity before it was time to present Tika's advisement.

She held her breath as the yibo man stood and began reading the speech that she and the others had spent so much time preparing.

She watched the expressions on the faces of the other advisors as he spoke, although she was still not adept at reading yibo facial expressions.

When the entire proposal had been read, there was a moment of silence before the questions.

"Am I to assume that this advisement was suggested by your human assistant?" asked one of the counsellors, someone who Alba recognized as the woman who'd spoken against the proposal to accept refugees.

"I do find it helpful, when drawing up advisements that are intended to affect a certain population specifically, to take that population's views into account," said Tika blandly, and Alba had to bite back a small smile.

There were a number of questions, some of which Tika answered himself, others which he turned over to Alba.

And then, at last, the vote.

She found she was holding her breath as the results came through.

"The advisement will move forward to a second reading," said the Master of Readings, and Alba closed her eyes, her entire body limp with a desperate, disbelieving gratitude.

Alba felt as if she'd barely stumbled into bed before a familiar tingling through her nervous system jerked her awake. She stared around groggily, still not sure, for a moment, where she was, or why.

As the heavy fog of sleep faded, she recognized the tingling as coming from her wavelink, and the sound as that of an incoming call.

She frowned, blinking. She'd set her link to not disturb her unless the call was from someone who was already a contact, and the others should still be sleeping.

And then she pulled up the retinal screen with a flick of her eye, and something caught in her throat.

It wasn't, in fact, a member of their party, at least not currently. The owner of the name that floated on her screen was someone who, the last time they'd met, had threatened to slit Alba's throat.

"Savina," said Alba at last, accepting the call. "I hadn't expected to hear from you again." She hoped her tone was ironic, rather than terrified.

"I don't like this anymore than you do, believe me." The sweet, innocent voice stung fear like an electric pulse through Alba's nerves. "But—" the girl drew in a long breath. "But I can't call Joska. If she knows where I am, she'll try to come after me and—and she can't."

Alba frowned.

"So. I have important news, but I won't tell you unless you swear Joska won't find out where you got the information."

Alba pictured the captain's weathered face, the worry that had been a constant behind her expression since she'd rejoined them, Rafel and Beni in tow, without Savina.

"Can I—may I at least tell her that you're alive and safe?" She wasn't entirely sure why she'd asked. Wasn't sure why it mattered.

"No," said Savina flatly. "She's better at getting information out of you than you think. Besides, I can't promise that Beni wouldn't simply cut you open if you didn't tell them where to find me.

They're pretty nonviolent as a rule, but—"

Alba sucked in a steadying breath, and tried to ignore the mindless panic the assassin's words shot through her. "And if I agree—that's the only way you give me this information?"

"Yes. And it's worth the lives of people you care about a hell of a lot more than I do."

"Very well," said Alba at last, ignoring the twist of guilt in her chest. "What is this news I need so badly to hear?"

"You remember the human refugees from the ship? Kachik plans to trade them to the raiders. Reka Soler and I are getting them away while we still can. But we don't have anywhere to take them." She paused. "I heard you're in the yibo capital. I was hoping they'd have a place for them. Because if where you are won't accept them ..." She trailed off, but Alba didn't need her to complete the sentence.

Alba paused a moment. "I'm ... working on that. It may take some time. This government isn't necessarily hostile to humans, but I'm not sure they'll risk a fight with the Nativists over human refugees at the moment. I am doing my best to convince them. How long before you'll need sanctuary?"

Savina gave a snort of laughter. "How long does it take to get from where I am to where you are? That's about how long we have."

Alba closed her eyes, feeling sick to her stomach.

Even at the fastest the advisement could progress, several weeks was the fastest she could possibly expect before any human had the political capital to accept refugees.

What Savina was asking was impossible.

"I'll do my best," she repeated at last.

"Let's hope your best is good enough," snapped Savina. "Because if we don't get them out now, they're not coming out at all, at least not alive. And if we have nowhere to take them—" she paused. "Well, my guess is, they'd have been better off dying in the ship break-up."

19

Savina

The flight through the city was quick and desperate. Reka led the terrified group of survivors unerringly down streets and through alleys that even Savina didn't recognize. Already Savina could hear the shouts of the guards in the background, and they hadn't made it more than halfway to the city gate before the citywide alerts had begun to sound.

Savina glanced over at a small noise, to see that Reka had fallen in beside her. "They'll catch us long before we reach the gate if we don't do something," Reka whispered. "I thought maybe we could get to the ships, but there's no way. It'll take both of us to get them out, and if we don't get them out now, we're not getting out at all."

Savina rolled her eyes. "Are you ready to leave them yet?"

Reka gave a long-suffering sigh. "How did you get out last time?"

"We shot our way out. But the raiders were after us, and the yibo are terrified of them. Otherwise, I doubt we'd have made it."

Reka nodded thoughtfully. She was wearing that small, dangerous smile that Savina had come to recognize as always preceding something Savina did not want to hear. "We don't have raiders this time. So I guess we'll have to find something else for them to be afraid of."

"Reka. What the hell are you thinking?"

Reka's expression did nothing to assuage Savina's concern.

"Also, for your information, they currently think we're from the yibo government, and trying to sabotage their interests," Savina snapped. "They're going to be very invested in killing us."

Reka's eyebrows rose. "That's interesting. Perhaps we can use that to our advantage." She paused. "If they think we're from the government, they'll think we have resources. The perfect solution would be one of us going for the ships, and making a distraction that way. But we don't have time—the yibo would catch and kill the rest of the humans before either of us could get back to where the ships are, and that would tip them off that we're not what they think we are. We'll have to get the people out and come back. But if one of us manages to make them think more government agents—maybe even an army—is coming from another part of the city, we could use that to get the rest of the humans out." She glanced at Savina. "You take the humans, I'll—"

"No," Savina snapped. "I can understand what the yibo are saying, you can't."

Reka turned to stare at her. "You're volunteering?"

Savina scowled, and tried not to think of how much of her irritation was a cover for outright terror. "Your part is going to be more dangerous anyways. They'll be running away from me."

Reka's expression turned to something complicated, her eyes tracing across Savina's face as if looking for something. "I ..." she began, her voice quiet.

Then she reached out, her hand brushing gently across Savina's cheek. The touch was so fleeting that Savina could almost believe she'd imagined it.

"Thank you," Reka whispered. "Good luck."

And then she was gone, as suddenly and quietly as she'd come.

Savina reached up to touch the place where Reka had touched her, her mind a momentary static white.

Then she swore viciously under her breath, and turned off down an alley

If she was going to do this, she wasn't going to run around like some damn action hero. If she had to distract the yibo, she was damn well going to do it at a walk.

She made her way through the alleys as quickly as she could without getting out of breath, glancing around her quickly.

She had to fool them into thinking she and Reka were from the government. The problem with that, of course, was that she'd never met this yibo government, and had no idea how someone from the government might react. Still—she'd killed enough damn bureaucrats in Colorida that she could make a guess, at least, at how this might play out.

She sighed, shaking her head at her own stupidity. To think she could have just walked away from this all …

Government agents would have resources. But what kind? What kinds of things might a yibo government have?

She reached the centre of what looked like the business district and glanced around at the deserted streets.

Then she smiled to herself.

If growing up in the damn compound had taught her anything, it was how to use what you had on hand as a weapon. And she'd grown up preparing for the end of the damn world.

She turned back to where she was pretty sure she'd seen a sign she recognized.

A yibo tavern.

It took her only a few moments to break inside, and once inside, she stooped behind the bar and examined the bottles.

Her memory of her last time in a yibo tavern was, in fairness, more than a little hazy. But she was pretty sure she recognized a couple of the bottles.

She pulled out an armful of the ones she guessed must have been damn close to a hundred and fifty proof alcohol, and grabbed a case of something thick and viscous that she was pretty sure was soap. She popped the top off the bottles with her teeth and cut a strip off the bottom of her yibo tunic, and in a matter of a few minutes she had a dozen functional firebombs.

She searched around until she found an incendiary device on one of the top shelves, then she grabbed her firebombs and slipped from the building.

The first of the bombs hit the side of the building, the mixed soap and alcohol sticking to the wall and flaming out like a flare.

It wouldn't last long, but she didn't need it to. She just needed to get their attention.

And it did.

It couldn't have been more than a couple of minutes before the first alarm sounded, quickly joined by more. It was only a few minutes after that that she heard yibo soldiers pounding down the street towards her.

She tossed the last of her firebombs and took off running.

"If you find them, don't kill them right away. We need them for questioning!" a yibo voice shouted, and then she rounded a corner, and the voices faded behind her.

At last, panting and gasping, she came around the corner of a street and into view of the city forcefield gate, where Reka had sent her coordinates. Most of the ragged group of humans was already through, but Reka stood at the entrance she'd opened, her body tense. When she saw Savina, she almost drooped in relief. "Come on!" she hissed.

Savina rolled her eyes. "I was going as fast as I damn well could," she gasped. She reached Reka and slipped through the gate, and Reka followed, closing the narrow opening behind her.

Then Savina and Reka were running after the others, Savina sucking in short, shallow breaths and wincing at the stitch in her side.

The rest of the group waited for them at the edge of the jungle. There were nervous looks on their faces, and Savina couldn't honestly blame them—she'd been in this hellscape before, more than once. And once had been more than enough.

"Stay behind me," said Reka tersely to the waiting humans. "It won't take long for the yibo to figure out where we've gone, so we can't afford to waste time. There are things in that jungle that will kill us a lot faster than the yibo will if we're not careful."

"You can't make me go in there," said one of the men who, from the looks of him, was one of Cavaco's soldiers. "Half my company was killed within ten minutes of stepping out of the craft."

Reka jerked her chin impatiently towards the city gates. "Go back, then. I don't have time to hold anyone's hand. But I won't come for you a second time."

"And what's the plan once we get—" another soldier began.

A shout from the direction of the city cut her off.

Reka swore. "We're leaving, now. If you want to go back, leave your weapons. You won't need them if you're dead."

Reluctantly, with many a backward glance over their shoulders, the huddled group started forward after Reka into the darkness of the jungle trees.

"What is the plan?" Savina whispered, coming up beside Reka. "Like you said, the yibo aren't going to take long to figure out where we've gone, and they probably know how to survive in this nightmare of a place better than we do."

Reka's face was tight with strain. "We get them into the jungle, find a clearing farther in so it'll hopefully take the yibo some time to find us. They might know this jungle, but they don't like it. I have a portable force field that should keep the worst of the jungle out for a little, at least. And then … you and I go back for a ship."

Savina sighed.

It was hardly even worth protesting at this point.

"If you can keep these idiots in front from cutting and running, I'll take up the rear," she whispered instead.

They hadn't made it more than twenty meters in before someone screamed, a short, horrible sound, abruptly cut off. Savina spun in time to see a massive jungle cat bounding off, a limp body between its teeth. It vanished before she had time to bring her weapon to bear, blending back into the trees.

The victim's companions were standing stock still, wide-eyed with terror, a perfect invitation for any other predators that might be waiting.

"Go," Savina hissed. "Keep walking, or you'll die where you stand."

"We—we can't—" one man began, his already pale face gone completely white with fear. "We have to go back." He turned to the others. "Come on. We don't stand a chance out here. We'll tell the yibo—"

Savina shot him in the face.

He fell, choking, and she turned to the others. "Anyone else?" she asked pleasantly. "Or shall we keep moving? Because there's a chance you'll escape the jungle cat. There's no chance you'll escape me."

The small huddle of people who'd been on the verge of turning to run stared down at the body at their feet, then up at Savina, faces cut with horror.

Savina raised her weapon suggestively.

This time, they started forward again after Reka.

Joska would have disapproved, Savina reflected as she walked. But at this point, one death was a small price to pay to keep the rest moving, and keeping them moving was the only way to keep them alive. So in the end, even Joska could hardly blame her. She'd been practically an altruist.

They lost five more people before they reached the clearing where Reka finally called a halt—two more to jungle cats, two to carnivorous trees, and one more to something long and sinuous and snaky that Savina had never seen before and had no desire to see again.

As the terrified, exhausted survivors huddled in the centre of the small clearing, Reka gestured to Savina, and the two of them set the makeshift forcefield.

When they'd finished, Reka looked around her, face grim. "This is going to have to hold," she whispered. "At least until you and I get back." She paused. "How did you get them all to stay together and keep from running off, by the way? I lost ten of mine who tried to go back. None of the made it more than a few steps before the jungle got them."

Savina smiled cheerfully. "The first man who said he'd run, I shot in the face in front of everyone. No one suggested running after that."

Reka stared at her. Then she shook her head with a resigned expression. "I suppose if it worked …"

"Believe me, it did," said Savina, her voice still bright.

For a moment, Reka looked like she was biting back a laugh. Then she straightened and turned back to the others, whose postures seemed to have relaxed a little now that there was a barrier between them and the horrors of the jungle.

"Stay here. The force field should protect you. In the meantime, Savina and I will sneak back into the city and bring back a ship."

"If we live that long," Savina muttered. But she made sure her words were quiet enough that only Reka heard.

20

Aran

Aran walked numbly back along the corridors of the raider ship, until he got to his small cabin. Once inside, he glanced around helplessly, then sank down onto one of the cushions.

He wasn't entirely sure what to do next.

He'd spent all this time trying to convince himself that he could live without Istvay. And he'd learned that he could. He could survive, he could stand up for himself, he could do what had to be done. Istvay could be dead, and he could keep living.

And that was the worst part of all.

He glanced down at his palmscreen. He could continue researching the cure, but—there didn't seem to be any point to that.

There didn't seem to be any point to anything, really.

Ani made a subdued little sound, and he pulled her off his shoulder, cradling her in his arms. "I guess," he said his voice coming out almost a whisper. "I guess we just—we just keep going."

Ani snuggled against him, and he stroked her tentacles automatically.

His thoughts were surprisingly clear. He would have imagined that if this actually happened, he'd be a wreck. But he couldn't seem to feel anything at all, his thoughts a cold, emotionless sort of logic.

The raiders would probably give him a day or two to recover. And then what? Istvay was dead, but that didn't mean the leadership war was over. He couldn't imagine he'd be much use anymore, but they may ask him what he thought about the star charts. What he thought Istvay might have told Sharda before they were killed. And he'd tell them. He'd help them as much as he could, because they'd treated him well and he owed them. And then when the war was over, one way or another, he would—continue. Just … continue existing. Maybe Krevai would keep him on the ship, or maybe he'd be dropped off with Dessi at her research station. It didn't really matter. His life stretched out before him like a dull, empty ache— long and interminable and unbearable, but you bore it anyways, because you didn't have a choice.

Meaningless.

Ani chirruped, and he looked down at her, somehow managing a smile. "You're hungry, sweetheart, aren't you?" His voice came out just as calm and dead as his thoughts.

He'd have to remember to feed her. He'd have to remember to feed himself, too. He could refuse to eat or sleep, but at some point his stomach would pinch with hunger enough that he'd feed it, and he knew from experience that at some point his body would shut down if he didn't sleep. So there was really no point.

Ani chirped again, questioningly, and Aran pushed himself to his feet and placed her carefully in the pile of blankets. His legs felt heavier than normal as he stumbled over to where he'd put away her snacks. He was fumbling with the latch on the storage compartment, his fingers strangely clumsy, when he heard the voice.

"Aran!"

It was quiet, and far away. He ignored it, still fumbling with the latch.

"Aran! Aran, can you hear me?"

He frowned, glancing around him. The cold, clinical part of his mind that was still functioning told him that hearing things was … probably not a good sign. He should probably let Krevai know that he shouldn't be in charge of things until the voices went away.

"Aran? Oh hell, I thought this bloody thing was actually going to work … Damn it to hell—" The voice choked off in a way that was unutterably familiar, and Aran froze, his entire body gone suddenly so shaky he wasn't sure he could speak if he wanted to.

He squeezed his hand to activate his wavelink. "Istvay?" he managed, his voice almost inaudible. He cleared his throat and tried again. "Istvay?"

There was a long pause, and for a moment, he was certain he'd been wrong. He'd been hearing things, none of this was real, it couldn't be real because Istvay was dead—

"Aran …" This time, the voice through his wavelink was unmistakable, even cracked and heavy with tears.

Aran clutched the edge of the storage compartment hard enough that his knuckles went white, trying to keep from falling over. "Pishti?" He was hoarse, his voice refusing to work the way it should. "Pishti. You're—you're alive—" And then he was sobbing, sinking down to the floor, squeezing his hand around his palmscreen like it was the only thing anchoring him to reality.

There was a rustle as Ani scrambled across the floor and planted herself on his chest, suckering herself down across his tunic with every one of her tentacles, and he held onto her with his free hand

"Aran! Aran, what's wrong? What happened? Are you hurt? Oh hell, Aran, can I—" Istvay's voice was thick with concern, and the familiar tone was only making Aran sob harder.

"Pishti," he managed at last, cutting through their panicked questions. "Pishti, I'm fine. I just—I thought—I saw the blood, and I thought Sharda had—that you were—" He couldn't say any more, his throat closing up in remembered horror.

"You thought ... *Hell!*" Istvay's voice was still tight with badly disguised panic. "Listen, I'm fine, that wasn't me. You need to breathe, Aran, can you breathe? Please, Aran, I ... you have to—" and then their voice broke as well.

Aran sucked in a deep breath, forcing back his tears, fighting the thickness in his throat. When he spoke again, he was able to actually speak, which was ... an improvement, at least. "Pishti. I'm—I'm alright. We're on our way, I found the clues you've been leaving." His voice cracked. "Just—just hold on until I can get to you, okay?"

There were a few moments' silence from the other end of the line. When Istvay spoke again, their voice was a little steadier. "Listen, Aran. Sharda took me on as her crew, so she's not going to kill me right now. I had to give up my allegiance to Krevai in order for her to do that, which means *he* may try to kill me when he finds me, but —" they gave a low, strained chuckle. "I thought we could deal with that when we came to it. My wavelink is still broken. I managed to rig something, but it's taken me this long to get it to work, and it's going to burn out the connections in just a few minutes. So listen. I'm going to send you some coordinates. That's where Sharda plans on making her stand. There are other ships coming to join her, and I can't tell you for certain how many will be there, but I think your best bet is to get there as soon as possible, before too many have the chance to show up."

Aran's wavelink buzzed, and he glanced down at his palmscreen automatically to see a line of coordinates.

"I'm—pretty sure Sharda is getting suspicious of what I'm doing," Istvay continued. "I've been trying to leave clues for you in ways she won't see, but I can't promise you won't be walking into a trap, and if you are, I probably won't be in a position to help you." They paused. "When you get here, she'll probably realize what I've done. So once you come into view, I'm going to try to steal a pod and come find you, and we can figure everything else out from there. But —please be careful. Please. Please don't sacrifice yourself to try to save me, because I—I don't think I'd actually survive that." Their voice wavered, and Aran closed his eyes and breathed in through his nose, trying not to remember just a few minutes previous, when he'd been certain Istvay was dead.

"I need to tell you something else." Istvay was speaking quickly now, their voice hushed. "Sharda is gaining allies here because she can promise them something that Krevai can't—human flesh."

"You mean she's going to use you—" Aran began, panic jolting through him again like lightning.

"No," Istvay cut him off quickly. "Nothing like that. One human wouldn't be enough. And anyways, what was it Dessi called me? The skinny, pale one?"

Aran chuckled weakly.

"This is my fault," continued Istvay, their voice once again grim. "I suggested that she find a way to incentivize other crews to declare loyalty before the battle begins, but I had no idea this is what she'd damn well come up with. She's bargained with Kachik for the humans so her allies can hunt them for food when the leadership war is over. And I can't bloody fix it." There was mounting frustration in their voice. "I've tried everything I could think of to talk her out of it, but she won't listen. But maybe if you can convince Krevai to come up with something else to motivate the raider crews, maybe she won't be as enamoured with the bargain. She's already starting to mistrust Kachik, after he sent that spy with his negotiators on our last meeting. So I think if Krevai were to find a way to lure her allies to him—"

The line crackled. Istvay swore, their voice distant and almost inaudible. "Dammit, this isn't going to last much longer. Listen, Aran, you … you need to stay safe, okay? I need you to be alright, I need that. I can survive anything as long as I know you're alright. So just—please just—"

The line crackled again and went dead.

Aran was left sitting on the floor in front of the storage compartment, staring down at his palm screen, his stomach tight, his face wet with tears.

He wasn't sure how long he sat there. By the time he pushed himself shakily to his feet, the muscles in his legs were cramping.

He realized, belatedly, that he hadn't grabbed Ani's treat, and he turned back to the storage compartment, his fingers almost as clumsy now as they had been before, when he'd thought Istvay was dead. At last he managed the latch and pulled out a handful of dried meat for Ani. She took it delicately with the tips of her tentacles, then devoured it, growling viciously, flakes of dried meat scattering across the room.

Aran smiled at the spectacle despite himself, and when she was finished, he held out his arm for her to clamber back up.

"Well, Ani," he said. Then he had to swallow against the thickness in his throat.

He made his way along the hallways towards the cockpit. He must look awful, he realized wryly—the raiders who saw him didn't even ask questions, just stepped aside to let him pass, averting their eyes. That small, scientific part of his brain that was still functioning wondered if perhaps this was a raider tradition around grief—leave the grieving person to themself, not try to intrude. Maybe it was true, after all, that humans and raiders weren't all that different.

When he reached the cockpit, Krevai and Dessi and a handful of other raiders were deep in conversation, heads bent together as they peered down at a data screen.

Aran cleared his throat.

Krevai looked up, frowning. "Aran! I'm glad to see you here. I thought after your Istvay died, you'd be—"

Dessi elbowed him hard, and he grunted, but stopped talking.

"Aran." Dessi's voice was quieter, but he could see the spark of interest in her eyes. "What do you need? Are you—is there human memorial service you'd like us to conduct? Because if there is, I'm happy to—"

Aran shook his head. "Istvay's alive," he said. His voice was still shaky. "I just heard from them. Whoever Sharda killed, it wasn't them. They gave me coordinates for where Sharda intends to make her stand."

Krevai and Dessi were both staring at him now.

At last, Krevai chuckled heartily, shaking his head. "So your Istvay managed to survive after all," they said. "The two of you never cease to surprise me. I'm always having to revise my opinion on humans these days. Give me the details, and we'll see what we can do about teaching Sharda some manners."

Aran stepped closer, squeezing his hand to activate the palmscreen, and held out the coordinates for Krevai and Dessi to examine.

"You're going to have to convert that into our notation," said Krevai after a moment, shaking his head.

Aran nodded. "Istvay told me that Sharda suspects you'll know where to find her. So there's a chance this is a trap."

Krevai's grin widened. "Ah, so she's playing that game, is she? Keeping on a crewmember who might be compromised, just to show she's strong enough to do it. Captains do that sometimes, if they have crew who they know are thinking of becoming mates with someone on a rival captain's crew. Impressive, but a risky strategy." He turned to Aran, his long fangs showing through his grin. "I'm sure she has a trap for us. That just means we'll have to make a better one for her." He paused a moment. "And did your Istvay mention how she's managed to get so many other raider crews on her side? I'm a bit surprised—usually the crews who aren't making a leadership bid sit things out. No one wants to be on the wrong side when the leadership war is over."

Aran sighed. "That's ... the other thing I wanted to talk with you about. Sharda's promised humans for hunting to the people who follow her."

Krevai raised his eyebrows. "A tempting offer. And where does she plan to find these humans?"

"Apparently, she's made a treaty with Kachik for the remainder of the humans who were stranded when our ship broke up."

Krevai looked faintly impressed.

Dessi looked outraged.

"Well, you can't say Sharda isn't a clever one," the captain said, turning to the raider pilot, who sat next to him.

"It's not a bad idea," the woman replied thoughtfully. "It would tempt a lot of raiders, especially since we've all just lost our chance at hunting the human system through the portal."

Krevai turned back to Aran. "Thank you, Aran, that's excellent information. We'll plan to take her and all her humans, and we'll put the word out that the winner takes the prize. That should cause those who aren't completely certain of Sharda's victory to rethink their position, maybe find their ships breaking down so they can't quite reach the battle until they figure out who's going to win it. That should make the battle more even, trap or no."

"Captain!" snapped Dessi. "Humans are a sapient species! They're related to raiders, we can't just—"

Krevai grinned, turning to the scientist. "If they're related to raiders, all the more reason to respect their abilities. We'll make the hunt sporting, of course. But it would be disrespectful to imagine humans can't take care of themselves. Look at our Aran!"

Aran blew out a breath. "Couldn't we—wouldn't it be better to force her to break the treaty with Kachik?"

Krevai chuckled, waving a hand dismissively. "Much better to take the humans ourselves. We'll gain more loyalty that way. You truly have no idea how much we like human flesh."

"But—" Aran began again.

"Aran," said Krevai, pushing himself to his feet. "You've proved yourself a worthy member of my crew, and I appreciate your help. But you have already asked me for the life of a person who's denounced their loyalty to me, after signing on as my crew. That's a hard enough favour to grant." He looked down at Aran, the dangerous grin still lingering on his face. "You're my crew. And my crew knows not to push me too far. Do you really want to take a chance with your Istvay's life?"

Aran's heart was pounding. He dropped his eyes.

"I thought not," said Krevai smugly. "Now, why don't you get something to eat, Aran, and then you can translate the coordinates from your notational system into ours. In the meantime, we'll work on a plan for when we track down our good friend Captain Sharda." He dropped back down in his seat and turned to the pilot.

Dessi yawned and stretched. "I'm feeling a bit hungry myself," she said in a tone of forced casualness. "I'll go with Aran."

Krevai nodded absently, waiting a dismissive hand, and Dessi brushed past Aran out the door, beckoning him after her with her chin.

Once they were outside, Aran turned to her quickly. "Dessi," he whispered. "We have to do something about the humans! We can't just let Captain Krevai—"

Dessi put a finger to her lips and gestured him to follow her back to the cabin she used as her lab. Once they were both inside and she'd closed the door, she turned to Aran, frowning. "You're right," she said in a whisper. "We can't just let Sharda or Krevai hunt down the rest of the humans—that would be a massive waste of potential data." She chewed on her lip for a moment. "You say all of them are from your system?"

Aran nodded numbly.

Dessi sighed. "There's got to be a way—" she muttered. At last, she looked up with a grin. "I think I have the beginnings of an idea."

"What is it?" Aran asked cautiously.

She shook her head. "I still have to think through the implications. Just leave it with me." Her tone was satisfied. "In the meantime, you'd best sit down and work out the coordinates for Krevai. The happier we can keep him, the more likely this is to work."

Aran nodded, and took the data pad Dessi pushed into his hands. But he watched her a little uneasily as he sat down.

It wasn't that he didn't trust Dessi. She'd saved his life, and Istvay's, on more than one occasion, and she clearly had no desire for the humans to be killed.

It was just—

He shook his head, pushing back the unease, and bent over the data pad.

At this point, it wasn't like he had a lot of other options.

21

Alba

"Tika."

"Alba? What is it?"

Tika sounded groggy, as if she'd woken him up.

Alba gritted her teeth.

This was not ideal. More than one life depended on her being able to get on Tika's good side.

"I apologize for bothering you," she said. "But sadly, a matter of some urgency has arisen, and I was hoping that we could speak on it."

He cleared his throat a couple times, and when he spoke next, his tone was more friendly. "Of course. I would be happy to speak with you later this morning." His words were noncommittal, though—he was, Alba had learned, the type of politician who would never commit to a position unless he was very comfortable that the end result would be personally beneficial.

"You impressed my colleagues yesterday," he continued. "I was getting questions all evening about you. Most of the advisors, pro-human or not, were impressed with your political acumen."

Alba closed her eyes and drew a long breath, forcing her voice to remain neutral. "I am flattered indeed," she said. "And I am thrilled that our collaboration has begun a process which, I hope, will end up benefiting both of us." she paused a moment. "And that mutually beneficial relationship is why I contacted you. A new situation has arisen, I hoped we could once again use our collaboration to benefit all parties involved."

There was a long pause from the other end of the line. At last, Tika said cautiously, "As you know, my dear Alba, nothing would please me more than another collaboration. But of course, we would have to talk it over and determine exactly what such a collaboration would entail."

"Of course," said Alba. She hadn't expected him to agree sight unseen, after all. "I would be very happy to come to your office the moment you are available."

"Why don't you come in now, and I'll meet you there?" Alba could hear the calculation in his tone, the wary curiosity. "It's early, but I see no reason why we shouldn't start our day with the sun."

Alba ignored the wry note of rebuke in his words. "I think that will be quite acceptable. I will see you as soon as I can get over there."

By the time she arrived at Tika's office, the nerves and worry in Alba's stomach had formed into a tight, sick knot.

She was risking everything on the assurances of a lawless, amoral assassin. The girl had hated Alba from the beginning.

And yet ...

When Alba had spoken with Yosip—she'd told the others the information had come from Reka Soler, since she wanted to stay as close to the truth as possible—he had nodded, his face wrinkled with worry. "I haven't been able to contact my friends back in the city since we took down the portal," he said quietly. "I assumed they'd been moved somewhere more secure. But considering what we've seen of Kachik's behaviour, what Reka is saying makes an unfortunate amount of sense."

And the raw fear in Savina's tone would have been difficult to fake, even for the charming young assassin.

Alba sighed and shook her head grimly.

At the very least, she was currently in Tika's good graces. That had to count for something.

He was waiting for her when the security officer unlocked the door and she stepped through. "Alba," he said, rising from his seat. "We were so busy yesterday I'm not sure I congratulated you on a successful presentation."

"Thank you." Alba had to force her voice to remain civil, rather than break with impatience. "I should congratulate you as well. If this advisement progresses through both readings and is passed by the Synod, I expect it to be a significant political advantage for both of our constituents."

"Yes, I think you're right," said Tika, smiling. "And now, please. Sit down. Tell me about this new collaboration you wish to discuss."

Alba settled herself into one of the seats, wincing unconsciously as her posterior met the hard wood of the stool Tika had generously requested specifically for her. She spent a moment longer than necessary arranging herself, trying to calm her sick anticipation. "I received some communication from a fellow survivor from our diplomatic ship," she began at last. "The Nativists are, as you know, holding the remainder of my associates in enforced captivity. We assumed that we would have the time to find a way to open negotiations and perhaps arrange for their release." She paused. "However, it seems the Nativists have decided, rather than hold the humans or turn them over to us, they'd bargain them off to the raiders in exchange for an alliance."

Tika frowned. "Kachik plans to form an alliance with the raiders? That's absurd. He wouldn't dare. No one with any sense makes bargains with the raiders, and whatever you can say about Kachik, he's smart." He shook his head. "No, I don't believe it. Your contact was mistaken."

"My contact seemed very certain of the fact." She drew in a deep breath, forcing herself not to react to the skepticism on his face. "Regardless, however, of whether my contact is correct, what is indisputable is that the remainder of my fellow shipmates are in urgent danger. They have perhaps a day, two at best. And if we do not find a way to find them sanctuary by that time, they'll be killed."

Tika was watching her, still frowning. "I'm sorry to hear that. But I'm not sure what you expect us to be able to do about it. As you know, the Advisory Body has already voted on the question of refugees, and has decided that, barring a negotiated agreement with Kachik, rescuing the human refugees from your ship is not a topic that will be passed on to the Hierophants. No one, I think, wants to go to war over … you'll forgive my putting it bluntly, but these are people who are not, in fact, citizens of our system at all. They're not even yibo, and it's a small number of individuals to begin with. And they did beg refuge from Kachik, and as he provided it, their complaints would have to be taken up with him."

Alba shook her head sharply. "Neither of us is served by you pretending to be less intelligent than you are, Tika. Kachik is going to kill those people—that 'very small number' of almost two hundred people. If these were yibo, and were familiar with the legal system of refuge and acceptance in your system, perhaps your argument would hold, although even there I have my doubts considering the clear directives of your Tenets of Clarity. But I believe the hospitality laws become unenforceable if the offeror breaks the implied terms. And one of the implied terms, unsurprisingly, is that the offeror of hospitality cannot use or sell their guests into chattel servitude, or put them in a position where their lives are in peril."

Tika raised an eyebrow, an expression on his face that was either amusement, or annoyance. "I see you've spent your last few days well, to be so conversant in our laws."

Alba gave him a wry look. "You know I'm right. And while I understand the reasons that the Synod doesn't wish to provoke an argument with the Nativists, you must see the situation could accrue to your benefit as much as ours. If your district is the one to champion the acceptance of the refugees, that only increases your voice in the additional advisor seat."

"And you must see how that would hardly be helpful if my constituents are dying in an unnecessary war," said Tika dryly. "It's not that I don't sympathize. And I agree that accepting the refugees could be beneficial, if we were to take time to create that proposal. However—" he gave a helpless shrug. "Our proposed advisement yesterday passed through the first reading by the merest fraction. Even with the expedited procedure, and even if all goes perfectly, it will take dozens of cycles before the Synod considers and approves it. So while I understand your distress, it's not practical for us to attempt a second radical proposal so close on the heels of the first." He sighed. "These are—what, a few hundred humans you're talking about? There are thousands more in the system who will be helped by the advisement you and I worked on together. We can hardly sacrifice them in the hopes of something that will at best save a couple hundred humans, and at worst do nothing at all. I know my colleagues. Those who are anti-human tend to be virulently so. I doubt there's an argument you could make that would convince them to be otherwise."

"And how many, exactly, of your colleagues are virulently anti-human?" asked Alba, modulating her tone carefully so as not to show her despair. "From what I could see, they do not hold a majority."

"A majority, no," said Tika. "But enough that we'd need a strong majority ourselves to overcome their vote. And there are enough on the fence that we can't risk upsetting them. Our proposed advisement barely got accepted into a first reading, and some of that came from the support of the anti-human faction, because they agreed with your idea of segregating off the humans. If we upset them, they'll withdraw their vote."

"And if we don't upset them," said Alba quietly, meeting his eye, "my people will be killed."

There was silence in the office.

For just a moment, Alba allowed herself to hope.

Then Tika sighed and turned away. "As I said, Alba—I appreciate your position. But there's nothing that I can do to help. With the expedited procedure, our advisement is scheduled for its second reading later this afternoon. I do hope you'll forgive me—"

Alba closed her eyes and drew in a long breath. Then she stood slowly and left, on legs that felt too weary to carry her.

The others' faces around the small table were grave as Alba finished her account.

"Bastard," Jair muttered.

Feliu gave him a scandalized look, but Alba was inclined to agree with Jair on that point.

"He's right, though," said Jair. "At least, he's right in that if we frame it as accepting more refugees, we probably won't get enough consensus for the advisement to even go on to a second reading."

"Then we'll have to work out a way to make this more palatable," said Yosip.

"No matter how palatable we make it, Tika won't agree to submit it," said Jair quietly, "I've had dealings with him before. This representation issue has been his baby since he won an advisorship. It's probably the only reason he agreed to work with Alba in the first place—the chance she might have some insight that would help him. So if there's as much as a chance of this turning his fellow advisors against his proposal, he's not going to agree."

"But he will agree to have me present at the debate after the second reading," said Alba slowly. "He's already indicated as much." She'd been chewing the matter over since she'd stepped out of Tika's office, and if the conclusion made her faintly ill—it was still better than standing by helplessly as the remaining refugees were bargained off to the raiders. "And if my understanding is correct, any member—including a member of the public—may present a suggested amendment to a proposal during the second reading debates. And if someone were to present an amendment that would lead to declaration of emergency measures such that the human refugees were accepted as part of the proposal ..."

Jair turned to stare at her. "Tika would see something like that as a betrayal of the highest magnitude," he said, his tone a mixture of shock and grudging admiration.

"As you pointed out, he and I are only allies because our mutual interests converge," said Alba sharply. "This morning, he made it very clear the limits of our mutual collaboration. I hardly see that he could complain if the same standards apply in both sides."

"Logically, I agree with you," said Jair wryly. "In practice, however—you are human, and a refugee, and he is an advisor to the Synod."

"A human and a refugee who happens to have gained some reputation among the Advisory Body," Alba countered.

Truth be told, she didn't like it much more than Jair did. But at this point, it was this, or simply leaving the remnants of the diplomatic ship to their deaths.

"I am not a politician," said Yosip. "But I'm willing to trust Alba's expertise on this."

Feliu nodded as well.

"We can't exactly stand by and let the humans be murdered," said Joska dryly. Her voice was subdued, but there was something in the way she'd watched Alba since Alba had mentioned her newly gained knowledge of the humans back in Chrr that told Alba that Savina's comment on Joska's intelligence was not an idle one.

Still, she could worry about Joska's finding out about her falsehoods later.

Jair sighed, strain in his expression. "We'd best get to work, then, if they're reading the advisement this afternoon."

22

Savina

No one was happy with being left behind in the jungle, but when Savina pulled out her gun and made it very clear what the options were, they eventually acquiesced.

"What?" Savina snapped as they started back through the forest.

Reka, who was clearly fighting back her amusement, raised an eyebrow. "I didn't say anything."

"You didn't have to say anything," Savina muttered. "I've worked with you long enough."

Reka gave a cough that sounded suspiciously like a laugh. "You know, Savina—" She paused, swore, and fired off a shot in Savina's direction.

Savina's heart jumped in sudden panic—had Reka decided to get rid of her? Then a squat, green, monkey-like creature she had never seen before, but, if its teeth and claws were any indication, was definitely a predator, dropped from the tree above her to land at her feet.

She blinked, shaken, and Reka calmly holstered her pistol. "As I was saying, I'm coming to realize that—you make a surprisingly good ally. I … don't like to ask for help. But I couldn't have made it this far without you."

Savina stared, heart still pounding. Reka gave her that bare hint of a smile, and started off.

Savina hurried to catch up.

By the time they reached the city, it was well past nightfall, but the entire place was lit up like an emergency beacon.

Reka gave a low whistle as they crouched together at the edge of the jungle. "It wasn't even like this when the diplomatic party escaped."

Savina nodded curtly, not trusting herself to speak.

The gunshot in the jungle had shaken her more than she'd expected. And she wasn't sure if it was the brief certainty that Reka had turned on her, decided to kill her after all—or if it was that Reka had saved her life yet again.

They watched for what must have been at least an hour before Reka pushed herself to her feet. "If we were really infiltrators from the government, we'd probably have our own ship," she whispered. "So I doubt they'll be expecting us. In fact, they're likely readying ships to send after us, which means ships on the loading pad kitted out, waiting for us to take them."

"And if they are expecting us?" Savina whispered.

Reka shrugged. "In that case, we try not to get killed."

Savina closed her eyes.

What was wrong with her? Why the hell had she agreed to this? And why the hell hadn't she killed this self-sacrificing lunatic while she had the chance?

Getting past the guards at the city force field was not as difficult as Savina had anticipated, honestly. There were enough yibo going in and out that it was easy enough to blend into the crowd, and the focus seemed to be on keeping people from getting out. No one seemed to have considered the possibility that the humans would do anything so stupid as to try to sneak back in.

Reka was taller than Savina, but where Savina was accustomed to drawing attention to herself, albeit the kind of attention that was harmless and indulgent, Reka had the ability to move in a way that was almost more shadow-like than a shadow itself—a flicker of movement, a brush of air, and she was past.

At last they were inside the gates, crouched in one of the alleys.

Reka turned a questioning glance on Savina, and Savina gave her a brusque nod, hoping it would hide the extent of her fear.

She wasn't used to being afraid. She was used to being in control of whatever situation she was put into. She was used to being the one writing the narrative. But now, she wasn't. Now, she was going back to a group of vicious aliens who had very nearly killed her on two different occasions. The flash of fear, the icy shivers up her spine at the thought of what they were going to do, were disconcerting.

"Are you alright?"

She jerked her head up to find Reka watching her.

"I'm fine," she said in a sour tone. "I absolutely love going back into places where I was almost killed, just for fun."

Reka was still watching her.

"It's not like we have a choice, at this point," snapped Savina, when Reka's gaze became uncomfortable.

Reka nodded, turning away. "Let's go then," she said quietly.

They made their way quickly and silently through the back alleys, Reka leading the way, until they were crouched in the mouth of an alley overlooking the loading pad.

The taste of fear was cold and sharp in Savina's mouth.

"Your friend Joska said it was easy to hijack the ship last time," whispered Reka. "After what she did, though, there'll be more security. I don't know if stealth is going to work anymore."

"This is how we're going to do it," said Savina shortly. "We go in, we kill everyone in our way. If you don't like it, you can go in alone."

Killing, she could do. If she thought of this as a job, it made it easier to push past the terror that weakened every muscle in her body and choked off her breath.

Reka smiled. "I'm not Joska, so you won't get any argument for me on that point." She pulled out her weapons. "Gun, or knife?"

"Knives are for close work," Savina whispered. "I plan to stay as far away from these bastards as I can get."

"Guns it is," said Reka. She tucked a small pulse pistol into her belt, then stood, and the two of them slipped out of the alley and into the loading pad.

It was maybe a minute before they were noticed.

A young yibo soldier—at least, Savina assumed he was young, more from the nervous tension in his posture than from any physical markers—turned, and started at the sight of them. He opened his mouth, his eyes going wide, and Reka raised her pistol and fired.

He was dead before he hit the ground, his eyes still wide with shock.

But the communication device held loosely in his limp hand was flashing a bright, impatient yellow.

"He got an alarm out," Savina snapped.

Reka nodded, her mouth set in a grim line, and they ran for the ships.

More soldiers caught sight of them before they were halfway across the ground, and within moments, the air around them hummed with shots.

Reka dived behind a stack of boxes, pulling Savina down with her. "Do you want to cover me, or go in?" she hissed.

"You covering me would mean that I would be running," muttered Savina. "If that doesn't answer your question, you haven't been paying attention."

Reka looked at her blankly, then gave a surprised snort of laughter. "Alright. You cover me, I'll go."

Savina expected … something. Some threat as to what would happen to her if she ran, or simply decided to let Reka get hit. But Reka just turned away, checking her weapons.

Savina tried to ignore the odd, uncomfortable feeling in her chest.

"Are you ready?" whispered Reka.

Savina nodded.

Reka stood in a half-crouch, drew in a quick breath, and slipped out from behind the boxes, breaking into a sprint.

Savina raised up on her knees, lining up the sights on her weapon, and as Reka stepped out into the open, Savina fired off a handful of shots towards where she'd last seen the yibo soldiers, then lined up and fired again as a shot hissed out over Reka's head.

She should probably be terrified. Once she had time to think about it, she probably would be. But right now, there was nothing but her and her weapon and the woman who had trusted Savina, even though she probably shouldn't, and whose life Savina was currently trying to save.

Reka was already halfway across the open space.

And then a shot hit so close that Reka staggered, knocked off balance.

Savina's eyes tracked where the shot had come from, and her entire body went cold.

A yibo soldier had made their way around behind the ships, and was now crouched beside a low wall, directly between Reka and the ship.

And there was no way Savina could hit them from where she was hiding.

They were aiming their weapon again, squinting down the barrel.

Savina didn't stop to think about what she did next. She simply reacted, jumping to her feet, shouting curses, running towards the soldier.

They jerked their head up, startled by Savina's approach.

And then Reka had slipped inside the nearest ship and to safety.

Savina allowed herself a quick, unconscious gasp of relief.

Then she realized what exactly she had done—she out in the open, alone, Reka inside the ship and likely in no position to help her—

She dived to the ground as a shot whizzed over her head, then scrambled to her feet and took off running.

Dammit, why was her entire life made up of nothing but running?

Another shot hit so close on her heels that the paving stones under her feet cracked and buckled.

She wasn't going to make it. There was no way she was going to make it, Reka had barely made it with Savina covering her.

"Reka!" she shouted desperately.

And then something picked Savina bodily up and threw her a solid metre away, a white wall of force and sound that left her bruised and stunned, her ears ringing.

For a few moments she lay there, certain she'd finally been killed.

And then she blinked her eyes open and glanced around.

The entire squadron of yibo soldiers were dead, bodies and body parts scattered across the courtyard in a gruesome tableau, blood staining the loading pad.

She turned automatically towards the ship where Reka had taken shelter, and realized it wasn't where it had been—it had swivelled, turning its gun ports towards her, and she could just make out a familiar figure in the cockpit.

Reka was smiling, her eyes narrow and dangerous.

"Mind on the job," she mouthed when she noticed Savina looking. Savina scowled and staggered to her feet, stumbling for the ship's loading ramp.

She made it before the yibo soldiers regrouped, possibly assisted by the fact that Reka was firing at random at anything that moved. But as she scrambled inside, she could see the squadrons of yibo running for their own ships.

"Are you hurt?" Reka's voice came over her wavelink.

"I'm fine," she snapped back. "But neither of us are going to be fine in about ten seconds. Get us the hell out of here!"

"We're going up. Hold on," said Reka grimly, and Savina lurched into the cockpit and managed to grab hold of the back of the copilot's seat just as the ship shot forward.

"You could have waited for—" she began, and then the first shot hit them. The impact shook the ship, and Savina landed on the ground, still swearing. Another shot hit home, and then they were off and bursting upwards over the buildings.

"I'm going to need all my attention to fly this thing," said Reka through her teeth. "You'll have to get us through the force field." She tossed something in Savina's direction, and Savina caught it automatically.

She glanced down at it. "What—" she began, but Reka had turned her attention back to flying.

Savina swore, glaring at the device in her hand. It looked like the same thing Reka had used to get them through the walls of the yibo buildings, but on a larger scale. She fumbled her fingers over it, then hit the button that she was pretty sure was the controller.

The force field, now so close she could almost have reached out and touched it, split around them, and their ship shot through, with a dozen yibo ships on its tail.

23

Aran sighed, shaking his head, and reached up to rub Ani as she pushed up against side of his cheek. "Alright, sweetheart, I'm done," he whispered. "I'll drop this information off to Krevai, and then we can get back to our cabin."

Ani purred, and he stood and stretched, glancing around. Dessi hadn't returned to her lab, and he had no idea where she'd gone. Probably to dinner or something. He'd grab something to eat and head back to his cabin, and then maybe he'd pull up the information on his data pad and go through some of the DNA analysis he and Dessi had been working on before … well, just Before. He wasn't sure he could think about it any closer than that before a hell of a lot more time had passed.

He certainly wasn't going to be sleeping, at least not until the sick panic had finished draining from his muscles.

By the time Aran looked up from his painstaking research, the ship had gone quiet and dark. He blinked, and glanced down at his wavelink for the time, then gave a rueful sigh. "Probably best get some sleep, eh, Ani?" he said, glancing around the small cabin.

A lump in the blankets of the foot of his bed wriggled, and Ani poked a sleepy eye out.

Aran chuckled. "Well, I guess only one of us needed that advice." He stripped out of the filthy clothes he'd never actually got around to changing since his trip planet-side, and into one of the soft raider tunics Dessi had procured for him—much too large, but functional as a nightshirt. Then he tapped off the artificial light, curled into the pile of blankets, and tried not to think of how quiet and still the room was without Istvay's soft, familiar breathing.

This was stupid. Istvay was alive and safe, and he was going to see them soon, and despite the overwhelming rush of emotions that still jittered through him, everything would be alright, he just had to stop thinking about it … He blinked back a tear, scrubbing at his eyes roughly. Istvay was fine, and he'd see them soon, and …

And then his tired body won out over his spinning mind, and he was asleep before he finished the thought.

He heard, somewhere in his dreams, a faint sound—a slight scuff, like the soft scrape of a footfall, just enough to pull him into a warm, slow semi-wakefulness. But the room had gone quiet again, and he was on the verge of falling back asleep.

And then he heard the first scream.

He jerked upright, staring frantically around the room, his eyes trying to adjust to the darkness.

The scream had cut off in a desperate gurgle, and now he could make out a shape slumped against the door, and a shadow that must be Ani detaching herself from it and flowing across the ground towards him. Even in the dark, he could tell by the deadly focus in her movements that she was hunting.

He opened his mouth, and then there was something cold and sharp at his throat. A terrified voice hissed in his ear, "Call your—

your creature off, or I'll slit your throat right here."

Now that Aran's eyes had begun to adjust, he could see two other slumped figures at the foot of his bed, make out the faint outline of acid foam bubbling from their still forms.

Whoever these people were, they must have boarded on the last planet the ship had visited.

Which meant they may know something about Istvay, and unless something changed very quickly, they were going to be much too dead to tell him about it.

"Ani!" he snapped, pushing the knife away from his neck and jumping to his feet. "Ani, come here, sweetheart—"

His attacker grabbed for his arm, but he ducked out of the way, his eyes scanning the room. "Ani! Ani, listen, let's—let's not kill anyone until we can—"

Ani's quiet hiss gave away her location, and he turned quickly, cataloguing the scene as he did so—at least two more people dead on the ground by the door. At least one still alive to threaten him, apparently. And Ani, in the corner, crouched like a spider waiting to spring at her pray.

The attacker's hand landed heavily on Aran's arm again, and Ani's hissing increased in volume. Aran grabbed the man's hand and yanked it away. "Would you please stop that? If she thinks you're trying to hurt me, she's not going to—"

Aran just caught the glint of metal across the room from him, and he dived to the ground as a pulse blast shuddered through the cabin. Almost quicker than the eye could follow, Ani pounced. There was a muffled scream, then the *clang* of something metal hitting the ground.

"Aran!" Dessi's voice was muffled through the door. "Aran, you alright in there? We caught some humans on the ship, and I think

—"

"Don't try to come in, or I slit the human's throat!" The man's voice was high-pitched with panic, and he grabbed Aran again, pulling him around between him and the door.

Dessi banged on the door. "Aran! Are you in there? Are you alive? What's—"

"I'm fine," Aran panted, yanking himself free of the man holding him and ducking out of the way as a figure with a knife dived at him. "For the Mystery's damn sake, would you stop trying to—" he began in exasperation, turning on his attacker.

His attackers clearly were not listening. One of them grabbed for him again, and Aran barely caught Ani as she surged forward towards them. "Hey, sweetheart," he whispered, trying to keep his voice soothing.

"Aran?"

"Look, Dessi, I'm just a little busy, we're fine in here, we've—we've got the situation under control—"

Someone grabbed Aran again, this time catching his ankle, and Aran fell hard, his other foot tangled in the mess of blankets. Ani slid free of his grasp, and he cursed under his breath.

Someone else stepped forward, their gun glittering in the reflected emergency lights from under the cabin door. "Call off your damn creature, or I'll—"

"Ani!" Aran snapped.

Ani looked up from where she was currently enveloping the face of a struggling human. The man yanked out his pulse pistol, holding it against Ani's bulbous body.

"No! Aran shouted, almost forgetting the gun at his own head.

The man pulled the trigger.

Ani gave a startled little jump of surprise, then hissed, raking her tentacles down her prey. The man dropped to the ground, convulsing.

"I told you," Aran snapped through his teeth, glancing up at the woman holding the pistol, whose hand was already beginning to shake. "I'm trying to calm her down so we can talk this out, but she's not going to listen if she thinks you're threatening me. Believe me, you don't have any weapon that will hurt her, the entire Joias System hasn't found a weapon that'll hurt her and they've spent five hundred years trying. So, please put your damn pistol away, and you —" he turned to the man who had him by the ankle, "put away your damn knife. Stand up very quietly and let me restrain your hands and feet, I'm pretty sure I can convince Ani to leave you alone."

"I'm not going to—" the man's voice was frantic.

"Listen," said Aran, in the same tone he used to try to soothe Ani. "Did Emeric, or whoever the hell sent you, bother to tell you what Ani is?"

There was a long pause.

"She's a great tree-dwelling venomous tentacled land-devil. Even if you were to kill me, she wouldn't stop hunting you. Wherever you went, she would hunt you down. Land-devils are very, very loyal."

"Why the hell would I believe anything you say?" The voice of the woman holding the gun was just as panicky as her companion's.

"Because," said Aran through his teeth, still very carefully, "you don't really have a choice, and I don't want any more people killed if they don't have to be." He paused a moment. "And besides, Ani always gets a stomach ache afterwards, and I don't want to have to get up fourteen times in the night to get her something for it."

The woman gave a hysterical little laugh, her pistol jerking up to point at Aran's face.

"No, don't—" Aran began.

The woman was dead before her finger had time to twitch on the trigger.

Behind him, there was the loud sound of a knife clattering to the floor.

Aran turned to see the man standing unarmed, hands up, his tawny complexion gone sickly pale in the reflected light.

Ani turned on him, hissing, and Aran swallowed down the sick in his own throat and crouched down quickly, holding out his arm to her. "You did such a good job, sweetheart, look, there's no one trying to hurt us anymore. What a good girl you are."

Ani was still growling suspiciously at the man, and Aran made a show of picking up the fallen knife and shoving it in his belt, then binding the man's hands and feet with rope from his supplies pouch. It wasn't until the man was completely restrained that Ani deigned to stop growling, and came over for a head rub.

Now that the excitement was over, Aran's hands were shaking a little, but he petted her head affectionately. "You did such a good job, sweetheart," he whispered. "What a good girl you are! So good at protecting! You want a treat?"

He tried not to look too hard at the bodies strewn about the floor, one or two still twitching. Yes, they'd been trying to kill him, and yes, he could hardly blame Ani for following her instincts, but still …

The man was watching in horror.

Aran followed Ani's hungry glance towards the dead woman at his feet, and sighed. "A different treat, sweetheart. Sorry."

Once Ani had been sufficiently praised, and was chewing on a treat in lieu of the bodies of one of her victims—although honestly, when he thought about it, there really wasn't that much difference between letting Ani deal with the victims and handing them over the raiders—Aran turned back to the man. "Whoever sent you didn't bother to tell you about Ani, did they?" he asked.

The look on the man's face confirmed his assessment.

"Maybe it's time to question who you really want to be loyal to, then. None of these people had to die." He glanced around. "Ani would be very happy to kill and eat you, as I'm sure you've discovered. And the raiders are outside, and I get the feeling they would also be very happy to kill and eat you. So why don't you tell me who you are and why you decided to kill me?"

When Aran finally opened the door to his cabin, it was to find a very angry Krevai, with Dessi and half a dozen of the crew behind him. When the captain saw that Aran was alive and unharmed, some of the tension dropped from his posture. But he ran his eye hungrily over the man cowering behind Aran, arms restrained behind his back.

"I told him we wouldn't eat him," said Aran hurriedly, putting out a hand to stop Krevai as he started forward. "I think he has information. He said he was sent by the yibo who are going to ally with Sharda, and I thought—"

"He tried to kill you," Krevai growled. "Nobody tries to kill my human."

Aran avoided pointing out the obvious fact that there was currently a very large number of people trying to kill him, and instead stepped quickly in front of the captain as Krevai went to step around him. "Listen. It's—" he paused a moment. "It's a matter of —of honour among humans. If we accept someone's surrender, we can't kill them. It's a … a cultural thing." He spread his hands in a gesture that he hoped conveyed his helplessness in the face of tradition.

Krevai narrowed his eyes, but at last, he gave a brusque nod. "I won't destroy your honour in front of the other humans, then," he said grudgingly, his voice still a dangerous growl. "But this one had better hope that the information he gives us is helpful."

The raiders cleaned the bodies from Aran's cabin with a brisk efficiency.

"Ani poisoned them, check with Dessi before you eat any of them!" Aran called after them.

He hadn't been certain that his captive's face could go any more bloodless, but it did.

And then, at last, they were gathered in the map room. Krevai was still fuming, and Aran could practically see the steam rising off the raider captain.

"I've sent my crew to go through the ship top to bottom, to make sure there aren't any more humans hiding on board," he said once they were all gathered. "They must have come on at the last planet. And if I find that man who we thought killed your Istvay knew about this, I'll make sure the cook prepares him for tomorrow's breakfast." He turned to the captive, who was still huddling behind Aran, doing his best to stay out of the way. "Alright, then," he said, his tone lowering once more into a growl. "Explain yourself."

To his credit, the man managed to make his story both quick and efficient, despite the obvious tremble in his voice. He'd been sent by Captain Mattin, under Kachik's orders. His original mission had been to find and kill Aran and Istvay, but when the portal had shut down, there had been a change of orders—a mission to negotiate with Sharda. Sharda had asked for a group of humans to negotiate in person, and Kachik had seen this as an opportunity for reconnaissance, as well as an opportunity to insist that Sharda send one of her people down to Chirr, supposedly to negotiate, but in reality as a potential hostage should things go badly.

And then the man and his party had received a further change of orders a few hours before Sharda landed: some of them were to get onto Krevai's ship, gather information, and most importantly, kill Aran and Istvay to keep them from passing potentially valuable information on to the raiders. Kachik had been hearing rumours of new raider technology, and he didn't want humans alive to pass on anything further. Yes, it was possible someone from the diplomatic ship may have encouraged Kachik's concern on this point, but the man didn't know first-hand. Yes, the man had seen Istvay, they'd been arguing with Sharda before she'd come to talk with the rest of the humans. The man and his team had given up the idea of going after Istvay when Sharda had disemboweled their companion, but he'd known Aran was on this ship because Sharda had mentioned it in the course of the negotiations.

The anger in Krevai's face grew more and more pronounced as the man spoke. When he finished, Krevai smashed the side of his fist against the wall. "How dare they think they can send spies to get information on me, and kill my human?" he growled. "And how can Sharda think to make peace with cowards like that?"

Dessi stepped forward. "Captain," she said, in a voice that was loud enough to make it obvious she meant to be overheard. "Sharda has made an alliance with the yibo, humans to hunt in exchange for her promise of peace. And the yibo just tried to send spies onto our ship and kill our human." She turned, glancing over the rest of the crew with the air of a dramatist. "We could take the humans from Sharda that she bargained with the yibo for. But that would mean alliance with the yibo, who have already proved they cannot be trusted. They tried to kill our Aran!"

There was a murmur through the rest of the cabin.

Dessi turned and gave Aran a small wink, which did absolutely nothing to calm his sudden unease.

"We've been at peace with the yibo for a long time," Dessi continued. "They think it's because of their force-fields, but they live in peace for one reason—we've chosen to let them. And now, they think they can insert themselves into our leadership war, send assassins after one of our crew!"

More murmuring from the raiders.

"Um … Dessi—" Aran began.

Dessi ignored him. "Why would a real raider crew be content to hunt down a few hundred tame humans? Perhaps that's alright for Sharda, but we are Krevai's crew!"

Shouts of agreement from the crew, growing gradually louder.

Krevai was watching her, a thoughtful expression on his face, but Aran could tell from the glint of humour in his eyes that he could see exactly what Dessi was up to.

"We don't need to go begging to the yibo for a hunt. That might be Sharda's way, but it's not Krevai's. I say, instead, we offer the raiders who follow us something more sporting. I propose we offer a hunt on the yibo themselves, once we win this war!"

Aran stared.

Krevai raised an eyebrow, but he didn't step in to stop the jubilation. "Perhaps that isn't a bad idea," he said finally, his voice cutting through the noise. "I know our Dessi is a little over-fond of humans, but truly, I think we raiders have had enough of being bated like tame uguio. It wouldn't hurt our cause to show our followers something a little different."

Dessi turned and caught Aran's eye, a smug grin on her face. "I told you I could find a way to save the humans," she whispered through her communicator as the rest of the raiders whooped and cheered.

Aran managed a weak smile in return.

She wasn't wrong, exactly. But—
But damn it to hell.

24

Alba arrived back in Tika's office minutes before the second reading was scheduled to begin.

The tension visibly relaxed from his posture when he saw her. "I was worried you were going to be so offended you wouldn't show up for the reading," he said. His tone was joking, but it held enough relief under it that she knew his nervousness had been more real than he wanted to pretend.

She gave him a small smile. "As I said, I have worked in politics before. I understand it's not personal. One simply must do what's necessary."

He nodded, but he was studying her a little more closely. "I'm glad that we understand each other so well," he said at last. "I could have made the arguments without your assistance, but as you were the original architect of the ideas, I'd much rather you be present to answer questions."

"Of course," Alba murmured.

The business of the Advisory Body took, as always, much longer than should have been possible. For once, Alba didn't begrudge the wait. Her heart was pounding, her nerves on edge, and she watched the advisors as they spoke, trying to gauge from their reaction to various proposals how they might react to her words.

Because Jair, and even Tika, had almost certainly been correct— what she was about to say would blow the coalition that had agreed to their proposal to shreds. If she couldn't get the support she needed, they'd lose both advisements, and Alba's desperate attempts to help would have succeeded only in making matters worse for the humans here, while condemning the Joias System survivors to their fate.

"Second reading of the proposed advisement by Tika regarding the humans' political representation in our system," called the Master of Readings.

Tika stood. "Esteemed advisors," he began. "I will outline once more the benefits that would accrue to all of us in the proposal I have put before you." He launched into the speech Alba and the others had prepared earlier.

Alba forced herself to sit impassively as he spoke, the training from long years of Council meetings proving as useful here as it ever had in the Joias System.

At last, Tika finished his speech, and read aloud the text of the advisement.

"Come forth with your questions for the advisor," called the Master of Readings.

A few advisors stood, calling out questions. Some were clearly asked in bad faith, but others bore the hallmark of genuine curiosity, and Alba gave a small sigh of relief. She and Yosip had compiled enough evidence of the prospective benefits of the proposal that the answers would likely not cause any noticeable decline in the advisors' support. Some of the questions Tika answered himself, others he directed with a wave of his hand to Alba.

It spoke to the acceptance she'd gained in the Advisory Body over the last few days that no one seemed offended by this, and she wondered, wryly, how well her newfound popularity would survive the coming blow.

"Come forward with your proposed amendments to the bill. Public come forward, advisors come forward," the Master of Readings intoned.

Alba took a deep breath and rose to her feet.

For a moment, no one reacted. Then a small stir fluttered through the assembled counsellors, whispers and muffled hums of laughter, as if they were under the impression Alba had misunderstood, or had forgotten the order of the proceedings.

"Alba," Tika whispered, amusement in his voice. "This is the time for—"

"I come forward with a proposed amendment," said Alba, her voice ringing through the silence.

Every head in the room swivelled to stare at her.

She consciously avoided glancing back at Tika. But from the corner of her eyes, she could see the outrage, the fury, and the dawning realization in his expression.

He opened his mouth, half-standing, but the Master of Readings gestured him curtly to sit. Her eyebrows were raised in what was much more likely curiosity at the upcoming spectacle than genuine interest, but she gestured to Alba to continue.

Alba tipped her head in acknowledgement and turned to the advisors.

"This advisement," she began, letting her words come slowly to allow the interpreter time to translate, "was one that, as you know, I, as a human, supported. It has the potential to help not only my fellow humans, but our friends the yibo as well. However, since the first reading, I have discovered new information which, I think, changes the calculus."

From the look on Tika's face, he would have happily strangled her to shut her up. But he also clearly understood that the time for that was long past.

"As I think you are aware, the ship that brought me and others from our home system was destroyed when the portal closed unexpectedly. We were forced to take refuge on the nearest planet, upon which Kachik had established his rogue government. This, I must assume, was his intention on opening the portal where he did."

"You told us all this when you spoke about the refugees," called one of the advisors. "Unless you have something further to add—"

The Master of Readings held up a hand to silence the interruption, and Alba continued.

"As you're all aware, a very generous reading of hospitality laws says that Kachik is entitled to repayment for the hospitality he offered. I say generous, because that would require accepting that he is sovereign authority in an area in which he has proclaimed himself free from the restraints of the Synod. However, for argument's sake, let us presume that analysis is sound. He is still obligated to treat his guests according to the principles of the laws of hospitality, one of which is, he cannot force them to pay the debt by selling them into chattel servitude, nor put their lives in imminent danger. I have learned, however, that the Nativists intend to break this cardinal rule, and perhaps worse. My friends who are held captive by him inform me that he intends to sell them off to their deaths for political favours."

After Tika's reaction earlier, they'd all decided it would be best for Alba to avoid mention of the raiders as much as possible.

There was a murmured whispering through the advisors.

"If the Nativists break the hospitality laws, we can discuss the consequences of that," said one of the advisors at last. "However, I don't see how it reflects on the advisement in front of us."

Alba placed her hands on the rail and leaned forward. "I will be frank, then. If the Nativists are willing to sell off humans, that is not only a moral outrage. It will be a political nightmare. Even if you are not interested in the knowledge my fellow citizens brought with them, there are those who are. That is a valuable asset that you are willing to hand over to your enemy, without even the bare pretence of legality. And raiders, too—I understand they'd pay a high price for humans, if the opportunity were offered."

This, of course, was the advantage of having someone advising on your proposal who had inside information from the military.

"All very well," broke in another advisor, "but accepting the refugees—let alone demanding them—may mean declaring outright war on the Nativists. Kachik said as much himself. And while you and I might disagree as to the legitimacy of his government, he certainly has a strong legal argument that the humans are his to do with as he chooses. Until we have concrete proof that he plans on breaking the laws of hospitality, there is little or nothing we can do."

"I'm not asking that the yibo government demand the Nativists turn over the refugees," said Alba. "I'm simply asking for an additional emergency measure. While the Synod considers this advisement, issue an advisory for the autonomous settlement. Allow the humans to be the ones accepting the refugees, with your role merely to protect your sworn allies. If the Nativists want war, it will be up to them to declare it, but now it will be them asking the question as to whether a group of humans is worth going to war over."

"And how would this autonomous human district retrieve the stranded humans from the Nativist's city?" asked another of the advisors. "I somehow doubt Kachik will hand them over on request, and if we are to judge from what you're saying, he plans on moving quickly."

"If the humans should escape, reach a neutral territory, and request aid—legally, the Nativists would have no claim. The autonomous district could offer them refuge."

"And you propose no additional change to the advisement?" asked the yibo woman who Alba had initially assumed was in charge. There was a note of warning in her tone, and Alba glanced up at her sharply.

This woman, perhaps, wanted Alba's proposal to succeed. Knew that without additional political incentives, it would not.

"No," said Alba, keeping her eyes fixed forward. "I propose an additional amendment. I propose that, in consideration of the risk that you, my friends, are taking to provide refuge to my fellow humans, that each district that aids in the resettlement of the humans, and each district whose resources are used to provide the temporary site of the humans' autonomous district, gains voice in proportion to their aid in the regent advisorship that will hold the vote until it can be filled by a human."

She could practically feel Tika's gaze burning into her back.

Her proposal would effectively strip him of any advantage he would have gained from the human inhabitants of his district.

But it would spread the advantage much wider, and Alba had to hope that this would be enough to keep it alive.

The advisors looked at each other, and Alba tried desperately to read their expressions, or even the expression on the face of the yibo woman who seemed to want her success. But she could read nothing from their faces.

"Come forward with your discussion on the proposed amendment," said the Master of Readings at last.

The discussion went on for what seemed like hours, although Alba had no real idea, and her voice grew hoarse from answering questions. But at last, the questions died down.

"Come forward with your discussion, before the vote," said the Master of Readings. She glanced around the chamber. "Come forward," she said again, and at the silence, she nodded. "Very well. Present your votes."

As the votes appeared on the holoscreen in the centre of the room, Alba swallowed back the sour taste of sick in her throat.

Jair had been right—the support they'd won on the previous advisement from the counsellors on the anti-human faction had disappeared like dew on a hot summer morning.

If she hadn't convinced some of the moderates, they'd lost utterly.

She closed her eyes, unable to watch as the remainder of the votes were counted.

"Let the advisors note," the Master of Readings said at last. "The proposal, as amended by the human Alba, will be passed to the Synod for consideration."

Alba's eyes snapped open, and she had to grab for the rail, her legs suddenly too shaky to support her.

"And in the interim, the emergency measures proposed in the amended bill have also been accepted."

She breathed out a long sigh of relief, her heart pounding in her chest.

They'd won. They'd gambled, and they'd won, and if Savina and Reka could pull off their part in this, get the humans to neutral ground—they were safe.

She glanced back at Tika involuntarily.

He was still glaring at her, cold hate in his eyes, and she repressed a shiver.

Jair had been right in this, as well. She hadn't just orchestrated a victory.

She'd also made a very potent enemy.

25

Savina

"We have the ship," Savina hissed as she pulled herself up and strapped into the copilot's seat next to Reka. "What's the plan now?"

Reka glanced over at her, face tight with strain. "The plan *was*, we get out without being seen."

"Yes, well that plan clearly didn't work!" Savina snapped. "So what's the new plan?"

"Your guess is as good as mine," Reka muttered.

"Do you always do this?" Savina said through her teeth. "Just throw yourself into situations without thinking anything through, and hope you come out the other side?"

Reka gave a faint shrug. "It's worked for me in the past,"

Savina narrowed her eyes, and then another shot bounced off the ship's shields. She gritted her teeth. "How many of these shots can we take?"

Reka shrugged again. "I'm not an expert in yibo ships, but I'd say not many more."

It was absolutely infuriating how calm she sounded.

A voice came through both their wavelinks, sharp with panic.

"Savina? Reka? The yibo soldiers are here. They're not through our force field yet, but if they reached the controllers—"

It was the voice of the woman Reka had left in charge of the ex-prisoners.

Savina and Reka exchanged grim glances. Then Reka spun the ship, and they started towards the jungle at top speed, flying low.

It was only minutes before Savina could make out the portable force field through the canopy of the jungle. It was sparking with the yibo shots bouncing off of it, and from her vantage point, she could see the small fireworks of shots in response.

Reka's expression was grim as she tipped the nose of a ship down and fired a warning blast at the assembled yibo soldiers. They stared up at the ship, then backed away quickly, shooting from under the cover of what looked like their own portable forcefield as they ducked into the trees.

"We won't have much time once we get in there," Reka whispered. "I'll take some of the soldiers, and we'll hold the yibo off while you get everyone else into the ship."

Savina nodded, and the ship swooped down. Reka whispered something into her wavelink, and the force field flickered for a moment to let them in, then reformed around them.

"Go!" Reka hissed as the ship came to a steaming halt. She was on her feet almost before the ship had settled onto the ground. Savina unstrapped and pounded down the gangplank after her.

By the time she ducked outside, Reka was barking orders at a handful of soldiers. No one seemed interested in contesting her leadership at the moment, considering the alternative.

Savina glanced around quickly to where the rest of the rag-tag company was huddled against the far edge of the force field.

"Let's go," she hissed at them. "Stop bloody wasting time!"

The looks on their faces were unmitigated terror, but at her terse command, they started forward towards the ship. Savina could see Reka and her handful of soldiers from the corner of her eye. The woman was holding a steady, calculated defence, firing only when an enemy was close enough for the shots to count.

The yibo ships following them were hovering outside the force field by now, and as Savina herded the first of the survivors inside their ship, the first yibo ship fired. The entire force field sparked and buckled, and Savina swore. "Faster!" she snapped, shoving the panicking people towards the gangplank. "Get inside, get out of the way."

A movement from just behind her caught her eye—a man pushing a slight woman to the side to shove past her. Savina spun and grabbed his arm, jerking him off-balance. He stumbled, cursing, and made to grab for her.

She smiled at him, her pistol levelled at his forehead. "No one leaves until everyone is in. So best rethink your strategy."

He opened his mouth like he was going to protest.

"I shot one of you in the jungle, for less provocation than this," she said in a pleasant tone. "I won't lose a single night's sleep over making you my second. Wait your damn turn."

He shut his mouth and did as he was told.

Another shot from the yibo ships, and the forcefield flickered again.

"Savina—" came Reka's terse voice through the wavelength.

"I'm getting them in as fast as I can!" Savina snapped.

There were only maybe two or three dozen people left in the clearing, but that was two or three dozen too many—

Another shot.

The force field flickered again, a burst of multicoloured light crackling across it in geometric patterns—and died.

"Go! Go!" Savina shouted, shoving people towards the ship. Above her, she could see the yibo ship turning its guns towards the ground of the clearing.

"Go!" She grabbed a woman by the collar of her jacket and shoved her bodily up the gangplank.

The whine of a ship's gun powering up split the air, and she swore and dropped to the ground, rolling under the gangplank as the clearing exploded in light and noise.

When the noise and debris died down, she looked up carefully, peering out from under the gangplank.

Yibo ships' guns weren't the atomizer weapons the yibo used for their handheld guns, but they may as well have been. There had been half a dozen humans, perhaps, who'd been caught outside the ship, and Savina had to fight back the sick rising in her stomach at the sight, blood and torn flesh smeared across the blast radius.

Someone grabbed her by the arm, and she spun, drawing her pistol.

"Come! There's nothing we can do for them," snapped Reka, and she dragged Savina out from under the gangplank and onto the ship.

Savina shook herself out of her shock enough to hit the controls to close the hatch behind them, and then the ship jerked and shot forwards and upwards.

"Where are we going, Savina?" hissed Reka.

Savina swallowed down vomit and opened her wavelink, scanning through for the information Alba had sent her. "We'd better damn well hope your precious Chief Justice does what she said she'll do," she muttered. "Because if she doesn't, every last one of us is going to be space dust."

26

Aran

The point in space that Istvay's coordinates had indicated looked exactly as Aran had expected it to: three planets formed an abbreviated triangle in the distance, their tiny moon circling them like satellites.

And in the centre, only visible on the ship's screens, was another ship, the size and shape of which had been burned into his mind that day a few weeks ago when he and Istvay had first met Sharda and her crew, and the raiders had promptly tried to eat the two of them.

Krevai, beside him in the massive cockpit, was grinning down at the screen. "Dessi. I was skeptical. But it looks like your suggestion had merit. The other ships seem to have liked our offer—look, they're hanging back."

The captain was right. Around the outskirts of the moon nearest Sharda's ship, at least half a dozen other raider ships were gathered, but none of them made the effort to come closer.

Dessi gave him a smug look. "See? It wasn't just to keep the humans alive."

"It was mostly to keep the humans alive." Krevai glowered at her, but there was amusement in his expression.

She glowered back. "Maybe I also didn't want you shoved into the middle of a fight where you're outnumbered ten to one. You're bad enough, but none of the other raider captains have even the slightest appreciation of science. I'd prefer you didn't die."

Krevai's smile softened. "Ah, Dessi. Here you are getting sentimental."

"I'm not getting sentimental," Dessi snapped.

His smile widened. "Well, if it makes you feel any better, I have no intention of dying. So it's a good thing Sharda doesn't stand a chance against us, then, isn't it?"

"I'm going to page the ships, Captain, see what they want," said Landru. She was grinning broadly. "I can't say I like our odds if they plan to stand with Sharda, but it'll be a hell of a fight."

Krevai's grin in return was vicious.

Landru hit the general ship line. "Krevai's ship, paging the captains Venti, Xonda, and Ikta. If you've decided to throw in your lot with Sharda, this is your warning. Krevai's not asking for a declaration of loyalty. He's just reminding you that you don't need yibo permission or yibo alliances, and that there are yibo settlements that have been getting a little too self-confident. And if you were to find something else to do while Krevai and Sharda fight, you won't be on the wrong side of the victor." She hit the channel off.

A moment later, it crackled on again. "Xonda's ship, paging Captain Krevai," said the voice. "I speak for the rest of the crews here. We've decided to sit this battle out. The captain who wins is the one who gets our loyalty. Word got out that the yibo have been sending out spies, not holding to their bargain with Sharda. We don't disagree with Krevai that they could learn a lesson."

Aran's head jerked up, his heart suddenly beating faster.

"This is your Istvay's doing, isn't it?" Krevai whispered to Aran. He was grinning. "I can see why you like them—crafty little bastard, aren't they?" He paused. "So. Are your ready for this?"

Aran gritted his teeth. But he didn't exactly have the option to not be ready at this point.

"Just … keep an eye out for Istvay," he whispered back. "They're going to try to get off Sharda's ship and make it back here."

Krevai nodded, and Aran blew out a short, quick breath.

Istvay was smart. They'd figure out a way to signal that it was them. Somehow.

He'd just have to trust them.

"Do we have Krevai's word that he'll respect the terms?" the other ship continued. "No retaliation for our sitting out, and no attacks on our ships without warning?"

Landru glanced at Krevai. Krevai nodded, still grinning.

"Your terms are accepted," Landru said back through the line.

Krevai leaned over and hit the communicator controls. "Alright, Sharda," he said, his voice thick with a mixture of glee and vicious anticipation. "Your proposal might have saved you some enemies. But it's not bought you allies, not yet."

"You think I need someone to fight my battles for me?" Sharda's cold voice through the ship's line sent a quick, unconscious shiver up Aran's back. "I bargained with the yibo to buy myself time, and it has, even if my little human going behind my back made it less time than I planned. My crew will feast on human flesh when we've dealt with you, and those who've helped me will be rewarded. But you're mistaken if you thought I'd need help killing you."

Almost before she finished speaking, a swarm of attack pods popped into view on the ship's screen, clustered around the outside of Sharda's ship, like wasps around a hive that had been hit with a stick.

Krevai hit the internal communicator lines. "Attack pods out!" he snapped. "First wave out, second wave ready. If a pod is struck, send in a replacement immediately. Let's test them first, find out what her plan is. I'm sure she's set a trap, she's been here long enough she's picking the terms of the engagement. But we'll see if we can't turn the tables in our favour after all." There was a maniacal grin on his face.

Sharda's attack pods were streaming towards them, but Krevai's pods flung themselves out the ship's bay doors to meet them. Within a moment, it was a messy dogfight, pods spinning and blasting, engaging each other with the ferocity of battling wood-bulls.

And then a second squadron of Krevai's attack pods emerged from the small moon behind Sharda's position, and her ships spun to meet their new attackers.

"Send in the third squadron!" Krevai shouted, and another group of ships went tumbling out the bay doors to join in the fight.

More pods threw themselves into the fight from the direction of Sharda ship as well, but within a few minutes, it was obvious even to Aran's untrained eyes that Krevai's pods were gaining the upper hand.

Then an ear-shattering alarm wailed out across the ship, and Aran clasped his hands to his ears reflexively. Krevai leapt to his feet, cursing. "Boarders!" he shouted.

He yanked out his pistol and ducked out of the cockpit, starting down the hallway at a run. Aran, gritting his teeth against the noise, pulled out his own pistol and followed.

By the time he reached the main deck, it was a jumble of battling raiders. The boarding party consisted of what looked like fifty of Sharda's crew, and they were now fighting a pitched battle on the deck.

The alarms wailed, raiders screamed and shouted, weapon-fire blasted out. Ani, hissing like a teakettle, leapt at the first raider who came for Aran, clamping down on the nape of their neck. They dropped, green spittle foaming from the corners of their mouth, and Ani leapt off, spreading her skin flaps and soaring across the room to her next victim.

The sound of the ship's boarder alarms pounded through Aran's head like an ice-axe, and twice he almost dropped his pistol, the screeching, disorienting sound loosening his grip unconsciously. Krevai glanced up at him in the midst of snapping someone's neck, let the limp body fall, and slapped the wall of the corridor. "Turn the alarms off, dammit! We all know there's borders!" He turned, bellowing across the open floor filled with struggling raiders, "Keep the noise down! Our Aran is in here!"

Aran wasn't entirely sure whether to laugh or groan, but Krevai's shouting had done the trick—the crews were still locked in a struggle across the open deck floor, but the cursing, at least on the part of Krevai's crew, was now done in harsh whispers, and every time one of Sharda's crew open their mouth to shout, they were likely to get pistol-whipped across the face.

Aran shook his head, then jumped back as someone grabbed for him. He ducked as a shot whispered over his head, slamming into the door behind him, and fired at his attacker, the shot sparking on their body armour. He twisted the settings on his pulse pistol and, as another raider started for him, shot the floor at his would-be attacker's feet. As it buckled under her, he brought the butt of his pistol down across the back of the woman's head, wincing at the *crunch* as it connected.

Ani was wreaking her own brand of havoc in one corner, but

keeping a worried, bulbous eye on Aran.

He jumped out of range of another raider's grasping claws, swinging the butt of his pistol down across their wrist in an awkward move that would almost certainly have made Istvay drop their head into their hands in exasperation. The raider readjusted their grip on their knife, grinning.

Then Ani landed on their head, her tentacles enveloping their face, and they dropped with a gargled scream.

Aran glanced around quickly.

Krevai was fighting three raiders at once, the combined force of them enough to push even him backwards. Aran raised his pistol and fired over their heads, and one of the attackers turned. They saw Aran, and started for him with an ugly grin. And then Krevai yanked out his own pistol and shot them full in the back.

They staggered as their body armour diffused the force, and Krevai stepped in, jerked the raider's head back, and slit their throat, shooting a wink at Aran over their head.

Aran turned away quickly as the hot blood spattered across the deck, swallowing back bile.

It was only then that he realized most of the boarding party were either dead, unconscious, or trying desperately to fight their way back to the ship's hangar bay. Krevai must have noticed the same thing, because he shouted, "Don't let them get away! If they're going to board us, they'll damn well stay on this ship!"

Krevai's crew leapt forward at his command, but a handful of the borders managed to get past them, running at full tilt towards the hangar bay. Krevai's crew took after them, but a moment later there was the *hiss* and whine of the airlock opening. Krevai cursed.

"Well, at least at least we took a tax," he said, glancing around the bloody deck. He turned to Aran, grinning. "You and your Ani are quite the warriors."

Aran sighed, and didn't even try to answer.

It didn't take long for the crew to clear the deck—a task which consisted, apparently, of grabbing the dead by whatever body part was more or less intact and tossing them into a pile, then hosing down the deck with some chemical mix that stung Aran's nose and burned his eyes and foamed up around the blood stains, leaving nothing but white powder in its wake, which was then sucked up by the cleaning drones.

"Keeps the decks from getting too slippery," said Krevai, noticing Aran's gaze.

The last of the cleaning drones was just finishing up, and Krevai had turned to go back to the cockpit, when Landru's voice came through the communicator. "Captain We've got an incoming message from Sharda."

"Put her through" said Krevai brusquely.

A moment later, they heard Sharda's voice.

"Congratulations, Krevai," she said. "Your attack pod pilots are good at what they do. And your crew—my boarding party was repelled quickly. But before you decide to declare victory, you should know that they took something with them when they left."

There was a pause. Then a voice that Aran recognized all too well came through the communicator. "Captain! Don't listen to her, it's a trap, don't try to—" He could hear the terror in Dessi's tone.

The sound cut off.

Aran glanced at Krevai. The captain's face had gone ashen, and he put out a hand to steady himself against the wall. "What have you done to my scientist?" he asked, his voice hoarse.

Sharda laughed, a soft, vicious sound. "I haven't done anything to your scientist yet. Your peaceful little scientist, who doesn't know how to wield a weapon. She talks very brave, but she's terrified. I can see her shaking. And then there's your other former crew, the human. They swore allegiance to me, but they've been going behind my back. So I thought it would be only just to kill Dessi and the human together. Since I know she loves humans, and she's the one who found them in the first place."

Aran stared, something sick congealing in the pit of his stomach.

"If you kill Dessi—" Krevai began. He sounded sick.

"I don't have to. You can save her, if you want. I can send a ship over, pick up you and your human pet. You can trade yourselves for your scientist and my human, give up the leadership war and let me slit your throat. Your crew will leave unharmed, and I'll release Dessi. Or you can watch over the general line as I kill them and feed them to my crew. Your choice, Krevai."

The line went dead.

27

Alba

Alba was almost giddy with relief as she made her way back to the public transport, her hands shaky, her legs trembling.

The Hierophants still had to consider the measure, but it was almost unbelievable that they'd made it this far.

But—she couldn't shake the tendril of unease that twisted up under her relief, the memory of the burning hatred in Tika's face when he realized she'd betrayed him.

She still felt a small sting of guilt at the thought, and the unconscious reaction was jarring. Here she was, powerless, a refugee, someone who Tika had made clear his interest did not cover, feeling guilty for having somehow betrayed his trust.

Her mind flitted back, involuntarily, to Ines, the way she'd always seemed to look to Alba for approval, although Alba was probably the one person in the system who'd caused her the most harm.

We're always trained to sympathize with those who hurt us, she thought, and winced at the discomfort of the realization.

She sighed. She had larger problems to worry about at the moment than moral philosophy.

Yosip and Feliu were waiting for her when the transport stopped a street down from the refugee housing.

"Madam?" asked Feliu, stepping forward to help her down. "How did it go?"

She took a deep breath. "They're going to put it to the Synod, and they've agreed to pass the emergency measures."

There was a moment of silence.

Then Feliu's face broke into a broad grin. "Well done, Madam!"

"It certainly wasn't me," she said sharply. "They were willing to consider it because of the hours of preparation you and the others put into it. I was simply the messenger." She raised her hand as he opened his mouth. "Please do not, Feliu. Modesty doesn't suit you, and I am telling no more or less than the truth."

He sighed, shaking his head, and she was once again struck with an overwhelming rush of fondness.

"Jair will join us later today, once he's off duty," said Yosip. "He'll want to know all the details. But you say they accepted it?"

Alba nodded. "They seemed amenable to my suggestion. They voted to go forward with a temporary measure, at least, to provide accommodations for the refugees. But—" she broke off. She wasn't exactly sure how to express her unease.

Yosip watched her, his expression more perceptive than she might have wished, but he didn't say anything, just nodded. "Why don't you get some rest?" he said softly. "We can't do anything until Jair gets here, and you were up early. This will be easier if we come at it with clear minds."

Alba gave a weary nod and made her way to the small, narrow quarters the group of them shared.

When she reached it, the door was standing ajar.

She frowned.

Probably someone had simply forgotten to close it behind them. Still …

Shoving aside her feeling of unease, she pushed the door open and stepped through.

Then she stopped dead.

The rooms had been completely destroyed. The beds were knocked over, mattresses slit. The few belongings she and the others still had, after the horrors of the past few weeks, and the few modest possessions the yibo had given them on charity were smashed on the floor. An outside window had been forced, and it swung open loosely in the breeze.

For a moment, Alba couldn't breathe. She felt as if she were watching herself from far away, as if the sick, overwhelming terror winding around her, choking her, freezing her in place like a small animal caught in the beam of a moving transport, was something happening to someone else.

She realized, in an odd, hazy sort of way, that she was going to be sick.

She backed out of the room, closing the door firmly behind her, and stumbled to the communal bathrooms, kneeling over the toilet and vomiting until her stomach was empty. She could feel the ghost of hands around her throat, the desperate panic of her lungs unable to pull in air. Watching the bloodstain, absurdly red, spread across her white yibo tunic from the person she'd shot.

She tried to steady her breathing.

It was a memory, that was all. Just a memory. No one had tried to kill her just now, despite the chaos of her room. Despite the hatred in Tika's gaze as she betrayed him.

But, some cold, logical part of her mind said it could happen again. It could very, very easily happen again.

She had no power here. She had no friends, except a handful of ragged political refugees and a human aide-de-camp who was at least halfway suspicious still of her motives and means. At least in Kachik's city, as dangerous as it had been, it had been in the yibos' best interest to maintain a showing of impartiality. To get her on their side.

Here, she was nothing.

Her mind flitted to the look on Istvay's face when they'd talked about their friend dying in prison, when she'd given them that sanctimonious, self-righteous answer.

Was this how they'd felt? Powerless and terrified and alone, unable to stop what was coming? Unable, no matter how much they shouted, to make their voice heard, because those who could change things either refused to listen, or didn't wish to believe them?

She took a long, shaky breath, then pushed herself to her feet. She paused for a moment before stepping into the hallway, then forced herself to move forward.

Yosip and Feliu both frowned at her as she came back into the main room. "Alba?" asked Yosip. "I thought you were going to—" He broke off abruptly.

Feliu stood quickly, his face tight with worry. "What happened? Are you hurt? Did someone—"

She shook her head. "No one's hurt, Feliu," she said. "But we may need to request another place to sleep for the night."

When Jair arrived later that afternoon, he must have already gotten word. His expression was thick with concern, his face drawn with worry. "No one was injured?" he asked, as he sat down at the table beside them.

Alba shook her head. "No one was injured."

She knew as well as he did how easily that answer could have been different. Had there been anyone in the room, for example, when whoever it was had arrived, and had they deemed the secrecy of their mission, or at least plausible deniability, more important than the life of a nameless, politically unimportant human refugee.

Plausible deniability was probably the right term—whoever had ordered this done had made no effort to hide what they were doing, or why.

"Was it Tika?" she asked quietly.

Jair sighed. "Possibly. There won't be proof either way. And it hardly matters—you've made more than a few enemies. And you only have the voice they deigned to give you. You can hardly afford complaining of something you can't definitively prove."

Alba nodded. She still felt sick to her stomach, although at this point there was nothing left for her to throw up. She wasn't sure she'd been able to stop shaking since the … hour? Two hours? However long it had been previous, when she'd stepped through the door and seen the destruction.

"That's not what's important at the moment, though." She forced the words out. "What's important right now is, we've got the votes, I think. They agreed to accept the refugees."

Jair turned to stare at her. "You—you mean—" he began, a mixture of shock and disbelieving hope in his voice.

And then he frowned, glancing down at his communicator, and she could see his posture stiffen.

"What is it?" she asked sharply, too worried to modulate her tone.

"I don't know," he said, his voice tense. "But I'm being called back to my post." He paused, still frowning down at the communicator. "And I've been asked to escort you back to the advisory chambers."

Alba's stomach dropped. "Right now? It's night. They'll all have gone home—"

He looked up, his expression grim. "This is an emergency meeting. All the advisors are being called back. As to why they want you, specifically—"

He didn't finish the sentence. But she could tell that he didn't believe it was good news.

Nor did she.

They left a few minutes later—only as long as it took for Alba to retrieve her handbag and re-lace her worn shoes. Jair walked ahead of her, his posture alert, his bearing military-straight. As they approached the political hall, his posture tightened further, the muscles in his shoulders stiffening. "There are more soldiers around the building than there should be."

Alba frowned and glanced around.

He was right. There were always soldiers posted at the gate, but there were significantly more tonight, and there were expressions on their faces that sent a sharp unease through her.

"Do you have any idea what this is?" she asked him.

Jair shook his head. "I'm sure I'll be briefed when I get in. But whatever it is, they're not willing to tell me over the communicator. If I had to guess, it looks like they're preparing for something."

Alba's frown deepened. "Surely they haven't declared war on Kachik."

Jair shrugged, but his expression was tight. "I doubt it," he said in a low voice. "No one wants a civil war. But as to what else it might be—"

Alba nodded, and, trying to keep her unease from showing, stepped forward into the building.

Getting past the security took longer than usual, and when she finally reached the advisory chamber, the entire building was an uproar. No one seemed willing to pay her the slightest bit of attention, and for a few minutes she stood near the back, watching the chaos.

At last, grudgingly, one of the aides approached her and beckoned her forwards.

"What's happened?" she asked, but he shook his head.

"You'll find out in a minute. They're calling the meeting to order, and you need to be in your seat."

Alba looked out over the rows upon rows of faces, which had become far more familiar to her than she'd ever expected would be possible in such a short time.

Still, there was nothing like the prospect of the murder of several hundred of one's fellow humans to burn faces into one's memory.

"Silence!" The Master of Reading's voice echoed through the chamber, and the chatter died down quickly.

Alba was not the only one, apparently, who was waiting to find out what exactly had happened.

"You have been called here today, advisors, because the Synod has asked that we reconvene. Something has come up that requires all of our attention."

There was silence in the room as the woman brought up her holoscreen in the centre of the room. The image fuzzed for a moment, then settled into a picture of Kachik's face.

And Alba recognized, with a sinking in her gut, his expression—one of calculating triumph. As if he'd been playing a long game, and now that he was certain he'd won, he could finally show his hand.

"You, the Synod, have been antagonizing me and the people who follow me for far too long," he said, his voice bland and matter-of-fact. "We do not want war. We have only ever asked for safety—

safety from the rapacious human culture that threatens to destroy us from within, strip us of everything we hold dear. But you have chased us out of your cities. You have refused to listen to our reasonable demands. You provided shelter to political saboteurs. And more than that—recently, you sent operatives to steal the humans that belong to me by the laws of hospitality." His voice was rising now, taking on a theatrical note of righteous anger. "I have been more than patient. But this is a clear act of aggression that I can no longer countenance. The ship your operatives stole is currently headed toward your planet. If you allow that ship to dock, I will take that as a declaration of war."

He smiled, and the sight sent a shiver down Alba's back. "You may think you have the means to win a war against me and my people. But I have allies. As part of our negotiations, I promised them the humans. And if they see you take what is rightfully theirs— believe me that they will not let it pass uncontested. So, advisors to the Synod, ask yourselves: are you ready to go to war with the raiders?"

He moved to one side, and the figure standing behind him, a vague blur in the background, resolved into a sickeningly familiar shape—tall, humanoid, with ice-pale skin, black hair hanging down below their knees, blood-red eyes and fangs poking from a vicious smile.

A raider, in the flesh.

The recording clicked off.

There was a stunned, horrified silence throughout the room.

"We are not equipped to go to war against the raiders," said the Master of Readings quietly. "I have spoken with the military, and Kachik's insinuation of government operatives in his territory is incorrect. But he seems to believe it, at any rate. Therefore, I suggest we rescind our previous vote regarding the human refugees. I suggest that if the humans attempt to land, we inform them we're willing to fire on them, or else give Kachik our assurances that they will be detained until he can send people to retrieve them. This is a matter of our very survival."

28

Savina

The ship burst through the atmosphere, and Savina sucked in a breath and fought back nausea, despite the fact that the grav stabilizers in the yibo ships were better than anything she'd experienced back in the Joias system.

"Coordinates," Reka snapped. "We're not going to be able to take many yibo hits, but if Alba's found us a safe place to land—there's a chance we'll make it."

Savina nodded, blinking to send the coordinates through to Reka, and Reka released the controls with one hand to pull up a holomap, clearly trying to get her bearings from the coordinates Savina had sent through to her retinal screen.

"You focus on flying. I'll get us there," said Savina sharply, turning to the control panel. This wasn't her specialty, but she'd worked with Beni long enough to understand the basics, and it only took her a moment to set the coordinates into the ship controls.

Reka glanced over with a terse nod of thanks, and turned to her screen.

Then she swore, her voice tight. "We're never going to make that, not as close as these yibo ships are. Call Alba. If they're going to offer us asylum, we need some protection getting in."

Savina hit her wavelink.

It only buzzed for a moment before Alba's voice answered.

"Listen," Savina snapped, not letting the woman speak. "We're on our way. The yibo's military ships are after us, though. We need an escort, or we won't make it. Can you get something—"

"Savina." Alba's voice wasn't loud, but something about the tone of it stopped Savina dead. "I'm sorry. I—I'm afraid I was unable to do what I promised. There's no safety for you here. If you get them here, you'll just be handed straight back to Kachik. I'm … sorry."

Savina stared blankly at her retinal screen.

"What is it?" Reka hissed.

Savina didn't say anything, just tapped the line open. She wasn't sure she could have spoken if she'd wanted to.

"Savina? Do you hear me?" Alba's voice was sharp with despair, but it still bore a trace of its usual arrogance. "Do not bring them here. If you bring them here, you'll either be shot down, or taken into custody. I'm sorry. I've done everything I can, but—" her voice choked off.

Savina wondered, distantly, how many people in the system had heard the Chief Justice cry.

Reka's face had gone slack with horror. "Madam Chief Justice—" she began. And then she stopped, shaking her head. "Understood," she said quietly.

Around them, Kachik's ships were catching up, settling into attack formation.

"What do we do now?" Reka sounded as if she were talking to herself, and Savina didn't bother answering.

There was nothing they could do, except die.

Someone was pounding on the door to the cockpit. "What's happening? The yibo ships are almost on us. What are you going to do?"

Reka glanced at the control screen, then cursed and yanked down on the controls. A shot hummed past them, and then another impacted against the ship, and the entire thing shook.

"We have a few minutes, at best." There was a flat, despairing finality to Reka's tone.

Savina glanced over at her, something tightening in her throat.

Reka had closed her eyes, slumping back in the pilot seat, and for the first time, Savina could see the heavy weariness in her posture. "I'm sorry," she said, without opening her eyes. "I brought us here." She took a deep breath and straightened with a visible effort. She opened her eyes again, her usual air of no-nonsense responsibility draping over her again like a cloak.

"Alright," she said briskly. "I'm almost sure the raiders Kachik is negotiating with belong to Sharda—her raiders have been trading with the city for some time, so it wouldn't be a stretch. And Sharda's the one I negotiated with … before. In the city." She had the grace to look mildly embarrassed as she said it. "I may be able to get her to talk to me."

Savina frowned at Reka. "You think you can talk a raider out of eating humans? You either know a hell of a lot more about raiders than I do, or a hell of a lot less."

Reka gave her an amused smile. "No. I couldn't do that. I have nothing to offer them. What I can do—" she leaned forward, her sharp gaze catching Savina's and holding it. "What I can do is tell her I'm willing to negotiate. Tell her I can get her the humans without a fight. She's not going to shoot the ship down if it's full of her dinner."

Savina stared at her in shock. "You'd give up the humans?"

Reka gave her that bleak, dangerous smile. "No," she said. "As I think you mentioned not too long ago, there's really no use for honour when it's a choice between that and allowing innocents to die. I'll go in to negotiate with them. And while I'm negotiating—" she shrugged. "You'll take the ship, and you'll get these people the hell out of here."

Savina blinked at Reka. "You'd call a parlay, and then have me break it?"

"I hardly expected you to lecture me on morality," said Reka coolly, raising an eyebrow.

Savina scowled, her heart beating faster than it should have. "This isn't about morality," she snapped. "This is about what the raiders are going to do to you when they see I've taken off with the ship."

Reka's smile this time was a little wider, and the humour in it a little more genuine. "Savina. You do care."

Savina scowled reflexively. "I do not!"

The truth was, it was a lie. Reka could see it, and Savina didn't even have the bare cover of a valid excuse.

It wasn't bloody fair. It wasn't fair that this should happen now. There had always been exactly two people in the system she cared enough to risk her life for: Beni, and Nicolau. And Nicolau had been more of a concept than a person, a vague, faded, rosy memory of a five-year-old, laughing in the small front yard of a farmer's cottage.

And now—

Now Beni was gone, hopefully somewhere safe, with Joska and Rafel, who, Savina knew without having to think about it, would protect her sibling with as much care as she herself would. Nicolau was all grown up, a young, stupid, idealistic boy who thought he was a man, who disobeyed, and fell in love, and risked his own life to save Savina. To save the system.

And Reka Soler was only the latest in a long, long list of people Savina had risked her life to protect.

She swore under her breath.

It wasn't bloody fair.

The pounding came at the door again. "Open the door! We need to know what you're—"

Savina scowled and jumped to her feet. "Don't do a damn thing before I get back," she snapped at Reka. "Not a damn thing, or I swear I'll shoot you."

She stepped to the door and shoved it open, opening her mouth to snap a rebuke—and then something smashed into her temple, sending lights sparking in her vision.

She staggered backwards, dazed by both the blow, and the unexpectedness of it, and before she had time to recover, someone grabbed her, yanking her arms behind her back and securing her hands. She opened her mouth to shout, but her attacker—a grim-faced woman she recognized as one of Cavaco's soldiers—slapped her across the face. "Shut up!"

Another soldier was holding Reka, although two soldiers lay motionless at her feet beside her fallen pistol, probably dead. Reka had clearly been taken by surprise as well, but she'd always been good at this sort of thing. Five other soldiers stood back, weapons drawn and pointed at Savina and Reka.

The soldier who seemed to be the ringleader stepped to the communications line. "Calling Kachik's ships," he said loudly. "Calling Kachik's ships. We surrender. Repeat, we surrender. We have taken the ship, and we are willing to trade the remainder of our company for safe passage."

Savina stared.

She'd thought, once, that she couldn't feel any sicker at what was happening.

She realized, distantly, that she'd been wrong.

Reka's face was bruised, blood trickling from a split lip, a sharp bruise in the shape of a fist across her cheekbone, but she hardly seemed to notice the injuries. Her face was as shocked and horrified asd Savina's.

"We surrender! We will give up the remainder of the humans in exchange for safe passage. Please acknowledge."

And then the line crackled, and an accented yibo voice came through. "We accept your surrender. Turn over the prisoners, and we will grant you safe passage."

The soldiers looked at each other and laughed in giddy relief, grinning at each other like schoolchildren.

And Savina and Reka could only watch in horror as their captors dragged them from the cockpit.

29

Aran

Aran sucked in a quick breath, fighting back panic. He'd almost lost Istvay too many times, he couldn't do this again. He couldn't, he couldn't handle seeing his friend in danger one more time—

Krevai, standing across from him, looked hardly better than he did. "If it was anyone other than our little Dessi …" he began. His voice was more broken than Aran had ever heard it. "She doesn't know how to fight, she's practically a vegetarian. And I told her she'd be safe here. That's the only reason she agreed to come along, she would have stayed back at the research station. I promised her."

He looked old. Shaken.

The rest of the crew were watching, their faces tense.

"We can tell Sharda we'll destroy the rest of her attack pods if she doesn't give our scientist back," ventured one of the crew.

Krevai shook his head. "She'll never agree to that. She knows what she has. Even if I were willing to sacrifice Dessi, the other crews will be watching over the general channel. If I let Sharda kill someone who's specifically under my protection, they'll know exactly what my protection is worth. They'd be all over us like space lice. It would be the end of my reputation, and without that to protect us, the end of our crew."

"Captain," said Landru, stepping forward. "I know how long you and Dessi have been friends. But if you give yourself up, Dessi will die anyway. Even if Sharda keeps her word and lets Dessi free, your name won't be able to keep her safe any longer. And you know how many of the younger captains would be happy to murder her and take the mountain for their own reputation."

Krevai gave her a weary smile. "Landru. Everyone knows you're my next in line, and you'll make an excellent captain. If I let Sharda slit my throat, she, at least, will be sworn to leave your crew in peace. I have every confidence that you'll build your reputation even higher than mine, after a few raids."

"Captain, you can't—" Landru broke off, her voice rough with what sounded suspiciously like tears.

Krevai's smile broadened, just a little, and he glanced over at Aran. "Come now. If our little human is so willing to die for his friend, a raider captain can hardly do otherwise."

Aran felt sick to his stomach.

Ani tugged on his trouser leg with a tentacle, and he reached out automatically, picking her up. Something scraped his arm as he lifted her, and he glanced down, pulling out a small sliver of metal that had caught in one of her tentacle spikes.

And then he let go of her so abruptly that she gave a little squawk of irritation and grabbed for his shoulder to keep her balance.

"Krevai," Aran said, turning slowly. "I assume when we go, Sharda will make sure there's no way we can fight our way out?"

Krevai nodded. "She'll insist we're unarmed. We could certainly try—it's what I plan to do, at least, go down in battle—but she'll be expecting that. Her people will have weapons, and they'll be waiting for us. We'll last a fraction of a cycle, no more. I may be able to kill one or two before I go down. You, likely fewer. If you had your Ani, I've no doubt you could make more of a stand than I could, but I'm sure she'll consider your Ani a weapon."

Aran nodded, his stomach tight with something that was either excitement, or terror. "But here's the thing about Ani," he said, keeping his voice low. "She can survive in space. She's done it before, held onto the outside of a spacecraft."

The thought of putting Ani in danger, no matter how well-equipped she was for it, made him ill.

But she'd survived on the outside of the diplomatic ship as it was breaking up. A short flight on an attack pod was hardly more dangerous than that. And the alternative was to watch Istvay die, because he'd noticed the conspicuous absence of Istvay's release in the list of concessions Sharda had agreed to if Krevai turned himself over.

Krevai was watching Aran consideringly, his face slowly turning up into a grin. "And they won't be checking the outside of the ship that brings us, because why would they? Do you think your Ani will listen to you if you ask her to do this?"

Aran swallowed, trying to fight back the panic.

This was for Istvay. He could do this, just like he'd done every other damn thing so far in this mission.

If it meant keeping Istvay alive, he could do it.

"I—I think she would," he said. "And once we get in—"

Now Krevai's grin was spread across his entire face. "And once we get in," he said, "I think, Aran, that our friend Sharda won't know what hit her."

"Ani," Aran whispered. "Listen, sweetheart, I—I need you to do something for me." His voice broke a little on the words.

He hated the thought of not having Ani with him. He hated the thought of potentially putting her in danger. She could survive out in space, he'd seen it, and she hadn't seemed to suffer any ill effects last time. But still, the lingering fear of what might happen was enough to make him sick to his stomach.

He'd lost one of his best friends. He didn't think he'd survive losing the other. But this was their only possible chance of saving Istvay, and the alternative was unthinkable. So in the end, it wasn't really a choice.

Ani gave one of her friendly, curious little chirrups, the sound she made when she was trying to cheer him up.

He smiled, blinking back tears. "Listen, sweetheart," he whispered. "I'm going to hand you to Landru. She'll hold you while I get on the ship, and I need you not to kill her, okay? And then she'll let you go, and I need you follow. I need you to hold onto the ship. Can you do that for me, sweetheart?"

Ani gave another small, reassuring chirp and twined herself lovingly around his arm. She probably didn't have any idea what he'd been trying to tell her, but as always, she didn't actually care. She just wanted him to feel better. To be alright.

"I just want you to be alright." He could still see the pain on Istvay's face as they'd said the words back on the diplomatic ship, the way their eyes had squeezed shut, their fists clenched, head tipped back.

He sighed.

He wished he'd had the words to tell them, back then, that being alright wasn't really about not having people trying to kill you.

Although that would probably help, honestly.

He closed his eyes again for moment and drew in a deep breath, rubbing Ani's head. Then he walked slowly over to Landru, who looked a bit like she was bracing herself to give her life for the cause.

"This is Landru, remember her?" he whispered to Ani, as she coiled herself tighter around his arm. "You know her, she's very nice. I—I need you to stay with her, just for a minute. I need you to stay with her until I call you, okay?"

Ani tightened her tentacles stubbornly around his arm.

He smiled, rubbing her head again. "I'm sorry sweetheart," he whispered. "If there were any other way—"

At last, reluctantly, Ani unclamped her tentacles from his arm and allowed him to pass her to the raider woman, who looked as if she weren't sure she'd survive the next five seconds. But Ani didn't try to spike her or spit acid, just huddled in a sulky lump in her arms.

Aran breathed out a sigh of relief. He hadn't been exactly sure how this would go, but step one seemed to have been a success.

He glanced down at Ani, swallowing back the lump in his throat. She would be fine.

The thing was, she didn't actually need him. She could take care of herself perfectly well. She wasn't here because she needed him in order to survive. She was here because she loved him.

Just like, he'd discovered, he didn't need Istvay in order to survive. He just … didn't want to keep surviving without them.

He stroked her tentacles one last time. "Alright, sweetheart," he whispered. "Just for a minute."

Krevai stood near the opening to the airlock chamber, his posture tense.

"Permission to board?" The raider's voice through the communication line was smug.

Krevai glanced around the deck, his expression grim. "You know what to do," he said in a low voice to the assembled crew. "I'll signal you from Sharda's ship the moment I'm able. When I do, send everyone you can spare. If you don't hear from me within the next quarter cycle—" he turned to Landru. "The ship is yours. And if Sharda tries anything at all, I expect you to knock her out of the sky."

"Yes, Captain." Her voice was unusually grave.

Krevai tapped his communicator. "Permission granted."

Someone hit the airlock controls, and the airlock doors yawned open, exposing the black of space on the other side of the plex bay windows.

Aran had to bite back a sudden surge of terror.

He hadn't thought this through. He'd be getting on a ship with people who wanted to kill him and blasting off into space, without even the comfort of Ani's presence …

He took a deep breath.

He could do this. He knew how to do this.

The airlock doors slid closed, and the plex dividers pulled back to reveal Sharda's attack pod, settled like a tumour, small and malignant, on the floor of the bay. Three of Sharda's crew disembarked cautiously, weapons drawn.

"Any tricks, and your Dessi and your human die," the leader of them called out as they stepped down.

"We're unarmed," Krevai called back. "I've instructed my crew not to fire."

Sharda's raiders were on the floor of the bay now, huddled close to the shelter of their ship. "Tell the ones that are armed to back off," the leader called, and Krevai gestured with his chin.

The rest of the crew backed away, leaving Krevai and Aran alone in the centre of the floor.

"And the human's … whatever the hell that thing is?" the leader asked warily.

Aran gestured to Ani, huddled miserably in Landru's arms. It wasn't entirely clear which of the two of them was more unhappy with the arrangement.

The raider nodded brusquely and jerked his head. The other two came forward and patted Krevai and Aran down for weapons. Then they clipped restraints onto their wrists and shoved them forward into the ship.

Aran turned over his shoulder as he stepped from the gangplank into the ship, to where Ani's anxious eyes tracked him. "Ani, follow," he mouthed, making a quick motion with one bound hand.

Her entire body perked up in enthusiasm. Then his captors shoved him around the corner, and there was the *hiss* of the hatch closing behind them.

Krevai shot him a glance, and he gave a small nod.

He'd done all he could. Now they'd have to hope like hell that Ani understood what they needed. Because they'd gambled their lives and the lives of the two on Sharda's ship that this would work.

30

Alba

Alba made her way out of the building and sank down on a bench outside.

Her head was spinning, and she felt sick and weak and oddly off-balance.

She'd heard the despair in Savina's tone, and in Reka's. They were going to die, within the next few hours, not only them, but every person who'd survived the breakup of the diplomatic ship.

She closed her eyes.

She'd done everything she could. Out here, in this system, she wasn't a politician. She wasn't anything. She was a powerless refugee, with no voice, no influence.

She could still hear the desperation in Savina's tone—an assassin, yes, but just as far out of her element as Alba was. And still, for whatever unknown reason, risking her life to save the refugees.

Alba swore, bitterly, then managed a bleak smile at how shocked her clerks back in do Sol would be to hear it.

The worst of it was, she could hardly blame the yibo advisors. Their duties were to their constituents, not to her. Not to any of them.

She dropped her head into her hands.

If she were in their shoes ...

She gritted her teeth and lifted her head.

No, dammit. If she were in their shoes, she wouldn't sit by and let this happen. Maybe she'd made mistakes, more than she really liked to think about. Maybe she'd hurt people she'd never intended to hurt, maybe she'd caused tremendous harm through her mix of ignorance and hubris. But she hadn't been lying when she'd told Yosip why she'd gone into government. She may have made a thorough mess of things, and she knew very well that good intentions were not enough to redeem anyone. But she'd always *tried*.

She'd never have agreed to leave innocent people to die, on purpose, merely because she didn't want to stand up to a would-be dictator.

And then, from the back corner of her mind, she remembered the older yibo woman who had, it appeared, been prompting her when she'd presented her proposed amendment.

As if she, too, wanted the amendment to succeed.

Alba frowned.

That had been before Alba had begun enumerating the benefits of her proposal. Before the woman would have known whether it would benefit her district in any way. And it could have been that she'd simply hoped Alba would introduce some benefit she could take advantage of, but ...

She pictured the simple, beautifully carved edges to the old buildings in the city here, her sudden, whimsical thought of the similarities between their species.

Humans could be crass, and greedy, and self-centred, and arrogant. She'd been all of those things herself, more often than she probably wanted to admit. And she'd seen first-hand that yibo could be the same.

But she'd also seen a yibo grandmother hold the hand of an indigent stranger to teach her how to work embroidery, and keep her from embarrassment. She'd heard Aran Romeu speak of a yibo scientist who, Alba now realized, had risked her life to give him information on the cure to the genetic disease, because she saw it was important to him.

She took a deep breath and closed her eyes, thinking back to the meeting.

She hadn't been consciously paying attention to the faces around her, too stunned by the horrific news, but she was so used to taking stock of votes and potential votes that she knew she'd been doing it in some corner of her unconscious mind.

It hadn't been everyone who'd voted against taking in the humans. There had been a handful—a small handful, admittedly—who'd voted against pacifying Kachik. And there had been another handful who had hesitated before passing their vote.

At last, she stood, straightening her robes. She glanced around, squared her shoulders, and started back towards the halls of the building gone frantic with panic.

She made it back inside, and pushed through the crowds of panicked yibo until one of the guards grabbed her roughly and hissed, "What are you doing?"

She drew herself up to her full, height—much more impressive among the yibo then it had been among humans—and snapped, "I am trying to get through to Advisor Tika. So if you would be so kind as to let me pass—"

At first, she thought he might not. But there must have been something in her expression or her tone of voice left over from her days as one of the three highest-ranking individuals in the Joias System, because at last, reluctantly, he stepped aside.

She was scanning frantically through her memory, trying to put names to the faces of the advisors who'd voted against abandoning the humans. Trying to remember the name of the older woman.

Karri. That was it. Advisor Karri. And she was fairly sure she knew where the yibo woman's office was.

She paused outside the door, drawing a long breath, then she tapped on it sharply.

"Who is it?" The voice from inside was terse and impatient.

Alba wasn't sure, in fairness, that hers would be any different, under the circumstances.

"It's Alba Espina," she said. "The human woman who spoke in the meeting earlier. I'd like to speak with you."

For a long moment, no answer came, and Alba's chest tightened with the strain.

Perhaps she'd guessed wrong. After all, there was a long and tortuous road between an advisor being unwilling to actively turn humans over to someone intent on murdering them, and that same advisor being willing to put their life, or at least the lives of people in their district, on the line in support of that proposal.

"Come in," said the woman at last, and an entrance opened in front of Alba.

The woman sitting inside the office looked just as imposing in her private office as she had in the Advisory Chamber, her face set in a stern composure that was impressive, considering the circumstances.

"Advisor," Alba said brusquely. "I apologize that I have no time for pleasantries. But I noticed that you were one who disagreed with the others' decision to turn the humans over to Kachik in exchange for peace."

The woman nodded cautiously. "I know there's hardly room for idealism in a government such as this one, much as we may wish that were not the case. But—" she shook her head wryly. "It seems to me that perhaps there ought to be. I am sorry I wasn't able to influence the outcome."

"As am I," said Alba. "But I learned long ago that regret doesn't do nearly as much good as we wish it would. My friends will be killed if we do nothing, likely before I would have time to make it back to my apartment in the city. If you are willing, I would like to try to stop that from happening."

The woman watched Alba for a long moment. "You realize that we are not likely to succeed," she said at last.

Alba gave a short nod.

"And you realize that if we do not succeed, you will have burned through any political capital you might have accumulated."

"I hardly see what good political capital is if it does not allow me to save the lives of people who are looking to me to keep them from being slaughtered," Alba snapped.

"It's not just your political capital you'll burn, but mine, too," the woman said.

Alba hesitated a moment. At last, she said quietly, "I worked in politics, back in my home system. I was, by all measures, relatively successful. But I will tell you this: if there are things that I regret from that time—and I assure you, there are things I regret—the largest are those times when I had a chance to use the power I had been so carefully accumulating to stop an injustice, and, through ignorance or fear or worry about my position … I did not. Those are regrets that will follow me for the rest of my life. I don't know you. But from what I have seen, I suspect that if you choose to do nothing, you will look back on this with that same regret, and be just as unable as I am to assuage it. I would like to save you from that."

"Save me from that, perhaps," said the woman wryly. "But it seems to me your greater interest lies in saving your friends."

"I believe that in this case, those two aims may be the same."

The woman studied Alba for a long time.

At last, she sighed and nodded. "Perhaps you're right," she said. "Well then, if things are as dire as you suggest, we should get started."

31

Savina

Savina didn't try to fight, and nor did Reka. It seemed they'd both come to the same conclusion—there was no way out of the situation, at least not right now.

The soldiers dragged them along the corridors of the ship, then pulled open the hatch to what must have once been a storage space. Inside, the remainder of the company, those who weren't Cavaco's soldiers, were huddled in terrified clusters. A few of them turned to look as Savina and Reka were shoved inside. Their faces showed, for a moment, a brief spark of hope, and then, as they noticed the bindings on her and Reka's wrists, a sick hopelessness.

The soldiers stepped back out, locking the hatch behind them.

Savina took a deep breath, glancing around at the faces of the prisoners. She tried, very hard, not to see a reflection of Joska's face among them. Not to see Nicolau in the young crewmen who stood to one side, shaking with fear, or Beni in the tall individual in the corner, who wore the same sort of dark outfit and visible piercings her sibling seemed to prefer.

"I'm sorry," one of the men said, coming forward to where Reka and Savina stood. "We—we didn't see it coming. They grabbed us and locked us up before we had time to get off a warning."

Savina didn't bother to answer.

It hardly mattered—even before they'd been locked up, they'd been about to be blown to shreds by the yibo military ships. They'd been doomed before they started.

She'd been so close to death so many times in the past few days that it was hardly a shock anymore, just a sort of weary resignation.

A young man in the battered uniform of the diplomatic ship's crew peered at Savina, frowning. "Wait," he said. "I recognize you. Aren't you ..." He paused. "When the ship was breaking up, I swear I saw someone grab my friend and drag him off. I didn't see him afterwards, so I assumed he'd died in the breakup, but ... Nicolau?" He gave a short, self-deprecating laugh. "Sorry, it's probably not the time. But do you ... did you ..."

Savina stared at the young man, jolted out of her despair. "You knew Nicolau?"

"Yes! We were good friends. I thought after the breakup ... I thought ..." He sucked in a quick breath, closing his eyes for a moment. "But is he ... did he make it?"

"He made it," said Savina. "He's ... he got out of the city. He's safe." Her voice came out strange.

So many times she'd glanced over at her brother, when he thought no one was watching. She'd seen on his face how much it had hurt him to leave his friends behind on the dying ship.

And now here was one of those friends, alive, at least for the moment. And Savina had brought him here, almost against her will. Saved his life.

Reka's words from earlier echoed in her head. *"People are ... more complicated than I like to believe. And sometimes you need help, whether or not you want it. Whether or not you deserve it."*

Whether or not you deserve it. Had Nicolau deserved it? He certainly hadn't asked for it.

Had this boy?

Had she?

For a moment, she pictured Joska's face, her stern gaze, the hint of a wry smile on her lips. *"You know, sometimes having friends can actually be helpful?"*

"I'm … I'm glad he's safe." The boy laughed, a small, shaky laugh. "Even if …" He gestured around him, trailing off. "If you happen to see him again," he said at last, "Tell him Mikel said hello."

Sometimes you need help, whether or not you want it. Whether or not you deserve it.

She closed her eyes for a long moment.

"Savina?" Reka sounded concerned.

"Just a minute," she said, turning away and blinking a command through her wavelink.

Whether or not you deserve it.

"Savina?" Joska's voice was sharp with surprise and thick with worry, a tone to her words that told Savina she was in for a long talking-to next time they saw each other.

But there was relief there, too. The same sort of boneless relief that Savina had felt on seeing Nicolau again after all those years apart.

"Savina, where are you? Are you hurt? Beni's hardly been eating, and Nicolau is worried sick. What the hell were you thinking?"

"Joska," she said, and found she had to swallow hard to get the words out. "I … I'm in trouble. I … I know you don't owe me anything. But you said once …"

Joska cut her off. "What do you need?"

And for a moment, Savina couldn't answer because of the tears welling in her eyes and tightening her throat.

"Alright, Vina, listen," said Beni, once Savina had explained the situation. Savina had joined Reka's wavelink line to hers, and now the government agent stood next to her, a hint of hope in her expression that hadn't been there a few moments before.

"If the ship is the model Reka's told me, then there should be a second cargo hold underneath the place where you're locked up. The hatch will be in the starboard corner of the deck, I'll send the specs through, and tell me it you need anything else. I'm sorry I can't do more."

"Beni, I—thank you," said Savina, her voice barely audible. "And … I'm sorry."

A moment later, a transparent 3D model of the ship floated in Savina's retinal screen, a red dot blinking in the corner of one of the storage decks. Savina turned to Reka. "What can we do with this?"

Reka was studying the diagram on her own retinal screen. "First thing, I think, is to get everyone out of here. Kachik's ships were close when the soldiers locked us in here, we don't have much time." She turned to the rest of the prisoners, who were standing frozen, watching her and Savina with wide eyes. "Is there anyone who's not restrained? If so, get the hatch. We may be able to salvage this yet."

There was a slow smile growing on her face, one that Savina recognize all too well.

After a stunned moment of silence, the prisoners jumped into action. Mikel, the young man who'd been friends with Nicolau, along with an older woman, bent over the hatch in the corner, and after some effort, managed to pull it back.

"Go," Reka whispered. "Everyone inside. You need to hide—there should be some hatches that will get you into the maintenance tunnels from there. Do whatever you need to, but you can't be here when they come for you, and you can't be easy to find. Go on!"

In a matter of minutes, the room was all but empty, Mikel still at the hatch helping the last of the stragglers. As the last man disappeared, the young crewman looked up at Savina and Reka. "Are you coming?"

Reka glanced at Savina.

Savina gave a long sigh. "It looks like Reka and I are going to be keeping the yibo too busy to come looking for you," she said resignedly, ignoring the brief flash of amusement on Reka's face. She paused. "If you open my jacket, there are some knives. Take a few, and keep your wavelink on. And be ready. We may need you."

Mikel nodded earnestly, stepping forward to open Savina's jacket. Then he paused a moment, gaping. "You were carrying a—"

"Just get the weapons, please," Savina snapped. "No commentary necessary." She ignored Reka's amused hum from behind her.

"Alright," said Mikel at last. "I took five knives. I'll hand them out to people who know how to fight."

Savina gave a quick nod. "Be ready to use them, in case you have a chance to take back the ship. And listen for a call over your wavelink."

He nodded again and tapped his wavelink line through to her.

Outside the door, they could hear the footsteps of one of Cavaco soldiers.

"Go!" Savina hissed.

The young crewman disappeared down the hatch, and Reka kicked it closed behind him a moment before the entrance hatch swung open, revealing a dozen of Cavaco's soldiers.

They stared around the room.

"What the hell—" began one of them, after a moment. "What in the Mystery's holy name happened here?"

A soldier stepped forward, grabbing Reka by the front of her shirt and yanking her towards him. "Where did they go?" he snapped. "Where are they?"

Reka's expression didn't change. "I couldn't possibly say."

The soldier yanked out a gun, shoving it into her ribs. "Tell me, or I'll shoot you and your girlfriend right here." He gestured, and another soldier grabbed Savina and pressed a gun to the back of her head.

Reka raised an eyebrow. "I'd be careful. Kachik's not a patient man. He won't hesitate to shoot down the ship if you can't give him something in exchange, and we seem to be your only option."

"You're on the ship too!" the soldier snapped. "You'd be shot down with us."

Reka smiled. "Since it doesn't seem like you have anything better to offer, I hardly think it matters."

The soldier turned away, muttering into his wavelink. "The rest of you, look for the others," he growled to the remaining soldiers. "Take a scan of the ship, whatever you need to do, just find them. In the meantime, I'll take these two over as an appetizer. I understand that Kachik has a personal interest in them, so it may be enough to buy us time."

Savina should, she knew, be terrified. She should be wondering if Reka's taste for suicide missions would lead to both of their deaths.

But she'd seen the look on Reka's face. And she found herself fighting to hold back a grin.

32

Aran

Aran's mind was so caught up in concern for Ani that it wasn't until he was pushed down into one of the seats, his legs secured, and a harness locked into place, that he remembered where they were and what would inevitably come next. He clenched his teeth, biting back a curse as the plex divider slid shut and the airlock doors hissed open. Damn it to hell, this wasn't even a ship, this was a pod, why in the actual hell would someone make a pod with so damn much plex? Why the hell would someone want to be able to see what was out there?

The ship lurched as it rose off the hangar bay floor, then shot forward, and he swore, swallowing back vomit.

The first marker in the genetic code. He remembered that. And if he closed his eyes, he could picture the comparative chart between human and raider genome that he and Dessi had been working on, trying to pinpoint the differences. And somewhere in that in those differences was a gene or a set of genes that made the defect deadly in humans and completely innocuous in raiders.

If they could find out what it was, find a way to replicate the effects—

At last, his spiralling brain slowed, his thoughts dragged back to a scientific problem that once again held meaning. As long as his and Krevai's desperate plan worked.

A soft bump jolted him out of his thoughts, and he looked up with a start to realize they'd docked.

Krevai shot him a questioning glance, but he shook his head.

They'd both know in a moment. And on the bright side, if it hadn't worked, if something had happened to Ani, he probably wouldn't live long enough to have to find a way to survive the crushing, horrifying guilt.

Sharda's crew came in a moment later, unstrapping them from the harnesses and pulling them to their feet, then marched them roughly through the corridor of the ship and down the gangway.

Aran turned his head a little, straining to catch a glimpse of the outside shell of the pod. His heart was pounding so fast he was actually dizzy, and he kept stumbling, hardly able to keep his feet under him.

And then, with a rush of relief so strong it almost made him stagger, he caught sight of a familiar tentacle, a bright, irritated purple.

He let out a long breath, his shoulders dropping with the released tension, and only then did he realize he hadn't actually been breathing for—well, he wasn't sure how long, but his head ached, and black spots were forming in the corners of his vision.

He glanced over at Krevai and gave him a quick nod, and Krevai's mouth turned up into a slow grin.

Aran had to resist the urge to grin back.

For the first time since Sharda had called to tell them she'd kidnapped Dessi—maybe, just maybe, they actually had a chance.

* * *

Sharda waited for them on the main deck. She grinned as they were marched in, her eyes narrowed, her sharp fangs clearly visible through her smile. "You checked them for weapons?" she snapped to the three from the pod.

They nodded, and she turned back to the small group from Krevai's ship. "Good. Check them again, in case we missed anything." She gestured to a member of her crew, who came forward and patted Aran and Krevai down, then stood back, weapons drawn and ready.

"Krevai." Sharda stepped forward, examining them with hands clasped casually behind her back as if she was inspecting a shipment of goods. The pulse pistol scar across the side of her face was an angry red against the ivory of her skin. "If only I'd known it was so easy to bring the mighty captain Krevai to his knees—just kidnap his little scientist." Her smile widened. "I'm true to my oaths. I'll show you your scientist before I kill you, and the little human who defected. The moment you're dead, the scientist goes free. The human I took stays with me. I plan to eat yours." She turned over her shoulder. "Hook through to the general line. We'll bring the scientist out, and then they can watch as I slit Krevai's throat. And let the others know I don't need Kachik any longer. I have no interest in dealing with someone who is so quick to try to take the advantage. Call our ambassador back."

There were a few moments' pause. Then, from the corridor behind Sharda, Dessi was prodded out onto the deck. Her normally pale face was sickly white, and blood stained her face and tunic.

"Dessi?" Krevai asked quickly, worry thick in his tone.

Dessi gave him a wan smile, although there were tears glittering in her red eyes. "I told you not to come," she said, obviously trying to make her voice sharp. "You never listen to me, Krevai."

Krevai grinned, but he was blinking back tears as well. "Ah, Dessi. You're my oldest friend, of course I listen to you. Just not when you're wrong."

"You see, Krevai. Your scientist is unharmed. And she'll be sent back to your ship as soon as I kill you and your human." Sharda's smile was sharp as she pulled out her long butcher's knife.

All the raiders in the cabin were watching them now, even the two holding Dessi.

Sharda stepped up beside Aran. "You first, little human. Maybe once you're gone, my human will stop trying to go behind my back."

She grabbed him by the hair, yanking his head back.

In the background, he heard Dessi gasp.

But from the corner of his eye, Aran could see the small, tentacled lump hanging from the ceiling behind his head, her body blending into the surface, but tense in a way that usually meant something or someone was going to have a very, very brief moment to contemplate their mistakes before dying horribly.

"Ani," he called. "Protect!"

And like a boiling, hissing, and very angry weapon of mass destruction, Ani launched herself forward, her skin gone a furious lime-green streaked with red.

Sharda stumbled back, her crew throwing themselves in front of her, and Ani landed on one of them, hissing like an angry cat.

The raider screamed and fell.

She killed two more before Aran managed to get her attention, and then she soared across the room to land on his shoulder, still growling. He held out his hands, and she nipped through the restraints quickly, then launched herself back into the fray.

Aran snatched a knife that had fallen to the deck in the confusion and sliced through Krevai's restraints, and Krevai shoved his way through towards Dessi.

"Krevai!" She shouted. "Tell Aran, red-rock valley—"

And then two raiders had grabbed her and dragged her out the door.

Krevai swore and started forward, but Sharda's crew streamed out of the corridor, knives and guns at the ready. Aran barely had time to bring up his knife as a raider lunged for him, and he braced himself—then the raider dropped, twitching. Krevai stood over him, a grim smile on his face. He snatched the fallen raider's gun off the floor and tossed it underhand to Aran. "This will be easier than a knife," he called. Then he turned back to the battle.

"Ani!" Aran shouted. "Come!"

Ani turned and soared across the room, taking down two raiders in quick succession as she landed, and then pausing on one of the foaming bodies to look up at him innocently.

A raider lunged for Aran, and he yanked up his weapon, firing at her point-blank. She stumbled back, and he grabbed her by the collar, jerking her head up. "Where the hell are Istvay and Dessi?"

"You'll just have to figure that out, won't you?" the raider snarled back, her voice garbled with pain.

"Ani!" snapped Aran.

Ani scrambled over, latching on to the raider's chest. She was hissing, and the raider's face went pale.

"You'll be foaming at the mouth in about three seconds flat," he said, turning back to his prisoner.

"They've—they've taken Dessi to the main deck," the raider choked. "I don't know where the human is." But her eyes flicked towards a small side-corridor.

Aran let go of her collar, and she collapsed to the deck. "Krevai!"

he shouted, shoving his way through to the captain.

And then something made him glance over at Sharda.

She was standing back from the melee, but there was a vicious glint in her eyes, and a look on her face that said their escape attempt hadn't been entirely unexpected.

"Tell Aran, red-rock valley—"

The message had to have been from Istvay. Istvay must have known he'd try something like this, and they were warning him.

"Krevai. Dessi's on the main deck, and I think I know where Istvay is," he called when he was close enough to be heard.

Krevai turned, dropping the limp body of one of Sharda's crew, their throat torn out. Blood dripped off his chin and stained his teeth, making his grim expression into something terrifying. "Main deck. That's what mine said, too."

"It's a trap," Aran said in a low voice. "They're trying to split us up, that's how valley wolves hunt. I assume they want to get me and Ani away from you so that Sharda can kill you and win the leadership."

"I won't let her kill Dessi," Krevai growled.

"I know. So—" he took a deep breath. "Take Ani with you. If that's Sharda's plan, she'll have most of her people waiting by the main deck."

Krevai frowned. "You'd send your Ani with me?"

"If Sharda kills you and takes your crew, I'll be dead anyways," he said. "And I don't want Dessi hurt any more than you do. Besides, if Ani's with you, I suspect everyone will be too busy to worry about Istvay. And if Sharda assumed I'd have Ani with me, she probably won't have too many crew guarding Istvay—no point. She'll probably have just enough guards to lock me inside whenever I find Istvay, something like that."

"So I take Ani and go after Dessi. And you?"

Aran gave the captain a small smile. His heart was pounding so hard he was dizzy with it, and he wasn't sure if it was fear, or exhilaration. "I'm going to find Istvay."

33

Alba

"Alright," said the yibo woman, pulling out her communicator. She tapped something into it quickly. "If you want a chance at this, there are a handful of people we'll have to convince." She held out the communicator screen so that Alba could see it. "This list here are the advisors who voted in favour of your amendment earlier. And these—" she gestured to another list, "are the advisors who rescinded their vote after Kachik's threats. We need to get most of them, if not all, to change their minds. And to be safe, we'll need to convert at least a few who didn't vote to accept your proposal earlier. I'll put together a list of the most likely candidates."

She gave Alba a sharp look. "I can work on them from my end, and I have some ideas as to what might convince some of them. But if you're correct, we don't have time for backroom negotiations. The bulk of this will be on your ability to convince them that your friends are worth saving."

Alba drew in a deep breath. "I shall certainly do my best."

"Do you need time to prepare?"

"I hardly think it matters, since we don't seem to have any," said

Alba wryly. "I do request, however, that my colleagues be permitted to speak as well."

Karri nodded slowly. "Very well. I shall contact the Master of Readings to inform her that your friends have additional information to add to the debates. And we will hope that she agrees."

Alba gave a short nod of thanks, hardly trusting herself to speak.

By the time the advisors had assembled, Yosip, Feliu, Joska, and the others had arrived at the building.

Joska shot Alba a grim look as she came in. "Chief Justice," she said quietly. "This is an emergency, and I'm happy to help. But I expect a very good explanation afterwards. Savina called me this afternoon."

Alba sighed. "I shall be happy to provide you with one, if we all survive this." She paused. "But I am … sorry."

Joska's gaze was sharp, but she gave a short, non-committal nod. "Best get through this first, and we can argue about it afterwards."

Nicolau was very obviously avoiding Alba's eyes, and Beni, for all their piercings and spiked hair, looked as vulnerable as she'd ever seen them, the way their head was cocked, as if listening to something only they could hear, telling Alba their attention was glued to their wavelink earpiece.

She shoved down the guilt. As Joska said, that was a matter for afterwards.

"Alba," asked Yosip, "what do you need?"

Alba turned to face the group of them, ragged, weary, faces pinched with privation and worry—this group of people who she'd come to trust more, even, than she trusted herself.

"Karri has bought us an audience. But we must help these

politicians understand why those people out there matter," she said. "I need you to help them see those people the way you see them. The way you've taught me to see them."

There was a long moment of silence.

At last, Yosip nodded. "We'll do our best."

"That's all any of us can do," said Alba.

The eyes of the assembled advisors followed the small group of humans as the Master of Readings brought them to the tall balcony alcove where Alba had stood the first time she'd come here. Where she'd given testimony as to how the portal had been closed, and begged for the lives of the survivors. An interpreter stood to translate for them, and Alba thought it might be the same one who'd been there for that same first meeting.

Tika was glaring at them with undisguised hate, and Karri watched them, her expression neutral.

"Advisors," the Master of Readings began. "Advisor Karri requested that we interrupt our debates on our best response to Kachik in order to hear what these humans have to say."

Alba nodded at Yosip, and he stepped forward.

"Advisors," he said, his voice just loud enough to carry. "I am not a public speaker. But I know some of you. I've spoken to your clerks. You have families at home who you worry about, people who are counting on you to keep them safe. I understand wanting to keep the people you love safe." He paused. "But there are people out there, right now. My friends. Marzal has two children back home, the oldest is going into primary school this year. Leiri's mother is sick, and until she was stranded here, she'd call her every night. Cascadi can carve the most beautiful things from wood, little animals that look like they're alive. They told me they used to carve them for their baby sister. These are the people Kachik has condemned to be killed. They're afraid, and they've lost everything they knew, and they're going to be killed. And I can't save them." His voice broke on the words. "But you … you can. I know you understand what it is to love someone, and see them in danger. And you hold the power we do not. You hold the power to save them. Please." He wiped a quick hand across his eyes, and sat.

Joska stood next. "I don't know any of you, and you don't know me. I'm no one important, just a cargo ship captain. But … there's a girl on the ship that Kachik is trying to shoot down. Just a kid. She's not perfect, any more than any of us are, but she risked her life to save a whole group of people she didn't know. She called me just a few minutes back, begging for my help, but there wasn't anything I could do from here. I'd risk my life to save hers, if I could, because she deserves a life too. Please don't let Savina be the only one who'll risk herself to save people who she doesn't know, but who deserve a life too. Please don't let your fear of a bully make you stand back and watch that girl—my friend—be shot down."

"My sister is dying," said Nicolau, jumping to his feet and striding over to stand beside Joska. His hands were clenched, his face tight with worry and anger. "My sister is out there dying right now, because you aren't damn well brave enough to do anything about it. Do you have any idea—"

Joska put a hand on his arm and shot him a look, and he subsided, but Alba could still see the tension in his shoulders, and his fists were still clenched like he wanted to hit something.

Rafel stepped forward awkwardly. "I agree with the captain," he said, his voice gruff. "That's all." He limped back to his seat.

Alba glanced over at Feliu.

He looked at her, eyebrows raised in surprise. "Madam?"

"Please, Feliu," she whispered.

He watched her for a moment, then, with obvious discomfort, he stood. "Esteemed Advisors," he began. "I … don't know what to add, really, to what my friends have said. I simply wish to ask you, please. Don't abandon us. Don't … don't let these people die. Don't …" His voice choked, and he sat back down quickly.

There were a few moments of silence. Alba couldn't read the looks on the advisors' faces, and she cursed her lack of familiarity with yibo culture and expressions.

She stood and stepped forward to stand beside the interpreter.

"My friends," she said, looking out over the rising tiers of seats. Her voice wavered, just a little, but she forced it steady. "I have spoken to you, before, on the political advantages of taking in the human refugees. I have worked with some of you, and with my human colleagues behind me, to craft advisements and amendments that would benefit all concerned. Now, it seems, such considerations have been overshadowed. I, too, am a politician, back in my home system. I, too, held the power to craft laws. And I understand the importance of working for the benefits of those you are appointed to serve. But …" She paused for just a moment.

"But, my friends, politics is more than simply taking the safe road. It's more than trying to gather as many favours as we can and go home at the end of the day with the shiniest collection of benefits. Your political system is different than mine, but at its core, every just political system exists to prevent tyranny. No system functions perfectly, and every person, I believe, human or yibo, holds within them a measure of greed, a measure of self-interest. But a just political system exists to hold that in check. It exists to keep the downtrodden, the underprivileged, the poor and the marginalized and the outcast, from being utterly trampled down. It exists as a wall

—a bulwark, a safeguard placed between them and the uncaring masses who would crush them. And as politicians, our highest and most vital calling is not simply to barter for favours. It is to uphold justice. It is to place our lives, our skills and our knowledge and our sweat and our very blood, in the service of protecting the rights of every sapient creature within our borders. To allow them to strive, as each one of us strives, for goodness, for the meaning that drives their lives as much as it drives ours. To care for their own families, their loved ones, to find beauty and joy in whatever it is they hold dear."

She gestured behind her at the others of her party. "You have heard my human friends speak. They have friends on that ship. Family. People who have risked their lives, selflessly, to save the lives of others. But the people on that ship have done all they could do, and we, standing before you, are powerless to save them. And so I ask you, my esteemed friends. I beg you to stand up, free of favours, free of benefits, free of any ulterior motive, and use the power granted you in the way it was meant to be used: to protect those who cannot protect themselves. To stand between innocents and the tyrants who would destroy them, and say, enough."

There was utter silence in the room as Alba finished speaking, the echoes of her words swallowed in the arching greenery.

And then, at last, one of the yibo advisors stood. "I, for one, am willing to bring this matter to a second vote."

34

Savina

The soldiers marched Savina and Reka, none too gently, towards the back of the ship. They stood for a few moments at the airlock, then it hissed open, revealing a narrow walkway between their ship and, presumably, a yibo ship.

"Go on," the soldier snapped, shoving the two women ahead of him. Reka stepped forward calmly, and Savina, with a quick glance over her shoulder, followed her lead.

She'd thought she wasn't afraid. She wasn't, really—at least, not as afraid as she should have been.

But still, her heart beat strangely. She'd never been good at trusting anyone. Trusting Reka Soler, of all people.

They hadn't even discussed a plan—there hadn't been time. But somehow, she knew that even if Reka would have been willing to sacrifice herself—she wouldn't sacrifice Savina. Not anymore, not if she could help it.

Neither of them spoke as they walked down the long corridor. The airlock on the other side hissed open, and the soldier prodded the two of them through onto the yibo ship.

This ship was clearly much larger and more important than the one she and Reka had stolen. At a guess, this one would fit at least ten times the number of crew, and it was spacious enough to have its own hangar bay—through one of the plex windows, Savina could see the bay doors opening and closing as smaller attack ships came and went.

She glanced at Reka again out of the corner of her eye.

Reka caught her gaze, and gave a quick, meaningful glance in the direction of the hangar bay.

Savina smiled to herself. Steal a ship and break out, then.

However they'd manage that.

And then a yibo woman who must be the captain of the ship, judging by her uniform and the deference the others paid to her, stepped forward, surrounded by a troop of guards.

And behind her …

Savina sucked in a quick breath. The tall, broad-shouldered shape was instantly recognizable—long black hair falling almost to the floor, the predatory glint in red eyes, mouth pulled back in a grimace of a smile that showed off the long fangs to best advantage.

The raider's eyes swept across the two women, and Savina found herself frozen, like a tree-mouse under the gaze of a blue-winged hawk.

"Reka Soler. Captain Sharda will be very, very happy indeed." The raider's voice was deep and rich, and they spoke with an accent that had been seared into Savina's memory—first, by a raider in a small yibo tavern, his hair hanging down to his knees, his red eyes glittering with amusement and hunger, a few seconds before Savina had shot him dead. And second, by a scarlet-cloaked raider captain blocking their exit to the city, her fangs glinting in the dim light of the moons as she surveyed Savina and her small party, as Savina would have survey the plum trees outside the compound walls back home, searching for the ripest fruit.

Savina's muscles had gone weak, her head spinning.

They were going to die. Even if they saved the others, even if the raider hadn't recognized her yet, she and Reka were going to die.

As if from a long distance, she heard the yibo captain snap, "What about the rest of the humans? You promised me all of them, and you deliver only two?"

And the soldier, defensive: "The others are coming. We're just getting them together."

It didn't matter. There was a raider here, and from everything she knew about raiders, this one would be able to hunt down the people on the ship with ease.

But that wouldn't matter to her, or to Reka, because she could see in the raider's red eyes that they'd be dead before they left this deck.

Savina forced her gaze away from the raider with an effort.

Her heart was pounding, quick and shallow, but she took a deep breath and stepped forward towards the yibo captain, giving her biggest wide-eyed smile.

"The soldier is lying to you," she said, enunciating her words clearly. "He and his friends don't have the rest of the humans. The rest of the humans escaped, and they have no way of getting them back."

The human soldier turned on her, the fury on his face overlaid with fear. "That's not true," he snapped. "She's lying. She's just trying to turn us against each other."

"Why would you tell us this?" asked the yibo captain, ignoring him.

Savina smiled wider, not allowing herself to look at Reka. "Because I know where they are. Reka does too, but she's not likely to tell. So, I'll make you a deal—I'll tell you where the humans are hiding. I'll give them up. And you can take this soldier back to the raiders in my place."

There was a long moment of silence.

The yibo captain was looking between the three of them with narrowed eyes. At last, she shook her head and gestured to the guards. "Lock them all up. Hold them here. We'll take this woman back onto the ship and see if she can do what she says she can."

The guards stepped forward quickly, and before Cavaco's soldiers could so much as protest, they'd been restrained.

The raider hadn't spoken throughout all of this, just watched, an amused half-smile on their face.

Savina glanced, almost unconsciously, at Reka. The woman was watching her with that sharp, sceptical gaze, and for half a moment, she wondered if Reka had been fooled by Savina's act as much as the yibo captain had.

And then Reka gave her a tiny, almost imperceptible wink.

Savina's heart stuttered in relief.

The yibo guards were gathered around Cavaco's soldiers, securing the restraints. And Savina had finally managed to slip her fingers around the knife hidden in the back of her belt.

She worked it free quickly and quietly. Then she cleared her throat and shifted, as if trying to get comfortable, and at the same time, she dropped the knife.

She caught it on the back of her calf, let it roll to the ground, and then, with a quick sideways glance at Reka, she tapped it across the floor with the tip of her toe.

From the corner of her eye, she saw a Reka catch it under her boot, then, with a quick, graceful movement that was almost too fast to follow, slide her foot over it and flip it neatly up, catching it between her fingers.

And then the guards had turned back, and they grabbed Savina and shoved her ahead of them towards the airlock.

Savina fought to keep her breathing steady.

She'd been certain, somehow, the Reka would have a plan, some way to turn this to their advantage—but she had no idea how. And the realization that she'd thrown away what could have been her one chance at freedom churned in her stomach like vomit.

But it was too late to go back now.

She and her yibo guards were at the entrance to the airlock now, waiting for it to open, and she could still feel the raider's eyes on her back.

And then there was the faintest sound from behind her.

Savina and the guards turned as one to see Reka spring to her feet, her hands unbound, and yank something from the inside pocket of her jacket. Before anyone had time to react, one of the guards holding Savina dropped, and then a second. The third was just opening her mouth to shout when she fell as well, a pulse-pistol wound burned through the centre of her chest.

There was a moment of stunned silence. Then Reka had reached Savina and grabbed her, slicing through the restraints on her wrists, and Savina pulled out another hidden knife and sent it through the stomach of one of the guards who'd started towards them across the floor.

"Cover me," Reka hissed.

Alarms rang out through the ship, and Savina grabbed the pistol Reka shoved into her hand as a door burst open and yibo guards flooded in, weapons drawn.

Savina fired half a dozen times in rapid succession, then dropped to the ground as a barrage of shots whispered over her head.

Reka was already at the door of the ship's hangar bay, and with a quick swipe of her keylock, she was through.

More alarms began to wail, and the outside hangar door slammed shut at the intrusion.

Savina rolled out of the line of fire, ducking behind the makeshift shelter of the bodies of two fallen yibo guards, and raised up on her elbows long enough to squeeze off another handful of shots.

Reka was paying no attention to the guards who were now sprinting towards her from all sides, just studied the yibo ships for a moment, as cool and collected as if she were in a purchasing lot. Then she stepped to the nearest, shot the pilot, and swung herself into the cockpit. Savina jumped to her feet and ran for the ship. She pulled herself inside, and the hatch slammed after her as she dropped into the copilot's seat.

And then there was an explosion of sound and light, loud enough that Savina had to blink for several seconds afterward before her vision cleared.

And when it did, she sucked in a quick, horrified breath.

The raider was no longer standing beside the yibo captain. In the confusion, they'd crossed to their own ship, and now the raider ship guns were pointed directly at Reka and Savina.

She could see their face through the plex windows, the satisfaction in their red eyes.

Reka's mouth was set in a grim line. She glanced over at Savina, and suddenly, Savina knew exactly what Reka was going to do.

She felt sick.

Reka leaned over to push the ship's communication button. "This is Reka Soler," she said, in her cool, matter-of-fact voice. "I'd like to negotiate a bargain."

"Negotiate?" The raider's voice on the other end of the line was amused. "Sharda's negotiated with you before, Reka. Prove to me that you're worth giving a second chance. What do you have worth bargaining for?"

Reka opened her mouth. But before she could speak, Savina leaned forward. "Believe me," she said in her sweetest voice. "Reka has something to bargain with."

Reka was watching her, confusion on her face, but Savina could see the beginnings of the dawning realization.

She hurried on, before Reka could stop her.

"My name is Savina Moya. I'm the one who shot one of you in a yibo tavern, when I was working for Yuur. And I'm the one who shot your captain as I was getting out of the city, when she came to hunt me down. I'm very sure she'll want to talk to me. So, what Reka is suggesting is, you stand down. You don't kill us. You bring me to Sharda. And we discuss what Reka gets in exchange."

She hit the communications off.

Reka turned, grabbing Savina by the front of the jacket, fury in her face. "How dare you?" she hissed. "They're going to kill you. They're going to murder you, Savina, slowly and painfully, and there's not a damn thing I can do to stop it. You told me you didn't do suicide missions! What the hell were you thinking?"

Savina realized, with an odd, detached sort of clarity, that Reka was—worried. For her. Reka was upset, because Savina was going to die.

"I—" she began, but her words were coming out as inarticulate as her thoughts.

The communicator flashed with an incoming transmission.

Savina reached out, without taking her eyes off Reka's, and hit the button.

"We accept your offer, Reka Soler," came the raider's voice.

Something in their tone made ice form in Savina's stomach. "Send Savina Moya out, and I'll contact Sharda, see what she's willing to give in exchange."

"I'm not letting you go out there," said Reka through her teeth. Her hand was still clenched in Savina's jacket, her face set, and her eyes bore into Savina's, as mesmerizing as they'd been the first time Savina had seen her.

Savina reached up a hand and laid it over Reka's.

Her skin was warm under Savina's palm, and Savina could feel the slight tremble in the muscles of Reka's fingers.

She cleared her throat. "This is the best option we have, you know that. Maybe the only option we have."

"I don't care. You're not going out there."

For the oddest reason, Savina felt like laughing.

Here she was—Savina Moya, the assassin. Volunteering to be killed to save the life of the woman who'd spent the last few months trying to kill her, and who Savina had spent the last few months trying to kill in return. And Reka Soler, government agent, was trying to stop her.

Savina flicked her other wrist inconspicuously, straining her fingers for the small blade she had hidden in the sleeve of her jacket, free now that her wrists were no longer restrained.

She knew enough about knifework to get Reka to release her grip, and to momentarily incapacitate her without causing any lasting damage.

She looked into Reka's face one last time. It was so close to her own that she could have leaned forward and kissed her, like she had back in the tavern, drunk off her skull and waiting to die.

Reka's breath was warm on her skin, anger flashing in her gaze, her hand still trembling a little beneath Savina's.

Savina smiled fondly, tightening her other hand on the knife.

And then there was a sound from outside, and both women turned.

The raider ship had moved, its guns no longer pointing at the ship Reka had stolen, but back into the interior of the yibo ship.

"Ah, I am sorry, Reka Soler. I have new orders, so we shall have to negotiate later. I've been informed that Captain Sharda has her rival captain trapped on her ship, no thanks to the yibo, and she no longer sees a yibo alliance as a productive step. And she wishes me to send her regards to Kachik in exchange for the honourable and trustworthy way he conducted himself in the negotiations."

Reka and Savina stared at each other blankly.

And then the raider ship's guns blazed again.

When the debris cleared, the yibo captain and her guards had been reduced to a bloody pulp across the floor.

The raider ship lifted off the hangar bay deck, hovered for a moment, then blasted open the exit doors to the hangar bay with two well-placed shots.

Then it disappeared into the blackness beyond.

There were a few moments of stunned silence, the discordant wail of the alarms the only sound.

"What the hell—" Reka began at last.

"It doesn't matter," snapped Savina. "Go!"

Reka's expression changed from shock to businesslike in a fraction of a second, and she shoved the controls forward, sending their small ship careening out into space.

35

Alba

For a moment, the room was silent, the one yibo advisor standing alone.

Then another stood. "I, too, request a vote on the matter of the refugees."

More advisors rose to their feet, one by one.

Alba could hardly draw in a breath.

She couldn't tell, yet, if it was enough, if they had the support to carry the vote. But the fact that the advisors were willing to bring it to a vote spoke volumes in and of itself.

Karri stood. "I suggest that the vote be on the following: that we accept the human refugees from the Joias System who are fleeing from Kachik, and that we send ships to their aid if necessary to bring them in." Her voice was as calm as always, but when she glanced at Alba, she was smiling.

Alba smiled back, blinking back tears.

"As the advisors have requested, I will bring the matter to a debate, and then a vote," began the Master of Readings.

And then Tika stood. "Advisors," he snapped.

There was a look of grim triumph on his face, and Alba's entire body went cold to see it.

"Advisors," he continued, surveying the room. "You've heard from the humans. They've made a compelling case—a sister, a friend, who risked her life to save innocent people from death. But Kachik has been broadcasting over the general channel from his ships pursuing these 'innocents,' to allow those of us who wished to follow along, information on what is happening." He smiled, thin and cruel. "Listen to this." He hit a command on his communicator, and, after a moment of crackling, the line cleared.

Alba recognized the voice, immediately, as belonging to Savina.

"The soldier is lying to you. He and his friends don't have the rest of the humans. The rest of the humans escaped, and they have no way of getting them back."

A man's voice. *"That's not true! She's lying. She's just trying to turn us against each other."*

A new voice, in accented yibo tones. *"Why would you tell us this?"*

"Because I know where they are. Reka does too, but she's not likely to tell. So, I'll make you a deal—I'll tell you where the humans are hiding. I'll give them up. And you can take this soldier back to the raiders in my place."

When the recording finished, silence hung in the room like a lightning storm, charged and sparking.

"These are the noble, innocent people these humans are asking you to risk yibo lives to save," Tika said, his voice thick with disgust. "Listen to them. Turning on each other like fungus beetles, tearing each other apart for the chance to save themselves. And if I'm not mistaken, the woman who offered to turn the rest of the survivors over in exchange for her life was none other than the sister and friend these people spoke of so touchingly just now."

He glanced around the tiers of seats. "So. By all means, let us call a vote. But don't let Alba fool you as to the nobility of her cause. Remember that for all her talk, she is simply scrabbling for any scrap of power she can grab, and she's willing to use these peoples' deaths as a means to get there. Let us not be mistaken as to what, exactly we are voting for."

In the silence, the rustle of Tika taking his seat was loud.

"The vote has been called, and will go forward," the Master of Readings said at last. "However, if the humans would like to make a response—"

Alba hesitated, glancing quickly back at the others.

Her eyes found Joska. The ship's captain stood still, lips pinched, face tight with concern. But when she caught Alba's eyes, she gave a quick, sharp shake of her head, and Alba read the message there.

Joska, at least, believed this was a ploy. Joska believed that Savina was trying, somehow, to save the rest of the humans.

Alba wasn't sure she believed it. She wasn't certain she could trust, like Joska so obviously did, that the charming, innocent-looking young woman who'd held a knife to her throat and threatened to slit her open was capable of the type of altruism that Joska and Beni and Nicolau had ascribed to her.

But Joska knew the girl better than Alba did. And Nicolau, too, by the look on his face, believed Savina had been trying to help, and so did Beni.

They were too close to her to be unbiased, of course.

But then … Alba had spent her whole life making decisions from a position of self-proclaimed detached disinterest. Perhaps the time had come to trust the people who cared about a thing because they had a stake in it. Because it mattered to them too much for them to pretend not to care.

"Tika is correct that the girl you heard on the recording is the same girl my friends have stated risked her life for these refugees. And—" She drew in a deep breath. "I do not believe that she has sold them out. I believe that if we were to continue listening, we would hear something different."

Beni stepped up beside Alba. They towered over her, and their face was drawn into a scowl of concentration. "Do you have a communicator?" they asked, their voice abrupt.

Alba nodded, and handed over the device.

Beni took it, their hands running across it in a practiced fashion. "I'll hook us into Vina's communication line."

For a moment, there was silence in the chamber.

A yibo voice crackled from Alba's communicator. *"Lock them all up. Hold them here. We'll take this woman back onto the ship and see if she can do what she says she can."*

And then, a moment later … chaos. Shouts, screams, the hiss of weapons.

Alba frowned, her breath tight in her chest.

Beni looked as if they might be sick, and from behind them, Joska swore quietly.

The chaos grew momentarily louder, than was abruptly muffled, then there was an explosion that, even through the communicator, made Alba's ears ring.

Then, *"This is Reka Soler. I'd like to negotiate."*

"Negotiate?" a raider's voice answered.

There were small hisses of alarm through the seated advisors.

"Sharda's negotiated with you before, Reka. Prove to me that you're worth giving a second chance. What do you have worth bargaining for?"

And then, at last, Savina's voice once more. *"Believe me, Reka has something to bargain with. My name is Savina Moya. I'm the one who shot one of you in a yibo tavern, when I was working for Yuur. And I'm the one who shot your captain as I was getting out of the city, when she came to hunt me down. I'm very sure she'll want to talk to me. So, what Reka is suggesting is, you stand down. You don't kill us. You bring me to Sharda. And we discuss what Reka gets in exchange."*

Beni grabbed for the edge of the railing for support, and Nicolau made a choked, horrified sound that almost masked Reka's next words. *"They're going to kill you. They're going to murder you, Savina, slowly and painfully, and there's not a damn thing I can do to stop it. You told me you didn't do suicide missions! What the hell were you thinking?"*

Slowly, as if they were moving in a daze, Beni reached over and shut off the communicator. They turned their face to the rows of advisors surrounding them.

"You've heard my sister." There was a bite of steel in their voice. "You heard her getting ready to give herself up to be killed. And if you're not damn cowards, you'll do something about it!"

They turned their back deliberately on the room. From the corner of her eye, Alba saw Joska stand quickly, laying a hand on Beni's arm, but Alba kept her face towards the advisors.

"Please," she said, turning to the Master of Readings. "If we do not call the vote now, I suspect it will be too late to do anyone any good."

She couldn't read the yibos' expressions, but nor could she force her eyes away from the tiers of seats as the advisors silently cast their votes.

She didn't look up at the screen in the centre of the room, tallying the votes as they came in.

She couldn't.

And then there was a small rustle through the chamber, and she heard Feliu's quick intake of breath, Rafel's muttered curse, a small sound from Ines.

She forced herself to look up.

Then she staggered, and might have fallen if Feliu hadn't jumped to catch her.

"We won, Madam," he whispered, his hand on her arm, his voice awed and almost disbelieving. "They voted to take the refugees."

"We will page the refugee ship immediately and let them know we are willing to provide sanctuary. I will also instruct the army to page any nearby ships and instruct them to escort the humans in, and to notify the Nativists of our decision."

And Alba almost couldn't make out the Master of Reading's words over the breathless, absurd, lightheaded relief that was flooding through her like a wave.

36

Aran

"Ani! Watch Krevai!" Aran snapped.

Grumbling, Ani obeyed, leaping to Krevai's shoulder.

"Go, Aran." Krevai called. "I'll keep as many of them busy as I can over here, me and your Ani." He yanked out his butcher knife in one hand and drew his pistol with the other. "Come on, Ani, let's see how many of Sharda's crew we can kill before we find Dessi!"

Ani gave Aran a last, soulful look. Then she turned and spat directly into the middle of a cluster of Sharda's crew, their screams echoing off the walls as Krevai waded into the fight.

Aran watched after them for a second. His stomach was tight, his brain buzzing with a mixture of terror and adrenalin.

He tightened his grip on the raider weapon and started for the hallway where, he was pretty sure, Istvay was locked up. It was probably a trap, yes. And Sharda was almost certainly expecting him to do exactly what he was about to do. But it didn't actually matter. He would get to Istvay if it killed him.

He sprinted across the main deck, ducking between the groups of raiders who'd started after Krevai, with much less resistance than he'd expected, and then into the hallway.

It wasn't until he'd gotten several steps down it that he realized what Istvay had been trying to warn him against.

Half a dozen raiders detached themselves from the shadows of the doorways, cutting off both his way forward, and his retreat.

One of them pulled out a knife, the sound of the metal slipping free loud in the sudden silence, and lunged at him, grinning. Aran gritted his teeth, swung his weapon up, and fired it point-blank at the raider's chest.

The guard staggered back as the weapon sparked off their armour, and then another raider grabbed for Aran. He ducked out of the way, bringing the butt of the weapon down on his attacker's forearm, and she hissed out a curse as it connected with a solid thud.

A third raider backhanded Aran hard enough that he staggered up against the wall. He blinked, dazed, and barely managed to dive out of the way of another blow, rolling.

The side of his face throbbed, and blood streamed from his nose as he scrabbled for his knife on the floor. His fingers closed around it just as a raider grabbed him by the back of the jacket, and he drove the point of it as hard as he could into the black boot in front of him.

The owner of the boot howled in pain, letting go of his jacket, and Aran scrambled to his feet and took off down the hallway.

There was the *hiss* of a weapon firing, and Aran threw himself against the wall as it blistered by him, then he was running again, down the corridor.

"Istvay!" he shouted. "Istvay, if you can hear me, answer! It's Aran!"

The raiders' footsteps pounded behind him, and then someone grabbed him. His momentum swung him around, and he hammered the butt of his knife down across the bridge of his attacker's nose, but they ducked out of the way, holding him easily in one hand and pulling out their own knife with their other. "Didn't think you'd get away that easily, did you, human?"

Aran twisted in the raider's grasp, the fabric of his shirt tearing as he jerked free. The raider grabbed for him again, claws digging into his shoulder, and at the same time, a sharp, hot pain lanced through his torso.

He sucked in a quick breath.

For a disconnected moment, as the knife was pulled out, there was only an odd, cold sensation where it had been.

And then the pain hit, and he staggered.

Damn it to hell.

His mind was spinning far too quickly, still oddly removed from his body.

This couldn't be fatal. He couldn't have been hit anywhere vital, because he still needed to get Istvay, he hadn't saved Istvay yet—

The raider was drawing back their knife for another blow, and Aran forced his arm up, the muscles clumsy and unresponsive, forced his fingers to close on the trigger of his pistol. The shot hit the raider in the hand, and the raider shouted in pain, letting go of Aran and the knife both, and Aran collapsed, landing in a messy heap on the floor.

He had the presence of mind to bring up his pistol, slippery with blood, and fire again. It must have hit somewhere more serious this time, because he heard, vaguely, a gargled cry and the sound of a body falling.

Wherever he'd been injured, he was losing an inordinate amount of blood—the floor around him was slick with it, his shirt and one leg of his trousers already soaked through. His head felt light, his body much heavier than it should be, but he splayed his hands on the slippery floor and shoved himself to his feet, staggering a little as he came upright.

A quick glance over his shoulder showed him the other two raiders were on their way, weapons drawn. He bit back a curse, and took off down the hallway at a stumbling run.

"Istvay!" he shouted. "Answer, damn you!"

And then, faintly, "Aran? Aran, what the hell!"

The sound was coming from the door directly ahead of him. He was almost there, just a few more steps—

He staggered up against it, catching himself with both hands. He noticed, idly, that he was leaving bloody handprints everywhere he touched. The raiders were shouting from behind him, and something hit the wall beside his head, and it took a moment for him to realize they were shooting at him.

He stared at the lock on the door for a few seconds, stupidly, then he yanked out his pistol and fired into the lock. He fired twice more before it gave, and then he shoved the door open and pushed his way inside. He slammed it shut behind him, grabbed a nearby chair, and wedged it up against the door latch, then leaned back against it, panting.

His breath was coming quick and shallow, his hands trembling, his whole body shaking and cold. He knew, in the back of his mind, that he was going into shock, but he didn't have time to pay attention to that right now.

He turned, bracing himself against the door for support.

There was a chair on the far side of the room, facing away from him.

And in it, hands and feet bound to the chair legs—

"Aran?" Istvay's voice was sharp with a mixture of worry and disbelief, and they were straining over their shoulder to look at him.

From the little he could see from where he stood, they looked worse for the wear—a wicked bruise purpling across their temple, clothes ragged and stained with dry blood, face even thinner than Aran remembered.

But they were alive. They were real.

Aran's vision was blurring, and it took a moment before he realized it was with tears. "Pishti!" he choked.

"Aran! I told you it was a damn trap!"

"Did you honestly think something like that would stop me?" asked Aran with a weak grin. The room was spinning, but he couldn't afford to pass out just yet, Istvay was still tied up.

"No, I knew bloody well it wasn't going to damn well stop you, that was exactly the problem," Istvay grumbled. There was something about the familiar strain in their voice that made Aran's smile grow wider.

He was so tired. So cold, and so tired.

His eyelids were trying to close, but he forced them open again. Getting across the room to Istvay would be a challenge, but he'd done worse. He was pretty sure.

"Aran?" Istvay's voice was sharp with a sudden worry. "Aran, what happened? What's wrong?"

The raiders outside were already pounding at the door. It wouldn't take them long to get through, and he had to get Istvay free before then.

"Just—just give me a second," he muttered. He braced himself, then with both hands against the wall, pushed himself upright and turned.

Istvay's face, already pale under its usual tan, went bloodless. "Aran, what the hell!"

Aran forced his heavy legs to move, and he staggered across the floor towards Istvay. Istvay was straining at their restraints, expression panicked. "Aran! Answer me, what the hell happened?"

"Don't—don't worry about it, Pishti, it was—it was worth it, I'd do it again in a heartbeat." He reached the chair where Istvay was bound, finally, and caught the arm of it, barely keeping himself from falling. With his free hand he fumbled for his knife. He managed to pull it out at last, and he sliced awkwardly at the restraints.

"Aran!" Istvay grabbed for him with their newly freed hand, and that was probably the only thing that kept him from keeling over. He brought the knife up again, although it weighed at least double what it had a minute ago, and sawed at the restraints on Istvay's other wrist. As the restraints snapped, the knife slipped from his bloody fingers.

He stared down at it for a moment, not terribly sure he had the strength to bend to pick it up.

Istvay had grabbed for him, pulling him around to look at him.

There were black spots floating at the edges of his vision, and he felt so, so tired. "Can't—sorry," he mumbled. "You're going to have to do your legs, I don't think I can—"

And then Istvay must have seen the injury, because their eyes went wide, their face taking on a sick look. "Aran, stay with me," they choked. "Dammit, Aran—" They supported him with one hand, reaching down with the other to grab the bloody knife and slicing quickly through the restraints on their legs, then jumped to their feet as Aran swayed. "Dammit, don't you dare do this to me! Don't you dare damn well do this to me—"

The black around the edges of Aran's vision was getting thicker, his vision narrowing to a rapidly shrinking point. He turned his head so he could focus on Istvay's face. He was fine, really, as long as Istvay was alright.

"Pishti—" he mumbled. And then his legs wouldn't hold him anymore.

Distantly, he could hear Istvay cursing as they lowered him to the ground in a sort of controlled fall. "Aran, stay with me, damn you to hell! If you do this to me, I swear I'll—I'll—" their voice choked off.

Now that he was lying down, enough of Aran's vision had returned that he could see Istvay stripping off their filthy shirt and folding it neatly, their hands trembling. "This is going to hurt," they murmured, and pressed it against his wound.

The sharp jolt of pain brought him back to himself momentarily, and he sucked in a quick breath.

"Sorry," Istvay whispered. "I need to hold pressure on it, just— just stay here, please don't leave me—" Their voice was thick and choking.

They were upset. Aran didn't want them to be upset, hell, all of this had been to save Istvay's life, now they were upset—but when he tried to open his mouth to say something, his tongue was heavy and the words wouldn't come. Istvay's face was wavering, and it was getting harder and harder to keep his eyes open, even with the glowing pain in his side.

There were shouts from the hallway, and something crashed against the door. Istvay cursed, head jerking up. "Sorry, Aran, I need to borrow this," they muttered, pulling the pistol from Aran's limp fingers.

The door burst open, and Istvay jumped to their feet. Through the mist clouding his vision, Aran could see them standing over him, their weapon held steady.

"If you touch him, I'll kill you," they snapped in a voice Aran had never heard from them before.

And then, from the fading corners of his consciousness, he heard a familiar bellowing laugh. "Istvay! So good to see you again! Don't worry, we don't want to hurt your Aran, we just—" there was a momentary pause. "What the hell happened to him?" Krevai barked.

And then blackness enveloped him completely.

37

As their small ship burst out of the airlock doors, yibo ships from surrounding spacc wcrc alrcady flooding after them.

Then, abruptly, they wavered and broke off, milling around the exploded airlock.

Probably more concerned with a dead captain and a rogue raider than two escaped humans at the moment.

Reka was grinning, and Savina, for some reason, found it hard to look away from her.

She shook herself mentally, and grumbled, "You really don't understand how to keep a low profile, do you?"

Reka laughed, her teeth flashing in the reflected explosions from the yibo ship, and for just an instant, Savina's chest ached at the beauty of it.

Reka's hands moved skillfully over the controls, and a moment later their small ship was lined up with the airlock tunnel connecting the humans' ship to the yibos'.

Reka hit her wavelink to the channel she'd given the rest of the survivors back on board. "Everyone back from the airlock," she snapped.

She waited for the count of ten, and then nodded at Savina to hit the guns.

The airlock tunnel exploded.

Savina found she was grinning as well.

Reka tapped the ship's communication over to the open line on the ship carrying the human refugees. "This is Reka Soler, paging Cavaco's soldiers. Give yourselves up, or I shoot to kill."

"Reka." The soldiers voice through the line was cold. "I'm calling your bluff. You'd never shoot a ship with innocent hostages. Stand down, or I gas them out."

Savina shot Reka a smug glance and leaned over to the communicator. "You're right," she said, in her most innocent voice. "Reka would never shoot down innocent people. But Reka's not the one on the guns. I am. And you've seen me shoot down innocent people just because I felt like it. I can blow your ship to space dust long before Reka has time to stop me."

"If you kill us, you'll never be able to save yourselves!" The soldier's voice over the line was much more panicked now. "You don't have the supplies to—"

Beside her, Reka was whispering into her wavelink.

Savina grinned. "I appreciate your concern," she said, her voice breathy and just a little too sincere. "But you know, I don't like soldiers. I don't like people who hit me over the head and tie me up. And I'm very good at surviving when I need to be. So. Here's what I propose: you surrender. You drop your weapons. And you send me visuals, so that I can see that you're properly restrained."

"I can't—" the soldier began.

"Your excuses are boring," said Savina with a bright little laugh. "I guess I'll—"

"Wait!" the soldier shouted. "Don't—"

The line went abruptly silent.

Reka shot Savina a satisfied smile and leaned forward. "Surprise," she said, dry humour in her voice. "Mutinies are less enjoyable if you're the one standing in the cockpit with a knife to your throat, aren't they?" She paused. "Mikel? Do you have everything under control?"

"Yes." Mikel's voice was shaking, but he sounded elated. "We've taken back the ship, just like you said."

Reka grinned. "Good. Lock the soldiers up, but put them in a room that's a little more secure than the one they had you in. The yibo are distracted for the moment, so get yourselves in position to move quickly when I tell you. Savina and I are going to see what we can do to get you out of here."

At Reka's words, Savina's grin faded abruptly.

Of course. They had nowhere to go.

She took a deep breath and turned to Reka. "Listen," she said quietly. "Maybe if the two of us—"

"Savina? Savina!"

There was so much panic in Beni's voice through her wavelink that in the time it took for Savina to open her line, she'd almost had a heart attack. "Beni! What's wrong?"

There was a moment of silence. "You're alive," Beni whispered. "Vina, I thought you were dead."

"It's … it's fine, Beni, it's alright. I'm fine." She paused, glancing out the plex window in front of her. "I … don't know if there's anything you can do," she said, her voice a little grimmer. "We got away from Cavaco's soldiers, but we don't have anywhere to take these people. We have a few minutes' breathing space, I think, while the yibo regroup. Reka and I are in an attack pod, but the ship the rest of the humans are on is fenced in. Once the yibo start coming after it again, I don't know if—"

"That's what we called to tell you." Joska's voice came over the line, calm and just a little wry. "I might have a thing or two to say to the Chief Justice for lying about your whereabouts, but ... she managed this, somehow. The yibo government has voted to accept the refugees, and to send the nearest military ships to act as your escort. They should be paging the main ship now."

Savina stood for a moment with her mouth hanging open, completely unable to respond.

"What is it?" Reka hissed.

Savina blinked and turned to her. "Reka. They're ... they're going to let the ship land. They're going to give us sanctuary. They're sending escort ships, the main ship just has to get to them."

Reka glanced out the cockpit window, and Savina followed her gaze.

The smaller yibo ships were still swarming around the flagship in confusion. But already, they were beginning to reform into military formation. And when she glanced down at the ship's screen, she could see more ships moving in from the direction of the planet they'd just left.

Reka activated her own wavelink and blinked through to Savina's line. "Joska," she said quietly. "How long until the military ships arrive?"

"They said something about half a cycle, which I think means a little over six hours," said Joska. "That's the best they can do. Fewer, likely, if your ship heads out to meet them. Are you going to be able to make it?"

"Savina and I will get the others there," said Reka, her voice still quiet.

There was a long pause on the other end of the line.

At last, Joska said, "Savina. I'm … proud of you. I'm proud of what you've done, you and Reka. I'm still angry that you ran off the way you did, but like you're so fond of telling me, I'm not your mother. You're old enough to make your own choices. If you decide to run off again on another crazy death mission, because that's the only way you can see to keep the rest of the refugees safe, I can't stop you. But—" She paused, and when she spoke again, her voice was a little thicker than usual.

"You don't have to do this alone. You don't have to try to protect me, or Beni, or Nicolau, or Rafel, or any of us. Your siblings are capable of making their own decisions too, and they want to help you. They care about you as much as you care about them. I have the *Dolphin* fuelled up and ready to go, and we can leave at a moment's notice, meet you anywhere. But I don't know where you are, and I don't know your plans. So it's up to you, Savina."

Savina stared out into the blackness of space around her, cut by the brilliant glow of stars.

Sometimes we need help, even if we don't deserve it.

She drew in a deep breath. "I'll … send you our coordinates. Beni will be able to track them. And you can meet up with us whenever you get here." She paused. "And … thank you."

Joska made a small sound of approval that lit something warm in Savina's chest. "You're growing up, Savina," she said. "Sometimes it takes growing up to learn to ask for help. Send the coordinates, and we'll meet up with you as soon as we can. And until then … be careful. There are people here who care about you."

The line clicked off, and Savina stood where she was for a long moment, staring out at the blackness.

She wasn't sure if the feeling twisting around her ribcage and squeezing was happiness, or pain, or something else entirely.

"Savina."

She blinked out of her revery. Reka had come over to stand beside her, and she put her hand on Savina's arm. Savina turned, and for a moment, she was staring into Reka's eyes.

Reka's gaze was dark and intense, the shadows in the dim light of the cockpit sharpening her cheekbones and accentuating her full lips, her elegant features, the way her hair fell around her shoulders. The place where she gripped Savina's arm was warm, and Savina could feel the hint of a tremble in her fingers.

For a long moment, neither of them moved.

And then, at last, Reka dropped her hand and gestured to the control screen in front of her. "They're forming up too fast, and there are too many of them. The main ship isn't going to make it out unless we give it a chance."

"I know," said Savina.

"But I think, between the two of us, we may be able to keep the yibo distracted for long enough for Mikel and the others to get their ship clear. Then they'll have to do their best until they reach the escort ships."

Savina sighed and rolled her eyes. "Little Miss Sacrifice Yourself for the Good of Humanity. Fine, Since I'm stuck on this attack pod with you, it doesn't look like I have much choice."

Reka grinned, a tiny little grin, quickly hidden, and turned back to the pilot's seat, tapping through to the ship's communication line. "Paging Mikel," she said quietly. "I assume the yibo already explained things to you. There's an escort coming in, but it will take a little while to get to where you are, and you're not going to get there unless you can get past Kachik's army. Do you have someone who can pilot the ship?"

"Yes." The boy's voice was subdued.

"Good. Savina and I will buy you some space. As soon as you see an opening—go."

There was a momentary pause from the other end of the line, then Mikel's voice, sounding a little choked. "Understood."

Reka turned to Savina, that familiar grin back on her face. "Alright," she whispered. "Shall we show the yibo a good time?"

Savina grinned back, resuming her place in the copilot's seat, and tightened her hands on the gun controls.

"I have a map of the system loaded into the ship," said Reka, her voice as bland and businesslike as ever. "Once we've caused all the damage we can, we'll likely have to head for the nearest terraformed planet and hope for the best. If we make it that far."

Savina nodded again. An odd sort of adrenaline was bubbling up through her. Maybe this was why Reka did what she did— something about the giddy exhilaration of flying into the face of almost certain death.

She'd done it often enough herself, these past few weeks. Maybe it was, after all, a little addicting.

"Serves me right for getting involved with someone who always has to be the hero," she grumbled, shooting Reka a mock glare.

Reka grinned back. "Ready?" she whispered. "Let's make them angry enough that we're the only thing on their minds." She shoved the controls, and the ship shot forward.

Savina pulled back on the guns, firing with every weapon she had as the yibo ships scrambled to get out of the way, then they were past, and Reka had turned them for another strafing run.

The yibo were shooting back now, and Reka's face was tight with concentration as she fought to pull them out of the way of the shots. A shot slammed into their starboard side, and the ship shuddered at the impact. But from the corner of her eye, Savina could see the human-piloted ship slip out from between the distracted yibo warships and streak towards the far distance, where, supposedly, their escort waited to bring them to safety.

"They're out," she whispered. "Just a little longer, to give them a good start."

Reka nodded, not looking up from the controls. She spun the ship in a tight turn and pointed their nose directly into the thickest knot of yibo ships.

The ships scattered as Reka dived, Savina firing into the middle of them so that her hands cramped around the gun controls. Then they were through, and Reka swung the ship around for another attack run.

And then something slammed into them hard enough that Savina was thrown roughly against her harness straps, her head connecting painfully with the back of the seat.

The control panel lit up with warning lights, and Reka cursed under her breath.

Another shot, and the ship lurched again.

"We get hit like that one more time, and we're dead," said Reka grimly. She glanced at the controls. "We may be dead anyways. But in the meantime—let's make them work for it."

Savina's heart was pounding, that tight knot of fear mixed with exhilaration buzzing in her chest, but she managed a grin.

She should be terrified. She probably would be, if she took the time to think about it. But honestly, from the moment she'd left the note for Reka and slipped out of the courtyard, she hadn't really planned to come out of this alive. This was better than she'd dared hope—a chance, at least.

"I'll tell Joska where to meet us, if there's anything left of us to meet," Savina said. "And I'll let her know the refugee ship made it through. She'll be glad of that."

Reka glanced over at her, and for a moment, her eyes caught Savina's, gaze as piercing as the first time Savina had met her, weeks ago and lightyears away on a small, dirty moonport. "Thank you," Reka said quietly. "Thank you, Savina. I … "

Savina rolled her eyes. "If you're trying to tell me you'd have completely messed this up without me, believe me, I already know."

Reka shot her a brief smile. Then she shoved the controls forward, and they streaked off towards the small, green planet marked on their map, with the yibo attack ships in hot pursuit.

Savina watched her for a moment longer.

She still wasn't entirely sure how this had happened. She wouldn't have believed it, if someone had told her earlier—that she'd be sitting here beside Reka, the woman she hated. The woman she'd kissed. The woman who'd saved her life. And Joska, who's ship she'd hijacked, coming to find her.

To save her.

She glanced back at the ship screen. The yibo ships were closing in, but she and Reka would almost certainly reach the planet before they were shot down. And everything else, they could worry about then.

"We'll meet up with you as soon as we can. And until then … be careful. There are people here who care about you."

She smiled to herself, blinking a haze from her eyes that could have been tears, and strapped in, preparing for a rough landing.

38

Alba

Alba stood with the others at the wide, open-air loading pad as the battered yibo ship came to a ponderous, steaming halt, and the loading ramp hissed open.

Yibo emergency medics stood at the base, and the moment it was locked in place, they jogged into the ship, accompanied by yibo soldiers—they'd heard, over the communication lines, of the attempted mutiny by Cavaco's soldiers.

At last, the human refugees began to stagger down the loading ramp in small clusters, accompanied by the medics. They looked awful—faces drawn and hollow with shock, eyes wide and staring.

Jair nudged her. "They'll be happy to see someone they recognize," he whispered.

Alba nodded, drawing in a long breath, and stepped forwards.

Yosip and Feliu kept pace with her—the last remaining members of their party. Joska had gone after Savina, and Rafel, Beni, and Nicolau had insisted on accompanying her. And since, Alba suspected, it would take nothing short of physical violence to separate the young crewman and Alba's diplomatic interpreter, Ines had gone with them as well. Before she'd gone, though, she'd left Alba with the final addition to her translation program, the component that would translate their speech into yibo.

It would come in useful, Alba was quite sure.

Still … she found it was an odd, uncomfortable pang to glance over and not see the young interpreter pouring over her documents, or conversing in low tones with Nicolau, her eyes shining and her face bright in the way it always was when she looked at him.

Yosip tapped Alba's arm, and she glanced up to realize she was standing at the base of the loading ramp.

The refugees were watching her, and the frantic relief in their faces on seeing her made something in her chest twist.

She may be nothing in this system, a powerless refugee exactly like the ragged figures on the loading pad. But these people looked to her as something more—their Chief Justice. The leader of their diplomatic mission.

The one who could save them.

She managed a small smile, and took a step forward. "Welcome," she said, pitching her voice loud enough to carry. "I am very, very happy that you have made it safely here." Her voice choked a little, and she found she was blinking back tears. She cleared her throat. "There have been places prepared for your accommodation, and you'll be fed and clothed and given whatever medical attention you may need. Now please, go rest. You are among friends."

The survivors were weeping openly, some of them, some of them turning their faces away to hide tears of strain and relief. Alba stepped back and let the medics escort them to the transports.

Jair had come to join her, and they watched as the last of the refugees were led away and Cavaco's soldiers marched down the boarding ramp, hands restrained behind their backs.

They, too, looked drawn and exhausted, strain and fear written deeply on their faces, but Alba found she could muster little sympathy.

As the last group was being led past, however, she stepped forward.

The yibo soldiers paused politely, stepping back a little to give her room.

The soldier in front of her was no one she recognized. But she frowned, examining his face.

"Why?" she asked at last.

The man scowled, his lips turning up in scorn. "Chief Justice Alba." He said the words like a curse. "You must be happy with yourself—trapping us behind the portal like this. Dooming us."

She fought back the sharp twinge of guilt. "You came here on Cavaco's orders. You came here knowing you were committing treason against the Joias government. And so, if you're doomed, regardless—then what? Why continue loyal to the man who sent you here, and who certainly will not come out a hero should we ever return? Why bind yourself to that?" Her voice was steady, despite the sharp hatred in the soldier's gaze.

"Because you've already lost the game, Chief Justice." There was a glint of triumph in his eyes, under the hatred. "Do you think Cavaco needed the yibo? They would have been helpful. But the threat of them was enough. He'd put his plans in motion before we entered the portal. If he doesn't already hold the full reigns of the Joias government, he will soon. You gone, presumed killed, and an alien threat at our doorstep? He has everything he needs, thanks to you, Chief Justice." He spat on the ground.

A yibo soldier prodded him forwards, nodding an apology to Alba.

Alba hardly noticed. She watched after the soldier, her heart once more beating quick in her chest.

"Madam? Could he be telling the truth?" Feliu stepped up beside her, his voice low.

"He … could be," said Alba quietly.

She felt a little sick.

He could very well be telling the truth. Her proposal to disband the military branch of the government had had enough support to pass, when she'd brought it up so many weeks ago.

She'd made very certain of that before she'd brought it up. Because she'd known exactly how powerful Cavaco was, and how very badly things could go wrong, should she bring up a proposal like that one and not be able to implement it.

And then the portal had opened, and she'd been very neatly got out of the way, and President Ander Seguer, she knew well enough, was a weak man. He didn't have nearly the constitution to stand up to someone like Cavaco.

The soldier could well have been telling exactly the truth.

She turned to Jair. "You say that the Nativists have not yet declared war over the refugees?"

Jair nodded. "It appears they had a falling-out with their raider allies. We can only hope that's enough to dissuade them."

She nodded, biting the inside of her cheek. "And with the temporary peace, then—how likely is it, do you think that we could convince the yibo to create another portal, guarded this time, for the sole purpose of allowing us, and whatever humans here who wished to come with us, to return to our system? In exchange, perhaps, for a pledge of mutual peace and non-interference?"

Jair frowned. "It's … possible. I would say unlikely, but then—" He gave a wry shrug. "I would also have told you getting those refugees in was unlikely, and here they are. But I will say, it would take some politicking."

Alba's mind was already chewing over the problem, breaking it down to its political components.

'Possible' was all she'd ever had to work with, in this system.

"Can we stop this happening, Alba?" asked Yosip quietly. His face was grave as well. "Is there anything at all we can do to keep Cavaco from seizing power?"

"I don't know," she said, her tone as quiet as his. "I don't know what Cavaco has done, and as of the moment, we're still stranded here. Even if we find a way back through the portal, I am certainly not arrogant enough to think my return would be the sole solution to the problem. But in Joias my voice will carry weight, and at least when I left, there was a coalition still willing to oppose Cavaco, given the means and leadership to do so. And in addition, all of us here have information that would leave Cavaco looking very compromised indeed."

She looked up at him and Feliu, who were watching her in concern, worry-lines deep on both their faces.

There were people they knew, people they loved, possibly trapped back on Colorida in a military coup. And even after all this time, after everything that had happened, after seeing the full extent of her weakness, her incompetence and inabilities and shortsightedness and hubris—they believed she could do something about it.

She took a deep breath. "It's possible we may not even make it home. And if we do, I don't know if we have the resources or the ability to stop this." She paused a moment, and raised her chin slightly. "But at the very least, gentlemen, I intend to try."

39

Aran woke to a feeling of something soft under his head.

He lay for a few moments with his eyes closed, trying to remember where he was and how he'd got there.

He was—exhausted, for some reason, and his whole body felt as if it was weighted down with a lead blanket. But there was something nagging in the back of his mind, something that was absolutely vital that he remember—

His eyes snapped open, and he stared wildly around the room. Istvay. The last thing he could remember was a muddled vision of Istvay standing over him, weak and pale, a raider pistol in their hands. And—Krevai's voice?

His brain was slowly making sense of the scene around him—a familiar small cabin, the pile of blankets replaced now with an actual bed. The lump on his chest that was not, in fact, a blanket, but Ani, huddled protectively on top of him.

And in the chair next to the bed—

His breath choked, his heart almost stopping completely at the overwhelming rush of relief.

Istvay was fast asleep, legs sprawled out in front of them, head tipped back against the wall. There was still the remnants of a bruise purpling across their temple, dark circles under their eyes, their usual five o'clock shadow more stubbly than what Aran was used to, and looking like they'd shaved it with a rusty bush-blade. They looked the absolute picture of exhaustion. And Aran had never seen anything so beautiful in his entire life.

He must have made some sound—maybe a gasp of relief—because Istvay's head jerked up, their body going rigid in panic as their eyes fluttered open.

"Hey, Pishti," said Aran, grinning weakly.

Istvay dropped back into their seat, closing their eyes for a moment, the strain written clearly across their face. "Thank the Holy Mystery in its everlasting mercy," they said, in half-whisper so soft it was almost a prayer. "Thank every higher power that exists." They pushed themself to their feet, then dropped down on their knees beside the mattress. Their face was so pale Aran was worried they were going to pass out. "How are you feeling?"

Aran managed to pull his attention from Istvay's face for long enough to take quick stock.

His side was … well, a little sore, but considering he was pretty sure he remembered a raider knife going all the way through him and possibly coming out the other side not very long before, he would have expected to be a hell of a lot worse than sore. And he was weak and a bit dizzy, but not nearly as much as he should have been, based on the sheer amount of blood he'd lost.

"How long has it been?" he rasped.

Istvay managed a wan smile. "I lost track of that when you damn well passed out in front of me and were bleeding out on the floor. But if I had to guess, I'd say … a couple days? Dessi got you back to

Krevai's ship, and the raiders doctored you up with a type of technology I've never seen before—they said they dealt with a lot of gut-wounds in their profession, and they needed to be able to get people back on their feet quickly. I've never actually seen something like it. And Dessi, for some absurd reason, had some artificial blood to use as an infusion, but this is the first time you've been conscious since then. I've been in here the whole time." They paused. "Aran?"

Aran blinked. He'd been staring at Istvay, he realized, his eyes drinking in their familiar features like they were food and water and warmth all at once. He cleared his throat, trying to pull his attention back to the matter at hand.

Just the sight of Istvay, the way they watched him like they couldn't pull their eyes away either, the thick relief in their expression, the way his brain told him that, wherever he was, Istvay was here and therefore it was home, was trying very hard to take up his entire attention, and it was very nearly succeeding.

He pushed himself up on his elbow, wincing at the expected pain. But whatever the raiders had done to him, it had been effective—his side twinged a little, but that was all. "Krevai?" he managed. "I assume he won the leadership battle, since you and I are still alive."

Istvay shook their head ruefully. "I ... wasn't exactly paying attention. Last I heard, he was still alive and so was Sharda. Krevai convinced Ani to stop before she murdered the entirety of Sharda's crew, and Dessi got the two of us back to Krevai's ship without any problems, so I assume they must have called a temporary truce. I don't know. Like I said, I wasn't exactly in a position to worry about that, seeing as none of us were completely sure you'd pull through even with all the raider's medical tech. Dessi said as long as your body didn't reject the treatment, you should be basically as good as new by the time you woke up, but hell ... I've been so damn worried, Aran—" Istvay's words choked off, and they leaned over, pressing their lips to Aran's forehead.

At the touch, Aran's brain went completely off-line, the feeling of Istvay's lips against his skin sparking through every nerve-ending in his entire body. At last, Istvay pulled back a few centimetres, cupping his face between their hands, studying him with that achingly familiar concern. "Aran, please don't scare me like that ever again, please—" Their palms were warm against his skin, their touch firm and gentle, and Aran still couldn't quite bring his brain back into focus. All he could think of was how close Istvay was, how overwhelmingly, sickeningly, shockingly good it was to be able to look into those familiar brown eyes again.

The way their thumb ran along his cheekbone.

The way they leaned in, their eyes closing, long lashes brushing the dark bruise-like hollows under their eyes.

Their lips pressed to his.

For just a moment, Aran was too frozen with shock to move. And then his body, apparently sensing it would get no help from his brain, took over, and he was kissing Istvay back, reaching up to pull them closer. Istvay made a soft sound, something that sent set off fireworks in every one of Aran's neural pathways, and the kiss went from gentle to desperate in a moment. Aran leaned up into them, every nerve in his body tingling, every sense full of nothing but Istvay—the taste of them on his tongue, the press of their body against his, their hands running down the side of his face, winding in his hair. There was nothing in the entire world except for Istvay, and he didn't need air, or light, or food, or anything else, just Istvay, like this, forever—

At last, shakily, Istvay drew back. Aran groaned unconsciously at the sharp jolt of disappointment as their lips left his. He was breathing heavily, and so was Istvay, their face still close to his, their eyes wide, their expression unreadable.

For a long moment the two of them stared at each other. At last, Istvay cleared their throat. They didn't seem able to break eye contact with Aran. "I—" they said, their voice unsteady. "I should probably—"

"Pishti," said Aran in a hoarse voice. "Please—"

Istvay finally managed to pull their gaze away. "Aran," their voice was rough. "I—should go let Krevai know you're awake. He'll want to know as soon as possible. And you're probably hungry, I'll bring you some food. You'll feel better once you've eaten something." They stood, avoiding his gaze.

"Pishti, no, please," he started, but they turned away, and he could see the strain in the set of their shoulders.

"I'm—I'm just going to—you lost a lot of blood, I'm sure you're dehydrated, I'll get you some water—"

Aran reached out and grabbed Istvay's wrist.

Istvay froze.

"Pishti," he said, in a voice that he hoped didn't shake too badly. "What the hell?"

There was a long moment of silence. Istvay's shoulders were so tight it almost made Aran's shoulders ache in sympathy.

"Let me go, Aran," they said, their voice almost inaudible.

Aran's heart was pounding, whether from nerves or anger, he wasn't sure. "No," he said flatly. "You don't get to kiss me like that and then just walk away."

Istvay could have pulled away from him easily—his grip was weak, and he wasn't holding them tightly. But they didn't.

"I won't let you do this to me again," he continued, his voice choking a little. "You don't get to just walk away and tell me we'll talk about it later. You don't get to—to damn well sleep with me, and then let me wake up in bed alone, and not say a damn word about it for seven damn years." His voice was shaking now. "I've loved you for so damn long, I just need to know. And if it's not what I thought, if you don't want a relationship, I can respect that. But you can't do this to me one more time, or I—I swear, Pishti, I'm not going to survive it." He had to clench his teeth hard against the tears welling in his eyes, and he turned his head away, trying to regain his composure.

Istvay didn't move, and they didn't say anything, and for a moment, he wondered if they would speak at all.

At last, they sat down on the bed beside him, running a hand across his forehead. And despite everything, he found his eyes closing, his face turning almost unconsciously into the touch.

They drew in a long breath, then blew it out again. "Aran, I'm— Aran, listen. I—I'm sorry." They paused a moment. "I—I didn't know for sure that I had the defect," they continued, their voice soft. "But I guess I always suspected I did. I always assumed that one day I'd—I'd die the way my mother had. And—" they gave a small, bitter laugh. "I knew how you felt about me, Aran. But I wanted you to be happy. I wanted you to be alright. You wonder why I kept setting you up with people? I just—I wanted you to find someone, and I wanted you to be happy. That's all I wanted. I'm sorry, Aran," they whispered, still not looking at him. "I'm so sorry."

There was so much pain in their voice that despite the pain that was washing through him, sharper than the residual ache from his wound, Aran found his voice. "Pishti, it's alright," he managed. "It's alright, it doesn't change anything, if you don't—if you didn't feel the way I did, if you didn't want the same thing I do, that doesn't mean—you don't have to feel bad that—"

Istvay turned to stare at him. "What?"

Aran stared back. "I said," he tried again, tentatively. "If you didn't feel the same way I did, or … or want the same thing, that doesn't mean you have to feel bad about it."

Istvay was still staring at him. "No. No, Aran," they said at last. "No, that's—that's not what I meant at all." They laughed, a small, almost hysterical sound. "I have been in love with you—stupidly, ridiculously, absurdly, sickeningly in love with you—since … oh hell, I don't even know. I honestly can't remember a time I haven't been in love with you. I—Aran, I—" their words choked off, and they stopped speaking, wiping at their eyes.

Aran was still staring. He wasn't sure he could remember how to speak. "You—" he began again, his voice sounding strange. "You—you mean this whole time—" There was a rushing in his ears. "What the actual—Istvay, what the actual hell?" His voice came out almost a full octave higher than usual. "You—Pishti, you said you knew how I felt. You saw that, and you lied to me, for—hell, how many years? Did you think I was stupid? Do you think I'm incapable of making decisions about my own damn life? What the actual hell?"

The shock and the sickness swirling in his stomach were hardening into anger, his breath coming too fast, his heart pounding, and for some reason, he felt like he was going to cry.

Istvay tipped her head back, their eyes closed. "I'm sorry, Aran." He could hear the weariness in their voice, and usually, he would have stopped, given them time to recover themself. But he couldn't, not now, not with this shaky, sickening anger flooding through his entire body.

"You were damn well setting me up with people! Every time we'd go somewhere, you'd point out some new person you thought I should date—"

"If it makes you feel any better, every time I set you up with someone, watched you head off to our rooms with them—I swear, I almost died of jealousy every damn time."

"And you—you didn't say a thing." Aran's voice was shaking. "You didn't say a damn thing."

Istvay was staring at the wall again. "No," they said in a low voice. "No, I didn't. I'm—sorry Aran, I—"

Aran closed his eyes, trying to bring himself back into some semblance of control, but it was impossible with the shaky adrenaline from the kiss still jittering through his muscles, the shock of—well, everything Istvay had just said. "And—that night in university, the night we graduated—"

Istvay dropped their head in their hands. "I—we were both drunk. And—oh, hell, Aran, even when I was completely sober, when you looked at me like that, I could hardly … and I wasn't sober, and you … do you have any damn idea how badly I'd wanted to kiss you? How long I'd wanted to kiss you?" They raised their head from their hands, and Aran was almost startled at the haggard expression on their face. "And then you kissed me back, and … and it was like every second of my entire existence I'd been waiting for that—for you—and I didn't even care about the consequences, I just … you were—you *are*—everything. You were the whole point of me, and that night was probably the best night of my entire damn life."

Their voice was so low that Aran could hardly make out the words. "And then I woke up, and I—I realized what I'd done. I realized how damn badly I wanted this, and I … I panicked. I didn't know what to do, and I just—I panicked. And then, afterwards, I was … I didn't know how to … what to …" they trailed off.

Aran stared at them. "Pishti," he said. His voice was shaking, he couldn't tell whether it was from tears or from fury. "Pishti, do you have any idea—" he broke off. "I spent the last seven damn years of my life thinking about that night, wondering what the hell I'd done wrong. Terrified that whatever it was, I'd do it again, and you'd leave me, and I'd lose you, and it would be my fault."

Istvay knelt, taking his face between their hands and turning it towards them, but Aran refused to meet their eyes.

"Oh, hell, Aran, I'm—I'm so sorry. I didn't—Aran, I would never —"

"You were just about to walk out right now!" Aran snapped, too angry to modulate his tone. "You kissed me, and then you were going to damn well walk out of the room without even saying a damn word to me about it."

Istvay grabbed his hands. "Aran, listen, I—I realized how stupid I was being, and I wanted to—it's been so many years, and I just—I thought, maybe if I had a little more time, I could figure out how to —"

Aran yanked his hands out of Istvay's and turned so his back was to them, his face to the wall. His entire body was shaking, and he couldn't seem to stop it. "I hate you, Pishti," he said, his voice muffled in the blankets. "Just—go away and leave me alone."

There was another long, long moment of silence. Aran was still shaky, and he was fighting hard to hold back stupid tears. Ani, he noticed distantly, had made herself scarce, probably under the bed. He could count on one hand the number of times he and Istvay had had an actual fight, but it seemed to disturb Ani almost as much as it did him.

The bed shifted again, and for half a second Aran was hit with a sudden jolt of panic, that Istvay was going to leave, just like he'd asked—

Then it creaked again and shifted as Istvay moved, scooting up onto the bed so they were sitting beside him. Their voice, when they spoke, was quiet, but for the first time since this conversation had begun, there was no uncertainty in it whatsoever. "Aran. I don't blame you for being upset. I don't blame you for hating me. You have every right to. I've had a lot of time to think about it these last few days, and I—there's really no excuse for what I did. If you want me to leave, I'll leave right now, and I won't come back until you want me to. But if … if you can stand it, can I … can I please apologize first? Then I'll go, I promise, I just …" their voice cracked a little. "I need you to know that I—that I'm sorry. That I understand that I hurt you, and I hate it, and … and that I'm sorry."

Aran lay where he was. He was trembling so badly he wasn't sure he could have moved if he wanted to. "Fine," he managed at last, his voice quiet and still so muffled he wasn't sure Istvay would even hear it.

They must have, though, because they let out a small breath. "Can I … can I touch you?"

Somehow, Aran managed a small nod.

The mattress creaked and shifted again, and then he felt Istvay's hand on his arm, and despite everything, his entire body relaxed at the familiar touch.

"Aran," Istvay began again. "You're right. What I did was stupid and selfish. I … I told myself I was trying to protect you, but I was really just protecting myself. Trying to hide from the fact that I was going to die, and I didn't know how to deal with that. And—and I've been realizing, these past few weeks, just how stupid that was. I love you, Aran. Dammit, I've loved you for so long that I don't know who I am without loving you. You're my entire world. And I knew I was hurting you, and I kept telling myself it was for your own good, but you're right—it was never my decision to make. I should have

—" They cleared their throat.

"I should have talked to you, told you. And—and that night after graduation—" they gave a small, choked laugh, resting their other hand on his forehead. "Aran, panicking and running away like that was the stupidest thing I've ever done in my life, and I'm speaking as someone who spent their entire life doing very, very stupid things. You're my … my everything. My whole damn reason for living. And there's no excuse for what I did, and I've spent the last seven years regretting it, and not … not knowing how to fix it. Not being brave enough to fix it." their voice choked again. "I—I hope that maybe, one day, you can forgive me. But—but whatever you decide, just know, Aran, I love you. And I will never stop loving you, and I was unbelievable stupid not to have told you that about fifteen years ago."

For a few moments, Istvay sat there in silence. They were running their fingers idly through Aran's hair, and his entire body had gone boneless at the touch. At last, though, they sighed and shifted. "Anyway," they said. "I—I just wanted to tell you that. I didn't want to make the same mistake I did before, and just … just leave without damn well saying anything. I'll leave you alone now, for as long as you need. You can—you can take as much time as you want, and if you do decide you want me to come back, I'll—I'll be there. Alright?"

Aran could feel the pressure of their hand softening on his arm, and he reached up quickly, grabbing it.

Istvay froze.

"Aran?" they asked at last, cautiously.

Aran took a deep breath. "You—you haven't finished apologizing," he said.

There was another long moment of silence. Then Istvay said,

"You know, you're right. I don't think I have." He could hear the smile in their tone.

The mattress shifted again as they repositioned themselves, so they were laying on the bed beside him. Their hand was still on his arm, but now he could feel the warmth of their body, not quite touching his.

"Aran." Their voice came from so close that he could he feel the ghost of their breath on his skin. "I am an absolute, complete, utter idiot."

Their lips brushed along the shell of his ear. He shivered involuntarily, and they stilled, waiting, but when he didn't stiffen or pull away, they relaxed, leaning in closer.

"The fact that I spent my entire life beside the most incredible, brilliant, intelligent, kind—not to mention unbelievably attractive— person in the entire Joias System, and I was too damn thick-headed to tell him that I love him—that was unforgivably stupid."

They nuzzled the soft skin behind his ear, then caught his earlobe between their teeth. Aran gave a quick, involuntary gasp, and their hand slid from his arm to cup his hip.

"So here's what I should have said years ago," they whispered, kissing down the side of his neck.

Aran wasn't sure he was still breathing. Hell, he wasn't sure his heart was still beating, and he wasn't sure if that was even necessary at this point.

"I love you, Aran. I adore you. You are my whole world, and I have wanted you for more years than I can possibly count." They pushed Aran gently back against the bed, kissing his eyelids, then the corner of his lips, lingering there for just a moment as their hand slipped around his stomach.

Aran's entire body was tingling, every nerve on edge. When at last

Istvay pulled back, Aran groaned involuntarily, turning his head to try to catch their lips with his.

They laughed, a low, warm sound, their fingers tightening on Aran's stomach and sending a rush of desire through his whole body.

"Pishti, don't—don't stop, please—"

Istvay sat up, swinging their leg over him so they were straddling his hips. They were grinning, a glint of familiar mischief in their eyes, their lips red and kiss-swollen, a pink flush across their cheekbones, and the sight almost took Aran's breath completely away. "Don't stop?" Their tone was teasing. They traced the outline of Aran's lips lightly with the tip of their finger. "Don't stop what, exactly? I thought I hadn't finished apologizing yet …"

Aran growled, bucking his hips to flip Istvay off, and pinned them neatly against the mattress with one leg. He pulled his shirt off over his head, then grabbed Istvay's wrists, trapping them against the headboard with one hand. With the other, he made quick work of the buttons on their shirt, then switched their wrists from one hand to the other efficiently as he pulled it off them.

Istvay's eyes had gone very wide. "*Hell*, Aran," they said, their voice catching. "Oh, hell …"

Aran grinned at them. His entire body was light, and he felt a strange mixture of euphoria and disbelief as he looked down at Istvay staring up at him, their breath coming in short little gasps, their eyes wide and dark. There was an unbearable lightness in Aran's chest, and he couldn't decide whether he wanted to laugh or cry, so instead, he traced his fingers along Istvay's jawline, their hint of stubble catching on the calluses on his fingers.

Istvay's eyes were fixed on him, their breathing gone quick and shallow.

He cupped their jaw in his hand, then trailed his fingers down the line of their throat, down their bare chest, down their stomach. He still couldn't quite believe this was real. "Pishti," he started, voice rough.

"Aran," Istvay choked. "I know damn well I deserve it, but I swear to the Mystery that if you stop right now, I'm never going to forgive you."

Aran grinned, leaning down to kiss the corner of Istvay's mouth.

Istvay's breath hitched visibly.

He grinned against their mouth, then caught their bottom lip between his teeth. When he pulled back, Istvay babbled out a string of choked curses, their voice hoarse. Their skin was shivering under Aran's fingers, their pulse as rapid and light as a bird's, and it sent a heady flash of warmth through Aran's entire body.

"Damn it to hell, Aran, how do you—how in the hell are you so— how can you—"

Aran grinned wider and leaned down until his lips were only centimetres from theirs. "Pishti," he whispered. "Shut up."

And then he leaned in, and Istvay's lips caught his, hungrily, desperately, their body squirming beneath him as if they couldn't possibly get him get close enough, and he let go of their wrists and slid his hand around their back, pulling them closer, and neither of them said anything even remotely coherent for a long time after that.

It was sometime later. Aran didn't know how long, and quite honestly didn't care. As far as he was concerned, time was a concept that had no meaning as long as he was here, with Istvay. They lay next to him, their body wrapped around his, one arm tossed over him possessively and holding him close, their breath warm and steady against the base of his neck.

Ani had tried to inject herself between them at some point, but had finally given up, grumbling, and settled at the foot of their bed, and the weight of her was warm and heavy on his feet.

Aran smiled, running his hand down Istvay's arm. Istvay sighed and pulled him closer, and Aran put his hand over theirs, tracing the lines and planes of it. Istvay mumbled something incoherent and kissed the nape of his neck.

"Pishti? I'm not going to wake up alone in bed again, am I?" he whispered over his shoulder after a moment.

Istvay's arm tightened around him reflexively, and for moment, they were silent. When they spoke, he could hear the thickness in their voice. "Aran," they said. "I—I wasn't lying when I told you that was the stupidest thing I've ever done."

The mattress shifted behind him, and when he half-turned, Istvay was propped up on one elbow, watching him. "I can't promise I won't do something stupid again. But I promise I will never, never do that."

Aran tried to smile, and then he found there were tears welling in his eyes. For half a moment he felt tinge of panic, because what if Istvay thought—

But Istvay just smiled back, their own eyes suspiciously shiny, and bent down, kissing him gently. "I promise, Aran," they whispered.

Aran sighed in contentment and dropped his head back on the pillow, and Istvay pulled him close again, nuzzling against the back of his neck.

Aran was almost asleep again when Istvay groaned.

"Pishti? What is it?" he asked, the sleepy, contented puddle of his thoughts spiked through with a sudden concern.

"I am such an idiot," Istvay mumbled. "I am such a damn, stupid idiot. All this time—all those years I wasted, that I could have spent being pinned to the mattress by my shirtless, incredibly hot best friend—" They groaned again, shaking their head. "I don't think I'm ever going to forgive myself."

"You shouldn't," Aran murmured sleepily, rolling over to kiss the closest part of Istvay he could reach. "You were a bloody idiot. But … I guess we could try making up for lost time."

A loud pounding at the door jolted Aran out of the comfortable fog of sleep. He jerked his head up, and a familiar voice behind him swore sleepily.

And he hadn't realized, until just that moment, how much the fear that somehow, despite everything, he'd wake up again and Istvay would be gone, had been tightening in his chest, until it was lifted, leaving him feeling lighter than a feather.

"Pishti," he whispered, turning. Istvay, tousled and sleepy-eyed, took his face in their hands and planted a lingering kiss on his lips that left him breathless and dizzy, and more than a little inclined to shove them back against the bed and pick up where they'd left off the night before.

The pounding on the door came again, followed by Krevai's voice. "Hello, Aran! Don't worry, it's just me."

Aran barely had time to yank the covers over him and Istvay before the door burst open, and Krevai stepped through.

Then Aran sucked in a quick gasp and shoved himself up into a sitting position.

Because beside Krevai was another raider, whose face was all too familiar—sharp eyes, sharper teeth, the red scar of a pulse pistol blast across her ice-pale skin.

Istvay was sitting up as well, the blankets pulled up to their chest, but their face was set in determination. "Sharda. If you plan on even touching Aran, you're damn well going to have to do it over my dead body."

Krevai laughed heartily. "Oh, no, Istvay! Don't worry, none of us wants to kill anyone, Sharda and I are just having a talk." He turned the other raider captain, raising an eyebrow. "See? I told you."

Sharda turned, examining Istvay and Aran. Her eyes were narrowed, her gaze sharp enough that Aran had the irrational urge to pull the blanket up higher.

She turned back to Krevai. "I don't believe it. Maybe this is just how humans normally interact. Maybe they're just very good friends."

"No, it's not, believe me. I know a lot about humans. And I'm not impressed with how you treated yours, by the way," he added. "Look at the shape they're in! I'm sure when you took them, they were in better shape than this."

Sharda turned her narrowed eyes on him, and Krevai spread his hands. "You were the one who took a human without putting any effort into finding out how you take care of them. I saw you grab your human without even asking—do you know how dangerous that is? You can stress them out, and Dessi's told me about how easy it is for humans that are stressed out to simply die from the strain."

Sharda gave him a sceptical look, and Aran and Istvay exchanged glances.

"But at any rate, don't mind us," Krevai said breezily, turning back to Aran and Istvay. "We were just in here checking on you. You were doing sex, yes?"

Aran stared at Istvay for moment, then turned to stare at the two raider captains.

"Um," he said, his mind gone completely blank.

"He asked—" Sharda began irritably.

Aran glanced between himself and Istvay, both naked and halfway under the covers, their clothes strewn on the floor, and decided there was really no point in denying it. "Yes, we were having sex," he said resignedly.

"See?" Said Krevai smugly, turning back to Sharda. "I told you. They said they weren't mates when I first met them, but when Aran got himself practically cut in half for his Istvay, and Istvay tried to shoot me to protect their Aran, I was pretty sure they'd changed their minds. And you see? They're doing sex, which means they're mates. So what can you do?"

"Um," said Aran again, helplessly. "It's—I mean, humans often have sex without being—without being … mates. And there are plenty of people who don't necessarily enjoy sex, and it doesn't mean they can't have partners, it's just another way of—"

"Yes, yes, of course," said Krevai, waving hand breezily. "But you and your Istvay both like sex, yes?"

Istvay sighed. "Yes, as a matter of fact," they said, irritation showing through their voice. "Aran and I both very much enjoy sex. And we did have sex. And if you hadn't just practically broken the door down, we would probably be having sex right now. Which would be a hell of a lot more enjoyable than this damn conversation," they muttered.

"So you are mates? Krevai's telling the truth?" Sharda snapped, turning to Istvay.

They sighed. "I—" they glanced at Aran ruefully. "Yes," they said. "If you absolutely have to put it that way, yes, we're mates. Although there are a hell of a lot more romantic ways of expressing it."

Aran tried to ignore the giddiness in his chest at Istvay's words.

Sharda watched the two of them narrowly for moment more, then turned back to Krevai. "I suppose you're right," she said grudgingly.

"I guess that leaves us to simply discuss details."

Krevai was still grinning. "Of course, of course." He glanced at Aran and Istvay. "I'm sorry, you can go back to your sex. I just had to come in here with Sharda—she didn't believe me."

Aran and Istvay looked at each other again.

"Believe you about—what exactly?" Istvay's voice was wary.

"Surely Dessi's mentioned it? If two raider captains have crew who are mates with each other, the captains are in a truce for as long as it lasts. You're humans, so we weren't completely sure it applied, but Sharda and I talked it over and decided that if you were mates, we'd let it stand. Besides, if the Ani killed all of Sharda's crew, and Sharda's ships shot mine out of the sky, whoever was the final winner, it would take them ages to get their strength back up, which would be very disruptive to either of our plans. So we agreed to a truce in the meantime."

Aran stared, not entirely sure his brain had processed the words correctly.

"We're—" Istvay began at last, sounding as almost as shellshocked as Aran felt. "You mean we're—" They turned to Aran, the disbelief on their face so close to comical that despite everything, Aran had to bite back a laugh. "Aran, we're … this is … it's like a damn political marriage!"

"Except of pets," Aran muttered.

Istvay stared at him for moment, then gave a snort of laughter and turned away quickly.

"Don't be silly, you're not pets," Krevai chuckled, winking at Sharda. "And now we just have to discuss the details of the alliance."

"Um," Aran said. "What—what exactly do you—so you mean the leadership war is over?"

Krevai grinned. "Well, I wouldn't exactly say over. I'm sure at some point we'll have to fight it out. But you humans have relatively short lifespans, I think, so in the meantime, you could say we're … allies in a common cause."

Aran glanced at Istvay again and saw the same unease in their face that he felt.

"In a common cause?" he asked carefully, almost not wanting the answer.

For the first time since she'd stepped into the room, Sharda smiled, wide and vicious. "Yes," she said. "It appears that Krevai and I will be sharing leadership of the raiders. And we've just declared war on the yibo."

40

Epilogue

"Kachik!"

Kachik didn't bother to lift his head from a study of the documents before him, just gestured with the tip of his tail for his assistant to open the door. He could hear the angry stomp of the human's boots on his clean floor, and he had to hold back a shudder.

"Captain Mattin," he said, looking up at last. He made an effort to hide the distaste in his expression at the words, but it probably didn't matter—the humans were singularly incompetent at reading yibo expressions.

The human was scowling, his heavy brows, drawn together on his hairless face, making an ugly, incongruous picture. "Kachik. I heard you told the Synod you did not intend to declare war. What is the plan here?"

Kachik studied the man—his pale-brown skin reddened and darkened by the sun, cracking in the heat, the messy fuzz of hair too sparse to be called fur growing in dirty whorls over the exposed skin of his arms and legs and spreading in uneven patches across his face, the longer hair on his head grown ragged and uneven over his skull.

He fought back a shudder.

The Synod had risked war to provide shelter to a rag-tag, desperate band of these creatures. They were willing to allow them to infiltrate yibo society, serve in positions—even, if the rumours he'd heard were correct, to speak in their advisory meetings.

It had to end. The creeping, insidious, mark these aliens were leaving on the simple, unadorned beauty of yibo culture was like a slug-trail on a leaf—a slime that marred the clean surface and warned of a coming destruction, should the infestation not be dealt with.

The Synod must have seen something in these humans he had overlooked—some promise of shared knowledge, likely, as unpromising as that appeared.

That, too, would need to be dealt with.

"Our raider allies abandoned us, in large part thanks to your people," he said, looking up into the human's angry face. "I told you Sharda was clever, and they would need to act discreetly."

"You were the one who insisted on sending my soldiers, instead of yours, to negotiate," Mattin snapped, his words coming out almost unintelligible in his odd, thick accent. "And you told them to send us back information, and spy on the other raider captain."

Kachik sighed internally and raised his hands. "Very well, Mattin, it isn't worth an argument as to fault. But the facts we are dealing with are, the raiders have reneged on our agreement. And I am not willing to send my people into a war we cannot yet win."

"So you're just going to give it up, after all this? We had an agreement, Kachik." Mattin was leaning forward, as if he believed his bulk would be enough to intimidate.

Kachik didn't flinch, or step back. "You forget yourself," he said quietly.

Even the human must have been able to catch the menace in the tone, because the man straightened a little, his eyes darting nervously around the room to the assembled yibo guards.

Kachik smiled to himself. "Mattin," he said, rising and tucking his tail gracefully over one arm. "You are correct. We made a bargain. And I still believe it will benefit both of us. However, attacking a squadron of Synod war ships over a band of stranded human ship's crew seems like an unwise way to go about it."

Mattin watched him, calculating.

The man was … crafty, in the way humans were. It didn't pay to underestimate him.

But for now, at least, their goals aligned.

"You have a plan, then," the man said.

Kachik smiled. "I intend that the Synod will not get whatever benefit they might have hoped from their captive humans. I intend that the raiders will not, either—you may tell that scientist of yours, it should make him happy. And even if we are not yet powerful enough for open war—that doesn't preclude other methods." He paused. "You are still prepared to do your part?"

"My soldiers have been drawing up the specs of all the weapons they're familiar with and handing them to your weapons designers, as well you know," said Mattin.

"And I have been providing you prototypes in return," said Kachik smoothly. "Very good. But you can still hold to your promise?"

Mattin looked at him and smiled, that threatening, open-mouthed smile that humans seemed to prefer. "I can assure you—Cavaco will be more than happy to uphold his end of the bargain."

"Very good," said Kachik, still smiling. "I shall be delighted to make your general's acquaintance, just as soon as I am able."

"And how soon will that be?"

"That depends very much on how well each of us carries out our part of the plan, does it not?" Kachik kept his voice light.

One more human system. One more pestilence to wipe from existence—not necessarily with yibo weapons, of course, he didn't need to outright break his bargain with Cavaco. A simple rumour passed to the raiders should be enough to ensure that there weren't enough humans left over to contaminate the system, like they had last time.

But Mattin and this Cavaco hardly needed to know that.

"I hope to speak with you again soon," he said, resuming his seat and glancing meaningfully down at his paperwork. "As soon as either of us has news for the other."

"Then I hope it will be soon indeed." Mattin shot him another gap-mouthed smile, turned on his heel, and strode out.

Kachik watched him go.

Disgusting creatures, humans. But there was no denying they had their uses.

And as a weapon against the Synod—he could think of no better tool.

Book five, Event Horizon, coming soon!

You might also enjoy The Ungovernable series, also by R.M. Olson.

A mouthy ex-smuggler pilot, a grumpy demolitions expert, a tech genius and a hacker. They're pulling a job on the most dangerous weapons dealer in the System. They're stealing tech that could change the course of history. And every one of them has something to hide.
What could possibly go wrong?
"Spectacular and thrilling! Olson's debut novel is filled with compelling characters and endless excitement." -SD Simper, author of the Fallen Gods series

You can order book one, Zero Day Threat, on Amazon.

I also have a Patreon, where I post character art, short stories, sneak peaks, and other fun stuff. You can get in on it for only $3/month, so if you're interested, check it out here!
https://www.patreon.com/rmolson